BAD VIBES

BAD VIBES

By Alberto Fuguet   Translated by Kristina Cordero

St. Martin's Press ⚎ New York

Endpaper photographs by Macarena Minguell

Design by Songhee Kim

Library of Congress Cataloging-in-Publication Data

Fuguet, Alberto.
    [Mala onda. English]
    Bad vibes / by Alberto Fuguet : translated by
Kristina Cordero.
        p.   cm.
    ISBN 0-312-15059-8
    I. Cordero, Kristina.   II. Title.
PQ8098.16.U48M313   1997
863—dc20   96-43468
                                    CIP

First Edition: April 1997

10 9 8 7 6 5 4 3 2 1

This one's for my family,
those here and those down there

ACKNOWLEDGMENTS

This book has two lives—one in Spanish, its natural language, and now English, which is probably the language it should have been written in the first place.

A thousand thanks to the International Writer's Workshop of the University of Iowa, mainly Clark Blaise who was like a father abroad and whose generousity is amazing. Also to all the Mayflower gang, Rowena and Mary, Toscana and Carmina and Oscar Hahn.

Corrine Stanley and Shyla Osborne, my first translators, who really helped. *Gracias.* All the crowd that gathered on Sundays at Glen's house, especially Nathan and Stephanie. And Aaron, too. You all made me feel part of what I felt I had missed.

What can I say about Thom Jones? You're the man. We once talked about Richard Price; after that, I knew we would hit it off. Thanks for your support and encouragement and your seminar, and Thanksgiving and letting me sneak into the famous Workshop. Don Fotheringham in Seattle, your buddy is my buddy, *tu casa es mi casa.*

Mike Patton, of course, for the inspiration, soundtrack, and good vibes.

In New York, Eric Simonoff, my agent at Janklow & Nesbit, who believed in me even in Spanish. Gabriela De Ferrari, who read and recommended me and even gave me a party.

Jim Fitzgerald at St. Martin's, for being the editor I always dreamed about.

And last, but not least, Kristina Cordero, who gave me the voice I always wanted, but made me understand, in the end, that my language is Spanish after all. Guess our E-mails make another novel, *¿no es cierto?*

For the Spanish version, once again *gracias* to Ricardo Sabanes, Marcela Gatica, José Donoso, Antonio Skármeta, the two workshops, Juan Forn and Rodrigo Fresán and all the McOndo gang, Iván Valenzuela, Sergio Paz, Zoom, María Olga Delpiano, Carolina Díaz (por cierto) and everybody at Planeta and (now) Alfaguara.

Sometimes I think I'm blind
Or I may be just paralyzed
Because the plot thickens every day
And the pieces of my puzzle keep crumblin' away
But I know, there's a picture beneath.
Indecision clouds my vision
No one listens . . .
Because I'm somewhere in between.
My life is falling to pieces
Somebody put me together . . .

Mike Patton
"Faith No More"

WEDNESDAY
SEPTEMBER 3, 1980

I'm lying on the beach, faceup, eyes closed. I'm sticky from the humidity, but I don't have the strength to go into the water. It wouldn't be a bad idea, I'd float for a while and then eventually disappear. I'm bored—bored, fed up. Thinking is a monumental effort. I've been sitting out here for an hour. My one distraction is this feeling of the sun pricking at my eyelids. Some ex-girlfriend is probably sticking pins into a voodoo doll on break in Haiti or Jamaica somewhere. Ouch. That bitch.

I left my sunglasses in the hotel. Great. I'm sure some idiot from my class is going to find them and give them to that cleaning girl they're all trying to pick up. Then I'll be left with nothing. Stupid to leave them there. I mean, you shouldn't go to the beach without sunglasses, unprotected. And they were right there, on the night table, too. I was even looking at them before coming down here. Stupid. Of course someone's going to steal them from me. I'm just the idiot for forgetting them and leaving them there for the taking.

I turn over and make myself think about something else, like . . . I don't know . . . the heat. The heat. It feels like the hottest day ever today. For me, at least—it's like, one more degree and it's all going to explode. I'm going to explode. They'll declare a state of emergency and evacuate the city. But nobody here will care too much. What's normal to them is a really big deal for me, since I'm the tourist here, which really pisses me off. It makes me feel like an outsider or some kind of little intruder, like I don't belong, which is my worst fear. I hate it.

It's probably around three or four. Whatever. Anyway, it's late. I got to the hotel around noon, but there wasn't anyone from my class around, not even the ones hung over from last night. And the creeps, those little teacher's pets, had been up for hours. Of course. They get up really early every day, go for their little jogs, play their beach volleyball games, or watch the sun rise together. Then they go to those shops in Rio Sul and buy those embarrassingly, shamelessly tacky fucking T-shirts they sell to all the Americans that come here for their little vacations.

I'm tired from all the sun. I'll go back to the hotel. I remember waking up there this morning. When I finally opened my eyes and realized where I was—which was not where I thought I was—I had to think for a while . . . figure out some kind of plan, so that I wasn't wasting my entire day away. There weren't a lot of choices, though—I mean, I could stay and suffocate in my room (which was starting to smell like the combined five-day body odor of my classmates) or I could go outside and take advantage of the last day of our trip, hang out on the beach one last time, get some more sun. It was either-or. So I got up—slowly— and just started walking down the sidewalk, all the way down to Ipanema, which is where everyone goes to check everyone out, to see and be seen. That sort of thing.

As I was walking, my mind kind of wandered. I thought about Chile and then, of course, about my life, which is what I seem to think about most of the time anyway. A few times, I felt that cloud of depression coming over me, then I'd just quickly change the topic—like, I'd study the T-shirts in the store windows. It was somehow comforting to see the same shirts in the shops and know that they're sold here too, not just in Chile. It made me feel more safe, or secure, somehow.

So I walked for a few blocks like that, not moving too fast because of the heat, and I was all sweaty and everything. I got to the plaza that's right in the heart of Ipanema. Ipanema is the artsy-bohemian neighborhood in Rio, where all the Brazilian beatniks hang out, in the bookstores and clothing stores and trendy bars and cafés.

Cassia likes Ipanema, especially this square where all the hippies sell their arts and crafts, their useless trinkets, roach clips, earrings—all the same crap they sell in Chile, at the entrance to the Quinta Vergara in Viña. Except, of course, here in Rio they don't sell Chilean rag sweaters or those ridiculous posters of Violeta Parra. The whole mood here is different. I met a bunch of Cassia's friends, who are these totally intellectual, left-wing university types—like, they all get together and hang out drinking *cachaza* with *maracuyá* juice and listening to Mercedes Sosa and Joan Baez. Really. Of course, the minute Cassia tells them I'm from Chile, all of a sudden, their conversation changes and its Pinochet this and that, and what an awful dictatorship, and why not come and hang out with *us,* compañero. And they're all telling me stories about the people they never knew in Chile who were exiled, and this, and that, and Neruda's the greatest poet ever, and what about that fascist bastard Figueiredo, and let's read some protest poems. Then they really start in on the military, the fucking military didn't screw up just Chile, they ruined the entire continent. And on and on and on. And me, I just kind of sit there, hanging out quietly, this hapless tourist, acting cool, you know, really agreeable and everything: sure, oh yeah, uh-huh, I totally know what you mean, *tudo bem, legado.* Whatever.

That type of conversation pisses me off more than anything. First of all, the guys all look like they're from California, but talk like Bolsheviks, which is kind of questionable to begin with. One of them wore this Che Guevara T-shirt (like a dummy, I of course looked at the shirt and asked him who it was), invited us across the bay to Niterói to listen to some really fired-up Panamanian sing those Silvio Rodríguez songs my family's housekeeper listens to all the time. Protest stuff—songs like "Ojalá." She, of course, is anti-Pinochet and will vote "NO" in the referendum next week. Once I heard their music, I knew exactly what to expect from this crowd. To Cassia this was all very normal, and fun to do on a night out with her friends. They said maybe Chico Buarque was going to come: it was going to be an unannounced concert or something—a protest thing: anti-Figueiredo, anti-Stroessner and Videla, anti-Pinochet, *man.* The guy that said that shook his left fist, all serious and defiant. I explained to Cassia that in Santiago, you had to search this crowd out a little: to check out the communists, you have to go to a place called Kafé Ulm. But I couldn't lie to her—I mean, it's not really my scene at all. At all. I don't have anything against them, but in Santiago, it's not so simple. It's like, you always have to be thinking what if the police come. They'll start by asking questions, then they'll arrest you. No kidding. It's like, one wrong move in Chile and you're fucked, and before you know it, you get kicked out of your house and that's it, you're finished. That was how I explained it to Cassia anyway, and she just nodded her head in sympathy. We wandered around and eventually ended up together on the beach, just kind of contemplating the night sky, looking at the lights of the city. Later, I took her to the hotel, but the school chaperone caught us, and naturally the bitch wouldn't let Cassia come upstairs. Cassia was very cool about the whole thing, though, and said it didn't matter. It was late, and she had to go home anyway. So then I offered to take her home, but she just said *brigado,* I can go myself, and disappeared into the night.

After watching her leave on the bus, I went into one of those pizza places by the beach, on Avenida Atlantica. I ordered a *pizza tropical* and a beer and entertained myself, watching the tourists go by. I saw a black guy in a straw hat and a massive set of teeth, banging the shit out of his portable bongo drums. Now that I think about it, lying here on the beach waiting for Cassia to come, I realize that it was the first time ever that I was all alone in a restaurant. It wasn't so terrible, actually. Kind of strange, though.

After watching the street scene for a while, I went back to the hotel, to my room, which was full of guys from my class, snoring, stinking, wasted, and passed out. It was really late. Cox woke up and started telling me about a *boîte* they went to, where there were these gorgeous Brazilian girls. "They were charging, you know what I mean, man, I don't know how many thousand cruzeiros, and at thirty-nine pesos to the dollar, that's a lot of money, man, you know." Whatever. I got undressed and into bed, but couldn't fall asleep right away, so I started counting all the streets I could name in Rio, like counting sheep, until I fell asleep. It wasn't easy. I had the added distraction of listening to Cox jerk off in the bed next to mine: his bed creaked ever so slightly, as if he was trying not to disturb anyone, so as not to give himself away. I'm sure all these guys jerk off anyway. Everyone does it—shit, no wonder the sheets feel so starchy.

So I slept. Sometime real early in the morning, I woke up to Patán puking in the bathroom. Disgusting. For about half a second, I thought of getting up and helping him, but it was too disgusting to even think about at that hour. I turned over and went back to sleep, dreaming about Cassia thinking about me. That was something like four or five days ago already. Shit, time flies. It really does.

I wiggle my toes in the sand. Not very much fun, I realize, but it's just a distraction—my mind is actually quite focused on one thing: finding Cassia. She did tell me to call her, it's just that I'm such an idiot, I lost her phone number. It was right inside my almost-empty wallet, which I lost. I left it at a party at this woman's house, this woman who I'm sure I'll never see again. The only thing I remember about the party was that it was in this really tall building, on the top floor somewhere in Leblon, which isn't even on the beach. And the hostess was some woman, kind of older, with red hair—actually, she kind of looked like one of the ladies in that TV show *Pecado Capital*. Anyway, she was coming on to Ivo, which was sort of weird because she was so much older, and it was funny—even though we were in Brazil, it reminded me of these parties my parents used to have when I was a little kid, where everyone would hit on each other. Ivo, who is one of Cassia's friends, knew this lady; he met her at some party at one of the embassies in the city. The problem is that fucking Ivo took off with her, and I left them—and my wallet—there, with everything in it, except for the little "origami" with those grams of coke I bought. Actually, it wasn't a big deal to lose the wallet except for Cassia's number—most of my money and my passport I left in the hotel safe. Just like my father told me to.

I think—in fact, I'm sure—that the only way I'll bump into Cassia again is if for some reason she comes by here, or to the hotel. I mean, I don't even know where she lives, or where the fuck her father's apartment is, or anything. Kind of strange considering how many nights we slept together this week. Total lack of communication, I guess.

I want to, I have to see her, though, and there's not much time left. My vacation is practically over. The plane for Santiago leaves later today. I bet she doesn't come by the beach today, it's way too hot. On the other hand, she's used to the heat—maybe she'll come after all. If she doesn't, though, maybe it's because I'm just one more silly tourist to her, some jerk from a country that no one's heard of and no one really cares about. At least Rio will always hold good memories for me, it will always remind me of Cassia.

She's also leaving Rio pretty soon. She told me all about it the day I met her, about how she's going to go back to Brasília to live with her father. He works for the government, Figueiredo's people, who everyone here seems to really hate. To me, Brazil seems incredible. Compared to Chile, at least. Cassia says Figueiredo is a dictator. Just like Pinochet, she reminded me. As if I didn't know. It's funny, because at first, her little communist act seemed like kind of a put-on, sort of poserish and fake, but I forgave her for it, mostly because of the way she said it, in that cute little accent. It was that accent of hers that did it for me, right from the start. Even before I saw her in that little calypso thong bikini and ripped Clash T-shirt that her ex-boyfriend had given her—he's this English guy who lives in Brasília now, who I'm sure would kill her if he knew that I'm the one wearing his T-shirt now.

Maybe she's packing, maybe she's visiting her grandmother, maybe she's out shopping for those baggy pants she was talking about the other day. I fast-forward for a few seconds and imagine her: Cassia watching television, Cassia drinking a Brahma Guaraná, Cassia talking on the phone. Cassia. Maybe it's just boring to her—the idea of coming and hanging out here with me. What would we do anyway—come to the beach, go in the water, maybe walk down to the Praia do Arpoador and buy some joints from that weird guy down there—the one who claims he sells "the best shit on earth." And then we'd probably go hide behind the rocks on the beach, smoke them together, as if we'd known each other all our lives, as if it were our own secret little ritual or something. As if to prove how inseparable we were. As if we were a couple—both of us living here, all tan, me in shorts and sunglasses all the time, her in those thong bikinis and torn T-shirts. We'd have a tiny little apartment by the beach, with a view of the ocean, a good stereo, reggae music on all the time, and the only piece of furniture would be a mattress, our soggy mattress, which would smell like the two of us—my sweat and Cassia's aroma, our scents all mixed together.

I turn over in the sand onto my stomach. I feel nauseated, I probably have sunstroke or something. I smell my burned skin and peek out at the horizon through the strands of hair on my sweaty underarms. I try to sleep a little, but after the *cachaza* from breakfast, then the pot I smoked after that, it all got to me. And then jerking off in the shower, as I lathered up thinking about Antonia and Cassia—Cassia, who I left last night on the floor, in the apartment of one of her artist friends. I'm way too drowsy and weak to do anything but lie here. All that just left me totally wiped out, exhausted and thirsty, with a weird crav-

ing for one of those pineapples—*abacaxis*—the black guys sell
in the street here. I feel sick, like I could easily puke up everything I ate last night in the restaurant that I went to with the guys
from my class before meeting up with Cassia and João, all the
Brazilians, that Dinho, who's so cool, and Ivo, no, actually, Ivo
wasn't there. Alfredo was, Alfredo with the Lennon specs, and
Patrick of the Sid Vicious T-shirt and the acid blotters we licked
and tripped on. And the Grand Funk album, and Santana and
Janis Joplin, and the spicy smell of the *maconha*. And then there
were these guys who painted with all different colors, who all
blended together and created different forms with thick paint,
in large brushstrokes, and their paintings seemed to open up and
expand and expand. Cassia then put a video on, a movie with
Sonia Braga, and started dancing around naked, in a room full
of television sets, and all of a sudden, everything seemed to
slow down, really slow down, and then we were all screwing,
like some giant orgy. And the music, the colors, Cassia laughing
as she danced around naked and hot, on the terrace—just like
in the movie, with the lights shining, the white mark of her
thong bikini on her ass that looked good enough to bite and me
singing in Portuguese, half crying. And all of us were dancing
around, spinning, slow and fast and fast and smooth with Jim
Morrison in the background somewhere or was it a fat bald guy,
like Demis Roussos, that Greek guy my mother's so crazy about,
talking about philosophy, opening a box, throwing a sack full of
powder onto a table, a little flour on the glass table, Jimi Hen-
drix's guitar playing and dozens of credit cards cutting lines on
the table—try it, man, come on, it's cool, don't be lame. And then
the explosion. I came down hard. A big fat tear burst out of my
eye, and my nose felt like a pimple that finally popped. There's
really nothing like those red and yellow McDonald's straws, Alfredo observed, as he put a nice long one up his nose just as some
great Brazilian music came on—or was it African music?—I can't
remember. Anyway it was great stuff, and so was the coke
Cassia spread out on her chest for me to lick off, to breathe in

and ingest as Jimmy Page then Eric Clapton went on playing.
It was one of those numbers where they just played the same
notes, over and over and over again, like a broken record, never-
ending, and the singer about to explode from the monotony
and me all of a sudden scared, scared shitless, but totally mes-
merized . . .

I wake up and open my eyes with a start. I inhale. That smell
of red, sunburned skin, of sweat mixed in with deodorant, turns
me on. I'm soaked; even my hair is dripping. I wet the tip of my
finger and relieve my nasal membranes. I breathe in again, and
Cassia's aroma washes over me. That smell that comes from
being together, hours and hours in bed, fucking over and over
again, in and out and exploring each other's body to the point of
exhaustion, surprised—trusting, satisfied—and happy, just being
next to her, not thinking about anything else but her and me.

The second time we did it was in the afternoon, with the sun
shining on us. We were in Alfredo's unpainted little studio apartment, on the double bed with no sheets, and a black-and-white
television set turned on to an episode of *Combat* I'd already
seen. Afterward, I woke up, feeling like I was melting from all
of the sex and the heat, wondering what I was even doing there,
lying naked next to a virtual stranger who I had just barely met.
That was when she, busy reading some dense, intellectual book,
reached over me to grab a bottle of red wine sitting on the floor.
After taking a gulp, she leaned on top of me and kissed me. The
wine, warm and sweet and thick, went from her lips to mine and
down my throat. She winked at me and then rolled back and just
kept on reading. A few moments later, as if nothing had happened, she turned the page. I swallowed.

I feel a dry breeze float over me but nothing changes. The
beach is packed, like in the middle of the summer even though

it's only September. I attempt to look down at my feet and every-thing gets blurry and starts moving around like crazy, as if I—now I move ever so slightly off my towel and onto the sand—were the broken hands of a watch gone berserk, the round face of the watch just spinning and spinning uncontrollably, like the eyes of some whacked-out cartoon character, like an end-less spiral, like Cassia's tongue that wiggles around and around, impossible to catch hold of. I decide to run in the water, which is hot as hell, like me, full of mossy green things, like asparagus or something. I pee in the ocean a little and then swim a bit. Nothing. It doesn't work, it doesn't do anything for me. I sub-merge myself a little more, slowly, slowly, until my eyes are be-neath the water's surface. But it still doesn't work. Right now, nothing will.

THURSDAY
SEPTEMBER 4, 1980

We've all been sleeping on the floor of the Rio de Janeiro airport for almost two hours now. Thank God for air-conditioning. A little while ago, Lerner and I went to the bathroom to smoke a joint, our last one. It was that really excellent Amazonian weed, which that idiot actually thought he'd try to smuggle into Chile, hidden in the lining of his boots. I'm also planning on bringing back a little memento, only mine is a fine granulated substance, in honor of Cassia. But that's my business. It's about three in the morning, I think, and our plane is late. It's coming from Spain, or Africa or somewhere. Who knows, who cares. Whatever. This whole return thing is depressing me—I mean, I feel sick, that's how much I hate the idea. The fact that we actually have to go back to Chile is enough to ruin the entire week for me.

I separate myself from my crowd of classmates. They're all sleeping, wearing the straw hats they all bought on the beach and those stupid little bracelets that supposedly bring good luck. The head chaperone, one of our teachers, is on some duty-free spree, buying a bunch of little branches that they say turn into plants when you put them in water. Another lady is with us too—Rubén Troncoso's—excuse me, I mean *Guatón* Troncoso's mother, who came on the trip with us just to keep an eye on her son. She's buying a bottle of *cachaza,* so I go over to her and ask her how much it costs.

"Wow, that's a lot more than it cost in that liquor store by the hotel," I say to her when she tells me the price.

"I don't know, young man," she says. "I certainly never bought anything there."

"I did. I stocked up pretty well there. They had a good port, straight from Portugal, I think."

I notice her eyeing the chains hanging from my neck. I bought them from some Bolivian guys who were selling souvenirs on the plaza at Ipanema. Actually, I can't stand that kind of stuff, that cheap, trashy jewelry only tourists wear, but for some reason, when you travel, it's like required or something that you go out and do stupid shit like buy bracelets and necklaces. Or get some kind of surfer haircut. Both of these things, actually, were Cassia's inspiration, so I can't be too critical, I guess.

"You know something," I say to her, "I'm just short ten *cruzeiros* to buy a bottle. And the bank isn't going to open in time. Can I ask you a favor—I'll give you all the money I have left, and then you could buy me a bottle? I'll settle up with Rubén when we're back in school. I promise." I learned this trick from my mother, who is the queen of manipulation. If you really want to bullshit someone, you have to make your little speech, sure, but then to really make it work, shoot them one of those meaningful stares. Direct, penetrating, without blinking, sort of a faggy, princely kind of a leer. It works like a charm, every time. It inhibits the enemy, makes them nervous, turns them into easy victims. No kidding.

Of course it works with Guatón's mother. She's easy prey. Typical Chilean wife, one of those who got married really young and already looked like a grandmother when she was about twenty-five. The old bag falls for it in about half a second and buys me the bottle.

"I assume this is for your father," she says.

"Maybe. Maybe not, though. Anyway, thanks very much—I owe you one."

I go look for a seat and she moves away, fumbling with her orthopedic shoe. She's really from another planet—even the perfume she wears, that cheap shit you buy in a drugstore, like something a housekeeper wears. It's like she's from another decade or something. And Guatón is the same: he's always walking around with calculators and digital watches and all sorts of electronic crap. He's also living in some other dimension, some other time. For all the money that family has, they really are like a Grant Wood *Chilean Gothic*—everyone thinks there's something strange about them.

I remember once I went to their house, to do some homework, I think. Creepy shit, like so creepy I couldn't sleep at night after hanging out there. It was this really old, creaky house with a greasy old oven that smelled like yesterday's dinner. And they had one of those aqua-green bathrooms with rusty faucets, really scummy. Typical of that Ñuñoa neighborhood. The whole family lives like that, totally isolated from the rest of the normal world. They clean their porch with a fire hose—I mean, they're just from another planet. I don't know—I'm even kind of surprised that Guatón goes to our school, with parents as weird as that. And the three of them together, that's something else. They all speak to each other in the formal, all the time. Strange, really strange.

I'm also convinced that Guatón is a Nazi at heart. That's really why I can't stand him. When he was little, he'd do things like kill cats, burn rats, and boil frogs alive. Seriously. And his notebooks were always filled with swastikas. One day, he came to my house with this book, filled with pictures of concentration camp victims. It was horrifying, all skinny women and men who were living skeletons. I was so shocked I didn't know quite how to respond, and anyway, there were still a lot of things about myself and my background I didn't understand then. Guatón, in a moment of weakness, decided to confide in me about something: he confessed that he jerked off looking at the concentration camp photos. He said they turned him on, more than *Penthouse* or *Hustler*. He hid the pictures in big old marmalade jars. So I listened, even though inside I felt like throwing up—just imagining that chubby little greaseball, in his army fatigues and his sweaty, smelly armpits, and those awful vests his mother knit for him, and those grimy flannel pants, his oily hair, naked in his bed, jerking off into a glass container. I shudder now to think about it, I really do. Anyway, inspired by a surge of confidence or something, all of a sudden Guatón saluted Hitler, just the way our military officers salute, Prussian style. Then he started telling me about some uncle of his that had been in the secret police. If that wasn't enough, he then started in on how much he hated his sister. Really hated her guts, so much that he once decapitated a bunch of her dolls and buried them underneath their house.

Lerner, who lives in ritzy Las Condes, on San Luis Hill, comes over to me and makes me an offer I can't refuse: he's got one little roach left to share. With my bottle of Brahma, they make a nice mix, so we head off to the bathroom. I'm still thinking about Guatón Troncoso, though. So weird, that guy—the entire trip he slept in the same room with his mother, who's just as much of a Nazi as he is. Lerner and I go down this long hallway with a big map of Brazil on the wall. I follow him into the bathroom, which reeks of baby poop, and we shut ourselves into a stall.

"I feel like I've been in here before. All these little cubicles are getting to look the same, aren't they?" I say.

"Yeah, the only thing missing is graffiti. And coke. We *could* have had half a gram right now, you know."

"Well, we're not in the fucking Disco Hollywood, asshole. We're in an airport. In another country," I remind him.

I don't dare let on that coke is my most recent diversion, just because I don't want to share what I have with him. I mean, nothing against him or anything, Lerner is fine to do coke with. Whenever he has, he always offers me some, but it would never even occur to me to share with him. If he ever found out that right now, inside my new neon-pink nylon wallet, I have a tiny little envelope, a little piece of paper folded like origami, with four grams of the shit, he'd kill me. First he'd kill me, then he'd snort it all. I almost offer him some, but think better of it, because I want to bring it to Santiago. I have a funny feeling that I'm going to need it there.

"Come on, light the joint," Lerner says. "If they catch us, we're fucked. They'll strap us down on the landing strip and run us over."

We smoke the joint and take a few gulps of the Brahma: two, three, four swigs and then . . . what the fuck are we doing here, we're such assholes, the plane probably took off already. Not that either of us cares, at least I don't. I really don't want to go back.

We leave the bathroom and head back toward the others. Either the terminal is more crowded, or I'm more stoned than I thought. The latter, most likely. A silky, almost seductive voice announces over the loudspeakers the flights coming in, like lyrics to some bossa nova music: *VASP a Recife, Pan Am a Nova Iorque, Varig a Lisboa, Iberia a Santiago.* Lerner's wasted, I can see it in his eyes as he walks next to me, in sync with my footsteps. We look like a couple of cowboys marching into some dusty town. Or a couple of soldiers in formation. All the other losers from our school are just sitting around exchanging tourist brochures and reading *Playboy* in Portuguese.

At the other end of the gate, I watch a big blue-and-yellow Lufthansa jet take off into the darkness. I turn around and bump into Luisa Velásquez, who I'm sure had a terrible time this past week. She's a nice girl, though, and sometimes even lets me copy off her exams, so we get along. I start talking to her:

"When does our plane take off? Now? Do you know?"

"Not for another two hours," she answers in her typical Spanish-teacher voice.

"Fuck. This is such a drag."

"Look on the bright side—it extends our vacation, sort of."

"What? Are you crazy? It's over. If we have to go back, it's better to do it in one quick shot. Why prolong the pain, you know what I mean."

"I thought you had a good time, Matías."

"Well, yeah, of course—I mean, the best ten days of my life. But it's over now, get it?"

"They all told me that you had a good time," she repeated.

She says it like someone who wants to be quoted for saying it. Then she gets all serious, really melancholy. She almost starts making me feel bad, as if it's my fault that she has no friends, that she studies too much, that she's a virgin, that no guys ever go for her, or that inside she's dying to be different from everyone else, special in some way. The sad thing about Luisa, though, is that no matter how hard she tries, it'll never happen. She's already got her reputation—everybody knows she's constantly depressed, a real downer, always analyzing everyone and acting all condescending. It's like, she'd be the one on the beach reading while the rest of us played paddleball. That sort of thing.

Luisa is weird. She knows it, too, and hates herself for it. She'd probably hate herself more if she were like Antonia, I bet. But maybe not. That's why I talk to her, though, because I understand her weaknesses. She knows it, so she's different with me. In a way, she kind of hates me, for having friends and for going out with girls who are her polar opposite. But for some reason, she accepts me anyway. It's hard to explain, but when we're alone together, I feel like she doesn't look down on me so much. In fact, I think I sort of entertain her, in a weird way, because if it weren't for me, Luisa Velásquez wouldn't know very much about the real world. I'm always telling her she should go out more, get a life, you know, but she never seems to listen. She thinks it's bad advice or something. The only thing about our friendship is that I don't feel like I can really open up to her totally, like right now I wish I could tell her how I'm feeling, how

I don't want to go back to Santiago and everything. Nobody knows that about me, least of all her. In a way I guess I don't want to reveal it.

I think I know why I don't open up to Luisa: it's because deep down inside she looks up to me. If she knew all my secrets, I wouldn't be as attractive or as interesting to her anymore. I like to have her this way, on my side, kind of unconditionally. I'm sure that underneath it all, she hates (and probably denies) the fact that she's attracted to me. I bet it just rankles her, and I know she chastises herself for it, tells herself to channel her energy toward a guy she's more compatible with, a guy who's more sensitive, tender, more of a sweetheart than me. Like Gonzalo McClure, for example. But she's got her masochistic side to her—why else would she keep coming back and playing games with me? I love provoking her and she knows that. I like things that way.

Just to fuck with her and make her a little jealous, I move over toward her, close enough so she can smell my breath. I say to her, in a low voice:

"Fine, you win. I did have an incredible time. So what? Everyone did, I guess. Although there are always the losers that manage to have a shitty time, who are so lame that they don't even realize that they're the ones who ruined the trip for themselves. They'll regret it, you'll see. You're only seventeen once, you know."

"Actually, I didn't have a very good time," she says to me.

"Hey, real fascinating conversation, guys, but I've got to sit down a second, okay?" Lerner, who's been staring out at the lights on the runway this whole time, suddenly interrupts us, as Luisa and I sit there philosophizing about the trip.

"Hey, later, okay?" I say to Lerner—I don't know why, since all I want to do is get away from this girl. Something tells me I should just get the hell away, leave her alone, but something else compels me to stay there talking to her. It's weird, but I'd rather be with her right now than by myself. I notice that Antonia is with her little clique; she doesn't even know I exist. I continue:

"You didn't have a good time, huh? That sucks."

"Yeah, well. Come on, let's go have a cup of coffee. I'll treat," she says.

"No thanks."

"Well, then, let's just sit down together."

"Legado."

"You just smoked marijuana, didn't you?"

"Yes, how terrible, right? Marijuana. Ma-ri-jua-na. *Maconha.* Kids today, I tell you, they're just bent on self-destruction. Nothing we can do about it."

"Have you got any left?"

"Hey, calm down now, Luisa. It's a little late to get with the crowd all of a sudden, don't you think? I mean, I know the trip was a bomb for you but let's not get carried away, huh? Anyway, I'm out."

"You love being a jerk, Matías. You do it on purpose." She pouts.

"We all do our part."

"And if you did have any marijuana, would you give me some?"

"For free . . . no. If you paid me, sure. I'm not your father, you know. If you want to ruin your academic career and throw away your future running around with the wrong crowd, fine. Go ahead and do it. Dig your own grave, my dear."

"It's just that I can't take it anymore."

"Come on, of course you can't—it's three in the morning. You're exhausted."

"Seriously, I can't believe the amount of money my parents wasted on this trip, this stupid trip, full of snotty jerks I don't even want to be with. The guys are all pathetic virgins desperate to lose it to the first *mulata* they see, and the girls are just spoiled princesses who came to get their little T-shirts and blouses and bikinis and hook up with Argentinian guys."

"Hey, calm down. I was here too, and so what? School's a load of shit, everyone knows that. This trip was a total bomb, more of the same bullshit. Even the hotel was shitty, but at least we got a chance to get out of Chile, do whatever we wanted for a few days, get to know people who were a whole hell of a lot nicer than the jerks that hang out at the Vitacura mall. That's what matters. The rest is all bullshit. You know that. I mean, what did you expect anyway? To go out dancing till dawn every night?"

She looks at me for a second or two, and she actually looks kind of pretty. Strangely enough, the fluorescent lights flatter her. I feel like I should say something meaningful right now, she's sort of waiting for me to, like she always does, but that's what bugs me about her. She's always expecting me to say certain things, like, so she doesn't feel abandoned or something. That drives me nuts, when people start expecting things like that from me. It brings me down, complicates things, forces me to be nice all the time. She continues looking at me. I go through my options, breathe deeply, and then back off.

"Listen, Luisa, nothing personal, but don't forget—a trip isn't going to change your life, you know. It's good because it makes you feel better, gives you some kind of perspective about Chile. Cassia's the one that said that to me, and she's traveled all over the world. Going to a different country shows you more options: new faces, new places, that kind of thing, you know. It's up to everyone to decide whether or not to take advantage of those options. We both know that Chile's a drag, but it's different here— you can do whatever you want. You can reinvent yourself, be someone else. If I can convince my asshole father, I'm going to come back next summer and screw Reñaca beach. I'm sick of it there."

"And you really believe that you were someone else here, is that it?"

"Yes. I matured a lot on this trip. I tried it all and I don't regret a single thing."

"Well, congratulations, then."

"Thank you."

There's a silence between us for a while.

"You just don't get it, do you, Matías? You're unreal. Even sarcasm goes over your head. It really does. I don't even know why I get involved with you in the first place. 'I matured a lot,' what a load of shit that is. Don't make me laugh. Go tell that to Antonia, not me. We're not even good enough friends for you to make up a story like that. Really."

"Hey, what's your problem? You're so uptight, you know that? You and your pop psychology—go analyze someone else, okay? Not me. I like to think of myself as normal, and frankly, I'd rather hang out with normal people if you don't mind. So if you don't like that, go leave me alone."

"The truth hurts, doesn't it?"

I keep looking at her and I almost smile at her, because I think that maybe, just maybe, she has a point, and maybe I was more of an unbearable jerk than usual and maybe I should try to make up for it a little. She flips her hair, turns around, and starts picking her nails as she looks out the window at the lights on the runway. She looks sort of distant. She must be really hating herself right now. Luisa Velásquez is like that—at the drop of a hat, she'll just get depressed and fall into a real existential rut, kind of a Pink Floyd thing. When she gets that way, there's nothing you can do about it, she just shuts off and closes up and you can't break in. I feel bad, but I shouldn't. She shouldn't start in with me like that. She knows that.

I wake up with a jolt. The airport's still here, and so am I, unfortunately. My eyes sting like hell, and I'd kill for some Visine. I tried to talk to Lerner earlier, to explain to him how I was feeling and everything, but he just wanted to talk about that Brazilian girl in the disco last night who gave him a blow job—"was she really a girl? She didn't actually take off all her clothes and her tits were too big to be real, don't you think?" He's next to me now, asleep, curled up on the floor, like Boris his famous German shepherd. I'm sure he's dreaming about his little Brazilian girlfriend, or boyfriend, or whatever. His return ticket falls out of the pocket of his linen jacket.

Almost on reflex, I look for mine too, and discover it's not there. I panic. I knew I was going to lose it, I knew it, I bet it's at the hotel, I left it in Leblon. Great, now I'm going to have to call the consulate and reschedule my flight and the chaperone's going to kill me. I look through my Adidas bag. It's there. False alarm. For a second, though, I could just imagine the ensuing chaos: "He'll have to stay here, the stupid jerk." And I, secretly happy, would leave the airport, find the highway, and probably hitch a ride back to the beach with a Jeep full of surfers. They'd take me down to the Rio Palace, right in the middle of it all in Copacabana. I'd rip off my T-shirt and Levi's and run headfirst into the ocean. And then Cassia would appear from behind, stroke my wet hair into a little ponytail. And then she'd say to me, like she did that one time, "You'd look so sexy, Matías, with long hair." And then I'd turn to her and say, "Oh yeah, really?" and her nose, her beautiful, elegant nose, would be all shiny and sunburned and I would lean over to her and kiss it, and the waves would splash over us and in between caresses and tickles she'd say to me, "Now it's your turn, time to go, time to swim . . ."

Instead, I walk around the airport a little, feeling sick. My fantasy didn't really do it for me, it was sort of second-rate, so I'm left feeling kind of bad, and sleepy too. It's just never-ending, I always feel this way, kind of like this plane that doesn't ever seem to take off. It really is just torture, senseless torture, dragging out like this. My head is killing me, my stomach too. Over the loudspeaker, I hear our plane is stuck in Dakar, Africa, a problem with the landing gear or something. When I get to a telephone, I contemplate before picking it up. Of course, I don't even have her phone number; there's no way for me to get in touch with her. I knew that, too, but for a split second I forgot. I lift the receiver and listen to the dial tone, different from the phones in Chile. I peek out and around the curve of the terminal, catch a glimpse of Antonia reading—just sitting there reading a magazine with a calmness, a serenity I can only imagine, and feel jealous of. I can't understand that at all, couldn't even if I tried.

I study her: she's perfect. In my eyes, at least. That's why I feel so far away from her at times; she seems so unattainable. That's the way I like it, though. Over her straight brown hair, she's wearing the hat I got for her, or rather, that she stole from me: it belonged to Tata Iván, my grandfather. I stole it from him at his eightieth birthday party. The hat—which is amazing—is a *calañé* from the 1920s, Hungarian. My grandfather used to use it to pick up girls in Budapest, and, thanks to his success, the hat quickly became the envy of all his friends. I was actually the one who started the trend in Las Condes. On the plane ride over to Rio, everyone wanted to try it on, but I gave it to Antonia. Right here in this airport, in fact, when we had just arrived. It had started to rain and I noticed she didn't want to get her hair wet, so I offered it to her. It was funny, because she's not the kind of person who usually accepts things like that, but I remember she looked at me and said, "Thanks. You saved me from getting soaked."

I'm holding the phone to my ear, listening to that strange dial tone. Luisa Velásquez is nearby, and I can sense she's trying to hear what I'm saying:

"You know I am, of course I'm coming back. . . . Really? . . . Yeah, me too . . . No, no, he's sleeping. . . . You're really going to miss me? Come to Chile, I'll teach you how to ski. . . . Yes, I love you, too, Cassia."

Then I hang up. I don't know why I did that, lied like that.

"I hope I'm not interrupting you," Luisa says, moving closer to me.

"No, no. Not at all. I just had to talk to her again, that's all."

"Aren't you two the little lovebirds."

"Come on, now. Don't be jealous, Luisa."

"Jealous? Please. Don't be ridiculous. I just overheard it, and it caught my attention, that's all. Oh, uh, and Antonia, she's fine, thanks very much."

"Who's side are you on anyway?"

"Not yours anymore, that's for sure."

She looks straight at me, tilts her head, and puts on this sat-isfied, smug little smile. Then she changes the subject:

"This whole thing with the plane being late is such a drag. Margarita already called some official in Santiago to tell him we'd be late."

"Yeah, I'm sure they're real broken up about it."

"Shall we take a little walk, Matías?"

"Sure, why not."

We go toward the Varig counter and pass behind Antonia, who stopped reading and is now talking to Rosita Barros and Vir-ginia Infante. My hat's sitting in her lap, and she's stroking it. The one she should be stroking is me, I think to myself.

Luisa takes me to the entrance to another gate: Rio–New York, direct. We sit down next to each other. We are silent. There are loads of Brazilians swarming around us, full of packages and bags and boxes, and of course two sexy *garotas* are waiting near the gate.

"So, what's up?" she asks me.

"Fucking lay off, will you? Why don't you just change the subject?"

I've already scanned the room once, fixating on a whole bunch of different people—a really pissed-off-looking guy reading a book in French, an older, elegant lady doing some needlepoint, but my eyes settle on a group. A family, actually.

"Look over there," I tell Luisa.

"Yeah, I noticed them before. That's why I brought you over here."

It's easy to see the tension between them. They're Brazilian, I can tell, but I can't hear anything they're saying because they're speaking very softly. The father, though, is the only one who's traveling. That's pretty clear. He's carrying a raincoat and a huge bag. Next to him is his wife, the mother, who's pretty young look-ing, and actually looks kind of like my mother when she's look-ing good. She's not traveling and neither are the kids, and there are three of them, two of them boys. One is about my age, and the other one is younger—about fourteen or so, athletic, a beach kid for sure—I bet he plays beach volleyball from the O'Brien T-shirt he's wearing. There's also a girl about the same age, nothing too special: green skirt, and she's got something wrong with her eyes—she's been crying, you can tell. And she's going to cry some more, I'm sure.

"He lives in the United States," Luisa tells me. "His whole world is there and he can't come back until he retires. He doesn't have anything here and the U.S. is where he can make a living. You take what you can get—that's what they say, isn't it?"

"How do you know all that?"

"The daughter told me. I asked her for a cigarette before. We were bored and so we got to talking. Her name is Gabriela and she lives near Botafogo but she just hates the beach. She wants to study biology."

"And what's up with the father? Why doesn't he stay?"

"Well, he has his whole life in the U.S. His wife and everything."

"What?"

"Yeah, yeah. This all happened years ago. He split all of a sudden one day. He just decided his marriage wasn't working anymore."

"I can't believe this girl told you all this. I mean, just like that?"

"Well, I guess some people just naturally confide in me, you know."

"Really, Luisa, come on."

"I'm serious."

I keep staring at them. The father looks at his watch again, like he's escaping or something, but he doesn't want to ruin the moment. You can tell he's taken something for his nerves and is kind of regretting it. Like maybe he's feeling like this is really his country, his home, and that he needs his wife more than he realized.

"So tell me," I say to Luisa, "is his wife over there American?"

"No, no. She's Brazilian. She followed him to Boston, in fact.

They live there now. He doesn't really love her, but they live together because it's worse to be alone, but now he's just realized
that he never stopped loving his first wife, this one here, and that
he truly despises the United States. There he's nobody. The only
thing good about his job is that he makes a lot of money. It hurts
him to leave his children behind, now that they're getting older.
Gabriela's thinking about getting married soon."

"And the son?"

"The older one, you mean?"

"Yeah, that one."

"What about him?"

"That's what I'm asking you. What about him? What's up
with him?"

"Well, this whole thing is hardest on him, actually. It's the first
time he's confronted his father."

"God, let's get out of here already, can we?"

"No, I want to see what happens to Gabriela . . . I kind of got
to liking her. Anyway, these things really mean something to me,
you know? I can use people like this as writing material. I mean,
in my family, everyone's always coming and going, you know
that. And no one ever cries, or gets sad, it's all the same to them,
they just board the plane and that's it."

I look at the older son, who sort of looks like me—if I dressed
like he did, that is. He turns around, looks out the window, then
talks to his brother. But he avoids his father, who looks just like
him, his father who's leaving again.

"I'll be right back," I say to Luisa as I edge away.

I lock myself up in another bathroom stall. I open my new pink
wallet and find the origami. I think the older son looked nervous:
almost childlike, vulnerable. You could tell he was trying not to
cry, but that he might not be able to hold it in, which he thinks
would disappoint his father. Maybe not, though. I find the sacred origami with its blessed, precious granulated grams. I open
it up and the powder looks perfect, bleached white and pure; I
could snort it all in one shot. I don't even have a straw or a spoon

or anything, so I press my finger into the envelope and then into my nostril, as far up as it will go. I breathe deeply. Peace. Calm, calm, I tell myself as the coke quickly takes effect. I smell Cassia too right now. I repeat the action with my other nostril and soon I get that bitter taste in the bottom of my throat, bitter like the guy who's leaving his family outside there in the terminal. Worse than that, even. I close the origami and carefully place it back in my wallet.

I exit the bathroom, and instead of looking for the group from school, I try to find Luisa and that guy who's trying not to cry.

"They're just about to leave. I mean, it's been like high drama here. The father is crying like a baby, he's so sad to leave."

I look at the older son's shoes. He's got these Top-Siders on, like the ones I left in Santiago. He stays off to the side, sort of outside the loop, separated from the rest of the family; it's hard for him to find his place. My throat starts to feel numb.

"Do you have a piece of gum?"

"Only cinnamon Dentyne."

The mother puts on her sunglasses. She's anxious; in her heart she just wishes he would leave quickly, so it would be less painful. She hugs him goodbye, but she holds back a little, she doesn't give herself over to him fully. The daughter also hugs him and turns away, crying, and at that moment, the father breaks down. He hugs the younger son, says something, a private joke or something, and they laugh. Then it's the older son's turn, and I'm getting more nervous by the second. My leg starts twitching. The father goes over to his son, his eyes all wet with tears, and hugs him. The son doesn't give him a real hug back, he's kind of like his mother that way. Then he says, "See you. Everything will be fine," or something like that. The father looks at him, a meaningful stare, a look that kills me, really rips through me. It's a look that says "We've lost so much time," or "You'll never forgive me for not seeing you grow up," or maybe, "I wish I were as strong as you are, son." The father turns away, devastated, and hugs the mother, hanging on to her, like he's asking for forgiveness. Then he disappears behind the door. That's when the guy, the older son who was so stoic before, starts sobbing uncontrollably. He falls into a chair, covers his face, and cries, and his brother and sister stare at him, and he says, "What are you looking at, assholes?" in Portuguese and you can just tell he's in a really bad way, feeling fucked all around. I stand there staring at him, thinking I understand him. I'm no good with these situations—I turn away and start crying also, I can't help it, it's like something out of my control. I close my eyes and the tears spill out effortlessly, and I feel this terrible sense of failure, of loss, and I'm scared. Something's been lost or is going to be lost and I don't know what it is.

The guy gets up, and disappears. From far away, I can hear a plane take off. I can hardly move. I think to myself: I'm not like that, I don't cry. Something must be happening to me. I let go of Luisa's hand, which I've been holding throughout this all.

"If you tell anyone about this, you're dead."

I dry my eyes and try to laugh a little; I never thought that coke would have that kind of effect on me.

"Are you okay?" Luisa asks me.

"I guess. It must be the drugs: sort of an aftereffect."

"Sure," she says, smiling as if to say "I get it . . ."

Fatigue really hits me all of a sudden, so I lean back into the folds of her skirt, rest my head in her lap, and close my eyes.

"I really want to get out of here," I say to her.

She doesn't say anything, but I can sense she feels the same way. I'm sure she's imagining all sorts of wild fantasies with me lying in her arms, but I don't really care. I'm just wiped out, and I turn over, facedown. I feel her hand stroking my hair, and I feel her wiping away my tears, my stupid tears, with her fingers.

FRIDAY

It was a turbulent flight. No, wait, I take that back, it wasn't really. Not at all, in fact. It was actually pretty calm, no air pockets, nothing. It left me sort of numb, out-of-it, partially because of the time in the air, but also because of that endless wait in the airport that had us all climbing the walls. I was ready to do anything to get out of there. It was so tense, such heavy stuff, I'd just as soon forget it ever happened. It was like this big anticipation, big buildup, and then nothing. As if all the bullshitting and fun and going out in Rio with Cassia and the beach and the drinking and the pot and everything just went away, never happened. As if, in a dream or something, someone pushed Record instead of Play and erased what was on my favorite tape forever. The memories are there still, sure: I can even remember the lines, but the thing is that I'll never get to hear them again. Shit. I'm back for good. Now I'm back in Chile.

I remember almost all of it now, even the things I thought I forgot about. Once I tied up all the loose ends in my mind, I absorbed everything that happened, and now I actually remember it pretty clearly. Better now that some time has passed.

I hated to have to leave Rio. I really miss it. Somehow, some way, the plane finally arrived in Chile, and by that time, I wasn't in great shape. That whole situation in the airport with the father who was leaving his family got to me, and my reaction embarrassed me. Coke has a way of distorting reality much more than a person realizes. When we boarded, Luisa took me down the aisle and we sat together for a while. I remember the hum of the engines, the plane picking up speed, going down the runway, taking off, the lights of Leblon and São Corrado shining underneath us, looking out the window, thinking about Cassia, who was down there below, maybe dreaming about me . . .

Santiago, Chile. I go into our kitchen. Carmen, our housekeeper, with those smudgy Coke-bottle glasses, wearing that blue apron I can't stand, is older and uglier than I remember. She doesn't even look at me. She's washing a pan, and I can tell she's about to leave. It's her day off. No one's going to be home tonight anyway, so it's a good day for her to take it. I notice that Rommy isn't here. She's a redhead, Irish, or so she says: "Just like O'Higgins, the founding father of our country." That's what she said to my mother anyway. So maybe it's true—she's from Chillán, so it's possible.

"Rommy's not here, Carmen?"

"No, and that little cunt isn't coming back either. Your mother fired her while you were away. She was stealing. What a whore— I never saw a hornier bitch in my life . . . what a nerve she had. So a friend of mine is going to help out for a little while. I can't do all this work by myself. You people in this house are trying to kill me."

"Oh, shut up. Just give me a glass of tomato juice, will you?"

Rommy sure didn't last very long. I never even got a chance to make a move on her, much less get her in bed, and she was pretty hot. Not even twenty years old. One time she went out with Lerner and they ended up in bed together in some sleazy hotel near the train station. He told me all about it—said it was amazing, that she was insatiable, etc. She overheard the conversation, though, when we were on the phone and afterward told me that he was all talk and that the whole thing wasn't so hot and heavy. Not at all.

"Here's your juice. Hurry up and drink it because I want to get out of here. I've got to take two buses."

"Well then, go if you want to."

I go over to the bar and pour a little Stoli into the juice and bring it to my room. Nobody's around. I close the door and turn on the stereo: Earth, Wind and Fire, "September." The pits. I put on "Tangerine Dream" instead. Familiar, predictable, nothing great, but lets me think for a little while. I take a sip of my Bloody Mary, lean back, and feel the effect. I try to sleep a little, since I'm still wiped out.

The trip continues. It's as if the bed is spinning, as if my body continues on in the air, like one of those physics laws they teach you in school. That whole thing about how a body in motion tends to stay in motion. So to make up for the plane being late, Iberia gave us an open bar during the flight. Just what I needed. I ordered a bunch of those little bottles of Johnnie Walker Red Label, and I mixed them right into a Coke bottle, then looked out the window and stared at all the landing lights and colored lines and vectors and X-Y coordinates on the runway. Luisa kept saying that I shouldn't drink any more, but then she fell asleep, so I got up and walked around the plane, a DC-10. McClure was awake, so we hung out for a little while, talking about the tapes he bought in Rio. Then they brought dinner, so I headed back, and found Antonia sitting alone by the window, with an empty seat next to her.

"Am I interrupting something?"

"No, of course not, stupid."

"Great, great."

The stewardess gave us our dinner trays. I ordered a beer, and Antonia got a Fanta.

"You're on something, right?"

"No, no, I swear."

"Don't lie, Vicuña."

I had no appetite whatsoever, but that didn't stop me from wolfing down the shrimp cocktail with ketchup.

"You want mine?" she asked.

"Yeah, please—that's right, I remember you don't like them."

We didn't talk much. She was tired and was playing the bitch, acting as if she didn't really care whether I sat next to her or not. The stewardess passed by again, took away the trays, and gave me two little slips of paper to fill out. Customs stuff.

"She must think we're a couple," I say.

"Well, she's wrong."

"I wouldn't be so sure about that."

"Matías, please. Cut it out. If you really want, fill out that thing for me. Those forms drive me nuts. You know all there is to know about me."

Just then, I remember it well, the plane took a sharp turn. I noticed it but I don't think anyone else did. Then they turned out the overhead lights. I fell right asleep, just as these iridescent clouds passed in front of the almost full moon that reflected off the wing of the plane. I dreamed of Antonia: I remembered an afternoon at her house, the two of us playing Scrabble with her little brother. I was coming up with these tender, special words that would make her fall in love with me, trying to subtly change the mood, so that she would open up to me and really express herself, just that once.

A little turbulence woke me up, and I felt Antonia resting on my shoulder. She was unaware of what she was doing, and it felt like the most natural thing in the world. I gently took her hand in mine, and with my other hand, stroked her hair. That lasted for about two seconds but I swear I saw her smiling. Or at least, inside, subconsciously, her heart opened up just a little, and she let down some of her defenses, even for that brief period. She woke up with a start, and quickly readjusted herself, as if embarrassed for letting her guard down. She straightened right up and jerked her hand away from mine.

We both remained silent, then listened to the hum of the plane's engine and the chatter of the stewardesses down the aisle. Antonia didn't say a single word to me, and didn't look at me either. For a few minutes. Or maybe it was hours. I don't know. Not too long after, the plane began to lose altitude little by little, and our ears started to pop. I didn't know what to say to her, so I got up to go to the bathroom, to see how I looked: horrible. I washed my face with that strange water that comes out of those little plane faucets, and I almost took out my little origami but something made me stop.

When I returned to where I thought my seat was, I realized I'd screwed up; I was in the wrong aisle, and Antonia was five seats over. I saw her, past all the other heads in the same row, a ray of orangy light shining in from the window next to her, not just on her hair. It put her whole face in silhouette, in such a way that made her appear to be lit up from inside, in the middle of that dark, sleepy plane. I just stood there staring at her. I think she realized, because she opened her eyes all of a sudden, looked out the window, and then turned around and caught my gaze. We both held it there—that I remember perfectly. Antonia doesn't ever smile, and she doesn't really communicate with her eyes. She just looks out, and she looked at me as if I were some sort of stranger. As if she couldn't care less who I was. Then, in the blink of an eye, she turned back around and looked out at the horizon, a horizon that was a black sky opening up to a yellowish purple light. I didn't know what to do with myself, that's how hurt I was. I just fell into the nearest seat, wounded. I looked at her again, but it was useless. I lost her. The captain then ordered us to fasten our seat belts and turned out the lights as the plane began its descent, slow and sure, into Buenos Aires, where I could see the lights spread out below, underneath the clouds.

The TV is on. It's on mute, though, so that I can watch, but not listen, to those idiot Bee Gees, who seem to be singing "Jive

Talkin'." Channel 5 has shown that Midnight Special concert over and over. They probably don't have the budget to show any new stuff. In my hand I have one of those luscious little Freshen-Ups that they just started to sell here. I pop it into my mouth and chew it until I squeeze all the green syrup out of it: *love that squirt!* Then I spit it out.

The housekeeper's gone now. But my mother should be coming home soon, I guess. I turn on the TV, it's Rod Stewart singing "Hot Legs," I've seen it about a hundred times. Channel 5 is the worst, I don't know what that Pirincho Cárcamo is doing on it. I turn away from the TV and poke my head out the window. From there I can see down to the street, and it looks like there was some kind of accident, I think someone got hit by a car. There's a horse lying on the pavement but apart from that, I can't see much—I can tell there's a lot of blood on the street. A mess. There's an overturned truck next to the horse, and there's fruit strewn all over the road, and a totaled Fiat in the middle of it all. I look back into the room. With the remote control, I change the channel. Afternoon movies. An old one with Kristy McNichol, who's on *Family* now. She looks young and scrawny, not nearly as cute as she is now. Like the way she looks in *Little Darlings,* where she sleeps with Matt Dillon and loses her virginity and wins the bet she makes with Tatum O'Neal, who plays the precious little rich girl. And Tatum almost does it with Armand Assante but doesn't. Or something like that. The phone rings.

"Why didn't you call when you got back, fucker?"

"Nacho! What's happening?"

"Nothing. What do you think is happening? Bullshit, that's all. Bored as shit."

"Yeah, that's what I figured."

"And? So? How was the trip? What happened?"

"I don't know, lots of stuff. It was awesome, really cool. I mean, I can't believe it's over. I should have never come back."

"Oh, fuck. No offense."

"Yeah, yeah, I know. It sucked for you."

"No, no, I know . . . whatever . . . it doesn't matter anyway. So hey, let's meet up or something. I've got some shit from Los Andes."

"I don't think I can. I can't, man. I've got one of those family parties to deal with, and I've got to make an appearance. I mean, I don't want to go, it's just that I can't get out of it, or maybe, well, maybe I won't go. It's my cousin, that loser, it's his graduation party. You remember him, don't you?"

"When's it over?"

"No idea, man."

"Well, let's meet later. I'll be at Juancho's."

"Maybe."

"No, no, you have to come, Matías—you owe me one, come on. And I missed you . . ." he jokes.

"All right, all right, maybe. Bye."

"You're stoned, aren't you?"

"Yeah, a little."

"Good deal. See you later."

I hang up and change the channel. Jeff Cutash is giving disco lessons in some unbelievable club in New York. *Hot City.* They showed it in Rio too, Cassia told me about it. She hated it—all these greasy Latin lovers in polyester shirts teaching each other the hustle or the shuffle, or whatever.

Then Alicia Bridges comes out on the stage. Her hair is high-lighted all silver, and she looks like a total slut, even worse than she did on Raúl Matas's show. I'm about to turn the volume down but then I hear her start singing, "I love the night life, I've got to boogie . . ." and she totally wins me over. I love that song, I don't know why. I know all the words by heart. Actually, that kind of music really annoys me, all that disco stuff does. But this particular one is one of those songs you love to hate, or hate to love, or something. Whatever. I don't know. That song in particular is kind of like a guilty pleasure. So I listen to it. I don't know how the fuck I'm able to remember those ridiculous lyrics.

I'm getting restless: Alicia stops singing and Tavares threatens to appear on the screen again. I push the mute button.

I punch out a number on the phone:

"Nacho."

"Matías. What's up?"

"Who are you going to Juancho's with?"

"A bunch of us are going."

"Girls?"

"Some of them. Maybe Pelusa, maybe Maite."

"Maite's still alive and kicking?"

"More than ever, dude."

"Well, anyway, whatever . . . Hey, I brought you something from Brazil."

"You did?"

"Yeah, what did you think? I wouldn't forget about you. You'll love it, I promise. So yeah, let's meet up later."

Nacho's a good guy, really cool. We get along. He's by far my best friend, much more so than Lerner. But who cares; if you start analyzing your friendships too much, you'll end up all alone and bored and that's not the idea at all. I could control Nacho if I wanted to: he's the type who can't make a single decision for himself. He's constantly asking my advice on stuff, which sometimes I give him. I do care about him, love him maybe, in a weird way, but I'd never say it to him, or to anyone else, just because, I mean, that would seem sort of lame, kind of faggy or something.

Nacho, a devoted surfer who dances samba like nobody else I know, didn't come to Rio with us. Too bad, too, because Rio's a place he's dreamed about ever since he was a little kid. They really fucked him on this one, and it was all his father's doing. He punished Nacho, said he couldn't go with the rest of us. And it wasn't a money thing either, because his family's loaded, more than mine, even. His old man is in the military, in the navy. He's some kind of decorated officer, even though he doesn't actually navigate ships. He works here in Santiago, in some kind of gov-

ernment job. I personally think he's involved in some pretty un-
kosher business, but nobody here would ever dare say anything
about it. He's definitely connected—he's got this unbelievable
olive-green Mercedes and he promised Nacho a new Mazda
when he turns eighteen. Now, though, it looks like Nacho would
be lucky if he got a ten-speed bike for his birthday. He'll never
forgive him for this one, though, I'm sure of that. His father's really serious—like he doesn't even speak to me anymore. Like it's
my fault or something. And I'm actually the one friend his father used to like.

So Nacho's old man has an office in one of those modern
buildings by La Moneda. From his window you can see how
they're fixing up the area, down to every last little detail. Nacho
and I have gone by there a million times, to borrow money from
his father. Every time we go there, we have to pass through a
security check, with those military jerk-offs that guard the entrance, all prepared with their guns. But now Nacho's father
can't stand him, really hates him, because Nacho finally decided he couldn't take any more of that Escuela Naval, something I always knew but never said to his face. I mean, nobody
with their head screwed on straight would voluntarily put up
with the shit there. They order you around nonstop, make you
do all sorts of crap, they take out their shit on you and make
your life hell for no reason. Nacho lasted about six months at
the Escuela Naval, and I'm surprised he even made it that long,
after the things he described to me. I mean, there was some stuff
they put him through that could really fuck with a person's
mind.

But anyway, typical, his father totally denied that it was any
kind of "sadomasochistic experience" (which it was), and forced
Nacho to go, took him out of our school and registered him
there, but also told him he would make sure that he'd be able to
go on the yearly trip on the Chilean sailing ship the *Esmeralda*.
He said he would personally make sure the trip went to California and Hawaii so that Nacho could surf. Nacho never wanted

to go, but just figured why not, how bad can it be anyway, maybe he would even look good in a uniform.

The phone rings:
"Hello, is Francisca there?"
"No, she's not. Sorry."
"Okay, thanks. Bye."

A group of us from school went to say goodbye to him, in Valparaíso. We had a party at my beach house in Reñaca, and everyone came, everyone except Nacho, that is. If there was anyone on this earth totally wrong for military life—especially naval life—it would have to be Nacho. Or me. Lazy, sloppy, disorganized, easygoing. In Valparaíso they buzz-cut his hair, made him get up at sunrise to exercise, and forced him to salute the members of the Junta Militar.

"Listen," he said to me once. "Remember the book *Time of the Hero,* by Vargas Llosa, that book that Flora Montenegro made us read? Well, that book is like fucking kindergarten playtime compared to what went on in the Escuela Naval. What a shithole, I'm telling you . . . no way could I take any more of that. I'm like terrorized there, it's so fucking scary."

He finally worked up the guts to leave the school. Of course his old man found out, and when he did, refused to allow Nacho in the house anymore. So now it's Nacho's mother who pays for his school and gives him money. But she can't give him that much, and didn't have enough to pay for the trip to Rio. So that's why he didn't go. Even if he had the money, his prick of a father probably would have refused to sign that form you need in order to leave the country if you're underage. That's how much he hates Nacho. He's accused him of being everything from a communist to a traitor to a coward and a hundred other things in between. Parents are just like that, I guess: they're just a big pain in the ass you have to deal with somehow. I haven't figured it out yet. So Nacho lives with his sister now, he's crashing there for as long as he can, which sucks, but he somehow gets through it. And his hair is growing back.

I don't know how my mother does it. She puts on her makeup without looking into the mirror once, as she runs around the apartment in her mustard-colored caftan. One hand is holding the phone, and the other is holding her blush. She's talking with my aunt Loreto, her sister, supposedly my godmother as well as the mother of those cousins of mine. Every so often my mother breezes into my room, looks around, then says something to me, as my aunt on the other end of the telephone line orders around the hired help in her house,

"Hurry up, Matías. Let's get going."

"All right, all right. Stop hounding me, Mother."

"Don't play games with me. You're going to this party. That's it. That's final."

"So what you're saying is, I should go. Maybe yes, maybe no?" I mess with her a little.

"Matías, please. Don't try to be funny right now. I'm in no mood for this. We're already late, I'm not nearly ready, I still look terrible, and I'm sure your father's going to arrive late. So do me a favor and get ready."

I look up at the ceiling but there's nothing interesting to see, so instead I cover my face with a pillow. Just the idea of getting together with my family depresses me. To put it mildly. Makes me suicidal is more like it. It makes me want to look in my mother's little orange-colored phone book, in her "emergency" listings, for one of the psychologists she sent my sisters to. I hold back, though.

I feel trapped. I never should have come back from Rio, that's my final conclusion. Barely one day back and I can't cope. I should have taken photos, I think to myself. Now I regret not having taken any. "If I can't picture it in my mind, it isn't worth saving," that's what I said to myself. Just to be different, I decided to hide my camera in the bottom of my bag during the trip. So I didn't take any photos. I hope Rosita Barros had hers developed. She took about a million snapshots. One, in particular, of me and Cassia at the entrance to the hotel. And another one of me and Antonia in Buenos Aires on the way there.

I wonder what Antonia is up to. Bored, in her house probably. I bet she won't go out tonight. I hope that *huevón* Gonzalo McClure is too chicken to call her tonight. He's always devastated whenever Antonia says no to him. Me too, though. I guess. I don't know, I mean, I don't really care that much anyway, I don't regret anything. She's probably hanging around with her girlfriends, showing off her new clothing, and bad-mouthing me. Actually, I bet she stays home tonight and watches television. I could call her, but maybe I should go to Javier's party. Go with the crowd, or whatever, until I hit bottom.

"All right, all right. I'm coming. I'll go with you to Javier's big night. Only back off, okay? Don't hassle me. I really can't take it."

"Fine. That's nice. Only it would be even nicer if you'd put on some nice clothes and shaved, maybe. All our friends are going to be there."

"Yes, okay, fine."

She finally gets out of my way and goes into the bathroom to finish making herself up. The hot air from the central heating feels fresher without her there. I turn on the stereo, put on Radio Carolina and listen to some awful song by the Village People. Boy, are they really on their way down. Still, though, that song about the eighties is kind of good. Another one of those "guilty pleasures" that I sing along with every so often. I'm obsessed with that line: *Get ready for the eighties, ready for the time of your life.* I don't know whether or not to believe it, because inside I feel like this decade is going to be all right. And it makes me think of something my friend Lerner sometimes says, just says without even thinking: "The eighties belong to us, dude." For some reason, that keeps sticking in my head, I keep remembering that, over and over again.

"Goodbye, Matías. We're leaving. We'll see you there."

The door closes behind them. I feel better already. She's gone to the party with my two sisters, who came home while I was sleeping. There are four children altogether, plus my parents. I'm the only boy, the third child. Pilar is the oldest and she's married to this jerk. All he ever talks or thinks about is rugby and getting laid. They've already got three kids and they've only been married for two years. The first one came six months after the wedding too. My mother always says he was premature, but the rest of us know. Whatever, though. I mean, that's not the first time my mother covered up for one of us, to preserve the "family honor," if you can call it that. Maybe that's why she's constantly running away from me, she feels guilty or something.

The other two are fucking vain, nobody takes them seriously. They spend all day on the phone gossiping with their friends and buying 45s at Circus. They sound like total stereotypes, but they're for real. They get all emotional at the stupidest things, and they're totally unaware that they're wasting their lives away. Francisca, the cutest one of all three of them, is around eighteen, and she studies advertising at this exclusive, really expensive school, run by a friend of my mother's. She used to be really wild but now they've got her a little more under control, especially after all that happened. Bea, who's the youngest, is around fourteen. She doesn't even merit analysis, really, until she grows up, gets past that immature stage of hating me and talking about me to her little friends, all of whom think I'm the hottest thing ever. When I'm not around they go into my room, go through my underwear, that kind of thing.

I try to read the paper. No way, though, too depressing. Gustavo Leigh, the guy who bombed La Moneda, switched parties and now he's voting for the "NO." And Jaime Guzmán, that fucking nerd, talks all day about justifying the "SI." Pinochet, as always, is on a big political trip through the south, to get votes. And of course he'll get them, he's going to win anyway. Pinochet himself is pathetic, but he's smart, because he surrounds himself with good advisers, like Guzmán. This month's slogan is: "Good today, better tomorrow."

My sister Francisca, who is now old enough, is going to vote for the "SI." She and all her poser friends are for Pinochet's *Constitución de la Libertad*. They talk nonstop about how Chile is now the most important country in Latin America for advertising. All the other countries come here to film their commercials. I could care less about politics. The truth is, I just don't know very much, outside of those documentaries on TV that are against the Allende administration. They're the ones they show on Channel 7. They're actually kind of entertaining, because Chile seems like such a different place on them. It's as if it were another country: men with long beards, girls in miniskirts, and posters and demonstrations and sit-ins and riots. My mother says it was the worst time ever in Chile, but I don't see that at all—it looks great to me. She's always exaggerating, my mother. Some of what she says is true, I guess. At the very least, though, it's a hell of a lot more interesting than what's going on these days.

I feel like lighting a stick of that incense I got from those Hare Krishnas on the bus before the trip. But the smoke nauseates me and the smell vaguely reminds me of those summer nights we would go out to Quintero, to pick up those slutty girls and get laid on the beach at Loncura. Or Ritoque, where the girls were even easier to nail—they'd actually hop in with us and we'd do it in the car. This incense doesn't smell like sandalwood, though, I think it's patchouli. Whatever. Anyway, it's awful. I grab the stick and put it out in a half-empty Coke bottle that's been sitting on my windowsill since yesterday. The Coke's dead anyway. A curl of white smoke drifts up. I get up, leave my room, and close the door behind me.

I decide to walk around the balcony for a little while; it's cold but I don't really care, at least it's clear out there. The smog is practically gone, the sun is shining this bright orange color behind the Torre Entel, and the Costanera thoroughfare is nothing more than a large ribbon of lights moving slowly toward me. Our apartment is pretty big and takes up the entire top floor of the building, which is pretty neat, because there's always sun no matter what time of the day it is. My bedroom looks toward San Cristóbal Hill, where I sometimes pedal my Benotto up, up to the pool and the monument to the heroes of La Concepción. That's where Pinochet holds his annual ceremony to decorate the little ass-kissers of the year, our very own Hitler youth from the military academies. I'm sure my cousin Javier is doing everything humanly possible to win that award for next semester.

My father, looking really studly, bursts into the house, all tan from blowing off work and going up to ski at La Parva. His shirt is halfway unbuttoned and his hair in calculated disarray. He makes his triumphant entrance just as *Eight Is Enough* comes on TV. I see him through the glass, and when he catches sight of me, he waves. Going back inside from the balcony, I notice how fucking happy the guy looks, like always, which, of course, always makes me withdraw from him. It makes me feel bad that I can't ever just take it easy, have a good time in life the way he does. He turns on the stereo and puts on Olivia Newton-John's latest album, the sound track from *Xanadu.* It's by far her worst. But he likes that shit. He thinks it makes him youthful, he actually thinks this is what kids listen to all the time.

He starts preparing drinks for us.

"Here, have one."

"I can't. I have to study," I lie to him.

"Hey, kid, life isn't all about studying, you know. Take it easy, have a drink with your old man."

He practically forces me to down a screwdriver. It's not bad, actually. My father, in a way, feels like a real winner. He knows he's good looking, that's how he got my mother to fall for him. The priests kicked him out of high school, so he started making money at a pretty young age, before the rest of his friends. He got married when he was this young stud, and I guess still looks younger than he really is.

"Matías, hurry up and get dressed. We don't have that much time. I don't want to be late to Javier's."

As if Javier's party is some major social event. My perfect cousin, Javier, who was selected to be on the national ski team. Javier with the bulging biceps and the Peval T-shirts. Javier the windsurfing champion. He's one of those guys who always seem to have everything. He gets everything he wants so effortlessly. So he's turning twenty-one. He's just about to graduate from Hotel Management and Tourism at INACAP, *of course.* My uncle, his father, wants to open a hotel near Pucón. He thinks he can turn the place into an international resort. Highly doubtful. I can't think of a more boring place for tourists than Pucón or Villarrica or Licán or the whole southern part of Chile for that matter. All those annoying little boats. The only thing worse is the people that sail on them.

Javier's graduation has everyone all excited, especially my fucking grandmother, who always melts at the sight of her little darling. Actually, the guy isn't that bad. I mean, he's finally finishing up something that has some merit, something that's slightly more meaningful than picking up girls in bars. Before going south, my uncle is sending him on a trip to Atlantic City to do some kind of internship at some major hotel with a casino. He also wants to send Javier to some cooking school in France where they specialize in sauces, patés, *petits bouchées,* and things like that. This is a guy, everyone says, who's really going to be a real success.

I go into the shower, wash my hair, and then get out. I start shaving what little hair I have on my face when my father comes in. I forgot to lock it. Shit. He turns on the Jacuzzi, placing his drink on the water faucet. Without giving me a moment to react, he gives me a little whack, trying to take off the towel around my waist. He almost gets me naked. I just barely manage to cover myself.

"What are you hiding, kid? A lot of people say you've got a lot to show off there."

Now it's confirmed in my mind: my father definitely wants to see me naked. This has happened before. The other day, for example, he invited me to come with him to the Sauna Mund, this Turkish bath. I said no, of course, but he's always saying how being naked is the ultimate form of complicity; it's the most basic trust that can exist between a father and a son. Maybe he has a point, but it still sounds kind of suspicious to me. He doesn't mean any harm, though. Guys are always showering together, in locker rooms or other places like that, and nobody questions it. No big deal. But that doesn't mean you automatically trust each other or anything. That's why it's different with my father. It's something he's kind of pressuring me into and it pisses me off. I just can't stand the thought of him looking at me. It's as if I'd be revealing my deepest secret to him, really turning myself over to him. I think that there should be things, certain things, that a person has a right to keep to himself and not share with anyone. My old man dreams of my becoming a mirror where he could see himself. There's one thing I'm sure of, though: I will never give him that pleasure.

When I wipe the mirror, I realize that with the jolt of his smacking me, I've cut myself. I watch the blood trickle down my throat and mix in with the foam. It drips in big globs into the sink, filled with water.

"What happened? Did you get your period?" he laughs.

I give him my most withering look as I fix my towel, firmly. I'm sure I'm red in the face, embarrassed, so I splash water on my face and put a little cotton on my nick. My father slips out of his blue, Japanese-style robe and gets into the Jacuzzi, which he brought from Houston. The fucker stays in shape, I have to admit. Always tan, lean, he's a real exhibitionist too. I sleep in pajamas, but my father struts around the house in the nude, even in front of my sisters. They make fun of it all, and laugh at him and how ridiculous he is.

I close the bathroom door and go back to my bedroom. I lock the door, but even with the lock I don't feel very safe. My father is always trying to talk to me about sex, he's always giving me condoms, porno magazines, money for hookers, that kind of thing. One time, we were downtown, drinking coffee at the Haití, looking at the waitresses in their minidresses, and he invited me to come with him to a massage parlor he frequented. I said no. He never forgave me for that. I know it. He went alone. Maybe I should have gone with him. Later, at home, he stopped me in the hallway and tried to bond with me a little: "She completely drained me," I remember him saying to me. I'm sure he thinks I'm a virgin, or gay. He always tries to act really cool and mess around with me, and I have no idea why. I don't know any other fathers that are like that. Most of them barely take the time to even look at their kids. Mine never stops hassling me. Just my luck.

I put on a striped shirt and a pair of slightly worn-out FU's that my mother brought back from her four hundredth trip to Miami. I sit and wait for my father. He finally emerges, wearing his Azzaro cologne, a gray wool suit, from Milan, and a burgundy silk tie. He looks good, I guess. In the elevator, he starts playing again, this time punching me, Rocky style. He waits for me to retreat and jump up, to start throwing some punches myself, but instead I don't pay attention. I've found it's better just to ignore him. Maybe someday I should nail him with a good left hook, leave him knocked down and unconscious for a few days on the elevator floor, as punishment. Maybe then he'd learn.

In his car, his beloved Volvo, he puts in a KC and the Sunshine Band tape—his taste really is the worst—and sings at the top of his voice in his Chilean Spanglish, as he tears out of the parking lot, cutting people off whenever he can, racing whenever possible. As we stop for a light, two blondes in an orange Datsun check out my father and smile their little flirtatious smiles. That whole thing. My father gets this really sexy look on his face, a real killer, eyes the girls, and lights a cigarette as if he's in a Viceroy commercial or something. Then we continue, full speed ahead, running from who knows what, burning rubber and screeching the tires for blocks and blocks. The Datsun follows us. The driver is really scary looking. She looks like one of those heavily tanned Argentinian women who summer in Viña, wearing tight, ratty old T-shirts. Not gorgeous, but probably a good fuck. Like a real party girl.

"So what do you think, stud? You get the one in the passenger seat, and I get the fox that's driving. Whoever scores first, wins. At the next light, offer them a smoke."

My father's always calling me "stud." He drives me crazy with that "stud" shit. He's totally obsessed with picking up women on the street. He goes for any woman that gives him the nod, wherever and however he can. And he's constantly trying to rope me into these *affaires*. Too bad they don't interest me in the least.

"What do you think? We could get that lovers' suite in Valdivia for the four of us. Let's see who gets it first."

"Stop your dreaming, will you? We've got the cocktails, the party . . ."

At the next light, I'm supposed to lower the window and offer them cigarettes. I throw them the box.

"Are you two brothers?" the driver asks me before accelerating and leaving us sitting there.

My father is overjoyed. The triumphant one, he wins again. At Calle Luis Pasteur he turns right and we're off again, at full speed.

"Another time, stud. One of these days your father is going to get you some pussy you'll never forget," he says as he leans over and ruffles my hair.

We continue on in silence for a few more blocks. I try to mentally distance myself as much as possible from him. All of a sudden, almost as an aside, he says to me, "I sure as hell love you, stud."

He doesn't even look at me, but just keeps on driving. I don't know quite what to do or say. I suddenly feel tense and nauseated. I'm no good at this kind of stuff, and even worse when the

feelings aren't reciprocal. I don't say a thing. It just doesn't occur
to me what to say. "Thanks" wouldn't exactly do it. I focus on
the mansions hidden behind the huge stone fences that are covered with antigovernment graffiti. It's all against Pinochet, huge
"NOs" that some genius majordomo or butler has tried to cover
with whitewash.

My father takes out the tape then turns on the radio. I think
about him. He's got girls by the kilo. They're not all in his imagination, they're for real, with great asses and great tits. And they
all fuck a lot too. I can't even fathom it. I'm too romantic, I guess.
Or shy. Or better yet, a plain old nerd. For my father, nailing a
cute girl is as easy as turning on the television. And that's probably his greatest virtue, that adolescent quality he has. He's like
Nacho almost, the way he insists on recounting every last detail
to me. I'm his confidant. If he didn't have me to tell all those
things to, I don't know if he would have such a burning desire
to fuck all those girls: it just wouldn't be as fun. He reaches his
orgasm again, I'm sure of it, in the retelling of the story, sharing
it with me. Since he doesn't have any friends, he tells me everything. Except I'm his son, not his friend. I listen to him anyway.
I feel guilty, though. Since I don't share my confidences with
him, the least I can do is listen to him. All his stories are always
the same. They never change. The sexual stuff never changes
very much. It's not like when a person falls in love and despite
all his experience, he's still the little boy inside, unsure of himself, vulnerable. All his experiences are the same, that's why it's
so lame. He tells me everything. He even shows me photographs:
Polaroids of orgies at his friends' houses, girls with their legs
wide open, that kind of shit.

The one thing he never talks about, though, is his relationship
with my mother. Probably because it doesn't really exist. They
don't even flirt. Sometimes, when they've both drunk enough,
though, they mess around a little, dance together, or even make
love, and all of us, my sisters and I, die of laughter listening to
their moans and groans. I know they got married in a hurry, that's

my sister Pilar's fault. I'm the only one who knows it, because I'm the only one who took the time to make the necessary calculations. In any event, though, for my father it was a big move socially, because his family, the Vicuñas, were definitely on their way down. He said something to that effect once when we were driving home to Santiago from Reñaca. He was pretty drunk, and it was just the two of us. I was chewing on some beef jerky. I remember there was a green '59 Chevy in front of us the whole way.

"It was in the backseat of a car when we conceived you, kid. That was my first car. Your sisters were little and we left them with your grandmother. We went to the Cajón del Maipo and had a few bottles of pisco. We stayed out late, dancing the twist with the radio on. We were like teenagers. I looked pretty hot too, no kidding. I was wearing a jacket like James Dean, and was the best-looking out of all my friends, seriously. So we settled into the backseat and ended up doing it. We hadn't talked about having another baby because I still didn't have much money, you know? Economically, the country was nothing, not like it is now. So when you were born, I didn't want anything or anyone else. I took you around everywhere, where all my friends were, to show you off. I was the only one married out of all of us back then, and you became our little mascot. I was so proud of you. Even before knowing your mother, or getting married, I always wanted a son. A little guy just like me."

All right, Matías, *the night is young.* I imagine that I'm in Rio or Los Angeles, speeding down a street lined with palm trees. If only Santiago had freeways and highways to roar down: I could get up to 100, maybe even 110, on my parents' Accord. But Santiago is in Chile and the only things we have are those four-way intersections and endless, useless traffic circles packed with cars going round and round and round. I'm in the traffic circle at the Portada de Vitacura, going around and around, as usual.

I've already gone around four times; I suppose I should try to exit already. First, I look at the digital clock on the dashboard: 22:18. Early. The curfew tonight is 3:00 A.M. Nacho said "late" so I have some time to kill. I decide to go for a ride, to get lost for a little while.

I go up Avenida Kennedy, which shines, wide and white, under those mercury lights, and I continue changing the radio station, horrified by all the disco music that's on. What happened to good old rock and roll? I pull out a tape, one of my mother's: Anne Murray. Not exactly my taste. "Country love songs," that's what that *huevón* McClure would say, with all his records and tapes and superior knowledge of music. I bet he's with Antonia right at this instant. I open the window: the air is cool, nice, refreshing. I feel it on my face and in my hair, which flies out behind me now. I know the way by heart. It doesn't do anything new for me. I go down on the clutch and change into fifth. Then forward, up the hill, Anne Murray singing ballad after ballad: "You Needed Me," "Someone Always Saying Goodbye," that kind of shit that's usually true. I'm anxious, I might as well admit it. Only slightly drunk, but I'll be cured soon enough. Cured from the shock, maybe . . . I'm not cured of anything. That's the real truth, isn't it?

I dream about buying a bottle of pisco sour, I need to keep drinking. Or something. Maybe some potato chips. As I think about it, I realize I've reached Gerónimo de Alderete: I signal, turn onto Calle Espoz, in the direction of Vitacura, to the right, there. Suddenly, I'm on the street where Antonia lives. It was inevitable, of course it was. Who am I kidding anyway? So now I should do something, why waste the trip, right?

I park next to that house, the house I know so well. What am I saying? I don't really know it at all. Anyway, no action is visible there; her parents' car isn't in, so maybe she isn't either. I go into first again and drive up to the liquor store and ask to use the phone, which, of course, they charge me for. I dial and ask to talk to Antonia. My breathing almost halts as the housekeeper decides for herself and answers: "She's not here . . . who's calling, please?" she asks. "No, nobody. A friend. Ricardo," I lie, which ends up leaving me mute, dumb, and pissed off. I buy two bottles. As long as I'm there. No chips this time. I almost ask for a pack of cigarettes, even though I don't smoke. Straws. I ask the fat lady behind the counter for one, and she gives it to me, no charge. I buy a pack of cinnamon Freshen-Up, pay, and leave.

I keep driving around and around. I try to remind myself the night is young, but I keep looking at my watch. Bored, I put in some music: Anne Murray again. I take out the tape and throw it out the window, which I immediately regret. I brake, then look back. A car behind me runs over it, crushes it, and the tape is left there, scattered across the road, blowing in the wind. My mother is going to kill me.

I go on, just as life usually does. I get Concierto on the dial. That's the radio station I rely on most; the best one. Julián García Reyes talks about peace, love, and then reads some liner notes from an old Stones album, about he who waits and he who gives up, or something like that. Then they play "Emotional Rescue," which sounds good. Solid, and quite appropriate. I reach Avenida Manquehue, cross Apoquindo, continue to Colón, and then go straight down, passing McClure's house. McClure, my rival of the evening. I stop. The song ends. I open the bottle and drink some. My body shakes a bit, then stabilizes. I get out and ring the doorbell. It's his mother.

"Hello, good evening. Is Gonzalo here? I hope it's not too late."

"No son, not at all. Although actually, Gonzalo left a while ago. I lent him the van. You know, he's turning eighteen and it's really not long before he'll get his license. The best thing he can do is practice, that way he'll pass the exam, without a problem. I mean, look, a daughter of a friend of mine flunked her driving test, and she almost died of embarrassment. That's just terrible, don't you think?"

Uh, yeah, sure, I think as I drive off. McClure's going to pay me back for that. I go down Isabel la Católica in silence, except for the beeping horns and a bunch of patrol cars escorting a Mercedes, which is definitely some government official. They say the head of the navy lives around here. McClure is probably out with Antonia, I know it. It's been a while now that he's been going out with her; why else was he hovering around her all the time in Rio? What about me and Cassia? I don't ever remember that. It's the same thing, I guess, to each his own, right? How predictable, though, that she'd go for a guy so boring, so common, so totally ordinary. He's just like all the rest. I mean, I'm the superior one here, even though she'd never realize it. But she doesn't believe that, really, and anyway, I don't know if I do either. Antonia just wasn't meant for me; everyone's told me that a hundred times. And now she's really out of reach. I really screwed that one up. Sucker. She's with someone else, someone who doesn't annoy her, who doesn't bother her, who doesn't disagree with her all the time. That's what happens all the time with us anyway. I always try to challenge her, and change her mind, hoping that I can make her see it my way. I'm the loser on this one, though. It looks like I fucked up.

I check the time again: 11:43. I stop on a dark street, lined with trees. I can tell it's spring from the leaves and the smell of flowers. A dog barks behind a big wall, but who cares, I'm on the other side anyway. I open my wallet, take out the little book from the Automóvil Club, pull out the origami, and shake out a little of the powder. I push it around, line it up with my school ID card, and with that little straw from the grocery store, sniff what there is left to sniff. For a second, I think of my father, for whatever reason. I don't know why. I turn on the radio, full blast. Again, it's all disco music: Anita Ward, Sister Sledge, Cheryl Lynn, "Born, born to be alive . . ." and I go on drinking. I finish off the second bottle, throw it out the window, and listen to the crash. As I turn down Avenida Vespucio, two hookers, sort of hidden, motion to me. I want to cross Apoquindo but the construction work for the Metro is going on over there, so I go around, up Nevería, and manage to pass around the other side, down Riesco, and cross (very slowly) in front of the military guards with their machine guns, who are patrolling the Military Academy.

I finally get to El Bosque: I park in front of Juancho's. The green and orange light from the neon sign falls on my skin. I check in the mirror: the lights actually make me look good. I turn off the engine. Is it really worth it to get out of the car, go inside the bar, and bullshit with all the same people I always bullshit with, and then go God knows where? My rational side tells me: "Go home, go to sleep, you've had a rough week," but my other half orders me to stay out now that I'm out and at least try to have a good time. As good a time as possible, that is. With that last thing in mind, I get out, cross the street, decline the rose wrapped in cellophane that a vendor lady tries to sell me, and I walk into Juancho's, hoping secretly that I'll somehow forget what I don't even know is bothering me. That's just a thought, a secret wish: if it works, good; if not, fine. It's not like it's my first time in Santiago. Or maybe it is. But that's another story anyway, isn't it?

Juancho's is the place where all the "chosen ones" go; the hangout of the "golden children," as Luisa calls us. Luisa, who never even comes here. She's right, though. Not just anyone can come here. There's a bouncer at the door who checks that everyone coming in is "people like us." Before, I thought it was just lucky getting into Juancho's, considering my age, and being a student and all. But El Toro, the owner, believes in cultivating his future clientele, if you will, and has no problem letting me and my friends in. He also knows that underage shits like us will pay whatever it costs. And it's true. Everyone under eighteen—pre-PAA, pre-driver's license—that comes here, everyone I know, spoiled little fuckers that come from the country club or Reñaca or from school, all have the good fortune of not looking their age. They all dress well, get their "look" just right, and spend shitloads of money. That's why everyone gets in.

One of the major selling points of Juancho's is that El Toro (whose real name is Juan) trusts us. What that means is that he has various "open" accounts where he keeps tabs on what people spend. If, at the end of the month, you don't have enough money to pay it off, he and his little gang bill your parents directly. The great thing about this arrangement is that the parents always pay, because El Toro is somehow associated with the local Godfather as well as with Pinochet's nephew. That's what connects this whole network of bars, pubs, cabarets, drug dealers, hookers, massage parlors, saunas, and who knows what else. That's how Nacho's account works. They just add his expenses to his father's bill. And every time his father leaves Krazy Kat or Private VIPs, he's so nervous that Nacho's mother is going to find out he's been screwing some hot little Ecuadorian woman that he just whips out his Mont Blanc and signs. And Nacho, of course, drinks and drinks. I guess everyone gets their revenge in their own way. In my case, though, it's harder to charge me. My parents only go to Regine's, where they're members, or else they go to the Red Pub. So what ends up happening is that when I'm broke, it's Nacho's father who ends up subsidizing my vices. That's why I come; it works out great for me. No loss on my part.

When I go inside Juancho's, the latest, horrendous Queen album overtakes me, penetrates my ears. I almost lose my balance. The place seems smaller somehow, slightly more Chilean than I remembered it. The big movie screen is still there with its bad picture and bad tracking. Jim Morrison is puking all over some flowers. The sound never quite matches the video. El Chalo, the disc jockey, is more into changing the music than the music itself. He then plays "Another One Bites the Dust," full blast. As I look at him, he just lifts those bushy eyebrows of his that just about meet in the middle, smiles a shit-eating grin, and then puts on "Bohemian Rhapsody" to piss me off. Fuck him.

Alejandro Paz, who is sort of my main connection to the place, says hi to me, noticing my newly bronzed state. He asks me about Antonia, if it's true that there's nothing going on between us.

"Give me a *caipirinha* and lay the fuck off, all right?"

"You've come back quite the Brazilian, haven't you?"

"You wish. Nacho—have you seen him?"

"Not yet."

I like the bar at Juancho's. It's the best part of the place, and it might just be the best bar in Chile. It's all done out in chrome, chrome and black, with a slick, stylized "look," kind of like Richard Gere's apartment in *American Gigolo,* that kind of thing. Instead of going for the *Saturday Night Fever* atmosphere, like Disco Hollywood, El Toro and his partners found and hired some fabulous, faggy American to decorate. I guess it works.

"Hey, Paz. Have you ever seen *American Gigolo*?"

"Sure. And you?"

"Of course. I saw it before it left. I slipped the usher some money and he let me in. No sweat. We went, it was me, Nacho, and Lerner. Great clothes. So much fucking clothing. All Giorgio Armani, you know? My father told me. He saw it too. Three times, actually. He's got a few Armani suits himself that he brought back from Europe, so he knew."

In the bar at Juancho's, where Alejandro Paz works, there's these lights, a ton of secret little neon lights, hidden, and they bounce off the mirrors and the glasses, creating these strange contours and shadows which give the place this weird effect, transforming everything into a movielike atmosphere.

"This isn't bad, Paz, you know? The way they redecorated the bar. They should fix up the rest, though—still too Chilean, you know."

"Easy, old man, one thing at a time."

"Yeah, fine, but all the chrome and steel just doesn't go with those dainty little lamps on the tables."

Paz gives me my drink.

"Fuck, this stinks," I say to him.

"What do you mean, stinks? It's perfect. I put in a lot of *cachaza.*"

"It's the lemons, Paz. In Brazil, they're different somehow: really bitter, or something. You should use the ones from Pica. Or mix lemons and limes. Whatever, I don't know, you're the bartender. Shit."

"Well, nobody ever orders that fucking drink. Anyway, if someone wants a real *caipirinha,* they can go to the Doña Flor."

"I guess."

The Great Alejandro Paz of Chile does a lot more than just serve drinks. He hangs out, talks to everybody, fulfills all the standard, stereotyped requirements of the bartender. Just like you see in the movies. He's a good guy, and I get along pretty well with him, better than most around here, and I kind of think I know why. He's sort of a working-class type, so his favorite thing is to piss off all of us who come into Juancho's. He criticizes and criticizes. So I tell him he's a spy, a secret agent from Frei's regime, or maybe even of the "NO." Yeah, sure. He dies laughing whenever I tell him that.

"To undermine this society, Matías, you have to get at it from the inside," is what he once said to me. "You'll understand when you get to college. Mark my words."

He's in his third or fourth year of literature and philosophy at the university, totally antiestablishment, that whole thing. The place is full of little party politicians, from La Jota and MIR, who all listen to Silvio Rodríguez and La Cantata de Santa María. The kind of people who've never heard of the Talking Heads. But it's that type of contradiction that kind of saves Alejandro. At the university, everyone thinks he's really arrogant and "imperialized" (the poor guy suffers from an unmistakable, almost unforgivable *"yanquimanía"*); here, on the other hand, at Juancho's, he takes on the role of proletarian-exploited-by-society-who-feeds-alcoholic-drinks-to-the-children-of-the-ruling-class.

Alejandro Paz, of course, is a member of the bourgeoisie. Four years older than me, he tells this (far too familiar) story of his life, that's just a little bit beyond my understanding. But I do get it. He lives alone, he's told me, and spends all the money he earns at Juancho's (plus the extra he makes off trafficking his joints and other "medicinal substances") on music, books in English, and subscriptions to magazines like *Rolling Stone* (which I also get) or *Interview* (which I hate). His dream is to go to the United States, a country that he has turned into his total obsession, almost like a sickness with him. He idealizes it to the extent that he probably knows more about América than practically any normal American does.

I've only been to Miami, with my parents and my sisters, a few years ago. We also went to Orlando: Disney World, Cape Kennedy, the usual. I liked it, sure, but it wasn't an obsession or anything. It all seemed incredible to me, though, like the ideal place to go, to be whoever you want to be, in a country where everything happens, where nobody notices you, nobody judges you, zero opinions, and full of things you never dreamed of. It seemed like a place where it would be impossible to get bored. For Paz, it's all that and more: it's heaven, the only perfect place. That's exactly why I think he's never gone there, though, and he probably won't, ever. Because if he gets there, and the United States disappoints him somehow, and treats him badly, the poor guy will just crack up. It'll destroy him.

In any event, it's this strange communion with the United States that continues to bond me and the Great Alejandro Paz of Chile. We always talk in English. Me with my good little accent and everything. According to him, I speak it well because, just like him, my background has been "nontraditional." Meaning, more than in school and those classes at the Norteamericano, you learn "American" from the radio, the movies, music, magazines, or screwing some American girl over here on one of those "Youth for Understanding" programs. In fact, Paz once introduced me to a girl from Texas, Joyce something, who was here on an exchange program. Paz is the kind of guy who loves making exotic drinks. He invents these concoctions with names like "A Drink on the Wild Side" or "Atlantic City Blues," which no one ever dares to order. It's inevitable with him—when we get to talking, he always starts doling out advice. Before I went to Rio, he said to me:

"You should go on a real trip, one that'll hurt you, get it? So you can see how things really are. Not with your teacher or with those little spoiled brats in your school. You should go alone. Go cross-country on Greyhound, for example. Get stranded in Wichita, eat a taco in front of the Alamo, sleep in a cheap motel full of bums in Tulsa, Oklahoma. Or go to New York, man; go to CBGBs, go see Patti Smith in concert. That's life, man, not this! One day in Manhattan is like six months in Santiago. To come back to Chile is insanity, it sucks, with all the fucking military all over the place, and all its phobias, and the total backwardness, it's so *heavy.* It's more than heavy, it's *hard-core,* man." All you have to do is turn on the radio to see how bad off we are, Matías. When are they going to start playing the Ramones or the Sex Pistols here? Listen to me, man, and take a trip: *go west, my son, go west."*

El Chalo puts on Fleetwood Mac, and some girl I vaguely recognize, from the Maisonette, goes onto the dance floor with this goofy guy who probably wouldn't even know where to eat her out if she told him to. The girl shows off her body, which is actually pretty hot, and clearly underused as of yet, underneath her dress with its plunging neckline. Her tits are in full view, she's wearing heels and a necklace which, no doubt, is some religious relic of her grandmother's.

"This fucking place is boring," I say to Paz, who is washing some glasses. "It's as if nothing ever changes, all the images just repeat themselves over and over again."

"That's what I always said to you, and that's exactly what I've always thought."

"Everything's so small, so familiar. I feel like I know everyone in this little world of Chile, and I know exactly what's going to happen here."

"You've got to get out. Escape before it gets too late. Nothing happens, and nothing's ever going to happen here. Much less now. This whole thing with the referendum and the constitution and that mess, these motherfuckers are going to stay in office at least another eight years, and maybe more. Eight years, and then another sixteen. That's twenty-four years, buddy. That's serious, *hot stuff,* you know, no bullshit. Just imagine what that'll be like. The worst part of it all is that it's the little assholes like you who are going to vote for the 'SI.' "

"I don't vote. I'm not even eighteen yet . . ."

"But if you did, you'd vote for the 'SI.' You know you would."

"I'd have to think about it."

"Think about what! It's because of people like you that we're in the situation we're in. Thanks to you, I'm stuck here, only dreaming about escaping. What do you think, Matías, that it's fun to feel like you have no country, that you have no future, and basically no way out? Do you?"

"Stop it, okay? Get off my back. I'm wired and annoyed enough as it is, and the last thing I need is to listen to your bullshit little speech, that I don't believe and neither do you anyway. What's this 'no future' crap you're talking about? How much money do you make here on a good night? God only knows you make enough to buy all the music you could ever want. On top of that, you're a student, you study the most indulgent, useless subject that you'll never be able to use to make any money, but that's your problem, man. If you wanted, you could switch to business. In this country, that's where there's opportunities for everyone."

"Who are you trying to kid, motherfucker?"

"Eat shit, Paz. You're a communist who dreams about the United States. You'd sell your mother to write an article for *Rolling Stone* or serve drinks at that famous Palladium you're always talking about. Give me a tequila, straight up, will you? With limes and salt and everything. And put it on Nacho's tab. That motherfucker should've been here a long time ago."

Half an hour, maybe twenty minutes later, Chalo is sweating like crazy and changing record after record. It's like he can't take all the pressure or something. I go over and offer to help him.

"Buzz off. Don't fuck with me. I play what I want here."

"Put on something by the Clash. In Brazil they play tons of that stuff."

Instead, Chalo puts on "I Was Made for Lovin' You." He knows I hate Kiss, even though this song isn't so bad. Antonia loves it, it's one of the few things that actually turns her on.

Nacho still hasn't shown up. I feel like killing him. The jerk is going to pay for this. Maybe I should just go, I think to myself. Leave, go for a walk, whatever. On the dance floor, everyone is dancing beneath the neon lights, which makes their teeth and eyes shine. Everything has a weird, sort of white glow. Even the oil on their skin looks fluorescent: if you look closely, you can see how some people's noses and foreheads shine. How awful. Now, there's one thing I can't stand: I cannot look at pimples and blackheads without wanting to throw up. Luckily I have neither. The only thing I get is those tiny blemishes that my mother's beautician deals with when she comes to the house.

I go into the bathroom to look in the mirror, just to see if I didn't jinx myself by saying I don't have any pimples. Nothing. Quique Saavedra is in there too, and he's probably the best-known rugby player in Chile. He's really famous for his biceps, underarms, and other body parts as well, now that he's done a commercial for Rexona deodorant. It comes on every five minutes on TV, and there's Quique, smelling his well-groomed armpits.

He's looking at himself in the mirror. The whole bathroom reeks of pot, and his eyes are as red as China.

"I'm shocked, Saavedra. An athlete, a university student, a television star like yourself, you shouldn't be doing things like that to yourself. It's not good for you, you know."

He doesn't respond. Instead, he checks out his biceps. He's got a little short-sleeve shirt on, as if it were the middle of the summer or something. The guy really is a first-class moron. He looks in the mirror and fixes his hair for the hundredth time.

"How do I look?"

"Older, Saavedra, older. Aren't you a little heavier than you were before?" I ask him after I finish peeing.

"Pure muscle, my friend. Pure muscle," and he jabs his stomach to show me.

"Sure, pure muscle. I doubt it."

"Some respect, please, fuckhead. The only reason I don't beat the shit out of you is because I know you, that's all. How's your sister?"

Saavedra went out a bunch of times with my sister Pilar, a whole summer, actually, before his teammate Guillermo Iriarte ended up marrying her.

"She's still around. With your friend Iriarte. On Sunday they baptize Felipe, their latest addition."

"Oh, really, huh?"

"Yes. Just think . . . we could've been brothers-in-law."

"Unlikely, kiddo. I always take care of myself. Condoms, always, just like they say. None of that 'Let me put it in just a little' stuff. With me, she never would've ended up pregnant, so even if we had screwed, we wouldn't have had to get married in such a hurry."

"Yeah, I get the picture. Are you leaving?"

"Yeah."

"Then go."

He leaves. I shut myself in a stall and lock the door, take out the little origami, and pull out a straw. A little more, just a little. My sister is a slut, I think. The other one is too. We all really should take better care of each other.

Back at the bar I ask Paz for a margarita.

"A lot of mixing, man. You're going to puke."

"Then make it a tequila with orange juice."

"A Sunrise, you mean?"

"Yes, whatever the fuck you feel like calling it. Just hurry up about it."

Everyone is still dancing. I settle into a corner, alone. Paz put a ton of grenadine in this lousy drink he made me. I watch Saavedra, dancing with a girl who looks familiar. She's wearing a tight white skirt and you can see her underwear lines. Saavedra squeezes her there. That asshole thinks he's perfect. Chalo puts on the remix of "No More Tears" by Barbra Streisand and Donna Summer. Things on the dance floor are beginning to unravel. A really suspicious-looking Middle Eastern guy, with a silk shirt and beads of perspiration showing through, dances this really dirty dance, with La Tortuga, the one from *Música Libre.* She's never been to Juancho's before. I get a good look at her, because she's the one I like best. She looks a lot better on TV, that's for sure. Right near her, I see six or seven guys from *Música Libre,* really annoying types. They all talk shit about women because they're on TV, and get tons of fan mail from all the teenage girls in the suburbs. All they ever want is to get in bed with them.

"You're Matías Vicuña, aren't you?"

"Yes. And you?"

"Miriam. But you can call me Vasheta, please. That's what everybody else calls me."

"Yeah, sure," I answer, thinking that she is some kind of ridiculous joke. But no, it seems like this kook is for real. She's like that, sort of a freak, a little weird but real.

"You're Antonia Prieto's boyfriend, right?"

"No. Well, more or less."

"Yes or no?"

"Let's just say no. Why do you ask? Got a problem with it or something?"

"Just gossip, that's all. I know her and I think she's just great looking. I've known her brother forever. He used to be really tight with a guy I once went out with."

This girl can't be for real. I should get away while I can and just let her talk to herself.

"Vasheta?" I ask, just to be polite and break the pregnant silence.

"It's sort of a family joke, you wouldn't get it. Sort of a private code. It's Yiddish. You know what that is, right?"

"More than you'd think, sure: kibbutzes, the State of Israel, circumcisions . . ."

"Exactly. You're not circumcised, Matías, are you?"

"No," I answer, laughing, half thinking, "Maybe I should be."

"How nice. I am so sick of guys with everything al fresco, if you know what I mean"

This girl really is something else.

"Would you like a drink, Matías? I'll pay."

"I don't know. I'm waiting for some friends," I say in my most indifferent-but-still-intriguing tone of voice.

"Hey, I don't bite, you know. Or if I do bite, it doesn't hurt. Relax. Anyway, it's early. Come on, we'll wait together. I've wanted to talk to you for a while. I've heard so much about you."

I decide to head for the bar. She follows me over there, to the chrome bar, and Paz looks at me, as if to say, "I've seen you down before, but this is . . ."

"Hey, how are you? What can I get for you all?" he says. The fucker.

"For you, Matías?" she asks me in her most sensuous voice, this crazy little curly-haired girl, who's just a little chubby, with her little roll of baby fat popping out from under her black T-shirt. It has an iron-on photo of Barbra Streisand—naked—embracing Kris Kristofferson, also naked, clearly uncircumcised, even though you can't really see anything.

A Star Is Born," I say to her.

"Exactly! Did you see it?"

"With Antonia," I counter.

Her eyes, beady and blue, widen, and penetrate my gaze. This girl is jealous, I think.

"Excuse me for interrupting," says the Great Alejandro Paz of Chile, "but what do you both want to drink?"

We order two margaritas. I don't want to mix my alcohols.

"I love Barbra Streisand," Vasheta says, as if I asked her. Her *Enough Is Enough (Is Enough)* still makes me want to puke. But that's what you get with girls from the Jewish high school. It's so totally Instituto Hebreo to identify with her and idolize that overrated walking nose.

"She's my idol. I think she's incredible: fantastic, great actress, great singer. Have you heard her album *Wet*?"

"Great title: *Wet*. I like it. *You're kind of wet . . .*"

"Not yet . . ."

This girl wants action. She's dropping hints left and right.

"One thing at a time, okay?" And I laugh, my most cynical, biting laugh.

Continuing to flirt, she tosses back her drink, which is already mostly backwash anyway. I study her profile. She has had a nose job, I conclude. It's too perfect, and doesn't really go with the rest of her face. Totally anti-Streisand, I think to myself.

"Nice nose," I say to her, without meaning to. It just slips out.

"Thank you. I'm glad you like it. It's been fixed. I got it done last year. By Dr. Zarhi, you know. It cost a fortune, but my father thought it was worth it. I did too."

"I've never been operated on."

"You don't need anything fixed."

I laugh a little, sort of a nervous little titter. Who does this girl think she is? I'm the one calling the shots here. I take a sip and lick the salt on the rim of the glass. She tries to imitate my action, and her shiny tongue laps the glass with more gusto than grace. Then she fixes her eyes on mine, and neither one of us blinks. If looks could kill, I think to myself. Why won't Nacho get here already, where the fuck did he go anyway?

"So what do you do, Miriam?"

"Whatever you want, baby."

She's asking you for it, buddy. This girl is easier than gym class. Keep playing the game . . .

". . . but don't call me Miriam, *please.*" She bats her eyelashes shamelessly.

"No, really. What *do* you do?"

You're changing the subject, watch out . . .

"I'm in Pre. I messed up my aptitude test. Now I go to CEACI so maybe I'll pass it this time and actually make it to college. I go in the morning, of course, not in the afternoon with all the little high schoolers."

"I was thinking of going there—next year, that is."

"God, you really are young."

Where *did* this girl come from? Who told her about me, I mean what is this?

"I also go to classes at Levinia Manfredini's. The famous cosmetologist, you know. If you want, I could help get rid of those little blackheads tucked under your nostril there."

"I barely have any. The sun in Rio dried them all up."

"Yes, it did you good. But you have to take care of your skin, you know."

"Yeah, I know. Astringent every night, scrub the face, no butter . . ."

"How do you know so much?"

"From an old lady who takes care of my mother and sisters. And my father too. Sometimes the old bag attacks me after she's done with them. She removes little things, puts me under a humidifier."

"And which astringent does she recommend?"

This conversation is not happening. It's some figment of your imagination, it has to be. You deserve better than this. Either go and do it or get out of here. Just shut her up, that horrible annoying voice, like Olive Oyl or something. Worse, even.

"Who knows? I don't care."

"And you don't have little pimples on your back?"

"How would I know? As far as I can remember, no girl has ever mentioned it."

"We'll have to see about that, inspect a bit. Another drink?"

No, I don't want another drink; I'm beyond drunk already. Hasn't anyone ever told you that you couldn't turn someone on if you tried—not even the most desperate, pathetic loser? Why don't you just go away. Pushy girls turn me off. Go hit on someone else.

"Tell me something about your life. Are you as mysterious as they say? Or is it just a mask?"

"What mask? What's the matter with you? What do you want from me, my life story? You must really be hard up. What do you want to know? What my ideal woman is like? If I cry at night from loneliness? If I do drugs because nobody loves me?"

"Calm down, it was just a question. I'll tell you whatever you want to know about me, if you want."

"Paz, give me another drink," I say, moving away abruptly. As if anything about her life could possibly interest me. I've already got more than enough to deal with.

The phone rings, interrupting my train of thought.

"It's for you. Nacho."

"Finally. Give me the phone."

Miriam looks at me, nervous.

"Where the fuck are you, man?" I shout over the music Chalo is spewing out.

"Relax, relax, Matías. Change of plans. I went with Papelucho for a little while. We were looking to get some shit, and we bumped into Julián Longhi and Patán. They were also trying to get some shit, so we hooked up and bought six joints. Anyway, now we're headed over to Cox's house. It's his birthday, and his parents are in South Africa, so everyone's over there. Want to go?"

"Yeah, sure. Why not? Where are you now?"

Miriam's staring at me.

"We're at Pollo Stop."

"What about Maite?"

"At Cox's, I guess. It's supposed to be a surprise party. Well, actually, Cox knows about it, he organized it and everything, but it's still kind of a surprise. At the last minute he figured why not. So, like, why don't we all meet up there? You know where it is. Los Dominicos, near Las Flores. You've been there hundreds of times."

I glance over at Miriam, at her brown curls, her thighs encased in those black stretch jeans.

"I'll see you there, then," I say to Nacho.

"All right."

I hang up, and before I even replace the receiver, Miriam's pale blue eyes are already interrogating me.

"Are you going somewhere?"

"Let's hope so."

"Can I come? I've got a car."

"I do too. But listen, it's kind of a small party, just friends, you know? Invitation-only sort of thing. No crashers allowed. Sorry."

"You're sick of me, that's it, isn't it?"

"No, no, it's not that at all. I swear."

"Well then, don't go, Matías. We could go dancing. Or out to eat."

Paz is washing some glasses, talking to some girl I don't recognize. I've seen her hanging around here, though, before I went to Rio. My back hurts, I feel like I've got a slipped disk or something, or whatever you call it. I should lie down on the hard floor, or on bricks or something. I'm so overtired, I can't relax at all. When I touch my face, I barely feel it. I know I've got tequila infiltrating my pores by now anyway. Miriam's waiting. She wants an answer, and I'm annoyed that I even have to think about a response.

"No, no. I don't think so," I say, feeling a mixture of guilt and relief.

"What are you hiding from, Matías?"

"Listen, enough, all right? Stop being such a pain in the ass. If you want to play therapist, go bother someone else. I mean, I don't know what you're looking for, but you're not going to find it with me, all right? Got that?"

"I thought you were different, Matías."

"Don't think anything, how about that? Do me a big favor—don't get involved in things that don't concern you. You don't even know me."

"Excuse me . . . you don't have to get all huffy, it wasn't anything personal, really. If you change your mind, give me a call. Here, I'll give you my number."

"Do what you have to do."

She grabs a napkin and writes her number down with a fountain pen from her bag. As she writes, the ink spreads, and the whole thing turns into a big blue blob.

"Wait," I say. "Paz, give me a matchbox, will you?" I write down her number and her name: Miriam.

"Vasheta, Matías. Vasheta."

I cross out "Miriam" and replace it with "Vasheta." It takes so little to satisfy some people.

"So, I'll call you sometime," I say before my escape.

"Give me your number."

I ask Paz for another matchbox. I start telling her my number but in the middle, I switch around a couple of the digits.

"Thanks. I hope you have a good time."

"You too. Sorry I can't bring you along."

"Sure, sure. Next time."

I edge away from her and go over to Paz.

"Nice way to treat a girl, my friend. Hit and run . . ."

"What's your problem, man? The girl is nothing, she's about as subtle as a ton of bricks."

"But she's hitting on you. Come and get it. Get it?"

"No big deal, man."

"Look at her. The poor girl, she's going to end up alone tonight, thinking about you, alone with her pillowcase, with nothing more than her little finger for company."

"You're sick, man."

"You too."

"Well, I'm leaving. Before I start feeling guilty. Anything, messages, whatever, I'm at Cox's house. It should be in El Toro's address book."

"Get out of here, you traitor. You've got no excuse, leaving her this way. Thanks to you, I'm the one who'll have to take care of her, entertain the bourgeoisie, satisfy her . . ."

"Resentful sonofabitch."

"Don't project, Matías."

"I've had it with you already. I'm going. See you later."

"And? Did you read what I gave you?"

"What, the *Penthouse*?"

"Read. Not jerk off, idiot."

"Oh yeah, the book."

"Salinger. More respect, buddy."

"I haven't had time yet."

"Read it."

"Another time, all right? Bye. See you."

"Yeah. Just read it."

I take a deep breath to change my mood, and feel the cool air up here in the foothills. It's like skiing in Portillo at sunrise. Not so far off, beyond those major Mediterranean-style villas, is Santiago. It looks like a pile of illuminated Legos, scattered around at random. Legos that would fall apart if there were even the slightest tremor. You can see it all clearly from up here, the eternal city. All those orange and yellow lights, endlessly perfect. It all has such strong impact on me—I'm really wired tight right now, really wound up—that valley, for example, that *plateau of intermediate depression* that's here below me, seems to me to be the most incredible thing in the world. Without warning, squealing tires dissipate the chimera, and I realize that Nacho and company will soon be making their big entrance. And in that big illuminated valley down there, all warm and inviting, crackling away with people and voices, is my house, a little black dot that isn't sparkling at all. Maybe it is, though. What do I know. As if I care that much anyway.

I'm sweating. My hair's all wet, and I look awful. I've been doing nothing but dancing at this party. Everybody's here, nobody new, nothing interesting, except for that little midget from Pelusa Echegoyen's, who just came back from La Serena, where she hung out for a year doing nothing, just hanging out in the sun at La Herradura. Now she's going to school at the Monjas Francesas, still doing nothing. Story of her life.

I dance for about an hour with Pía Balmaceda, who's finally gotten over the trauma of her freckles. I'd say she's gone so far as to be proud of cultivating so many over such little territory. We have a good time, though, and even dance to "Coming Up" by Paul McCartney (which was the only Top Ten song that Cassia liked). We don't talk: we just dance and practice some new moves. I really don't know how I got into dancing so much. We do the entire *Spirits Having Flown* album by the Bee Gees. It's fun, though, because I forget about everything, and when "Love You Inside Out" comes on, we cut out our flirtatious little dance moves, and we just about fuck in Cox's living room. Then the song ends. Nothing happens.

I breathe deeply to catch my breath and I realize that my hair still looks disgusting, all sweaty, like my shirt. Nacho is now sitting next to me, drinking.

"We could see *Mad Max*. It opens right after the referendum. They say it's awesome. Paz says that *Rolling Stone* gave it a really major review, that it's totally violent and gory."

"Well, that's better than what we usually get here. The only thing that has been any good lately was that movie about the gigolo we saw. Did you see anything else in Rio?"

"This porn thing, at a movie theater near the hotel. Almost all of us went. It was Lerner's idea. It was a bunch of erotic stories, kind of like those movies at the Alessandri or Mónaco but sleazier. They showed everything. The best part was with this one guy who falls in love with a watermelon and ends up fucking it, man. The amazing thing about it was you could see everything. The camera lens went in and out of the melon."

"Wow . . ."

"It was insane in Brazil. I mean, really insane. Patán and Lerner saw one that was even worse. I didn't go because I was hanging out with a girl I met there. We had an incredible relationship. Everything about it was awesome. It was perfect. Her name was Cassia."

"Brazilian?"

"Definitely. From Brasília. You should've seen her, man. You would've fallen in love with her in a second."

"And some fight that would've started, right?" he says, sort of sarcastically, as he nonchalantly moves over to the bar. It's as if what I'm telling him doesn't really interest him. The truth is probably that it does. So I decide to shut up, and I follow him over to the bar.

This party kind of sucks. Julián Longhi changes the tapes on the stereo, and Pelusa Echegoyen stands there, making drinks, as if she's some bartender or something, like the Great Alejandro Paz of Chile. At the bar, Nacho prepares his attack. He's hiding something, I can tell. From the moment I saw him, I sensed he was different somehow. Envy, that's what it's all about. Although I can hardly blame him. I would've been burning up with jealousy too. The whole thing of all my friends going on a big trip that I should've gone on also, that's really heavy; I mean, it would cause a pretty big trauma for anyone, and could really create a void inside a person, a void that could last centuries. Of course, at this party, like any good party in Santiago, there's a bunch of jerks from school who won't shut up about Paquetá and Leblon and São Corrado and that monstrosity of the Rio Sul mall where those assholes all bought the same Fiorucci jeans, the same Adidas Roma sneakers that they're all wearing tonight. And Nacho, who's pissed off and out of it, doesn't want to listen to what a fantastic, awesome, incredible time all of us had.

"Want another drink?" he asks.

"Definitely."

"They give Cox's old man all this liquor for free. Connections. I know, I'm sure of it."

"Maybe."

He doesn't say anything else. I notice something strange, but I can't figure out what it is. My head hurts a little. I'm exhausted, but not sleepy at all. He's hiding something, and it's something that in some way—I can feel it—is against me.

"I can't stand being in Chile," I admit to him.

"Go, then. Nobody's forcing you to stay. It's not like, if you're gone, the 'NO' will win, or Argentina will invade us because of the Beagle Channel again."

"It was just an opinion, okay? I just wanted to share something with you. Nothing personal. If you'd been with us, you'd understand."

"Well, I wasn't, all right? So I don't really understand what you're talking about. I haven't traveled very much at all, and I'm just stuck here, dealing with all this like everyone else."

"Okay, okay, enough."

"Whatever."

This party is really beginning to get on my nerves. Nacho is too. McClure isn't here, which probably proves that he's with Antonia. I shouldn't be here. I should be back in Rio, fucking till the end of time. Snorting every which way I can.

"Would you like to see what I brought you?" I ask Nacho, just to say something, to grab his attention. To show him I'm on his side.

"Sure."

We cross the living room. I take a straw off the table. Every-one's dancing: "Get Off, Hot Number." God, it's awful. Cox's se-lection, no doubt. I was with him when he bought the record, that much I remember. It was at the Los Cobres mall in Vitacura. Antonia was there skating and it was Virginia Infante's birthday. Her father rented out the whole rink. We were all quite a sight. Free hamburgers, drinks too.

"Remember Virginia Infante's party?"

"The one at the mall? The skating thing?"

"Yes. That one."

"Of course I remember it. How could I forget? You screwed me over that night, hooking up with Maite. I remember it perfectly. More than you think."

Nacho sure knows where to hit. Below the belt. He knows how to lay a guilt trip on. And he doesn't even know the whole story. If he knew that I screwed Maite in Rosita Barros's car, in that un-derground parking lot behind the Multicines, he'd kill me. He'd puke. He'd think it was some sort of blow to his manhood. Well, he'd be wrong. I don't even remember how it all happened; the truth is, I could care less, but I do remember that I did my best to get her, because this competition thing was far too seductive to say no to. There was just no way I could play fair or back off. Nacho himself was the one who started the contest, figuring he could show me up, or make me jealous, or something stupid like that. That was his big mistake. A person should only compete if he is sure, completely sure, of winning. The saddest part of the whole story, though—and what makes me feel worse about it— is that Maite really liked Nacho. I never would've guessed that the girl was a virgin, what with all those stories about her. So it was all a big mistake, your typical hot-and-heavy situation. She was totally wasted, and I did it faster than I should've. The point is, she liked Nacho, not me. Sure, she thought he was a little nerdy, a little bit shy still. So when I came on her shirt, she actually asked me to please not say anything to Nacho. She didn't want him to be disillusioned with her. She'd rather use me to mess around with and Nacho to go out with. That's what she said to me.

Now she's onto other things. In Rio, she hung out with Patán and with some Brazilian friends of Cassia's. Even Julián Longhi, with all his pimples, has eaten her out. That's what infuriates Nacho: that everyone else has had her except him. I still think he turns Maite on. But he can't stand her now. He hates her. The truth is, I don't know how he can tolerate me. Dependencies are tough to break, though, I guess. They keep plaguing you, over and over, even if they're bad and even if they piss you off. It's just that the idea of living without someone, of being alone and stuck in a void, is too harsh to contemplate. It's like deciding to be totally healthy and saying fuck everything else. That's why Nacho sticks with me, I think. And vice versa.

"You always remember the bad stuff. It's as if you keep a record of it or something," I say, annoyed with him, as I lock the bathroom door.

"It's nothing."

"I don't know about that."

"Maybe, then. What happens is that all the bad stuff, all the bullshit, the betrayals and all that, that's what gets remembered. Those thoughts eat away at the good stuff. They're more damaging. That's why they stick. A good memory fades away, and you have to really work at remembering it. Whenever you've felt like shit, you remember it in a second. That's all, simple. You just don't understand because you always have it so good. That's your problem."

Nacho is really jaded, I think to myself. Upset. Sitting over there on the edge of the bathtub with that rugby shirt of his that he never takes off. He has that typical look of those pretty boys on Paseo Las Palmas. Nothing special, never a big deal. But he's got a lot of shit that's been building up for a while, and it's beginning to show. It's making him distant, sort of. His father really screwed him over when he didn't let him go to Rio. He was actually this way before we all went, but he's worse now. Not that he's clinically depressed or anything. It's just a phase he's in. He acts like everything's all right, bullshits about how everything's fine, but he's just not there. It's inside of him.

"It's not such a big deal," I say to him. "Seriously. I mean, I think you're right and all that, but with your attitude, you're just making it worse for yourself, you know? You're the one that loses in the end."

I'm his best friend. By far. That's what distorts everything, makes it all more complicated. And it's his silence now, his ruminating over what I've just said, and not saying anything, that affects me. It really hits home.

"Yeah, I know. It's a phase, that's all, just a mood. Nothing serious, Matías. I'll shake it soon enough. Now show me what you brought me."

I close the lid of the toilet, sit down, and clean the lid of the water tank with my shirtsleeve. Then I see a mirror on the wall, so I take it off and put it on the lid.

"It's coke, isn't it?"

"You said it, man."

I open the origami and carefully spill out a good little mound of the powder onto the mirror. I leave the tiny packet balancing on the lid of the toilet tank. Nacho gets up, opens the medicine chest, and takes out an unused disposable Gillette.

"Cut it with this instead of your ID."

"You're the expert, huh. You go to lots of movies."

"Papelucho showed me how. We did a ton of it in Punta de Lobos when you were all in Rio. That's where I learned. Now hurry up, will you?"

This stuff hits me like a dump truck.

"So this isn't your first time."

"No, I'm not a virgin, no. I hope I haven't disappointed you."

"I thought I was bringing the latest, greatest thing."

"Well, it's all the same. No big deal. The main thing is you brought it. Good shit. Go ahead, do a couple of lines."

I do them, but it doesn't seem so appealing now.

"You went with Papelucho to Pichilemu, to Punta de Lobos?"

"Yeah, to surf. He's really into it, and he's not bad at it either. Learned it in California."

"I didn't know."

"Well, I just told you."

"Whatever. Just take some of this stuff, will you? This line looks like a killer."

He takes the straw and inhales the entire line.

"Man, this is good shit, isn't it? Papelucho would kill for this. Should we call him?"

"No."

The line is sort of crooked so that when I inhale it, it's a bit thick, but it's good. I see my eyes and my nose, and everything, reflected in the mirror. It's as if I were there below in the mirror, looking up, desperate. I also see Nacho, who's looking from farther away, behind my shoulder, vigilant.

Someone bangs on the door. Hard. They wait and then bang again.

"Give me another."

"Did they do a lot of coke on the beach there?"

"A little. It wasn't even good stuff. It was Rusty that brought it. He's Papelucho's friend, this totally disgusting, crazy American from Nido de Aguilas that he met on the plane."

"So you didn't go alone, then."

"No, man."

Someone keeps banging.

"Should we open up?"

"You want some toothpaste?" I ask him.

"Yeah, maybe."

As I open the Odontine, Nacho licks his fingers to take advantage of the last little remnants. He takes the mirror and hangs it back up. I move over to him, and he opens his mouth. I squeeze a little blob of toothpaste on his tongue. Then I open the faucet and clean my face, but I don't feel a thing. Nacho pees. At the same time, he takes the origami, which is on top of the sink, and stares at it.

"Open up! Who's in there?" some girl yells from the other side of the door.

I turn off the faucet and look down. The origami is floating in the yellow whirlpool of Nacho's pee.

"Shit, it just fell. I'm sorry, man. I got scared. This shit is seriously strong, you know. Was there a lot left?"

I feel really shivery and strung out. For a second, it's all the same to me. I move over, flush the toilet, and clean the powder that's still covering the tip of his nose. Then I lick my index finger; I feel the usual numbness.

Nacho just looks to the side.

SATURDAY
SEPTEMBER 6, 1980

It must be around five in the morning. I've already drunk an entire bottle of Bilz but I'm still thirsty. The air in this apartment just won't let me sleep. The sheets are on the floor, all tangled and sweaty from my tossing and turning, I'm drunk, fucked up. All the mixing is no good for me. I'm seeing visions, these strange images are coming into my head, I feel horrible. I wish I were in Rio, not here. I wish I were with someone right now. Having a conversation. Someone to talk on the telephone with. Tomorrow's another day, I guess. I know, you can't go home again, you can run but you can't hide, etc. But anyway, it's not fair. And I keep on thinking: I'm alone, I want to love a little more, I'm afraid, my Levi's have a hole at the knee. I should go into the bathroom to throw up, to puke, get it all out of me, but no, it's not just that. It's something else. I think I'm about to get a nosebleed. I feel like there's a big canal that's rising, steady and direct, toward my brain. The coke was too strong, it was cut with something. Or maybe it was really good stuff and I need more of it. I hope that Nacho didn't trash it on purpose, but who knows? Who ever knows, anyway?

It's dark in this room. All I can see are the red digits on the clock radio: 5:03. I think about going over to the window, to look at the lights from the city down below, empty, to see if the moon is out, the same moon that they're looking at in Rio and in

Brasília, but just the thought of having to get up and open the miniblinds totally depresses me. I'd rather just hug my pillow as if it were that old Winnie the Pooh bear I once had, even though it's not the same now. All this depresses me. My bed is spinning, but that's nothing new. Part of the game, it always happens. I should try to sleep.

I lost another day yesterday.

Let me recap:

We were playing pool with Patán, Julián Longhi, and Papelucho in one of those pool halls near the movies at Las Condes. It was really late then. The party was probably still going on, but none of us wanted to go back, so we went out in search of something better. Those lines we did in the bathroom really affected Nacho; he was in a strange mood and wouldn't stop talking, about the north coast of Hawaii, the pipeline, and that he was out of board wax or that in *Surfer* magazine there was an article about how Chile was the last remaining paradise for surfing, even though the water was really cold, and that Punta de Lobos was nothing more than an inlet with some fishermen.

Papelucho was more annoying than anything, but that was to be expected. Ever since they kicked him out of school and he ended up going to Marshall, and after his famous foreign exchange program in the U.S., he just seems way too sure of himself. It's like he does only what he wants to do, feels no guilt, and for some reason feels compelled to let the world know what a great time he always has. It's like we're supposed to admire him for that. Or something.

At this late stage in the evening, though, Nacho's obvious admiration for Papelucho had transformed itself into hate. Or something like it, because all of a sudden he was on my side. It's as if the incident with the coke made him feel guilty. Or maybe he was just happy to see me; even I felt better next to him, closer, and less aggressive and less hassled by everyone. That's not important. The point is, Papelucho was unbearable. He started in on Nacho when he caught on that Nacho was wired and hadn't bothered to invite him to join in. Which was an insult; after all, Papelucho was the one who introduced him to the stuff in the first place. Then he went off on his usual anti-Chilean lecture, talking about what prudes we all are, so provincial and petty and prejudiced, and how nobody ever dares to do anything new or different, how we all think that Chile is the be-all and end-all of everything, the California of South America, and how that's really the worst part of it all, because he knows better than the rest of us what the real differences are between the two places. So many things he couldn't even begin to list them all. Actually, I agreed with him, but it seemed kind of disloyal to support him at the time, so I kept my mouth shut.

So, after watching a couple of (boring) fancy pool shots that Papelucho himself assured us he learned at Los Manilas, Nacho and I decided it was time to go.

First we drove around Apoquindo and Providencia, and then we stopped to buy a couple of bottles of pisco in that little twenty-four-hour liquor store near the Scuola Italiana. There we were, tossing the drinks back, having a good time just talking about movies, avoiding the obvious, more touchy subjects like Rio, Cassia, Punta de Lobos, and Papelucho, when we ran into Cox. His surprise party was over, so he was wandering around with some guys from the San Ignacio, in a jungle-green Mitsubishi Galant that had some "SI" bumper stickers on the windshield. After making a couple of jokes about Brazil and telling Nacho how jealous he was of me for scoring with Cassia, who was really, really hot, Cristóbal invited us to follow them. There was going to be a killer of a road race down Avenida Kennedy, like in the old days. Chico Sobarzo was going to be racing against some buys from San Gabriel, or some people who had been teasing him at some party. We'd have to go immediately. The start of the race would be at that pedestrian overpass that nobody uses, the one that has all the AC/DC graffiti.

It was late and there wasn't much time before the curfew. Kind of time to go home, actually, but I looked at Nacho and sensed that he wanted to go and check it out, mainly because Chico Sobarzo was involved. Sobarzo is a character both he and Luisa Velásquez found fascinating, and not because he's a good guy or anything, the opposite, in fact. Luisa has always threatened that she's going to write a novel about all of us. According to her, Sobarzo would be one of the main characters since he "represents decadence in its purest, most unconscious state." He also wields the same kind of authority over a specific sector of our school, like Herman Hesse's Demian did over Sinclair, for example. I absolutely disagree with her: I think *I* would make a much more interesting literary figure than Sobarzo, even though she doesn't see it. But since she's the one who's going to go through the hassle of writing the fucking thing, I guess I can't complain too much.

I find the fascination Sobarzo seems to inspire in some people is really kind of overrated. In every obsession there's always a morbid element at work anyway. The thing with Sobarzo (who is short, ugly, ordinary, and dresses so badly I can barely stand looking at him) is that not only is he loaded (his old man is new money: he owns a used-car lot, but the truth is that he works for the Godfather), but he's also self-confident, especially now that Oscar, his brother, is dead.

Oscar was a classmate of mine, just like Sobarzo is now. What happened, though, is that Sobarzo, who is two years older, has had to repeat the same grade two times already. He's kind of slow, not too bright, although neither was Oscar, actually. Oscar was crazy, and on the soccer team. He always seemed to have luck with girls. He also had a tendency to get into fistfights about almost anything, which gave him a reputation as sort of a rebel and bad boy, and all those things that seem so important. The truth is, he was unbearably annoying, and I really could've cared less when he smashed the shit out of his horrible little orange and black Fiat 147. It wasn't just Oscar that died, though. He also killed two girls who had gone out for a ride, just out of boredom or something, in a Peugeot 404. The accident got a lot of cover-

age in the papers, and even *El Mercurio* ran an editorial on the
sorry state of today's youth, with all their money and all their
drinking. They treated it as if it were the story of the year.

Without Oscar, Sobarzo rose in status. It sounds awful, but so
did I. Oscar had this ability to attract everyone's attention, even
when he didn't do anything. He called himself the king of the
"chosen ones," and in a sense, that's what he was. Without him,
all the kids who consider themselves part of the scene lost a
leader. The position was then split among a bunch of different
people. You could say that it went from a situation of social authoritarianism to one of a slightly more democratic and civilized
manipulation. Sobarzo picked up on this immediately and took
advantage of the situation. To improve his own image, he now
tools around in another black and orange Fiat 147 (a family obsession) that his old man gave to him from his corrupt used-car
lot. That was the car he was going to use this evening in the race
down Kennedy. He was like one of those gang members in
Grease. But everything got fucked up.

We followed Cox and his friends down Avenida Manquehue,
to the overpass where Sobarzo, the black and orange Fiat 147,
and his quasi-disciples waited. When we got to Kennedy, there
was already a little group there, all hanging around as if it were
some sort of pit stop, near the little park by the military zone.
Sobarzo was wearing one of those Mario Ramirez olive-green,
safari-style shirts, the kind that are made out of distressed denim.
Nacho (who does have a good memory but who's also known for
being a vicious gossip) told me that the shirt had actually belonged to Oscar, who used to wear it constantly. Sobarzo must
have a really weird, fetishistic streak in him—not only was he
trying to imitate his dead brother in a pathetic way, but now he
was wearing his clothes.

There was an ominous atmosphere surrounding the whole
event. Sobarzo was clearly annoyed with the crowd from San
Gabriel, in their puffed-up feather-filled parkas, imitation
Nevadas. They were involved in some lengthy dialogue about

some guy whose body was so flexible he could suck his own dick. When we got there, nobody was sure anymore what the reason for the big confrontation was. It didn't make a difference, though, because the race was now what mattered. Sobarzo, sort of unwittingly, represented our school, so he had to make it good. This was his one chance to succeed purely on his own merit, and also to humiliate someone else.

There were other cars waiting for Cox up on Avenida Kennedy. Word had traveled fast. Lerner and a bunch of the others from our class were there, except for that *huevón* McClure and Antonia, who weren't showing any signs of life. Cox took charge of everything and laid out the rules: up to the traffic circle at Avenida Vespucio, U-turn, and the finish line would be here, at the overpass. The rest of us would watch from above. A girl who seemed to come out of nowhere, wearing a too-tight pair of leather jeans, was given the charge of dropping an empty bottle of pisco to signal the start of the race.

Fate has a way of taking care of things. Pinochet, unfortunately, doesn't agree with the philosophy that young people should be in the streets late at night. Maybe it was that we had just spent so many nights out in Rio doing whatever the hell we wanted that we had forgotten the basic rules in Chile. The curfew is ironclad.

Just when Sobarzo had gotten in his car and turned on the ignition, a patrol van with two cops drove up. Huge machine guns hung from their shoulders. It was obviously all over right then and there, because the bastards got down from the van, thinking we were terrorists, screaming at us: "Identification! Identification!" This little intrusion scared Sobarzo, so the idiot came down hard on the accelerator, and tore off, burning rubber as he left us. Of course, this totally pissed off the cops, making their attitudes even worse, because they didn't even have time to get his license plate. To retaliate, they started interrogating us, demanding answers in the most brutal and demented way possible: who were we, who was the motherfucker who took off in

the car. After the interrogation, they started in on civil disobe-
dience, and the time of night it was, and how the enemy is everywhere. One of them finally stopped lecturing us long enough to
convince himself of what he was saying, and put in a radio call
to the central police headquarters, to summon another patrol car
to arrest all of us. Then they forced all fourteen of us to line up.
Each one of us had to show his identification card; as one cop
looked at our IDs, the other had his Uzi on us.

Nacho was about six people down the line from me. When it
was his turn to show his ID, instead of showing his school card,
he gave them his membership card from the Naval Officers'
Club, or something like that, as evidence of his connections to
the government. It tied him, irrevocably, to that motherfucker of
a father of his, who, for the first time in his life, did something
good for him. Good for all of us, in fact, because the cop quaked,
and Nacho then took control. In a sickeningly patronizing, stern
voice, he launched into a tongue-lashing the likes of which he
could have only learned at that military school in Valparaíso. All
the while he was haranguing the cops, he made sure they knew
exactly who his father was. He even threatened them by saying
that the curfew officially started fifteen minutes later, and that
instead of wasting time bothering a group of youngsters who
were only trying to hang some posters in favor of the "SI," they
should have been busy protecting the neighborhood. It was hard
to believe that it was Nacho saying those things, but I guess if
you've got the military in your blood, it's there whether you like
it or not. The cop, surprisingly enough, reacted really well and
let us all leave. He apologized to Nacho, saying that in these
times, you never know, and that no precaution is too extreme.

The policemen's presence forced us all out of there, fast. There
were only a few minutes left before the curfew, so everyone left.
The nicer of the two cops offered to accompany me and Nacho
home. He even admitted that some military patrolmen were so
scared that more than a few times they would fire at any car
cruising around after the curfew.

I didn't think this was a good idea at all to associate ourselves with the authorities, even for a little while, but I caught on pretty quickly that we didn't really have much of a choice. I started my car and drove slowly, sticking close to the police car. He escorted us, with his siren light on, through the deserted avenues and streets, in the direction of Nacho's sister's house. The car radio wasn't working (I don't know why), but I didn't turn it off, so the static from the lost radio waves accompanied us during the trip home. Nacho was pretty wired from the coke, and I'd even venture to say that he got kind of a rush from the power of his recently assumed authority. Was this his inherent contradiction? He hated his father, but somehow that didn't make him ashamed of being his son. He had beaten the system tonight because he was part of it. That's how simple it was. That was what made him feel like one of the "chosen ones," of that new aristocracy that to me, every day and more and more, seems like such an overrated load of crap. I wanted to tell him what I thought of it all, to confront him and tell him what I really felt, but it wasn't the right moment. I'd already fought enough for one night. When you're running around stoned, it's better to leave things the way they are.

When we finally arrived at his sister's house, I flashed my headlights to let the cops know this was where we were stopping.

"You're going to your house, right?" Nacho asked me as he got out. "I'll tell them to escort you. No problem. That's what they're there for."

There wasn't too much to say at that point. I watched him go over to the cops to say good night and—I suppose—to tell them about me.

"It's all set. They're going to go with you. And you don't have to tip them either. Chau. Keep in touch."

Nacho always has this uncanny ability to rope me into situations that I want nothing to do with. Like driving through Santiago in the middle of the night, through an endless string of red traffic lights and calm, quiet, treelined streets, escorted by a military patrol van. Driving like that, totally alone, down streets that I had never seen empty before, so deserted that it looked like there'd been a bomb or something, I saw a few windows with lights on. They seemed suspicious to me somehow. I couldn't help but feel wrong, out of place, and totally useless.

Something was going wrong. Returning to Chile was more complicated and less appealing than I could ever have imagined in Rio. The great thing about traveling, I thought, was to be able to go home and then remember all the things you did when you were away. But this time was different. It was like I just couldn't take being back here. It was fear, a silent noise, like when a soldier fires blanks; it was disgust, it was exhaustion, it was mistrust that was screwing me up, that wouldn't leave me alone. But it wasn't just that: it was my family, maybe, my friends, the lack of girls in my life, my mood, my lack of mood, the bad vibes that seem to cloud over everything, in such a subtle way that it's hard to even notice or identify it. It can really make a person believe that there's no way things could be any better. But I can't realize that, even if I tried right now.

I was scared. I was restless. I just wanted to get home, and didn't like the idea that one of these patrollers would know where I lived. Later, I thought: of course they know where I live, they all do. Like when we landed at Pudahuel and the plane was so full that the customs line didn't move an inch. A man in front of me, with a tweed jacket and eyeglasses and this intellectual look that he just couldn't hide, gave his passport to the guy at the computer terminal. When the guy punched some stuff in, loads of information started coming up on the screen, and it was just at that moment, when I was opening my bag, that I looked at the tweedy guy in the face. He turned around and looked back at me, as if I were the only person that existed on earth, as if I were his son or his brother or something. It was the same way I'm feeling now, because I realized that he was not only scared but somehow happy despite everything. He had won in some way. Then an alarm went off and a bunch of uniformed men with helmets and machine guns suddenly surrounded him. One of them pushed me out of the way, then a group of plainclothes, secret-service types confiscated his bag and examined his passport. I just watched, stood there observing the whole thing, wanting to understand what I had just seen. I could barely believe what was happening. I felt so bad for the tweedy guy, who I hadn't even noticed was on the plane. He started shouting, "Let me in, let me into my own country, I have every right," but a sharp punch, right to his jaw, shut him up. Blood spilled from his mouth as he murmured, "She's sick, she's sick . . ." Then they took him away, and he disappeared behind a door. I just stood there, mute, unable to utter a word, until the traitor at the computer terminal yelled at me to move up. I gave him my passport, shaking, and he punched up my name. I saw that a Vicuña came up on the screen, but it wasn't me, it wasn't even a relative or anything. I still couldn't breathe any easier, all I could do was resign myself to the situation, accept the stamp on one of the pages of my passport, and listen to the guy at the counter, who said, "That's all, you can go through now . . . and keep what you just saw to yourself, kid."

I wake up late, but that part is easy. The hard part is buying into it, finding the strength to go the next step. Should I stay in bed or jump up and open the blinds, like that idiot in the margarine commercial? I look at my watch: false alarm, it's not that late. It's barely ten. The sun's out, strong, like the sun in Rio. For a split second I'm afraid I'll never be able to get up out of the bed, so I finally get up (not jump up) and open the blinds. Santiago is weird, it looks weird, all bright and cloudless and clear and green and full of trees, with new leaves and flowers, and you can see out to the mountains, zero smog, and there's even a tiny bit of snow at the top of El Colorado, I think.

Something's up: nobody's around. Not even Carmen. Today's Saturday. And this fucking place should be full of people, but nothing's happening. *Is anybody out there?* The refrigerator is empty: they all must be at Jumbo. Or maybe they were all murdered by a Chilean Son of Sam. I brighten up a little. Wishful thinking.

My head is killing me. Two aspirin with a swig of grapefruit juice, a little bit of cheese, yellowish and acidic. In the shower, I shave off what little stubble I have. I look at myself in a round, two-sided mirror: one side of it is normal, and even there I look worse than I thought. The other side magnifies everything and forces me to come to terms with a big blackhead just under the base of my nose. It reminds me of Miriam. I soap myself up well, but I don't get turned on, so I get out, dress, comb my hair back, as if I were John Travolta or something (something worse, probably), and I realize that I am absolutely, utterly, totally bored.

I find the latest issue of *19* in Francisca's room and flip through it, but not without feeling sort of embarrassingly horrified at the number of idiotic events I've read about in my short life: the divorce of two members of Abba, Donna Summer's religious awakening, Peter Frampton's drug addiction, the post–Partridge Family future of David Cassidy, and other equally important bits of trivia. Something that depresses me all of a sudden is the realization that I am addicted to the column called "Querida Márgara." It is written by some lady, Márgara Urzúa. It's clearly the worst part of *19*. My obsession with her must be some kind of oedipal thing because the lady is old, like around my mother's age. According to Francisca, she's crazier than cotton candy, has a bunch of ex-husbands and a really hot daughter who sleeps with just about anyone now that her mother can't control her anymore. Obviously she can't be a hypocrite since she isn't that way in the column.

I take the magazine to my room, flop on my still-unmade bed, and turn on the stereo. I'm jolted by that horrible song "Píntame con Besos" by Albert Hammond, which the host from *Música Libre* lip-syncs over and over again on his stupid TV show, like a Chilean Denny Terrio. The truth is, it's actually the best back-

ground music I could choose for reading this trash, so I revel in
my decadence and leave it on. I even prepare myself for a little
Air Supply or Andy Gibb to come on next. I open the magazine,
check out the Top Ten listings, then look for it. "Querida Márgara" is the only column where you can really read about what's
going on in people's lives and realize that there's tons of people
going through the same stuff as you. But, that said, it is also true
that "Querida Márgara" wouldn't be nearly so successful if it
didn't include that splashy photo of Márgara herself. It's my
own theory, and there are many who agree with me on this, including Lerner and my cousin Camila, who I am sure was the
person who wrote a detailed letter in which a girl announced to
Márgara that she had lost her virginity, guilt-free, at someone's
big fifteenth-birthday party—a party that I had been invited to
but didn't go to.

The theory about the photo is twofold. One has to do with
credibility: it assures us that Márgara really exists. My mother
even thinks she knows who she is, because she used to take yoga
classes at this center run by a friend of hers, and says she was a
classmate of my uncle Sandro's sister. It's because of the photo
that you believe in her. It's not like *Coqueta* or *Intimidades,*
those moronic, Miami-based tabloidy magazines that girls read
in class, the ones that are supposedly for "modern women" because they talk about vaginal discharge and stuff like that, but
in reality are just totally stereotypically female.

The other part of the theory is more masculine, more sexual,
I think. Márgara is what you would call a *vieja tirable,* in other
words, she's been around. In the photograph, she's sitting on the
floor, on a big cushion, with a tight bodysuit on. From what she
writes, you can tell she gets around and likes playing the field,
and definitely does not lack experience (even though she may
not be getting any these days). Also in this photo, she's holding
a little dachshund, with bright little eyes, and looking straight
into the camera, suggesting a certain pleasure or contentment
that's hard to explain but it's a turn-on. All you need to do is read

one or two of her pieces to see that she's obsessed with younger men. So that's why we all read her. And that's why we all write to her too, I guess.

She's definitely a turn-on. But it's all in what and how she writes, which is the best thing about her. I was with Nacho when I read the letter that we now attribute to my cousin Camila (who's only thirteen but both of us would do her in a second). She completely denies it, but it all seems suspiciously familiar. One of Nacho's cousins was at the party in question, which was at a weekend cottage near Pirque. Camila was there, wasted and totally drooling all over this Argentinian polo player who said he was the best player around. In the letter, Camila says that it was "a Uruguayan rugby player" but she really gives herself away when she starts relating the whole deal with the horses they rode there (my cousin is quite the equestrienne, wears those tight white pants, etc.) and the location ("There were palm trees, and I felt as though we were alone on an island," the little slut wrote). So anyway, the thing is, Nacho and I decided to invent a couple of stories to see if Márgara really answered the letters (where she includes her "advice for living") or whether it was all just bullshit. After smoking a few joints, we each took a pencil and paper and launched into writing.

Nacho's letter was definitely the more far-fetched of the two, straight out of a TV movie: it involves two best friends arguing over a girl who's gotten pregnant by one of them (they don't know which one). She gets an abortion and then hooks up with the older brother of the one who got her pregnant. He's a doctor and helped her with the whole abortion thing. The younger brother gets furious and starts in with the doctor's girlfriend, but when he discovers that the girlfriend is sort of a lesbian and in the throes of trying to seduce the girl that got the abortion, he takes a mess of drugs and ends up in bed with his best friend, who ends up totally confused and falls for him. The main guy (the one with the doctor brother who forgives and makes up with the lesbian after all) tells the whole story to the girl, goes back to her, they get married right away and end up parents of a pair of fat little twins. The other guy, dying of jealousy because of the double betrayal, turns into a flaming homosexual (a codependent who can't get over what his best friend/lover or the girl did to him), and ends up getting involved with some millionaire hood who pays him with cocaine and expensive Italian clothing. When he realizes that his life is a total sham, he injects himself with something in the men's bathroom at the Red Pub and dies.

Nacho wrote the piece as if he were the guy who ends up with the little fat twins and the truth is that the letter was quite entertaining, but not really all that believable. According to him, it was all true, and part of the story was based on what happened to a friend of his from another rich school, Craighouse. Maybe.

My letter, in comparison, was much more predictable and conventional but far more romantic, I think. I didn't even believe it myself. It's about a girl (I wrote it as if I were the girl myself) who loves her boyfriend "Matías" more than anything else in the world, but won't sleep with him because she wants to stay a virgin. Her best friend, who's considered sort of loose, is also in love with "Matías". It's more than that: it's that he's the love of her life and that's why she's so easy. She goes from guy to guy in an effort to forget about him, and she's never even touched him. The girl who writes the letter—I signed it "Antonia"—is really in the middle of a mess because her friend's mother tearfully confides to her that her friend, "Sara" (a small tribute to Fleetwood Mac on my part), has cancer and is about to die, even though she doesn't say anything about it. She wants to live her last few days in happiness. The doubt that "Antonia" has, though (who is a very Catholic and good person), is whether she should abandon "Matías" (who would definitely make a move on "Sara"), and make her friend's last few days a little happier, by allowing her to finally know what true love is, before it becomes too late. That was the question posed, one that only Márgara could supposedly answer.

Of course she didn't answer me, much less Nacho. Neither one was ever published, but I still keep on reading her column because you never know and anyway it's fun and she's always kind of surprising. You always wonder if a letter is from someone you know (she only answers letters from people with good addresses, I've noticed). Like this one from the latest issue: a teenager who can't decide if she should go on an international exchange program. "Everyone tells me that Americans are very liberal and that I'll end up abandoning my Chilean morals to fit in with my American classmates, and that scares me . . ." Papelucho should answer that one, I think to myself; nothing seems to scare him. Antonia, on the other hand, would tell her to stay here, I'm sure. She denies reading *19,* and Márgara's column, but she reads it, just like the rest of us. I remember how furious she was when she heard about my letter and how I had signed it "Antonia." According to her, it was the vilest and lowest thing we could do to her. Ever since then—this is her excuse—she reads Márgara religiously, terrified that the letter will be published someday and that her name (but not her last name) will appear in print.

"Hello? Uh . . . Is Antonia there by any chance?" I ask as I put on my Top-Siders.

"Miss Antonia left," the housekeeper says over the telephone. A bad sign.

"Oh . . . You mean she didn't come home last night?"

"Of course she came home last night. I meant just now. Shopping, I think. Who's calling, please?"

"Uh, it doesn't matter . . . it's Ricardo," I lie.

"You called yesterday, didn't you? I gave her your message."

"Thank you. Um . . . do you think she would have gone to Providencia?"

"Probably. She was going to meet a few of her friends. But she'll be back for lunch. Late, though. You could call back then."

The clock says 11:14. I shut *19* and leave it in back where I found it. As I pass the bar, I take out a bottle of Stolichnaya and take a long pull off of it. A shiver runs down my spine.

"So you came back an alcoholic? Some shithole country that

is, Brazil. I told your mother not to let you go. A cousin of mine ran away from Chile and all the commies and went there. She ended up a dancer in a topless bar, showing off her tits to all those horny black men."

It's Carmen: ugly, closed-minded, and judgmental, as usual.

"God, I hope your cousin isn't anything like you."

"Just leave me alone. I have to work. Lunch guests today. That lunatic Loreto is coming over. This place is turning into a restaurant, that's how busy I am, for Christ's sake. Are you staying for lunch or going out?"

"I'm going out. But I'm coming back. I think. Where is everyone?"

"I was up buying some shellfish at the store up the street. Your mother and sisters are at Jumbo and then off to the beauty salon. Waxing, the little darlings. Some people don't fucking know what to do with their money . . . Mr. Esteban has a meeting at the Country Club and isn't coming home for lunch."

"He went to play golf, right?"

"Who am I? Kojak? I have no idea. He took his clubs."

"Whatever. See you later. Make a note of all my phone messages. And learn how to spell, will you?"

"Fuck you, how's that for a message?"

Providencia, the very epicenter, is teeming, just the way it's supposed to be. It's one of the few places that saves Santiago. Lots of crazy, space-age buildings and everyone I know in the world walking aimlessly around, shopping for clothes, walking in circles, really.

The sun washes over it all. It's calm and clear today. I go into a stark, postmodern eyeglass store. There's a bunch of posters showing an overtanned Julio Iglesias wearing eyeglasses, broiling himself on the beach. The salesgirl is wearing one of those horrible, slutty little angora sweaters that are all the rage now thanks to Gina Zuanic, the TV announcer. I ask to look at the Ray

Bans. I like them, and she tells me they look good on me. Since I still have money left over, I buy them. Way too expensive. I'll have to ask my father for more money later. No problem. I assume.

I walk as far as the ice skating rink, but there isn't much action down there; it's filled with girls like my cousin Camila, wearing those little shorty skirts, all trying to seduce older guys. So I go in the other direction; down to Dos Caracoles and up the elevator that nobody uses, all the way up to the very top. I decide to look at each little boutique as I make my way down the circular walkway. I've suddenly got this feeling that I'm near her, so I check out all the shops with a calculated, mathematical thoroughness. But she's not there, so I move on, and walk down a couple of stores.

Pumper Nic is full, like it is every Saturday. The smell of french fries, of grease, engulfs me. I like it. It's the smell of the United States, I think. The smell of progress. It makes me think of Paz, it makes me think of Orlando and Disney World, of Miami, of McDonald's and Burger King and Kentucky Fried Chicken and Carl's Jr and Jack-in-the-Box. Pumper Nic—even the name sounds pathetic to me, way too third-world. It isn't all that bad, but it's a bad copy, that's the thing. It's not authentic.

The only real thing in there, though, is Antonia, who's standing outside near the entrance to the drugstore. Alone.

"Antonia . . . I was looking for you."

"I'm waiting for Flavia Montessori. She was supposed to be here half an hour ago. I think she's stood me up. Maybe she went to sleep late last night."

"She was at Cox's party. I saw her with Pelusa Echegoyen. I left after that. Sobarzo was going to race down Kennedy."

"What a worthwhile activity . . ."

"And you, what did you do last night?"

"I went to the movies. I went with Gonzalo."

"Oh . . . what did you see?"

"*Ice Castles,* nothing special. It's the one about the blind ice-skater. An ice skating champion, who . . . well anyway, I was just leaving. I guess it doesn't matter about Flavia . . . I want to see if I can find a pair of pants. I promised my mother I wouldn't come home too late, for lunch . . ."

Then, with those eyes of hers, she asks:

"Would you come with me, Matías?"

I practically fall over, from her sudden change of mind.

"Excellent. I'll go wherever, whenever you want."

"Just around here, dummy. And only now. Don't get carried away."

"It's too late for that. But don't worry, I'm used to it."

I enjoy walking around with Antonia. It's something I rarely get to indulge in, but I could get used to it. It would be perfect: walk and walk with her, fall into step, and strut around together, like that time that the officers from our school made us march around and salute the flag and get into formation and memorize the song "Orden y Patria." I remember they gave Antonia (who has always been tall and perfect) a pair of white gloves that made her look like one of those old film stars. She led the officers around the soccer field; it was late, the sun was low, and the light was about the same color as my mood. At that moment, with the breeze swirling around, and her not-very-long hair reflecting in the gleam of her eyes, I realized that she was the one I wanted, the one I wanted but would never have, because girls like Antonia don't fall for guys like me. Definitely not.

Or maybe they do. It's hard to tell. A person can't go around analyzing these things, much less expressing what he feels, because there's just nothing worse than saying: "You know that I love you, don't you?" and have her reply, "Yes, I love you too, but . . . only as a friend."

That's really uncool. Totally uncool.

I didn't used to be like that.

"So what do you want to buy?" I ask.

"Jeans, I think. Let's go to FU's."

It's obvious that there's something about me that she's attracted to. But I also repel her in a way. And vice versa. That's why we were made for each other and that's why nothing ever happens between us. I hate almost everything she does, I can't stand the way her mind works, I think her morals and her family life are middle-class and stupid, her proper manners drive me insane, but the way her clothes fall over her body fascinates me, her intelligence turns me on, and so does the way she always refuses to change her point of view once she's stated her opinion, even if I might be right. Her voice alone just makes me want to melt. I can always feel it. That smile of hers, when she's mad, I love to think about it. She looks much older than she is, and I know that if we got married (for argument's sake), she would never abandon me or cheat on me; she would just stop talking to me and acknowledging my little idiosyncrasies, she would just erase me from her mind and that would be that. She isn't shy at all; in fact, if anything, she's overconfident and she shows it. Her pride and her ego are so huge that she'll probably never realize how much she needs affection. Or that she misses things. Or that she can't stand being alone.

"How do they fit?"

"What do you think I'm going to say?" I tell her. "I'm not the most objective person, you know."

"Don't play games with me, all right? They're either good, or they're too tight. Tell me."

"They're perfect. Seriously."

"Fine. I believe you."

She closes the little curtains and I look out onto the street, onto General Holley. I watch all the blond girls walking by, loaded with bags, licking those soft ice creams that are everywhere these days. The curtains don't close all the way, and I manage to catch a glimpse of some skin, a leg. She knows I'm watching her but it doesn't seem to bother her; in fact, I'd almost say she enjoys it. That's so typical of her: yes but no, take but never give, convert everything—kisses, gazes, gifts, confessions, caresses— into accidents, little meaningless coincidences that should never be analyzed as anything more than what they are.

"Don't tell anyone about this," she whispered to me once, right after our best kiss, in her kitchen, while we were making tea and I was crushing an avocado.

"Extremely Chilean attitudes," Cassia would say. One day, on the beach in Rio, I explained my whole relationship with Antonia to her. She came down on me, saying, first of all, that it wasn't a *relationship* at all. And second, that Antonia, or "the girl," as she called her, was way too Chilean for her own good. Cassia said she could just picture the way things like that worked here. But it's easy to judge everything from the outside. Cassia doesn't know, doesn't understand. She doesn't get it, that things here just can't be loose and relaxed like: "Hi, what's your name?" and let's sleep together and no big deal, everyone does what they want, and that's it. That's what life is like in Rio, not here. Not on General Holley, not on Vitacura, not anywhere in Santiago I don't think. It's not that nothing ever happens here. Sometimes too much happens. It's just that you never really feel it or something. You just have to deny. And forget.

"I bet you can't stand the thought of going back to classes," Antonia says to me as we wait for the bus on the corner of Los Leones.

"Sort of," I say. "Anyway, I don't think there'll be too many of them, because starting Wednesday we're on vacation again. It's only three days. I bet they'll cancel school on Tuesday also, for the elections. I hear the 'NO' crowd is going to come out and picket."

"They should shoot them all, just to stop them from bothering everyone. I just want the referendum to happen and be over. We're all going to Vichuquén right after."

"You'll celebrate the holidays there?"

"Yes."

"You always miss the most entertaining stuff, don't you?"

"What? Spending the Eighteenth in Santiago is entertainment for you?"

"It's all the same to me, really. You don't understand. I was thinking that we could do something together. That's all. Here comes your bus."

"What are you going to do this afternoon?"

"Just hang around, I guess."

"Let's do something. We could go for a bike ride. How about it?"

"Sure."

"Get your bike and come over to my house, then."

"Do I have to?"

"What do you think?"

It's still kind of early to go home, so I go into Circus to look at records and check out the *Billboard* list, which has become an obsession with me. McClure comes up from behind me. There's no way to play dumb, I can't escape. Shit.

"Hey, what's up, dude? My mother said you stopped by last night."

I hear Elton John's "Little Jeannie" come on. The song is horrible and the guy behind the counter really should know better, but the album is at number five, so I guess I'd better get used to it. I turn and look at McClure. He sure does dress like an engineering student, but he doesn't look all that bad, to be fair.

"I did stop by. I was kind of wasted, actually. I hope your mother didn't notice."

"Never. She doesn't ever catch on to that kind of stuff. Anyway, she loves you."

"Good taste," I say, I don't know why.

The guy behind the counter (black T-shirt, with an iron-on picture of Kiss) takes the Elton John off and holds the record for a second. I look at him and smile ironically. This disturbs him slightly: he realizes that anyone who wears the kind of shirt he has on cannot play Elton John, even as a joke. Distressed, he puts on the new Billy Joel album, which isn't so bad, but doesn't quite correspond, as background music, to this kind of encounter.

"So what's going on?" I ask McClure.

"Nothing much. Just killing time. I'm going to buy something. I changed all my leftover cruzeiros, so I'm pretty loaded."

We go through the records: imports, obviously. *Empty Glass* by Pete Townshend intrigues me (the overly intellectual result of reading *Rolling Stone* for hours on end, clearly). There's also *Duke* by Genesis, but I'd have to listen to it first, because without Peter Gabriel, the group just isn't the same. McClure, who is obsessed with fashion, in spite of his conservative appearance, carefully studies "Eat to the Beat" by Blondie and also "In the Heat of the Night" by Pat Benatar (a step in the right direction for him, since at least they're women and actually pretty hot, especially Deborah Harry).

But what really grabs us is *The Blues Brothers,* because John Belushi himself sings on it. McClure and Lerner and Nacho and Papelucho and I are possibly the only people in all of Chile who saw the movie, at the Metro theater. It barely lasted three days there. We were very, very stoned when we saw it, and the record is sort of a symbol of it. Belushi is hilarious, and, as Alejandro Paz says, *Animal House* is an indisputable classic, even though to me it was just a really good laugh and a reflection of what we all wished life was like, that's all.

During our reviewing Belushi and Electric Light Orchestra albums, I suddenly sense that I'm on pretty good terms with McClure: he's not nearly as annoying or sickening as I wish he were. In fact, anyone that saw us right now would think we were a team. And they wouldn't be so wrong, I think to myself. He's really a nice guy, and actually very easy to be around. A thousand times easier than Nacho, that's for sure. Like he doesn't bother anyone, except me, obviously. Before, we used to be better friends, we went to the movies together, we shared notes from social science or chemistry formulas, we'd crash parties together, that sort of thing. That was before Antonia, of course. Or, more truthfully, before Antonia noticed him, because Gonzalo—like all of us—had always paid attention to Antonia. He's only human anyway, it's not his fault. But, that said, it still doesn't redeem him. I hate him just the same, and one day he's going to have to pay. I doubt they sleep together, though. That's pretty clear, and a great comfort to me. They also don't share this common thing for records either. She goes out with him to make me jealous, that's what it is. This afternoon, I'm going to tell her all about his little escapades in Rio and then maybe I'll ruin their romance . . .

"Should I get these or not?" Gonzalo interrupts my thoughts.

"If you have the money, definitely."

He decides on *The Blues Brothers,* the sound track to *American Gigolo* (including "Call Me"), and Led Zep's *In Through the Out Door.* He's in the process of collecting the complete works of Led Zeppelin. Looking at all those shiny records in their cellophane wrappers, I feel this anxiety—or is it anger?—coming on, and decide to buy something too, so I don't feel inferior or something. Without thinking twice, I buy Christopher Cross for Antonia (I tell McClure it's for my sister) and *Breakfast in America.* Nacho once told me it was a very good record and that Supertramp would never be able to outdo it. I also get a copy of *The Blues Brothers*: sort of as a little preventive-medicine, before-the-blow kind of a thing. If McClure keeps going out with Antonia (and all indications seem to show that this will be the case), I sincerely doubt that he will be inviting me over to listen to his.

We leave Circus. It's getting hotter every second and the mood outside is sort of like it is during the Fiesta de Primavera, that is, before they suspended it, because everyone threw eggs and sacks of water and flour.

"I have to get a haircut," McClure tells me. "Want to come along?"

I say sure, and decide to get mine cut as well, because my surfing look isn't exactly right for school and the last thing I need is for the disciplinarian to start hassling me. We walk in the direction of Yamil slowly, no rush. We cross the street, making our

way through the crowds of girls hanging out in front of the drugstore and Pumper Nic, but I'm already thinking about something else.

"What did you do last night?" I ask, all innocent.

"I went to the movies. A terrible movie, actually. Really
predictable . . . about an ice skating champion who goes blind
but keeps on skating. A total copy of *The Other Side of the
Mountain*."

"Did you go alone?"

"No, with a girl, who of course loved it. She was practically
crying at the end."

I'm not sure whether I should continue this line of conversation or not. Up until this moment, he's been telling the truth. He
just omitted the name, that's all. My obvious question that would
follow is "Who's the girl?" or "Do I know her?"

"I can't stand girls who cry at those tearjerker movies," I say
instead.

I look at the floor and at his Adidases, and I think how risky
and uncomfortable it would be to make him lie. It would be even
worse if he were to confess and say something like, "Yes, I went
with Antonia, and we made out. She's so hot, and everything's
going great between us and she even let me touch one of her tits
before getting out of the car." I'd rather not know this kind of
thing. But the silence—the curiosity—is killing me.

He breaks the silence.

"I remember once I took a girl out to see one of those police
movies, and the bad guy, some actor nobody's ever heard of, reminded her of an ex-boyfriend who went to live in Australia. The
girl cried and cried every time the actor came on. It was really
a tragedy, a total fiasco. She left the theater with her nose all
stuffed up. Never again."

"It's weird, the thing about crying," I answer. "One night, I was
with Antonia at her house, watching this movie on television,
She Lives, that has all the Jim Croce music, and it was really kind
of embarrassing, because I started crying before the movie was

over. She caught me and I tried to make myself out to be strong and silent but she was also crying . . . I don't know, it turned out to be kind of a nice moment, I mean, sort of moving. I think it kind of brought us together. Then she confessed to me that every time she hears 'Time in a Bottle' she thinks of me. Despite it all."

The anecdote, obviously, is a total lie. But it works. McClure is pale, shocked. He's somewhere between jealousy and anger. Obviously, he's hiding something, and his Catholic upbringing is weighing heavy on him right now. There's hundreds of people around us, and I'm sure he's thinking that they are all saying to themselves: "That's the guy they say is a *liar.*" But it's not just that: it's the lowest form of jealousy. McClure now realizes, clearer than ever, that for what little there is between me and Antonia, at least it's serious, and deep. Deeper than anything he'll ever have with her. I almost tell him that I'm going out bike riding with her today, but I decide that would be an unwise tactic.

We continue walking. We're just about up to the Torres de Tajamar. Neither of us says anything. In any event it is true that I cried during *She Lives,* so the lie isn't that big a deal.

The barbershop is a mob scene, and the attendant, who looks more like a hooker than a hairdresser, tells us there's a twenty-minute wait. We sit down and they give us each an espresso. McClure grabs a *Penthouse,* and I get a *Hustler.* I flip through the magazine awhile and am drawn to a spread of a mother eating out her daughter, 69 style. They're both blond, all oiled up, and both have these little pink vaginas. The attendant then calls me over, sits me down, and flirts with me a little as she starts to wash my hair, massaging me as if we're in a whorehouse or something. It's a good massage too, so good that I start to get a little turned on. McClure is to my right, all lathered up. He's still silent. Distant.

The attendant—Yenny—then dries my hair and hands me a copy of *Oui.*

"All right, my friend," says one of the hairdressers, "what can I do for you?"

The inquiry catches me by surprise. I almost say, "Shave it all off." When you're in a bad mood, a haircut is a good idea. It builds your ego. Or ruins it, if you don't like it. McClure is still sitting there, still pissed, he's not even listening, I'm sure.

"I don't know . . . something like . . . like John Belushi in *The Blues Brothers.*"

McClure looks at me.

He laughs.

My aunt Loreto is carefully peeling the shells off a pile of shrimp, just like I bet she takes the condoms off all the men she sleeps with. I'm only guessing, but I'm sure it's true. Absolutely. She's really kind of a slut, but I guess that's part of what makes her so funny.

"I can't stand people who confuse shrimp and prawns," she says. "Or shrimp with crayfish. Prawns are just large shrimp, right?"

"Yes, Loreto," says my mother, who knows something about shellfish. "Think fried prawns. With sweet and sour sauce. I adore them. Did you know that the best Chinese food in the world, outside of Peking, is in London?"

"Actually, I thought it was in San Francisco."

My aunt Loreto has traveled a lot. She's spent a lifetime in airplanes. She's also lived overseas, just to escape Salvador Allende. She tells the story as if it were just an anecdote but the truth is, it's kind of embarrassing. She and my uncle Sandro and their daughter Judith (who now studies marine biology up north in Iquique because she hates her mother) left Chile on August 11, 1973. The liner they were cruising on hadn't even reached the port at Los Angeles when La Moneda, the Presidential Palace in Santiago, was bombed. Her "diaspora," as she calls it, lasted a month. They stayed in Los Angeles for a while. Like two years or something, and Judith learned to speak English just like a perfect Valley Girl. Then they came back, with a BMW, a two-door refrigerator with one of those ice-making things, various color television sets, etc. Brought it all back without having to pay any taxes on anything. They took advantage of one of Pinochet's laws that was passed as an incentive, to encourage the people who escaped during the "red period" to return to Chile. My father always criticized that law, saying, "Sure, reward the cowards who took off. Those of us who stayed around fighting off the communists, we don't even get so much as a thank-you." That's what he thinks. But I think it was more an issue of envy than of politics. It was the envy he felt for that cobalt-blue BMW Uncle Sandro brought back with him.

"And how is Judith?" my sister Francisca askes Aunt Loreto as she takes another shrimp with cream sauce that Carmen prepared.

"Terrible. She never comes to Santiago anymore, and now she's got these dreadlocks that come down to here. She's decided to take up surfing. When she's finished with school she wants to go to California."

I think of Papelucho. He should meet Judith. They'd be perfect for each other. In general, my aunt Loreto's vapid, gossipy nature entertains me. When I really study her in the sunlight that is cruelly beating down through the window, bouncing off the salad bowl and the silverware, she looks old. Shriveled, even. She isn't so perfectly made up right now, and she's not displaying her usual Andean beauty. She doesn't look sexy. She's not wearing one of her revealing dresses. Under her skirt I see a roll of fat, and her freckled arms seem flabbier. A year ago, I couldn't even sit next to her without getting turned on. It wasn't because she was so fantastic then either: it was more that she kind of invited it. Not anymore, though. It's like she's damaged now. It's not the divorce; that was a while back already. It's something else.

For my parents, the whole case of Sandro Giulianni–Loreto Cohn is a touchy subject. Sandro works with my father and Aunt Loreto is my mother's sister. That means either one or the other comes over, not both at the same time, because neither one will tolerate the other. Once they overlapped visiting my house, and it was a debacle, a huge scene. Never again, that's for sure. Aunt Loreto wouldn't speak to my mother for months. Her theory on this actually had a certain logic: she said she couldn't be friends with someone who was, at the same time, friends with someone she detested. According to Loreto, this indicated not only hypocrisy but a weak resolve as well. "I'm not interested in getting together with people who entertain and trust a person of the likes of Sandro," she said furiously at the entrance to the elevator just before leaving that day, my father's birthday. Aunt Loreto had arrived at the party and my uncle was there with a hot blonde.

"You make a good salad, Rosario," continues Loreto. "You'll have to give me the recipe, since now all I'm eating is vegetables and things that won't make me fat. I made it halfway through the Scarsdale diet but then I got bored. I hope our main dish isn't too high in calories. Right now, I'm telling you, the only calories I'm willing to ingest are those in vodka. And gin."

She isn't as open anymore either, I realize. She lost her old sense of humor, and now she sort of hides things. Before, she never spoke, she kind of expelled words. It was like a compulsion. She always used to be great to listen to through the walls, and now my conclusion is that she and my mother, even though they are sisters, aren't such good friends anymore, which bothers me a little. My mother says she puts up with her because she's entertaining, but she still criticizes her a lot. She deplores Loreto's way of life: going from lover to lover, sleeping with whoever she feels like. And it's true: Loreto would sell herself for a drink at the Red Pub or La Rosa Negra. She practically lives at Regine's. The guy that lasted the longest was from Mendoza, very good looking but working-class and fifteen years younger than her. He used to wear a jeans jacket with no shirt on underneath and he thought he was so fucking cool. He stuck around for an entire summer. In general, her conquests don't tend to last longer than through breakfast the next day.

"Matías, love, forgive my prying, but isn't that what they call a hickey on your arm?"

I accept the blow but my stomach jumps. Witch. With my hand, I cover the aforementioned blemish and, in a matter of milliseconds, unroll the sleeve of my shirt.

"It's a bruise, that's all," I lie.

No one believes me for a second and I'm probably turning red. I quickly think of Cassia and try to remember. I remain silent.

"Are you sure, Matías?" insists Loreto, who, all of a sudden, isn't nearly so interested in her prawns after all. "Come here, show it to me. I've seen one or two of those in my time, you know."

Francisca whispers something to Bea, who starts laughing.

"No, no, it's a bruise. I banged into the car door. I swear."

"Listen, you have to be careful with these things, you know," continues Loreto, totally unabashed. "Passion is fine, but not when it gets out of hand, if you know what I mean. Especially in a woman. These things don't just disappear overnight. Neither do bites or scratch marks. Or stretch marks . . ."

My mother doesn't say anything but I can tell the topic of discussion is making her uneasy. She finally breaks in.

"Enough, Loreto. If Matías says it's not a hickey, it's not a hickey. Don't torture him. Anyway, he never talks about anything. Hides everything. Who knows where that's from. From what I can tell, he doesn't even have a girlfriend right now. In a way, I would prefer not to know where Matías has been. You know better than anyone that he ignores everything I say or ask about. Entirely. I could be a grandmother and I wouldn't even know it."

My mother then gives Carmen (who's been spying on us this whole time) a little signal, and she comes to remove our plates. My mother is talking as if I weren't even in the room. Francisca, who's still wearing her gym shirt, is playing with the bread crumbs. Bea's doubled over laughing.

"They are all like that, Rosario. It's a stage. Judith is exactly the same. The poor thing has turned out to be a real 'wild child.'

It's her father's Italian blood. Neapolitan blood, actually, which is even worse."

All this complaining about us as if we weren't even in the room jump-starts my aunt, who gathers up her hair and tries putting it in a bun as she talks. Her hands are large and freckled, but her fingernails seem completely contrary to her personality. It's a characteristic I've never noticed before. They seem as if they belong to a nurse: pale, with a dull shine, no color at all. She wipes her lips with a napkin.

"Forget about it. The fights I've gotten into with that child . . ." she continues. "What really makes me mad is that it's rebellion for rebellion's sake, all because I told her I wanted her to take the Pill and be done with it. But no, it has to be an argument: that it's not natural, that it's just another form of abortion, and all sorts of other protests. Me, I'm not a prude about it at all, so I just said to her, 'Look, Judith, I'd rather you had a little nonsurgical mini-abortion than end up in some clinic begging some doctor friend to do something that's illegal and perform a real abortion. Believe me, that would be much worse. *That* would be a real trauma. And I'm telling you this from experience. So if you're going on a manhunt, go armed.' Ever since then, she hasn't been a bit of trouble."

I look at Francisca, who now seems to be losing color. There's a moment of silence that is only broken by the creaking of the door, announcing Carmen's entrance into the dining room, with her tray full of steaks with spinach and carrots.

"Thank God Matías is a man. So however much he fools around, at the end of the day, it's not my problem."

"Of course, Rosario, but, well . . . what about your girls?"

Aunt Loreto is much sharper than we all give her credit for, and she knows much more than she should. Or does she just infer it all? Is it that obvious? Whenever we talk about moral issues, she always wins. Her scandals are such public ones that nobody can really criticize her. That's what gives her that attitude. It somehow allows her to preach as if from a pulpit. If she has one mission in life, it's to uncover the truth about people, no matter what.

"It's all a matter of upbringing," my mother responds, somewhat offended.

"Do you think so?"

Francisca is clearly becoming more and more uncomfortable, and I am too. Bea, thank God, limits herself to listening only to the juicy parts. I look at my mother, focusing on her earrings, but she won't meet my gaze. I breathe deeply and prepare myself for her answer. Whatever she says, I probably won't be shocked:

"I'm sure it is. It's a question of trust, that's all. Something like that would never happen to one of my daughters."

Without meaning to, I realize that I am staring at Francisca. I try to shift my gaze over to Bea.

"Don't spit at the sky, as they say, love. It might just come back down on you."

I stare at the spinach. I haven't touched it. All of a sudden, I want to get out of here, say "I lost my appetite," and go lock myself in my room. In fact, I'm really not hungry at all. I just want out of here.

"It's true, Aunt Loreto," Francisca interrupts. "It is just a matter of trust."

Now I'm looking straight at Francisca. I can hardly believe that she, of all people, just said that.

"Sure," I hear myself saying. "It's a matter of trust. Trust, that's all."

I ride my bike to the edge of the hill and then look down. Santiago stretches out beneath me: my neighborhood, full of trees and white buildings, with balconies and bay windows, the Club de Golf Los Leones, with its sand traps, the gashlike Avenida Kennedy, the Jumbo supermarket, the Calán Hill and its silver-

plated observatory, the far hills that end so abruptly at the end
of town where Cox lives.

"Should we keep going?"

"Sure," I answer. If it were up to me, I wouldn't say anything,
after what just happened.

We're at the top of Parque San Cristóbal, Antonia and I. Well,
the truth is, *we're* not there at all; she is, I'm not. Or maybe it's
the other way around: I'm up here and she's the one who's off
somewhere else. It doesn't really matter. To me, at least, it
doesn't.

Now we're going downhill, not racing, just going downhill. A
self-confidence contest isn't exactly what I need right now. She's
on her red Torrot and I'm on my trusty Benotto. She's wearing a
pair of long socks, with little designs on them, over her jeans to
protect them from the bicycle grease. I'm wearing shorts. I put
them on thinking it would be hot, but despite the sun, I'm kind
of cold. Freezing, actually. And sad. On this part of the hill, the
wind seems the way it is in the south: humid, cold, and fragrant.
Like in a forest. I like being here, because the trees hide the view,
and if you really concentrate, you can imagine you're in Caburga
or Ensenada or on the banks of the Lago Esmeralda. But you need
to be focused, something I'm not right now.

Or maybe I'm too focused. But on something else. On her. She
has totally taken over my mind, which in its own right isn't such
a good thing. Sometimes I despise her. I really do. I wish it
weren't like this, but what can you do? She may drive me insane.

About an hour ago—forty minutes, maybe?—we got up here,
all sweaty and tired, but with a little bit of energy still, and then
we went all the way up to the Tupahue pool. It was a good ride
up. We left her house, crossed the river, and went up by way of
La Pirámide. When we got to the pool, we parked our bikes on
the grass. Then we stretched out for a little while on the side of
the hill, where that Spanish fortress is, next to the Enoteca,
which is some kind of wine-tasting place. We were lying there,
on the wet grass, like all the grass in Chile, to sun ourselves. As

I absorbed the sun's rays (pathetically weak compared to those in Ipanema), Antonia messed around with the back wheel of her bike. I reclined backward a bunch of times and with a "bedroom" look on my face, tried striking sort of a "sexy guy" pose. I pulled up my shirt just enough so she could see me playing with the little hairs on my stomach, but I don't think she noticed anything. Whatever. I tried.

Seduction may have been an overly ambitious goal, though. All I really wanted was a minimum of attention, maybe a little something romantic, or whatever it is they call "intimacy." All she did was play with her bicycle wheel. I'd almost go so far as to say that she had a bored look on her face. Plain and simple. Pure boredom. Maybe it wasn't that. Maybe she forgot that I was sitting next to her and that even my neon-pink shorts weren't enough to get her attention. She's thinking about McClure, I said to myself. Or someone. Herself, maybe. Since the moment we left her house, she's barely said a thing. What she did say was all those things I wished she hadn't said, like "Should we turn here or at the next corner?" "It's hot. And it's going to be worse this summer." "Matias? Remind me on the way back to oil the gears, will you?"

That's what I was thinking about, there, on the hillside. And other stuff too. Why does being next to her (which is exactly where I always want to be) make me feel even more alone? Nine times out of ten, our conversations just don't crystallize. To be with somebody and not be able to talk is much worse, much more uncomfortable, than being alone. Whenever I'm with her, I only think about myself, about my flaws, and everything about me that's no good, and then I get all depressed. It's such an overwhelming feeling that it leaves me drained, alone. Then I've got no chance at all with her. Isolated, and at the bottom. It's not a good feeling, clearly; it makes me feel about two inches tall. I think she gets bored with me easily, or something's missing for her, and I'm not enough. That's why her mind wanders when we're together, and then she distances herself from me. I wish it were the other way around: that *she* was the one who felt ignored and left alone; that *she* was the one who felt that she wasn't quite what *I* wanted; that *she* was a little jealous. But that's not the way it is. That is the prerogative (a word I got from Luisa) of people who aren't romantically involved. A person in love—or infatuated—doesn't have the right to question too much, can't have too much of an opinion. All they can do is cross their fingers and hope for the best. Hope, for example, that someone like Antonia will notice them, give them that bare minimum of attention necessary to keep their obsession active and alive. Like accepting an invitation to go on a bike ride and then not talking.

"I wouldn't mind smoking a joint right about now," I think I said at some point.

It was a spontaneous urge. One of those moments when your thoughts flow right from your brain to your mouth, without passing through that internal filter that screens and sort of protects you. We sat there in the sun, in silence for a while, me drowning in really negative, depressing thoughts, but also with a very real desire to take advantage of this moment. To touch her forearm, to bite her, even just a little earlobe or something. Maybe that's why I wanted a joint, a good joint, *maconha do Amazonas* like we had in Brazil, not *cáñamo* or seeds from San Felipe. A good joint that would relax me, that would change my frequency, my mood, and allow me to move in on her without thinking about it so much.

"I'd smoke a good joint, like those from Rio. Wouldn't that be excellent?"

Her bicycle wheel stopped spinning. A bit farther down, a man was cleaning the deep end of an empty swimming pool. Antonia looked at me with those eyes of hers, and before I could say anything else, I knew I'd just said the wrong thing. But I didn't know quite how wrong.

"You are the most egocentric person I have ever known."

Just like that. Fast and straightforward.

I closed my eyes for a second, to try and absorb her blow in the most private way possible, but I quickly realized that it was pointless, because it wasn't anger I was trying to hide, it was pain, which is a different thing entirely.

"So, you're not saying that in the positive sense, are you?"

"Who knows, Matías? There are some people whose main goal in life is to be like you."

"I can't stand this kind of argument."

"Who's arguing? It's only an opinion."

"Right."

All of a sudden, it was weird. Everything clouded over so quickly that I thought it was going to rain. What was happening here? I didn't need this kind of thing. It didn't go with my personality, or, better yet, I simply rejected the idea of getting involved in this kind of relationship. I'd had it with these attacks. If I was egocentric, fine. I'd be proud of it. I'd rather be egocentric, self-sufficient, equidistant—it's all the same anyway. As long as I'm not like her. Nobody understands me anyway, that was the rapid conclusion I came to. So who was she to go around saying things that don't concern her?

"It's more than that, Matías. Egocentric *and* out of touch is more like it. All you ever think about is yourself. Yourself and your drugs and being the center of attention and being number one and never being one second out of step with what's 'in.' Your vanity makes me sick. You think I don't know what you're all about. Or you think that I'm going to pay attention to you and smoke marijuana just to please you, so that later you can go back to your friends and tell them how you 'corrupted' me. Well, you've got it wrong, jerk. You are light-years away from ever doing that to me."

"It was just a thought. I don't even have any pot on me. And I wasn't even thinking about involving you anyway."

"Typical, you see. You even admit it."

"Listen, Antonia, no offense, but this kind of arguing shit

bores me. If we were going out, maybe. If we were married, like my parents, it might even be necessary to avoid worse problems. But this, right now, to me, is what I call out of touch. I mean, we're not even in love . . ."

"Who knows . . ."

That killed me, I couldn't believe what I just heard.

"I doubt that," I said to her.

"Okay, then. That's your problem if you can't see it. Your conceitedness knows no bounds, Matías."

"Hey, ease up, will you? There's no need to get cruel."

"You see? You didn't even make the effort to listen or ask me how I feel."

"Yeah, well, you've already made yourself pretty clear."

Silence.

She didn't dare move her bicycle wheel again. She was still beautiful, but I hated her. Maybe it was true: she liked me. Or loved me. Her own egocentrism cut me down to the size of a seahorse. She wouldn't admit it anyway. If there was one difference between the two of us, it was that I didn't hurt her—not intentionally, at least.

At Oscar Sobarzo's funeral, my mother lent me her car and I went to pick up Antonia at her house. She was wearing a long blue coat, a man's coat. She spoke very little (which was unusual for her); the only thing she said was how horrible it would be to know that you were going to be buried so close to a neighborhood as awful as Recoleta. "Just the thought of it makes me shudder," she said.

On our way back from the funeral, driving beneath icy, black clouds, I felt close enough to her to express a rather personal opinion:

"To think that he died before making something out of his life."

"As if you have yourself," she said. I remember it perfectly, she said it as she stared ahead, looking at Lerner's car that was right in front of us.

Lost in my thoughts, I dropped her off at home. I didn't talk to her for a few weeks after that. After she had gotten out of the car, I drove to the corner of her street, stopped, and I started to cry. Just a little, but I did start to cry. From there, I went to Julián Longhi's house, where we had all said we were going to meet afterward. I saw Nacho there, and when he noticed my eyes, he asked if something was wrong.

"No, nothing. I'm just sad. Not so much for Oscar, but for myself. As they were lowering his coffin, I thought that if I had been the one who died, nobody probably would've even come. Stupid, I know, but I couldn't help it." Nacho smiled with an air of understanding: he said that he had been thinking the exact same thing. We all hung around in the living room, around the fireplace, and Julián's mother brought us cakes and coffee, and someone put on a Simon and Garfunkel tape. I remember this really relaxed feeling about that afternoon, sad but peaceful. We were all together. It was then that I realized Antonia wasn't with us, but nobody noticed, nobody missed her. Her presence or absence just wasn't an issue. So I got up, careful not to draw any attention to myself, and went into the bathroom to cry what was still left inside of me. Because if there's anything I can't stand, it's seeing a guy cry in public.

"Maybe you're right, Antonia. What do I know? One should never assume things about other people."

"See what I mean, stupid?"

"Don't call me stupid."

I turned my bike around. She looked at me and just barely broke into a faint smile.

"Can we leave?" I asked her. "I'm cold."

"Let's go."

That was an hour ago. Or forty minutes.

* * *

But it's all the same anyway. It's really all the same to me. It's not even that important. Seriously.

You know this feeling well. It's been with you for as long as you can remember, right? It's always there, it never completely disappears, always looking for the precise moment to reappear and remind you that, yes, it's true, you're not the same as everyone else. You're worse. Even though, if someone were to take a survey or something, the results would probably yield something different. You'd consider yourself somewhere around average. Flora Montenegro and Luisa are always telling you this, but maybe that's exactly the problem. You're worse, but nobody knows it: that's what your secret is. It's a question of inequality, of not being able to adapt, of being different, that's all. Who knows? It's all the same anyway: it still hurts, it's still uncomfortable, it still alienates everyone, it still makes you alienate everyone.

All right, Matías, turn the tape over, distract yourself, this isn't any good for you. This doesn't get you anywhere. Move a little slower, okay? There's something about you, some kind of rage, a hate, a void, something that scares you, whatever it is, and it doesn't allow you to enter the game, to let yourself go, close your eyes and enjoy anything. It's your egocentrism, remember that. If it wasn't for that, you'd be with her right now. But that's impossible. Not because of her, because of you. Maybe she's right. You're the one who's intolerant, the one who can't open up, the one who hides, or whatever—all those clichés that seem to swirl around you, poking at you, pointing out how different you are from everyone else: you're a loner, on a dead-end street, an egotist . . .

Enough. This is getting you nowhere. Nowhere new, at least. You've fallen into this rut before, and every time, you've emerged worse than when you went in, right? So enough, change the

mood, the frequency, distance yourself from your mind, think
about something else . . .

It's nighttime, Saturday night fever here has already exploded;
there's a ton of traffic out on Las Condes, cars full of couples who
kiss while waiting at the traffic lights. I'm alone, but that's not
the reason I think I should die. I feel like the people in the other
cars are watching me, thinking, poor guy, all alone on a Saturday night. That's just what they see. In reality, they don't see;
they don't really see a thing.

El Canta Gallo is on the right, and on the other side is the
bridge, which crosses over the Mapocho and into Mampato,
with its ponies. From there, the road goes on toward La Dehesa.
Nobody's there, so I keep going straight, toward El Arrayán,
going and going, but there's nothing there.

Today has been endless, useless.

I imagine, for a second, that I'm in Rio, around Leblon, São
Corrado, going toward Tijuca with the hot breeze blowing
sweetly, and . . . enough. Enough. Back to earth.

I turn on the radio: some horrible propaganda in the form of
a jingle for the "SI." No, no more, please. I would vote "NO," I
know it: but I'm four months too young . . . I'll be legal in four
months. Almost. It's all the same, it makes no difference. I change
the radio station. Now it's Neil Diamond, singing "September
Morn." I leave it, though, because I don't have the energy to
change it, and I just keep driving. But the road ends, and there
are only rocks and trees and curves and a dam. I can hear the
river rushing underneath the rocks, which somehow seems
scary. Better go back. Back down, down into the bowels of this
walled city which I don't even recognize sometimes.

The clock on the billboard says 21:44. Extremely early. Or
way too late. There's nothing to do, and I've been out for too long
already. I don't know what's happening, what my plans are,

what bullshit the "chosen ones" have planned for tonight. Parties, get-togethers, gatherings, hot-dog parties, orgies, poker games. Boring. B-oooorrr-ing.

I pass by my building, but I know nobody's inside. The windows are all dark, except the one by the hallway. For some reason, I feel this tremendous urge to stop the car, go up, fill the bathtub, and submerge myself in hot water until I disappear. But that's not my home, it's just a house, a structure, and so I continue, speeding now, down Avenida Nueva Costanera, thinking about another house that's around here somewhere, about a party I once went to, who even knows why. Then, for some reason, I think of this guy I once knew—he wore a lumberjack's jacket and I always remember how he hated Saturdays. He would only wake up if there was a party to go to. His mother slept all day long. Anyway, our math teacher once said to him, "You'll never get anywhere in life," which he agreed with. In fact, he said that's why he had been expelled and transferred to Liceo 11. That's why he had long hair.

I change the radio station, Concierto, which, when it comes down to it, is the only radio station worth listening to. Thelma Louise sings with all her heart, "Don't Leave Me This Way." The neighborhood reminds me a bit of Antonia, and all of a sudden, the song lyrics don't seem all that stupid. I can almost relate to it, especially the part that goes, "I can't survive, I can't stay alive without your love, don't leave me this way . . ."

Red light. The song's a piece of shit; it doesn't even come close to what I feel. I'm now convinced that the kids at Liceo 11 are having a much better time than I am.

Now I'm in front of the Las Condes movie theater, although I'm not so sure how I got here and I haven't even been speeding, I don't think. Right now, the origami is probably somewhere in the pipes underneath Cox's house. The movie has already started. I look at the huge billboard that's supposed to be a reproduction of the movie poster, but it just looks pathetic. *Ice Cas-*

tles, Antonia's movie, the one about the blind ice-skater. I laugh. But not for too long.

I leave, moving into fourth gear, and feel like I'm flying over Santiago as I cross over the new bridge that raises Apoquindo over Vespucio and the new Metro station. But Apoquindo and Providencia aren't very entertaining tonight, not at this hour anyway. I pass by Juancho's, but the neon lights don't fool me: it's still way too early to go in, it must be empty, except for the Great Alejandro Paz of Chile and his drinks and his American obsessions, and maybe Miriam is already in there, but nobody else would be.

On Concierto, someone clearly addicted to metal plays "Highway to Hell," the very same song they played that night in that redhead's apartment in Leblon. The song injects me with a surge of energy, so I feel like driving a little more. I turn onto Avenida Isidora Goyenechea, but have to stop. Clearly, there's some action going on here. Something big, which is pretty rare. The streets are swollen with people. There are police, and a long lineup of Mercedeses and BMWs and Volvos parked on the street. There's a definite "Oscar night" atmosphere, real Hollywood. Just beyond all the trees, I make out the neon sign of Regine's, and that's when I understand what all this is about. I understand it only too well.

I hear a horn blow and turn around. A gray Saab flicks on its headlights. Through my rearview mirror, I notice that the guy driving is in the navy. Maybe it's Nacho's father. No, it's not him. He passes me, and I look at the older lady hidden in the gray fur stole, almost invisible against the gray passenger seat. I decide to park and check out the scene. Why not? I don't have anything else to do anyway, and it could provide a brief bit of entertainment. Anyway, my parents are here. They wouldn't miss this for anything.

About a block away from Regine's, there's a run-down grocery store that doesn't quite fit in with the new jet-set, swanky image of this area. I go in, and there's an old man with hairs sticking out of his ears, watching *Noche de Gigantes* on an old black-and-white television. The TV is on a shelf, between the jars of Milo and Nestlé condensed milk. The atmosphere in here is dangerously close to what it's like in Ñuñoa, and I can't help but remember that Nazi/anti-Semitic feeling I got from Guatón Troncoso and his grotesque family. The old man doesn't even notice me come in. If I had a gun, I would definitely shoot him, right in the forehead, so that his brains and blood would end up splattered on the counter, all over the imported chewing gum and chocolate. On the television, Don Francisco announces something about the Telethon, and drones on and on, talking to that Italian guy, Umberto Tozzi, who barely even speaks Spanish.

I look in the meat section, and even though everything looks kind of stale, I suddenly get a craving for beef jerky. Umberto Tozzi starts singing "Claridad," the Spanish-language hit of the moment. The old man finally decides to look up. I look at him as if he were the household help and order my beef jerky and then two bottles of Capel pisco sour.

I cross the street and sit down on a bench, hidden by the little square that faces the avenue. I wash each chunk of jerky down with a generous gulp of lukewarm pisco. One after the other, the cars line up in an ellipse, like the cadets in a military parade do in Parque O'Higgins.

My mother has been talking about this party at Regine's all week long. That's why she got all dressed up in the red dress she kept going on about, the one my father said was too expensive. He then shut up when he thought, why shouldn't he just buy a new dinner jacket for the occasion. Today is the famous, long-awaited Fiesta del Rojo y Negro. *Cosas* magazine has been talking about it for God knows how many issues.

My parents became members of Regine's before it actually came to Chile, according to my calculations. They bought into it, just like they had to with the Country Club. Like the way you buy stocks or something. As a result, they get into this party for free. They're sort of the hosts, in a way. I'm sure there are plenty more members who'd like to be in their privileged place. The real Regine, the one in all the photos, made a special trip over here from Paris to come to the party. I know this thanks to my mother. She was explaining it all to Aunt Loreto. "Everyone will be there," she said. In order to get in, you have to be a member or invited by one, and, of course, the dress code is strictly red and black.

I look at my Top-Siders and faded blue Lee's. I fucked up; there's no way they'll let me in. So instead, I just watch the scene: an overly polished Camaro pulls up and out steps a flashy Arab. He helps his date out of the car, she looks familiar, I think. Then I realize it's that girl on television, the one who was on Raúl Matas's show, Amanda Lear. I read something about her in "Temas del Hombre" of yesterday's edition of *La Tercera*. She's tall, really gigantic, and some say she's actually a man. Or that she was once, but that now she's a woman. She says no, it's not true, she's always been a woman, and that she'd be more than happy to take her clothes off to prove it to the world, if someone was willing to pay her $10,000 to do it. Regine only paid her $5,000 (I read it somewhere), so it's not too likely she'll take it all off tonight at the party. My father will be disappointed, for sure.

I've about finished my beef jerky, but still have a bottle of pisco. The cars keep pulling up, but I don't see my parents anywhere. They must be inside, either eavesdropping or maybe even hanging out with George Maharis or someone like that. Everyone knows he's a has-been, he's like an embalmed corpse that's somehow still alive. He's touring Chile now, because of his reruns, still living off his famous part in that TV show—*Route 66*—which I used to watch when I was a little kid and my mother would say to me, "Time for bed, Matías, you have school tomorrow."

Or maybe my mother, who's bumped into all her friends by

now, is with Aunt Loreto, criticizing Paloma San Basilio's red dress. She flew in all the way from Caracas just to go to the party, and her flight back is tomorrow, when me and everyone else will be in church, witnessing my little nephew Felipe's baptism. Poor little Felipe, he's got no idea what he's in for. It's not his fault he's got parents like my sister Pilar and that Iriarte. My father, sort of drunk off the Chivas, proud of his red bow tie and his spanking-new dinner jacket, is probably leaning against the bar, smoking his Gitanes, slyly checking out that Costa Rican model Giannina Facio, who's no doubt tan and gorgeous and bra-less, and caught in a useless but entertaining conversation with George Hamilton. He's also deeply tanned, clearly. Thanks to the tanning bed he subjected himself to after filming *Love at First Bite,* that stupid-piece-of-shit movie about vampires and models from New York City, who go to clubs and dance to disco music all the time. I saw that movie in the Cine California—yes, there, right in the heart of Ñuñoa—with Lerner and Nacho, just before that party where I threw myself on Valeria Reyes, who was so wasted she was convinced that the "Romans Punch" was spiked with Spanish fly, the idiot.

The second bottle is now empty, and I throw it with all my might against a wooden pole. It shatters into a thousand pieces but even that doesn't provide any satisfaction. My parents are assholes. Then immediately I feel guilty for even thinking it. But it's the truth, and I should always tell the truth. After all, that's what they taught me, right? It's weird, I realize, kind of drunk now from the pisco. If my family is so sick, then what does that make me?

Later, my question is: should I stay or should I go? What I need to confirm is, am I bored or is this another one of those blood-curdling passions that (in my present state) I am unable to rec-ognize and act upon? I mean, if this is happiness, why am I thinking about something else, why do I feel so useless? Why so many questions, why does everything seem so annoying and so irrevocable? Why, for example, are there so many ice cubes in my Frambuesa Andina, or so little cheese on my cheeseburger?

The bowling alley is not the best place to eat dinner, I guess. It's also, incidentally, not the best place for bowling either. That's not really why I'm in such a rotten mood. I just don't know what I'm doing here. I've been here far too many times since it opened, and I have no idea what inspires me to keep coming back. It's not bowling, that's for sure. I've never bowled a game in my life. I don't even know anyone who bowls. This is just some kind of stupid meeting place for everyone. It's like people come here, meet, then take off to go somewhere else. Or if you come here without a plan, like I did tonight, and want to meet up with someone, like I also did tonight, then the thing to do is sit down, have a drink, and act really distracted and aimless, and then stare at the crowd of idiots bowling, so it doesn't seem so pathetically obvious that you've got nothing better to do.

Nobody called me up tonight, I think to myself. Well, that's not one hundred percent true, because Nacho called me when I was at San Cristóbal, to ask if I had any plans and to see if I wanted to go out with him. Francisca took the message but it seemed so lame, to depend on him, that I didn't even make the effort to call him back. Anyway, he'll show up here in a matter of minutes. Or if he doesn't, he'll definitely be at Juancho's at some point tonight. I'll run into him somewhere. It's like my destiny, I think.

Cox had also called me. I spoke to him. He had a proposition for me. I just wanted to bad-mouth Antonia, but he wasn't the right audience, so I just listened to him for a couple of minutes, semidistracted. His plan was to get his parents' Blazer. Could I get the keys to my parents' place in Reñaca? We all could head out there for the day was his plan. You know, some time on the beach, a little hanging out before going back to classes on Monday.

"I have to talk to my father first," I said.

"Talk and then call me back."

"Well . . . tomorrow is my nephew Felipe's baptism. And I'm, like, the godfather, that's a little problem. And afterward there's going to be this huge luncheon thing."

"Great. I'm sure they won't care."

"I don't know. I mean, we wouldn't be able to leave that early. The baptism starts at around eleven."

"We'll get there in an hour and twenty minutes if I drive. The Blazer has one of those radar things, so we can avoid the police, no problem. We'll be lying on El Cementerio by lunchtime."

"Who else is coming?"

"The usual suspects: you, me, Lerner. We could ask Nacho too. What do you think?"

"Yeah, I suppose we could do it."

"So?"

"Let me talk to them here, and then I'll call you."

"Step on it."

My father was in his room, trying to knot his red tie which stood out like freshly spurted blood against his perfectly elegant, impeccable tuxedo shirt. He was totally decked out, like some Argentinian, and I could swear he was humming "How Deep Is Your Love."

"Father," I said to him. "I'm going to use the apartment at Reñaca, okay?"

Sometimes I call him "Father." A little revenge for his calling me "stud."

"You're bringing a girl out there?"

"No, just some friends."

"There won't be any girls?"

"No, and we're not staying overnight. It's for tomorrow. It's just for the day, tomorrow. Just for a little change of pace. We'll have lunch, go there for the day. I'll even water the plants for you."

"And the baptism?"

"I'll be there."

"And the reception?"

"Don't hassle me, come on. I'll go to the baptism and then leave. What did you think anyway? That I was going to spend the whole day in church confessing my sins or something? The luncheon is the last thing I want to go to tomorrow. Come on, if you were me, what would you want to do—go to Reñaca and hang around with your friends or have lunch with your grandparents and your whole fucking family?"

"Fine. You've convinced me, *stud.*"

"Thank you, *Father.*"

I moved closer to him and noticed that scent of his, that mixture of Barbasol shaving cream that he gets imported by the caseload and too much Azzaro.

"Leave it . . . I'll tie it for you."

As I knotted his tie for him, he remained quiet and obedient, like a kid getting dressed for school. In my case, of course, it was my mother who knotted my tie when I was that age.

"I hope Giannina Facio shows up at this party. You know, Julio Iglesias fucked her," he says to me.

I moved behind him a step and looked at him:

"You know, one day if all your businesses totally failed, you could become a model."

"Seriously?"

"Seriously."

On lane number five at the bowling alley, a forty-something couple (obviously not married) kiss each time one of them heaves the ball and hits a pin.

I move over to the Formica table and look at the retouched photographs of freshly grilled, juicy hamburgers, with slices of deep red, succulent tomato and just-out-of-the-garden lettuce leaves. They're faker than those bowlers out there tonight. A pimply guy behind the counter asks me what I want. I stare at him for a second or two, at his face with all its festering boils, and I suddenly feel this uncontrollable urge to pay him—whatever he wants—just so I can pop a couple of those zits. I think one of the greatest pleasures in life is squeezing and squeezing a pimple that's right in its prime and then seeing how the oil builds up to a tiny point and then spurts out onto the bathroom mirror, leaving everything bloody and pussy and disgusting.

"I'll have a cup of coffee. And a Coke."

"That's it?"

"Yeah."

I pay (probably double what I'd pay for the same shit anywhere else), get my drinks, and then return to my table, which is now occupied by two little jerks, who are probably virgins. I sit behind them, my eyes fixed on the parking lot, my ears tuned in to the conversation of these two Jerry Lewis clones—Jerry Lewis when he was on his way down.

I sip a little of the Coke and then pour the coffee into the plastic cup, which melts a tiny bit from the heat. My little experiment yields a thick, strong foam that reminds me of the time Luisa Velásquez, Antonia, and I made this same concoction at Luisa's house when we were studying for the final exam in social sciences. We drank a coffee-Coke combo to stay awake, even though all we did that night was sit around and bitch about the jerks in our class.

Being alone in a public place can be very uncomfortable. This feeling of paranoia begins to take me over, and I feel like everyone's staring at me. Being alone, even if it's only for a few seconds, is frowned upon in Chile; in fact, it's almost seen as a political crime, not like in Rio, by the ocean, at all the outdoor cafés. Or even in Juancho's, which is always dark, and where at least you have the Great Alejandro Paz of Chile to talk to. The biggest thing you notice here, though, in the bowling alley at Apoquindo, is the fluorescent lights. I hate them. They make everything shine, and look artificially attractive when the truth is, there's nothing attractive about the place at all, nothing happens here. Like with these idiots, for example, sitting behind me:

"And what about your sister?"

"She's down south, with the President, collecting votes."

"My father is going to do the same thing. He votes at Liceo 7."

"The 'SI' should do pretty well there. At least ninety percent."

"Do you think we're going to win?"

"No doubt about it."

"Yeah, I think so too."

"Well, I mean, obviously, the people are happy. Nobody's even read the constitution anyway. They're not voting because of that. They're voting because of the General."

"Are they going to have a concert, you know, in support of the 'SI'? Your sister mentioned something about it."

"I don't think there's time. But there's a ton of musicians on our side that have publicly announced their support. It's in today's paper, in fact. Scottie Scott, Pollo Fuentes, Willy Bascuñán, Francisco Flores del Campo, and who knows how many others."

"Well, they certainly are famous. And they're good singers too."

I can hardly believe what I'm listening to. All I feel is this overwhelming urge to spit on them, or shake them just to see if anything falls out of these robots. They're the reason this country is the way it is. And they're the majority, people who think Pollo Fuentes is "the best," and who call Pinochet "General," and they're not even twenty years old yet. I can't even comprehend what they'll be like at forty. The more I think about it, the more it seems that my own opinion is totally irrelevant. Sometimes I think that I must be from somewhere else, anywhere but here. That all this—it's one big movie and I'm barely an extra. It's like something just doesn't fit right, I don't know what. But there's something worse. Each time I go through this, I care less and less about figuring it out.

I look at the cup: there's only a tiny bit of dried foam stuck to the base. I look up, because I want to see exactly what these jerks look like. I see Gonzalo McClure instead, with his new Yamil haircut and his carefully unbuttoned Lacoste shirt. Next to him are various familiar faces, and Antonia, of course.

"Hey, Matías. What's going on?"

"I'm waiting for Nacho Detmers. He's late," I lie. "What about you?"

"We're just killing time. We're meeting up with Pelusa Echegoyen and some friends of hers. She's got some plan. A party, we hear, around Manquehue and Bilbao."

McClure is speaking in the plural, I notice. "We" this and "we" that. And he's not referring to the group; he's talking about the two of them.

"Can we sit down here?"

"Sure."

McClure signals, and his group comes over. Antonia is wearing the FU's jeans she bought when I was with her, and an olive-green wool blazer that makes her look older and, of course, gorgeous. Julián Longhi is there too, wearing an ultra-chic purple windbreaker. Next to Antonia, like good little chaperones, are Flavia Montessori and Rosita Barros with her new little Prince Charming haircut.

"Hi," Antonia says with a touch of guilt. Or maybe disdain. She's holding McClure's hand, I notice.

They don't all sit down next to me, because there isn't enough room. The girls move over, closer to the political jerks at the next table.

"I spoke to Nacho today," Longhi says. "He didn't say anything about coming here tonight. I think he's still recovering from last night's orgy. He told me he snorted endless amounts of coke. And that you ingested some grams yourself. Shit, you could've at least offered some to your friends."

"Sometimes Detmers talks a little too much. There really wasn't that much. It's all gone now anyway."

"Shit."

"Yeah, shit," I say without too much conviction.

"Do you want to go to the party with us, Matías?"

"No, but thanks anyway, Gonzalo. I've got other stuff going on."

McClure just doesn't get it. It's academic in any event.

Okay, so he's not as bad as I think sometimes, and maybe he does have a ton of good records, but nobody can be such an idiot and not realize it. That's the saddest part of it all. Or maybe he doesn't want to realize it, that could be it. Who really cares? It's all the same to me anyway. Regardless of what the "truth" is, I am, officially speaking, his enemy. He can't just invite me to a party like that. There is such a thing called dignity. Self-respect. Revenge. Hate. Just like love, these feelings have to be cultivated and nurtured, because if not, one runs the risk of forgetting the reason for the hate in the first place. But all McClure ever wants is peace. And harmony. I bet he's lousy in bed. He probably doesn't even sweat.

"Excuse me," I say. "I'm getting a beer. Does anyone want anything?"

"How about some french fries, Matías? Your treat," that asshole Longhi says.

"I'm not treating you to anything. I'll get them for you, that's all."

"What the fuck is the matter with you?"

"Nothing. Nothing at all."

Once again, I go over to the orange counter. Out of the speakers I hear some Ray Coniff type music, and it's pretty scary. The guy with the pimples is sticking some fried empanadas into a grease-stained envelope with tiny bowling pins on it.

"A beer, please."

Antonia doesn't waste any time: she comes right over. I knew she would. That she wouldn't let this little opportunity pass. She rests her hands on the table in such a way that I can tell she's angry. Very angry.

"Matías, don't take this in the wrong way, but I think it would be a better idea if we didn't run into each other like this so much. Seeing each other in school is already more than enough for me as it is, and it's annoying too. I'm not going to Juancho's tonight, and actually, it would never occur to me to go there. So why don't you just stop coming to the bowling alley? You know that this is *my* hangout. I always come here. Gonzalo loves it."

"Your hangout? How was I supposed to know? Although I can see how this place would be attractive to your boyfriend."

"He's not my boyfriend."

"But he will be. Eventually. Mark my words."

The pimply guy behind the counter brings me my beer. Antonia orders empanadas.

"I don't mean to butt into your life, Antonia, but I still can't understand what it is you see in that idiot."

"He's supposed to be your friend."

"Yeah, he is, but I'm not going to deny that he's stupid just because of that. And I don't know what makes me think it, but he just doesn't even get what's going on. Look at the way he's watching us. He doesn't even realize we're talking about him."

"Oh, and you, you're the smartest of us all, right? You barely scraped by on your exams, but you still walk around judging everyone else's intellect."

"That's a lie and you know it. If that were the case, I never would've gotten involved with you in the first place."

"Go to hell."

"I live there."

"I'm hurting, Paz, bad."

"I've seen you worse."

"No, it's not just the drink."

"You want another?"

"But you have one too."

"All right, but just don't say anything to El Toro, because if he sees me drinking, he'll fire me."

"What time is it?"

"Five-thirty."

"Half an hour before the curfew, Paz. I have to go to sleep. I've got a baptism to go to in the morning."

Juancho's is kind of empty and El Chalo is playing an entire

Cars album. Still, though, there are enough people here for El Toro to keep it open. He's got the permission from the military. That's why he stays open from curfew to curfew—in other words, all night. Those who stick around past the curfew start getting bored, and it gets kind of claustrophobic. So they drink and drink and drink. Like me. And spend and spend and spend.

"Another vodka-tonic for you and a Cuba Libre with Puerto Rican white rum for me."

"A *Chile* Libre," I kid.

"Not yet . . ."

"Invent the recipe. It has to have pisco, right? Then you patent it, put it in a safe, and when that old bastard is finally out of power, or dies in twenty or thirty years, you can debut your new drink at a huge party at La Moneda or someplace like it."

"You're so calculating, Matías. You're kidding, aren't you?"

"Well, yes, I guess . . . that's what I've been devoting myself to lately. Kidding everyone."

"I know the feeling."

"Paz, you have to help me. I'm your favorite customer, right? Get me some coke. From El Toro. Or Chalo."

"I can give you a pill. Free. They say it's for people on diets. It gives you energy, gets rid of sleepiness. And hunger too, obviously."

"Give me one."

The pill isn't a pill, it's actually a capsule. Half green, half white. It's homemade, you can tell.

"I thought this kind was yellow and blue."

"Those are different."

I swallow it, washing it down with the drink, which is more tonic than vodka.

"If I had my own house, Paz, like you do, I'd go home and crash, and nobody would be able to get me out. I'd lock myself in there. Calm, though, relaxed and everything. I'd only see the people I wanted to see, and not get involved with anyone who pissed me off. I'd pray. Or burn incense. I don't know, maybe I'd even become a vegetarian or something. Or a mystic, maybe, yeah."

"That's how bad off you are?"

"Bad, no. Alone, yes. You understand? I feel . . . I feel bored. Alone. Like as if nothing's happening, at all. Nothing is happening to me. Everything's just depressing. It's all annoying shit."

"Isolated?"

"Something like that."

"I just read this article in *Rolling Stone,* a guy unknown in Chile, they don't play him on the radio here. I was really struck by how alienated he felt. Do you know what alienation means?"

"What do you think? Of course I do, it's like Pink Floyd in *The Wall.* That's what that album is all about, right?"

"Yes, kind of. The guy has everything he could ask for, and countless girls hanging on him, but he's fed up, you know? Fame just brings problems. Nobody understands his lyrics. They're all about alienation and isolation, and that sort of thing. So, anyway, this guy, this rock star, starts talking about solitude, and he said something that really hit me. He said that when he's alone, he never feels isolated. He only feels isolated when he's surrounded by people. It's crazy, isn't it?"

"Crazy but true. Get me one of this guy's records, will you? I've got to listen to it. This guy seems to know what he's talking about. I know, I feel alone when I'm with people."

"It's like Salinger, Matías."

"Who?"

"The author of the book I lent you. You should read it. It's all about being fed up with living. About not being able to adapt."

"It's not hard to read?"

"You are going to love it, I promise you."

The vodka-tonic has come to its end. It's still not anywhere near sunrise, even though there are no windows here to see outside. I smell my hands: they smell like sex. A mixture of hot sex, pot, Orange Crush, and sweat.

I leave the bar, glance at Chalo, and settle into a leather sofa that's hidden behind a pillar. Two very boring-looking guys dance their little numbers to the strains of a black man singing something incomprehensible.

I close my eyes but can't fall asleep.

I came to Juancho's after the bowling alley. It was already full and the Great Alejandro Paz of Chile had a message for me from Nacho. He had already been by and wanted me to come to this guy Rusty's house, who I don't know. I rapidly started downing vodka-tonics. By the third one, I was gone, ready for anything, almost in a good mood, forgetting about that whole thing with Antonia. I stopped talking to Paz about Jimmy Carter's alcoholic brother and his affair with Margaux Hemingway, and just sat there, anonymously watching the people out on the dance floor. And there was Miriam. Or "Vasheta." I saw her right away and immediately tried to hide. No luck. She stopped dancing with the guy she was with, and came over.

We then danced for about ten songs. Enough for my shirt to soak through with sweat. Then we left Juancho's. It was so cold that I didn't want to talk. We went to her house, in two cars. I almost crashed into her, because I was following so closely. I even ran a red light right in the middle of Providencia, that's how intent I was on not losing her.

Her house was half hidden among some oak trees, I think, on one of those streets that join Avenida Ricardo Lyon. It was an old house, and enormous, like one for an embassy or a computer institute.

"What time are your parents coming home?"

"They're in Tel Aviv. I'm here all alone."

"What are they doing in Tel Aviv?"

"Grandparents. Relatives. The usual annual pilgrimage."

"I'd love to go to Israel."

"It's a big drag. You're not missing anything."

We went to the bar, which was in a sort of party room that had these awful geometric paintings hanging on the wall. I decided to stick with the vodka. Luckily, they had Stolichnaya, and a strange kosher cherry wine that I almost tried. There wasn't any tonic, but there were bottles and bottles of Orange Crush, so we invented a drink. Miriam turned on the cassette player and stuck in Donna Summer's *Greatest Hits*. I also think—I can't be sure, and I don't know why—she turned on the heat (central heating), full blast. I think.

I danced for only a little while, because the drink took its effect fast. I had this strange sensation that everything was wrong, but she didn't seem to feel the same way. Miriam, in her coffee-colored leather pants, was perfectly happy doing a little dance routine and singing the complete lyrics of "Bad Girls," prostrating herself on the center table and then reaching out to touch the hanging lamps. This girl is crazy, I thought, before crashing onto a huge velvet sofa and falling asleep.

"Hey, what are you doing?" I said to her. Before opening my eyes, I felt that familiar sticky, humid feeling and that light twitter that comes from oral contact.

Then I opened my eyes. Donna Summer was on full blast—"Love to Love You Baby"—and the lights were dimmer; there was just one little lamp, fashioned out of a bottle of Peruvian pisco, those black ceramic bottles that look like those statues on Easter Island. It was disgustingly hot. My pants were down around my ankles, underwear and all, and Miriam was sucking me off. I somehow remained asleep. Through all that.

"Are you awake?" she coyly giggled.

She was seriously drunk. And naked. I touched her neck and it was all sweaty. I thought of saying something to her, but I didn't know what exactly to say.

"Take it all off," she ordered me.

I looked at her, but I couldn't make out her body, only her back, which seemed eternal and white against the velvet sofa.

"This heat is unbearable," I said.

"I know."

I got up, took off my Top-Siders and the rest of my clothes without noticing if she was looking or not, and I went over to the bar in search of the Stolichnaya, feeling the saliva she had coated me with sliding down my thighs. The bottle was open so I took a swig straight from it and looked closely at the face of the Indian on the bottle of Peruvian pisco. A clock on the wall chimed one-thirty.

"We haven't fucked, have we?"

"Not yet, Matías."

"Good. I was only dreaming. I'm kind of wasted."

"Me too."

"Yeah, no shit."

I sat down on one of the stools at the bar, facing her. She stayed on the sofa, now with her back to me, touching herself.

"Come here," she coaxed.

"Here I come."

So I went. It wasn't any big deal—what did I have to lose? Kissing her was kind of gross, so I went straight for her neck, which was still wet with perspiration and smelled vaguely of some perfume I couldn't identify. That was when I decided to go down.

"Turn over."

We repositioned ourselves. She really cracked me up: her big slobbery slurps were absurd. Then suddenly she crossed her legs over my neck, and I couldn't breathe, my nose was all slick and slippery, and there was all this hair in my mouth, which I somehow managed to swallow.

"This isn't working," I said to her.

"Maybe not for you. For me it is."

"I gather."

"Let's go to one of the bedrooms."

We went into her *parents'* bedroom. She disappeared and I threw myself down on the huge bed, right in front of a picture window with a chestnut tree just outside, which was underlit by a yellow outdoor light. There was a phone by the bed, and I had the urge to call someone, but couldn't think of a single person. It was dark, except for the yellow light that reflected off the leaves of the tree. When she came back she handed me a thin, long joint and a lighter that read "John Player Special." She was short and none too thin, I noticed. She had a little roll of flesh right around her navel, and it bothered her when I bit it.

"You're tasty."

"Don't bullshit me."

She jumped up and turned on the television set and put in a video, but the tracking was all screwed up and the sound was terrible. It was about an American football team, hanging out in the showers. The guys were all sneaking looks at the cheerleaders in the locker rooms next to them, until one of the blondes turned around. At the end, they ended up screwing in the showers, amid all the steam. The main actress massaged a black guy with a special oil for his muscles, which gave him a polished sheen . . . With one hand, I was smoking the joint very slowly, and with the other, I was trying to get as close as I could to touching her fallopian tubes. I started getting a little turned on, so I put out the joint, breathed in the last of the burned pot, and we got down to business.

I decided to kiss her because without kisses I have a tough time getting it up. But I was still drunk. Or somewhere else, at least. On the TV screen, the greased-up black guy entered the blonde, who had cherry-red nipples, on top of a wooden bench. Miriam started licking my back as I watched the television. It was good. Really good.

"I'll give you a massage."

"Okay."

"Like the one she just gave the black guy?"

"Yes."

"Wait. I'm going to go find some Hawaiian Tropic. It smells like coconuts."

"Like my coconuts?" I grabbed myself.

"Tropical coconuts, idiot."

I was really turned on now, floating on air, thanks to the joint, the vodka, the yellow light from the chestnut tree.

"It's run out," she said, walking back into the room. "But I've got this."

It was a tube of Ben-Gay.

"My father's addicted to the stuff," she said. "He's always asking me to spread a little on his back."

She opened the tube and an intense eucalyptus aroma overtook everything. She squeezed a huge amount onto her hands and started massaging my back. The smell was incredibly strong. Like toothpaste. Or menthol gum. Or Hall's lozenges. The cream was cold, like a bathroom floor, but as she kneaded it into my pores, it got warmer and warmer and filled me up with its heat. Amazing.

"Give me some of that stuff. I want to put some on you too."

After a little while, the bedcover was slick with the grease and the two of us literally shone with the liquid menthol. It smelled like a hospital and she was on top of me, totally into it, as I massaged her humongous breasts with that magical poultice that woke us up and worked both of us into the frenzy that we now found ourselves in.

"You are fucking wild, you know that? Do you like this?"

She closed her eyes, lifted her body up a bit, and then let herself fall down, lightly but firmly.

"Goal," I said as she fell limp.

"Offside," she whimpered.

I closed my eyes, but no matter how hard I tried, I couldn't imagine Antonia in that position.

"Don't go."

"I'm bored."

She stood up next to the bed. I grabbed her thigh, squeezed it, and kissed her menthol-scented navel. She sat down, opened the little tube, put a small amount on her fingers, and then touched me.

"You're all sticky."

"You are. It's more you than me."

"Don't be vulgar."

Then she took me in her hands and started jerking me off, covering me with that icy cream. It felt good as her hand moved confidently and skillfully. That is, until the chemical reaction set in, or exploded is more like it. I came, practically crying, and let loose a scream so loud that I'm sure woke up her neighbors. I thought I was dying. The surge of the heat from the menthol felt like hot coals on my balls; it was a heat that I had never felt before. Intense and alive, electric. It came over me all of a sudden. It was like having lemon squirted in your eyes. Horrible.

That's what happens when you experiment," said Paz. "You deserve it."

It's six in the morning, and El Toro has just opened the door that leads toward El Bosque. A tiny bit of daylight peeks in. I'm flopped down on the leather sofa, in the middle of Juancho's.

"Does it still hurt?"

"Not anymore. I took a shower, so I'm fine now. But I can still smell it. And I feel ever so slightly, abnormally hot."

"And what did she say?"

"Nothing. She didn't even say thank you."

Nobody's left here. Chalo puts on the last song—"Upside Down" by Diana Ross—and moves over to the bar to make himself a vodka and orange juice. Paz also goes over and opens the cash register. El Toro turns on the overhead lights and all of a sudden the place seems dreadful, tiny and depressing. I get up, and, without knowing why, go onto the dance floor. I can see my image reflected in the glass of Chalo's music cubicle. I don't particularly like what I see. I move away and start dancing. First slowly, calmly, reserved, but then I realize it doesn't matter and start moving faster.

"Matías. The night's over," El Toro says to me.

"You're right," I say. "It's over."

SUNDAY
SEPTEMBER 7, 1980

My dream stretches out more or less like this: I dream that I'm
dreaming, dreaming a dream about a guy who's sleepy, who
clutches his pillow, who doesn't want to wake up precisely because he's sleepy and he's sure he's dreaming a dream that's more
real than anything he's ever experienced before. His manager has
come into the hotel room. He knows this because of the smell of
the cigar. The manager tells him to wake up, get up, he has a
press conference to attend, he tells him. The guy is a rock musician and has long hair, and he looks suspiciously like me. He
dreams in English, he dreams that he's sleepy, he dreams that
he's somewhere else, he dreams that he isn't actually so alone,
that this is just a scene in the dream, and that he just might be
okay. This manager talks too much, so much that he can't help
but open his eyes. The desert sun enters through the window and
hits him, just like a stone breaking the *vitreaux* of a church. The
rock musician then manages to get himself out of the king-size
bed and looks at himself in the mirror. He doesn't like what he
sees. Beneath a lamp, he notices, next to a neon-pink wallet, on
a wooden dresser that looks like marble, a bottle of Stolichnaya,
a half-empty plastic cup, and a mirror with some wiggly lines
of cocaine, that crisscross like the frayed ends of electric guitar
strings. The window is huge, it takes up the entire wall. From
up above where he is watching, the city down below looks

squalid, roasting itself under the hot sun. The musician then considers the possibility of committing suicide, of throwing himself into the void and falling out the window, right down onto the *moai* tree that serves as a welcoming sign to the Tropicana Hotel, the one from the postcard, the same one that my parents stayed in once.

That's as far as the dream goes: then everything stops. Everything. Nothing advances. It goes on and on and on. The image of the musician, the image of me, myself in the window, looking out at the city of Las Vegas, that urban sprawl out there, useless, endless under the sun. Thinking about the possibility of throwing myself into the void, falling on top of the fake *moai* tree, and exploding. Nothing more. That's the image. The image that stretches itself out, repeating itself over and over and over. It never advances. It's as if I pressed Pause on my tape deck forever.

"Matías, wake up. Breakfast is ready. The baptism, remember?"

It's my mother, but I try to go on dreaming. Dreaming about the dream that never goes anywhere.

"Matías, phone for you. It's Cox."

That's Francisca's voice. I open my eyes, and it's almost as if I were in Vegas, I think. Francisca is wearing pastels. Elegant. I realize I'm still in Santiago.

"You look awful. You shouldn't go to bed so late."

"Yes, I know," I say.

"You never learn."

"Give me the phone."

"We can't move the telephone too far. Bea threw it on the floor and messed it up. Someone's coming to fix it tomorrow."

I get up and follow the phone cord. It's in Bea's pink bedroom. Luckily, the bed is made and Bea is nowhere to be found. I flop down on top of the bedspread and place a Porotín doll with yellow pajamas on my stomach.

"Hey, what's up? I'm wrecked. Barely slept."

"We were looking for you. Where did you end up?"

"I'll tell you about it later."

"Sex?"

"More than you could imagine . . ."

"One of these days, man, you're going to end up with some infection that you won't be able to get rid of."

I put the doll down and hold out the waistband of my sky-blue cotton pajamas to see how I look this morning. I don't see any burned skin or irritation or anything too weird.

"So? Are we going?" Cox asks me.

"I guess. I talked to my father. No problem. You'll have to pick me up, though. In front of the church near the golf course. You know where it is?"

"Yeah. A cousin of mine got married there."

"There, then. At eleven-thirty. The baptism is for ten-thirty."

"That's kind of unusual, isn't it, to get baptized on a Sunday?"

"It's a superstition of my sister's. She has all her kids baptized exactly forty-four days after they're born, and since the priest knows them, he went for it. He'll charge them extra for it too. It should have been at nighttime, you know, because it's forty-four days exactly after the birth, down to the hour."

"You people are strange."

"Tell me about it."

"At eleven-thirty, then."

"Perfect."

When I go back to my room I feel like going back to sleep. I search my shirt pockets and find the other green and white capsule that the Great Alejandro Paz of Chile gave me last night. In the kitchen, I bump into my mother, who's all dressed up, like for a wedding. She's fixing Bea's hair, putting a ribbon or something frilly in her exaggerated curls.

"Hurry up, Matías. You can't get there late. After all, you're the godfather, remember?"

"Yes, I've already got my bodyguards alerted. The shoot-out will take place after the ceremony."

My mother hasn't seen the movie. Or if she has, she doesn't remember it. She never remembers movies that she sees, or books she reads. She's always thinking about something else.

In the kitchen, Carmen is preparing pancakes, like we live in the United States or something. After a trip to Miami, my mother became obsessed with brunch and big breakfasts. My father, for example, puts strawberry jam and orange juice in his champagne. It's a Sunday ritual. God, I hate it.

I open the refrigerator and look for some kind of surprise. I find an open can of Nestlé condensed milk, which I love, and I take a healthy gulp as I swallow Paz's green and white capsule, not without feeling a slight twinge of guilt for what I'm doing: drugging myself at this demented hour, just to gain some strength. To continue onward. But what the fuck.

I leave the empty can on top of the kitchen table. Through the yellow curtain, a mountain of light filters in, reflecting off the shiny can. Way back when, before all of this, before the green and white capsules, before the Ben-Gay and the vodka, before Regine's and Juancho's, my mother used to make desserts with the condensed milk. *Bavarois,* the dessert she made, was her favorite gift to us during Allende's years in office. Red or orange, even green ones; foamy, most concentrated in the bottom part, they were always perfect. In those days, it was easier to get condensed milk than Jell-O. My mother sent me, hanging on to Fresia, our old Indian housekeeper. We'd get in line in the Almac, which was close to the house we used to live in. "Don't fight with the communists," my mother would say. We didn't always get it, of course. One day someone gave us the address of a grocery store that had extra cans. They piled me and Francisca into the car—a navy-blue Fiat 125—and we went to an older neighborhood, maybe around Avenida Matta. My mother bought two cases of condensed milk, at an exorbitant, black market price, but she said it didn't matter, it was worth the effort, that she wasn't going to allow us to eat junk. The communists, she felt, could destroy a lot of things, but they weren't going to rob her of the pleasure of preparing her children some *bavarois* like everyone else.

Through the door to the dining room I see my father, on the sofa, reading the B section of *El Mercurio,* checking the financial reports. Carmen is still cooking. My mother practically doesn't even set foot in the kitchen anymore.

"Do you want eggs or pancakes?"

"Nothing. It all makes me feel sick. Maybe tea. But with lemon."

"You people. You make me prepare these ridiculous pancakes and then nobody eats them. Your father says he's on a diet, and . . ."

"Carmen, it's Sunday. Be quiet. Pray or something. I'm sure you have something to ask for from God."

"What I want, I cannot ask God for."

"You can ask God for whatever you want. It's just that he never answers."

"People like you go to hell."

"No, Carmen, we go to heaven. After hell, if you can survive it, you go to heaven. Nonstop flight."

The empty can of condensed milk doesn't shine anymore. Carmen, who doesn't understand, who doesn't know, simply throws it to the bottom of the garbage. Where it should have been in the first place.

The day is perfect, so beautiful that my idiot sister Pilar can't hold back from commenting that this only proves the existence of God and that Felipe can only expect the best because of that. The truth remains, the day is beautiful, but a person doesn't forget all his opinions and beliefs and convictions just because of that. The rain last night, for example, short but torrential, the same one that transformed Miriam's house and Juancho's into

something rather terrifying, gave way to one of those meteoro-
logical phenomena that they can never predict on television,
simply because they're impossible to predict.

The sky is so blue, robin's-egg blue. Everything outside looks
like something straight out of a bad airline commercial. Maybe
that's why not a single cloud dares to spoil the panorama. The
Andes are like I've never seen them before, totally snowy, with
that snow that looks like just-recently-whipped meringue. It re-
flects and refracts the pale sun that falls straight onto it. The sunshine is so bright that you can't go around without sunglasses.
Seeing the family all together in front of the church in this park,
full of trees with new leaves, everyone in their respective sunglasses, confuses things. More than just the cinematic connota-
tions one could make, and the feeling that all this looks a lot
more like a Mafia funeral than a baptism, I still can't help but
think that we all look good, attractive, enviable, all in pastel colors, against that incredible background. The whole atmosphere
the sunshine creates makes Santiago seem like one of the most
beautiful, luminous cities in the world.

But right now there's no sun, no heat, no glistening snow.
We're inside the church now. Or on one side of it. In the part they
call the sacristy. In my hands lies Felipe, totally bald, like a little skinhead, wrapped up in a light blue blanket that matches
my shirt. I'm surprised how little he weighs and how good I feel
having him so close to me. The boy is warm and awake, and you
can tell he's alert. Now and then he looks at me, and I can sense
that he agrees with everything that I think; I can even imagine
making him see me as his father, only because his is such a jerk
and all his sisters are such morons. It seems to me that, beyond
this ceremony, which is a drag and has no real importance, this
commitment does have a meaning. I—who practically don't
know him and am holding him in my arms for the first time in
my life—have signed a contract that says, no matter what, that
I am responsible for him and will do everything possible to protect and save him. Before it's too late, maybe.

These thoughts make me sort of nervous. I feel my arms start to tremble, and Felipe, who is so absolutely small and fragile, trembles a bit too, but nobody notices because all this is internal, I realize. Despite what Antonia says, I think I'm not so terribly egocentric. If people just gave me the opportunity, if I gave myself the opportunity, I might even be capable of doing something good. So I look at what I'm holding in my arms, and Felipe's toothless smile inspires me so much, it makes me feel so secure and useful, so indispensable and proper. Everything stops for an instant, everything relaxes at that moment, and seems perfect.

Then the priest speaks. All that rhetoric about our brothers, and he talks about Jesus Christ as if he were just talking about some guy named Sebastián or Diego or something. As I look at him, his face surprises me. It's not the regular priest. It's another one, and this one seems almost embarrassingly attractive, and at peace. He has the same features as Felipe, almost, a childlike face, but somehow different, like that of a savior. He can't be more than twenty-five years old, I figure, and the simple idea that it could be me there in his spot, in those solemn robes, with those carefully scrubbed hands, is both fascinating and terrifying. He has short brown hair, with a little wave to it. He looks like a model, like someone who's played polo in Europe, who's studied at one of those ivy-covered schools in New England. While he's talking and stretching out this ritual that gives him his power, he's enjoying the fact that he's the center of attention. There's a certain perversity in that thing of showing yourself off but never offering anything. I think that he's drawn to the idea of keeping his distance, remaining unattainable. Nobody draws him to that, except Christ, of course, who's a myth to him, an idea that came into his head one night at a party. Christ is a perfect refuge, a best friend who doesn't bother him or pressure him. He accepted him. I guess.

My sisters are absorbed in the ceremony, and the girl next to me (a cousin of my brother-in-law), who is now Felipe's godmother, doesn't even hold him; she just looks at the priest, at this pale and serene clergyman who has a little hole in his earlobe that's now closed up. This man—nobody knows what he's doing here—underneath this imposing cross?

I am brought out of this strangely theological and annoying state by the sound of Felipe crying, wriggling around in my arms. The baptism has occurred and I missed it. Pilar takes Felipe away from me, and I feel, at least for an instant, lost. And then this priest decides to look straight at me, and, I don't know why, crosses himself and then blesses me.

It's still early, there's plenty of time before Cox and company are supposed to arrive. Now we're in the central nave, which isn't even very pretty. There isn't even a Christ figure here, just a Virgin and some bad paintings, the work of some art student, probably the relative of someone who built the church.

The eleven o'clock mass is the best. People pray and recite the prayers that they have memorized, then they cross themselves and sing. I think of the sun and the bright day outside, but I can't abandon the gathering here just like that. The priest from a moment ago, the one who used to have an earring, is now gone. I miss him, because his colleague now in front of us doesn't seem too convinced by all this. He looks more like the headmaster of a strict boys' school, earning a few extra pesos. But in his sermon, he gained some momentum when he insinuated about how our country is experiencing a crucial moment, and that God only wants the best for everyone, and that hopefully next week we won't be lamenting the loss of the established order.

I'm sitting in the back of the church, near the door, with my Adidas bag resting on that plank of wood I never know what to call, where people kneel when their guilt weighs too heavy on them. From this spot, the view is a privileged one. What I see interests me.

There they are, everyone all crammed in here, totally absorbed and listening to the real priest and not "that priest-in-training they gave us," which is what my mother said, my mother, who, depending on the situation, makes herself more or less religious. Or Catholic is more like it. The strange part of all this is to see my mother praying, saying things like, "Hear us, Father, we humbly ask . . ." because—and this is the tricky part—she's not Catholic, apostolic, or Roman, not even Latin. If you want to get technical about it, my mother is Jewish. Just like me. Maternal law. That's how it works. I'm the only Jewish Vicuña. If I were to have a baby with Antonia, for example, he wouldn't be. With Miriam, yes, but that would be repulsive and I'd rather not even think about it. Felipe is Jewish, like me, because Pilar is. And Pilar is because my mother is the daughter of my grandmother Regina, who can be a righteous Catholic when she wants, but is actually more Jewish than kosher hot dogs. My grandfather, Tata Iván, is Jewish too, for sure. None of this is a coincidence. It's a question of blood, of genes. Of blood, obviously, but not of traditions, faith, or last names. It's a matter of convenience in a lot of ways too. It's sort of our "state secret" that, clearly, the whole world doesn't exactly know about. Pilar doesn't know; Guillermo Iriarte, my brother-in-law, hates Jews and he'd have a heart attack if he ever found out. I know about Iriarte's anti-Semitism because he told me himself. He even said it to Tata, who, unflinching, answered that it was a complicated subject to talk about, because people tend to manipulate the issue of racism, but that "between you and me," it's true that you can't trust Jews, because they never really take roots in the countries they emigrate to.

Tata is right up there in front now, as close as possible to the priest, saying his prayers and conforming to this particular audience, which, at this hour, is very jet-set. My grandmother, holding her favorite rosary, sits next to him. Maybe that's why they called my mother Rosario, because it seemed symbolic or something. That's why she isn't called Edith or Ruth, I think. My grandparents make me sick, but they're the only ones I have. The ones on the Vicuña side died when I was little, in an airplane accident in the south of Argentina.

The Jaeger grandparents, though, don't have the slightest idea that I look down on them and think that they're pathetic. They don't even know that I know. I'm sure they think that I'm just not interested or that I'm permanently stuck in puberty. The most complicated thing about the whole issue is that I don't totally hate the two of them. The truth is, my grandmother Regina is a bitch, and her little fetish with the rosaries makes my stomach turn. Her perfume, not only is it heavy, but sickly sweet, which kind of sums her all up. What bothers me the most about her is that she's ugly, objectively speaking. She's short, has huge tits, way too many freckles, and her hair is this light burgundy which is just frightening. She doesn't talk, she shouts. When she takes the floor, everyone has to shut up. Despite all the years that have gone by, and all the talking she's done, she still can't kill her hideous central European accent.

Tata, on the other hand, has the gift of being kind, amiable, and the perfect gentleman, who adores women and delights bankers. He has the look of an exiled prince and his eyes are so blue that sometimes it really makes me mad that his genes weren't enough to make my eyes cobalt blue, like his, rather than the green I inherited. His accent is almost flawless, and his demeanor is impressive. My father looks like a midget next to him. Another thing that's attractive about him is his elegance. I have always admired how distinguished he is and what good taste he has, and I'm proud that he's so much more worldly than that decadent ambassador uncle of mine on the Vicuña side of the family. Later, after I found out all this stuff about being Jewish and everything, his appearance became an obsession for me. He then seemed—by far—the most vile and base creature of any I'd ever known. Also the most difficult, because, whatever you want to say about Tata Iván, the one undeniable thing is that he's a first-class actor. He even kind of looks like Rex Harrison in *My Fair Lady,* which my mother (who idolizes and even fears him) has always said. He decided to be someone else, and he did it. He rose so rapidly in Chilean society that it never even occurred to anybody to call him arrogant or uppity, just aristocratic. That's why now he prays, he takes communion, wishes peace and goodwill to his fellowman, donates money. Afterward, he will greet everyone as they leave church, especially the ladies, who still adore him despite his age (which he doesn't look) and his business (which he doesn't really run anymore).

The story that the world knows, more or less, is that he was born in Budapest, Hungary, at the turn of the century. His father was a doctor and his mother an English actress who fell in love with this medical student who used to send her roses after her performances. From that union, my grandfather was born, and, like his father, he too studied medicine. But instead of becoming a general surgeon, he decided to follow the advice of his mentor and enter the arena of plastic surgery—or reconstructive surgery—which had become so fashionable after World War I.

My grandmother was born in Pécs. Her parents were extremely wealthy art dealers. Her sister had some problem with her leg and was ordered to undergo treatment at the waters in the spas and Turkish baths that are all over Budapest, in addition to having my grandfather operate on her. That's how they met, and after a three-month courtship, they got married: he was almost twenty years older than her. After spending some time in Europe, they left, and moved to Central America, where my grandfather was put in charge of a hospital in Managua. My grandmother, though, got sick from the climate. Instead of returning to Hungary, which was in the middle of a war, they went to Peru, with Nicaraguan citizenship in their dossier and a new last name: Jaeger, which was the second surname of my grandmother's father. Their original last name was an absolutely unpronounceable mess of consonants. Peru didn't go over so well; they only stayed for a few months. They hated the terrible climate and "dreadful people" of Lima, so that's when they decided to emigrate to Chile. My mother and Aunt Loreto were born here, shortly after they arrived. As time passed, they eventually became just as Chilean and elegant as the Castilian-Basque descendants, and Tata Iván even became a member of the Club de la Unión.

That's the official version, and there are people who believe it. Iván Jaeger Mills and Regina Soth Szabó de Jaeger, an impeccable and delightful Hungarian couple, descendants of the well-educated bourgeoisie and even linked to the power structure that controlled the operations of what our teachers made us memorize in school as the Austro-Hungarian Empire.

The truth is something else. I learned it by accident.

By accident, and that's exactly why this topic has made me live with my antenna up. I can smell anti-Semitism a mile away, and in Chile, that means my nose gets a lot of use. I know a lot more about Judaism than I should. It's always interested me. It's my genes, my blood, I don't know, but anything Jewish always grabs my attention.

I'm obsessed with it. Maybe that's why I didn't resist that crazy Miriam: more than her seductiveness, it struck me that she accepted me (if only for a little while), since that implied a total violation of anti-*goyim* laws, which are very severe. I know this because I've seen it in my own life. Judith, my aunt Loreto's daughter, introduced me once to a girl from *"la colonia"* named Mijal, who was unbelievably pretty and had God only knows how much money. So fine, we started to go out together, and there was even a little something more, but her parents refused to let me into their incredible apartment. Mijal, in the end, stopped calling me. Later I found out she was seeing a guy named Robi Silverman. Now that I know what really happened, I can laugh about it, but the truth is, it makes me furious, because in this case I was the one who suffered.

Ever since I've known this, that's the way my life feels: neither here nor there, not inside, not out. I'm the only one who knows my secret, a secret that would mortify most people, but fills me with pride. And power, I think.

This revelation—that's what it is—came to me by chance. And

thanks to my inquisitive, nosy nature. We were eating lunch at my grandparents'. It was a holiday, the 21st of May.

After the lunch, I found myself flipping through a *National Geographic* in Tata Iván's study when the telephone rang. I answered it, and it was a voice in English, calling from London. She wanted to speak to a Dr. Istvan Rothman. I told her she had the wrong number, and then the voice said, "Istvan Jaeger." I asked her who was speaking. She said Janice Ashmore, and that she was a lawyer calling on behalf of Mrs. Raquel Rothman. I went back into the living room and told Tata that he had a long-distance call, from England, from a lawyer. He stopped what he was doing and disappeared into his study. My grandmother got really nervous.

"They asked for a Dr. Rothman," I said.

My mother and grandmother went pale, right then, but everyone else just drank their coffee and went on enjoying their chocolates from La Varsovienne.

"It was a friend of your grandfather's. A dear friend. I hope it's not bad news," said my grandmother with a Chilean accent that sounded more forced than usual.

That same afternoon, I called my aunt Loreto Cohn. She was really depressed: she hates holidays, because she never has anything to do. I told her that I met a girl and wanted to know if she was Jewish.

"Why?" she asked me.

"Because I'm a *goy* and all that."

"What's her last name?"

"Rothman. Raquel Rothman."

"More kosher than Golda Meir. But I don't recognize the name. Who's daughter is she?"

"She's from Argentina. From the Barrio 11. Buenos Aires," I said.

"Are you thinking about marrying her?"

"No, Auntie, just curiosity, that's all. Thanks."

"Anytime."

Later that afternoon, I waited for my mother. When she got home, I made her a drink and sat down in front of her.

"Why are you looking at me like that?"

"I was trying to see if you looked Hungarian or not."

"I look Chilean, Matías."

I didn't know what to say to her. After ruminating over the subject for so long, I'd gotten confused about what I was going to say. So I decided to just go for it, one hundred percent:

"Why didn't you ever tell me we were Jewish?"

My mother turned green. She swallowed her drink in one shot.

"What?"

"Just what I said. Why didn't anyone ever tell me we were Jewish? That call from England, it was strange. They asked for Istvan Rothman. So I asked Tata, and he confessed the truth to me. But I want to hear your version."

"He told you?"

"Yes," I lied.

"I can't believe it. Well, anyway, now you know. What more do you want to hear?"

"Details."

"My father didn't give you any?"

"That was a lie. I didn't ask him anything. It was just a hunch. I needed to know. Now I do."

I didn't even see the slap coming. And it hurt.

"Don't you ever lie to me again," she said, enraged.

"Same to you, Señora Rothman."

Right away, she disappeared into the living room, and I didn't see her for the rest of the day. The next morning she came into my room. I could tell she hadn't slept.

"Listen," she said. "Now that you know, I hope you know how to keep the secret. I don't have anything against Jews, or my parents. But it was a question of life or death, and they've gone ahead with their lives. Religion, if you didn't know this already, is up to the individual. It's a question of beliefs. The last name is irrelevant. Just because they used to go to a synagogue doesn't mean they deserve to die. I beg you not to go around advertising all this, because even today, you can never be sure. Your father and your sisters don't know. Not even my sister Loreto knows. More than that, my own mother doesn't know that I know. That's all I can tell you. I hope I don't have to ever discuss this topic again with you for as long as I live."

"Who is Raquel Rothman?"

"My father's sister. She died a few years ago. She left an inheritance and now someone has found my father."

"And what does Tata say?"

"I don't know. And I wouldn't ever dare ask," she said, and left my room.

That afternoon I went to the Israeli Embassy to ask for some leaflets.

They wouldn't let me in.

"My triceps hurt," Lerner says, as if it were the most natural thing in the world.

I look at him with disgust, trying to distinguish what it is that hurts.

"I swear. They're like rocks. It feels like I twisted them."

"That's impossible, you can't twist your triceps. Or biceps either, since we're in that area."

"I don't know. I'm going to talk to my trainer. I signed up at a gym, I don't know if I mentioned it to you. I told you, right?"

"No, but I don't really want to know about it anyway."

"Your blood's getting a little thick, Matías. Lighten up, man."

Lerner is next to me in Cox's father's Blazer. We're near Viña, destination, Reñaca. Cox is driving. Out the window, I can see the usual local scenery of slopes and hills and poplar trees and cows and little country houses. We're entering the Casablanca Valley. The day is still perfect. We finished eating our empanadas, which we bought a little way back, from a stand on the side of the road, that had a coal stove and a Pinochet sticker proclaiming "SI." The Blazer reeks of onion and cumin.

I breathe in.

Incredibly, there's no music. The radio is all staticky, and the cassette player is broken. Nacho is sitting up front, and every so often he looks in the rearview mirror, to check the highway and see that his surfboard hasn't come off the roof. Nobody talks, all we can hear is the light hum of the motor. It makes me want to say something, to break the silence, but I can't think of anything to say. Lerner is still prodding his muscles, sore from so much training.

"The guy from the gym says that it's a secondary effect, perfectly natural. From lack of use. I considered myself an athlete. Even with all that, there are still muscles I never use. I had to ask my mother to spread some Ben-Gay on me, to relieve the pain."

"Be careful, Ben-Gay can be bad for your health," I say, but nobody laughs.

Patán, who's here, uninvited by me, is next to Lerner on the other side. He's rolling a joint on top of my Adidas bag, which has my clothing from the baptism inside.

"I'm bored with pot," I say.

"Antidrug campaign?"

"No, but joints are getting to be a drag. It's like an excuse. People smoke them to think they're getting stoned, but really, nothing happens. At least not with Chilean pot. Anyway, it's usually three or four people sharing a joint—it's more the ritual than the drug."

"And that's fine," says Lerner. "Because it's not about drugging yourself so much that you get to be an addict."

"Is that what they taught you in the gym?"

"It's got nothing to do with that. But it's better to feel good and healthy rather than going around drunk or stoned, like some kind of zombie. By far. Smoking and drinking and doing drugs and jerking off are no good. No good at all."

"Jerking off isn't so bad," Cox says without taking his eyes off the road or his foot off the accelerator. "It's the same as fucking. Just alone."

"Well, maybe," says Lerner. "But any excess is bad for you. I mean, I'm not against them, I'm not that cynical, but eating wheat bran and yogurt, doing exercises and riding your bike, is good for you. It calms you down."

"Bike riding is fucking overrated," I say, thinking about Antonia.

Patán lights the joint that began this argument with a "you're not invited to share" look on his face.

"Nothing personal, Matías, but hey . . . if you don't like this, fine. Better to share what little I have with those of us who can appreciate it."

Lerner looks at him and laughs:

"You're not going to share with me either?"

"No."

"That's what I thought."

At the side of the road, there's a silo painted to look like a bottle of aspirin. My head hurts a little. I open the window and a warm gust of wind blows in. It smells like alfalfa or oats. Or something like that.

"This joint isn't bad at all, Matías," says Nacho, who hasn't said too much today, something that both pleases and bothers me. "Try it."

"Hey, what I said before wasn't a moral declaration," I explain, sort of annoyed. "I don't have anything personal against joints. I love the smell, I don't know. It just annoys me that people believe the myth that they're getting all drugged up, breaking the law. Bullshit. To really escape, you have to take stronger shit. And need to have something to escape from."

"You're fucking crazy, Vicuña."

"I think he's right," says Nacho in my defense. And he, for better or for worse, knows what he's talking about, I think.

"Exactly, man. If you're going to do it, you should really do it right. And let go. Light drugs are a waste of time. They're not worth it. Too hippie."

"So what you're saying is that pot and peyote stink . . ."

"What I'm saying is that I hate those people with their stoned-out San Pedro highs. They make me sick. That whole thing of going out to the desert and hitching out to San Pedro de Atacama, trying peyote and getting stoned with the Americans, or the Dutch wearing those Peruvian or Bolivian sweaters, that's bullshit. It's all so bogus."

"Obviously you've never done it, Vicuña."

"And I don't ever intend to."

I should change the topic. Talk about the priest and mysticism, or my Jewish heritage, or something, anything else but this. It's like here I go again, in the line of fire. Like always. I don't even know how I got onto this stupid subject in the first place. And worse, I'm not even so convinced with my own argument. But everyone's suddenly quiet, waiting for my response. I decide to go with the crowd.

I breathe in.

Onion, cumin, marijuana, oats, alfalfa, Azzaro.

"Hallucinogens," I start in again, "are not real drugs. They're 'mediators.' They do something else. They're not really a help at all. They're more like an experiment. A game. Jim Morrison and Janis Joplin didn't die from mushrooms or peyote or whatever. It's a much deeper, more psychedelic matter. A trip, you know. You can travel but you always have to come back. That's what I think."

"Have you done acid?" Cox asks me. "That does make you hallucinate, they say."

"Yeah, it's true. I licked one of those blotters in Rio, with Cassia, at an orgy at the apartment house of some redhead television actress there."

That last part is a lie, but it sounded good.

This makes Nacho totally envious, I know. Now he feels out

of it. That everyone else except him got to go to the party, and he wasn't invited.

"It's so much easier to get acid now in Chile," he says. "Rusty brought a ton of blotters back from the U.S."

"El Preguntón, that guy on TV, he does acid," Lerner says.

"What?" I ask.

"Seriously. My brother told me. He knows the actor who plays him."

"El Preguntón? The faggy guy on Channel Seven who wears that mailbox costume?"

"Yeah, that's the one. The one with Tía Patricia."

"Your brother has some very strange friends," I tell him.

"Wait, wasn't it Florcita Motuda, the singer, who was inside the mailbox on that show?" Cox asks.

"He was, but not anymore. Now it's another guy. Very few people know him," says Patán, who clearly watches far too many children's TV shows.

"Look, believe me or don't believe me. I don't care," says Lerner, really annoyed. "But it's true. You can tell. When Tía Patricia sticks a letter in the mailbox, and the mailbox starts dancing, that's exactly the moment when he is just getting off. Some of the letters don't have normal stamps on them but instead they've got tabs of acid. One of the producers, a friend of my sister's, gets them for him. The guy licks them right on camera, it's just that nobody can see."

"I don't believe you," I say.

"Don't believe me, then. What do I care? But it's true."

"In this country, everyone's corrupt," I say.

"Yeah, look who's talking."

I don't say anything. I look at the scenery, the evergreens that announce we're getting closer to Viña and Valparaíso. Nacho bites his fingernails. Cox listens, expecting something.

"No, I'm not."

"You're not what?"

Nobody understands anything, I think to myself.

"I don't . . . Look, just forget it," I say to them.

"Thank God," says Patán. "That'd be the last thing, for Vicuña to become a priest on us or something."

I think about that for the next few kilometers. But I discard the idea, not without a bit of nostalgia, though, for something I'll never experience.

"Hey, Patán. Do you have a joint? I changed my mind," I say.

Everybody laughs.

I, however, don't find it funny at all.

But I laugh anyway.

I'm lying on the beach, faceup, eyes closed. I'm sticky from the springtime sun, but for some reason, I don't have the strength to go into the water. It wouldn't be a bad idea, I'd float for a while and then just eventually disappear. I'm still bored—bored, fed up. Even thinking is a monumental effort. This is already more than typical, and it has me worried. Thoughts that attack me, conversations that bury me, opinions I listen to, paragraphs I read, it's all the same to me, it's all too much for me. Like, so much anguish, it really bothers me. I'm bored, fed up. I can't even dare to think. Thinking gives me ideas. I have too many of those already.

I close my eyes and absorb the rays of sunlight. I smell like coconut oil, like Hawaiian Tropic Dark Tanning, no SPF, extra-fast-tanning formula. I like it, my face all shiny from the oil, feeling its greasiness, sticky and slippery, invading my pores, encouraging the sun to pass through, calmly, and leave its copper-colored mark on me. That's the only thing that really interests me right now. My natural state of being. I should have been a surfer, I conclude. Like Nacho, who's in the water right now, in a black wet suit with the little flashes of fluorescent green, on a pink surfboard, riding these tremendous waves that are breaking way too fast. Near him, a couple of the others reappear every so often: Papelucho, who's wearing a black and orange wet suit that reminds me of Oscar's Fiat 147, and that Rusty guy, an American with long blond hair, nobody really knows who he is, but they all love and idolize him. I am on the sand, on a towel that says "Sheraton Brickell Point" that I found in my father's apartment, listening to these three jerks who are entertaining everyone else lying here, in this little corner of Reñaca, on a beach that we all call El Cementerio. It's because all we do is lie here like we're dead.

The sun isn't as high anymore but the glare is still intense. I've clearly gotten bronze, or at least managed to maintain my tropical tan. Not everyone is sunning themselves. The only ones in the water are the California trio who, since surfing is kind of new here, are causing quite a commotion. The boardwalk and the terrace are both full of people. Packed. The usual off-season Sunday with good weather.

Cox is drinking Johnnie Walker Black Label with Coke. Lerner and Patán are too. They offer me some, but I've already drunk enough. It annoys me, the way they drink from the gigantic thermos they brought down from the apartment. The thermos is my mother's, the Johnnie Walker is my father's, and the Coke we all bought in a store on the Long Beach. We're like Argentinians, I think to myself. Or worse. I hate the Mendocinos and Sanjuaninos who invade Reñaca and Viña and the whole coast every summer. I hate the way they all drink and go around with their teapots—or *pavas,* as they call them—and prepare their stupid drink right on the beach, all to the horror of the Chileans, who would rather die before having a picnic in public. In that sense, my father is right. They should charge people to come into Reñaca. It should be the exclusively private property of all the people in the neighborhood who have invested so much money here already in their beach apartment houses. The truth is, it's not very pleasant to take the cable car down to the beach and get out, only to find thousands of Argentinians who think they own the place, all shouting in those hideous accents of theirs. On top of it, they take all the girls away, that's what annoys me the most. For Argentinian men, the girls drop like flies. They don't even have to beg them.

Like the three that right now are sleeping by my side: Maite Daniels, wearing a black bathing suit, minus her Bo Derek braids; Pía Balmaceda, trying to tan over her freckles, and Flavia Montessori, who doesn't have bad legs but who is totally, absolutely flat as a board. Maite is by far the best, I think. She drank way too much at lunch. She came by the apartment with her friends just when we were about to eat sea urchins and razor clams on the huge table my mother had installed on the balcony. Cox had told them we were coming. The three of them are staying at Balmaceda's house, her grandparents' house, really: just above the Playa Negra, in Con-Con.

"Nacho's surfing well, isn't he?" Cox interrupts my thoughts. He's wearing a pair of gym sweatpants and a sleeveless shirt emblazoned with the word "Rio."

"Definitely," I say. Although to tell the truth, Nacho's annoying the shit out of me right now. If it were up to me, I might never say another word to him again. That's how much he bores me. For example, he tries to make himself out to be the outsider, the rebel, or something, when in reality, he's more attached, and more dependent on, what is probably the most conceited and judgmental clique of all right now.

"This Rusty guy is okay," says Patán as he licks a Danky 21.

I don't entirely agree with his opinion. Ever since Papelucho came around without warning, to the apartment—my apartment—with Rusty Ratliff, I declared a mental war against them.

Papelucho is definitely a bad influence. He's going nowhere, but whenever I'm around him, I feel like he looks down on me. I could bet that he hates me and that he gossips about me to Nacho, who is so weak and easily influenced that he even believes the story that Papelucho is really his true friend. And the worst part about it is that he thinks that just being next to him and Rusty, who's all blond and American, he rises in stature.

That it makes his stock go up and increases his possibilities of
transcending me and my world. When I have nothing to do with
it. Now that I think about it, the omens are not good ones.
Nacho's on some independence kick, and I think he wants to
stick it to me somehow. It's like this: one part of his world is his
past—his family and me, and for better or for worse, I'm like a
brother to him—and the other part is these new friends, who are
all wilder and crazier than anything in his past. So naturally he
wants to get rid of me. I remind him of his past.

Nacho is a traitor. He got into the Blazer this morning with this
look on his face like a decapitated lamb, and he didn't say anything. So I started to worry, and I stopped thinking about Antonia, the Jews, Miriam, my future, all so I could concentrate on
him. After we settled into our canvas chairs on the balcony at
the apartment, and looked out over Reñaca and the hills of Valparaíso and the water, with its yachts and warships and—even—
the *Esmeralda,* the boat they never launched, we had a beer. The
music was on full blast as we sat there in the sun, talking, the
two of us, exchanging information, facts, advice, laughing about
whatever bullshit, both of us feeling less alone, kind of bonding.
Almost.

He's awful that way. He's learned a thing or two from me, so
I know what he's feeling and can tell what he's going to do a lot
of the time. He and Antonia wouldn't make such a bad pair, actually. They're cut from the same cloth. They talk one way and
act another. Both of them want a little piece of me. As a result,
the more they want, the less I give.

I open my eyes. Beyond the human wall formed by the paddleball players, the waves are crashing. Farther beyond, the trio
of Americans on their surfboards continue with their little show.
This whole deal with the ocean, the camaraderie, and the
friends, and I don't know what else, loyalty or whatever it is, that
bonds people forever and ever, makes me think of those books

Flora Montenegro made us read for Spanish. She split the class up into twos and made each pair read a different book. She chose both the pairs and the books. I, logically, got put with Nacho, and we had to write a paper—an analysis, really—of *The Cubs,* by Vargas Llosa. *Time of the Hero* is Nacho's favorite book. Everyone knows. Looking at him in the water now, I'm sorry I'm not there with him. Important things happen in the water, I think. Like in "Sunday," Nacho's favorite story. It was about the water and competition. For me, the story "Los Cachorros" was what did it—really ripped me apart. It reminded me of my father, I felt like one of those who annoyed Pichula Cuéllar. When we were writing our paper, I got into a raging fight with Nacho. Somehow he got the idea that I was like the others, and he was like Cuéllar. That's how we did our analysis: what would each one of us do in a situation like that, who would we identify with? The conclusion we came to was that it was perfectly possible to isolate oneself without necessarily suffering a castration. "Castration," wrote Nacho, "is the metaphor; it is the great metaphor." We got a grade of 7.

Now I realize that it's true. That's the metaphor, that (just like the rock star that the Great Alejandro Paz of Chile told me about) a person can feel totally isolated even when surrounded by people. A great statement, I think. It's something Nacho should listen to. He would agree, I think it would make sense to him. So I get up and walk toward the water.

As I go in, my body stiffens from the cold. This is not Ipanema. The water is almost glacial and leaves me anesthetized. I dive into a wave and feel my blood emptying, the water current carrying it away, but then the wave ebbs, I emerge above the surface, breathe, feel the salt on my lips, and let out a shout to restart my heartbeat and move forward. I swim. I swim underwater, riding out the waves, opening my eyes, seeing only the turbulent darkness of the Pacific.

I continue swimming, more secure and warm with each stroke. My feet don't touch the bottom anymore, as I look for Nacho and his fellow surfers, but they're not out here anymore. The beach, the hills, my building, are all so far away. Too far away. And Nacho and his surfboard are back on the beach. The other two as well. They're sitting where I was before.

I decide to go back, a little closer to the shore, to where my feet can touch the sand. I swim a little, trying to avoid the current that could catch me and carry me out to where the bay opens up. My skin is turning blue and the coconut oil isn't penetrating my body any longer. Again, I look back toward the beach and see how Maite and Pía and Flavia Montessori are drying the surfboards with special care, looking up at Rusty as if he were a rock star. I watch how Nacho takes the thermos and how Papelucho dries himself with my towel. I feel absent. I could drown and nobody would even notice, I think. Just the fact that I'm even thinking about it fills me with shame. And hate. And frustration. Nobody's irreplaceable, it occurs to me. I'd rather be outside than in.

I swim backstroke along with the current. But the current isn't there anymore. So I float, drifting, as if I were on some sort of mission, looking at the sky, thinking about how a person can feel alone, even when surrounded by people; and when a person's alone, on the other hand, when you're really alone, it's like you're with a lot of people.

The woman sitting next to me on the bus is asleep, sound asleep. Thank God she doesn't snore. The lights are out and the dense darkness is broken, every so often, by the headlights of other buses, trucks, and cars coming from the opposite direction. After that police checkpoint just before Peñuelas, I fell fast asleep. Since I was cold, I hugged my Adidas bag. But for a long while now, I've been wide awake. Anxious. I woke up from the heat. It's freezing outside. You can tell because the windows are frosted up. We must be around Curacaví, but I'm not sure. With my hand, I signal the steward and tell him, in a low voice, to bring me a Cachantún. I'm dying of thirst. He brings it over, with a straw and everything, but it's lukewarm.

This maybe is a mistake, I think. This thing of leaving the group without saying anything to anybody, just disappearing. I was fucking fed up, I just couldn't stand it anymore and I really thought it would be much more honest and truthful on my part to go with my impulse and take off. But take off—I think—isn't the word. Better, I left. I got out of there, I stopped being there, I wanted to be alone. Better alone than in bad company. When I felt that I didn't want to be around them anymore, I made my way out.

From that moment on, I couldn't think of anything but them. I got to my father's apartment, cleaned up a little, watered the plants, and I felt alone there, too alone. So I locked up and took a bus out to Viña. I walked and walked around the streets there. Free of summer tourists, Viña seemed even more pathetic and provincial that I had ever imagined it.

It was late and I was bored. I didn't have a thing to do. I bought a bottle of pisco sour and I drank from it as I walked down the road, to the bus station, which is in the ugliest, most dangerous part of Viña. Luckily there were seats left. I had to wait ten minutes in the lousy weather. It finally left. It was the last bus of the night out to Santiago. I just barely made it.

It seems that a person always just *barely* makes it, if they make it at all. Sometimes you feel that poisonous dart, headed straight for you, and you don't even flicker. Or the tension mounts and mounts, until the point where it becomes clear that it's beyond your control. The important thing then is to lose with dignity. It's hard.

This has happened, for example, with Nacho. It's unbelievable, but now he doesn't even pay any attention to me; he thinks I'm just dead weight and that I don't have what it takes to join their little aquatic league. Maybe he's right. It's just that I haven't fallen for Papelucho or Rusty Ratcliff. I'm not interested in being associated with them. Rusty, who's got blond, tangly hair, somewhere between café au lait and yellow, dried up and curly, is the man of the moment and thinks he's just the hottest fucking thing. He's an idol. Even the Great Alejandro Paz bows at his feet and talks about how excellent and cool this guy is. He's always going around with about four days' worth of stubble, straight out of— and this is what kills Paz—the San Fernando Valley of Los Angeles. He's from a place called Encino that's supposedly the home of America's "golden children." He's told us all about how he's surfed in Malibu and Zuma. But now he's in Chile and he's milking his *yanqui* power for all it's worth. Everyone believes him. All the girls drool over him. According to Cox, he's already screwed a bunch of them. Papelucho, who at one time was a lot of fun, has become one of his most fervent disciples, his right arm.

Nacho, from what I can tell, is just about ready to join the fold. I know, because while we were eating lunch, Rusty lit joint after joint and talked with that accent he knows so well how to use, and he shook his hair as if he were the only person on earth with a mane like that. I looked over at Nacho, sort of conspiratorially, as if to say: "Where did this asshole come out from, man?" But he averted my gaze, he totally avoided it, and without thinking twice about it, allied himself with the gringo, one hundred percent. At least that's how I saw it.

I've lost my patience; I see that now. Just about everyone on this bus is fast asleep. In a little while, I'll be back in Santiago. In the morning I'll be back in class, in my uniform, with my notebooks. In third year.

When I got out of the water, I was frozen. It was like I was coming out of a snowdrift or something. Clouds were starting to cover up the sun. I had to run awhile down the shore, and eventually got back to the group, threw myself down on the towel, and closed my eyes. Nobody asked me how the water was. They were all involved in some ridiculous, stupid game, like "Yes or No" but it didn't have anything to do with the referendum coming up. Rusty, who had a really nice T-shirt on, one that read "Bob Marley: Survival—African Tour 1978," was in charge of the game. It was Nacho's turn. I remained lying down with my eyes closed, feeling the salt air drying me, listening and trying to understand the idiotic game, which went more or less like this:

"Dead?"

"No."

"Man?"

"Yes."

"American?"

"Yes."

"Artist?"

"Yes."

Nacho seemed a little confused. He thought the guy was a painter or a writer, and, I don't know why, but he asked if the personality in question had a foreign last name. They said yes, and that's where he lost it, because he went off in another vein entirely. From what I know, Nacho isn't exactly an expert on North American poets of Hungarian and Polish descent. So I opened my eyes and thought of joining the game, but since I didn't know what the guy's name was either, I decided just to observe the whole thing. That's where I collided with Maite, who was looking at me in a strange, annoying way. So I put on my Clash T-shirt. Obviously, it caught Rusty's attention.

"Do you like them?"

"Yeah," I said. "Especially the song called 'I'm So Bored with the USA.' "

The asshole didn't even acknowledge my attack. Maite looked over at me and laughed a little.

"Does he dance?" Nacho asked.

"Yes."

"Have I ever seen him dance?"

"Yes."

Maite moved over next to me and lit a cigarette with all the confidence of someone just on the cusp of becoming famous.

"Have I seen him dance in person?"

"I hope so," said Flavia, who's stupider than a can of tuna.

"It's 'yes' or 'no.' You can't use any other word," said an annoyed Rusty, who, like all Americans, takes these games very seriously.

"No, then. You have not seen him dance in person."

"In the movies?"

"Yes," said Cox.

"It's John Travolta," Maite whispered in my ear.

Then she asked me to walk her down to the terrace to get an ice cream.

"They sell pisco-sour-flavored ice cream, I swear."

Sure, I thought: Travolta is a foreign last name. Italian. But I bet Nacho thinks it's a Russian ballet dancer. Someone classical. He should ask if the person also acts or sings.

"Does he sing?" he asked.

I felt calmer.

After that, I left with Maite and we went down the boardwalk, toward the Long Beach. She asked for her cone of pisco sour, and I got a little envelope of french fries, to warm up a little. Then we sat down on a bench, to watch the people walking by. The sun was just beginning to set.

"Okay, so tell me about it. What's going on with Antonia? Is it over, or what? I saw her this weekend. I know on Friday she went to the movies with Gonzalo."

"How do you know she went with him?"

"I spoke with her on the phone, before going to Cox's party."

"How come you didn't tell me?"

"You didn't ask. We didn't even talk. You were acting really weird. Like today."

I should've just stopped our conversation right then and there.

You should never let a girl confirm for you that you were or weren't acting a certain way. And never allow a girl to make herself out to be the sincere little friend, when the only thing she wants is to manipulate even the most minimal, insignificant information. Now I understand why it's better sometimes just to keep your mouth shut. I should have answered her, "You're the weird one," and left it at that. But I was curious, and I needed to talk to someone, even if it had to be her, Maite Daniels, the least trustworthy and most gossipy girl in Chile. So I let it all out.

"And what do you think of Gonzalo? I think he's just right for her," she said.

"I don't think so."

"We're not talking jealousy here, are we?"

"Look," I said, "now that you're here, playing detective, I'll give you my opinion. That way you can messenger it back to your friend Antonia. Tell her that she makes me sick and that it's all over now. That nothing else can happen between us. Especially if she's going out with McClure. Not so much because she's going out with someone else, but because she's going out with him. Let's say that I'm not interested in going out with someone who is seeing, or has been seeing, McClure. Totally incompatible personalities. Tell me who you go out with and I'll tell you who you are."

"That's not true."

"What would you know?"

"A person doesn't always go out with, or get involved with, someone exactly at his or her level."

"That's true: I forgot about us."

"*Us?* Don't be gauche."

"Gauche, never. That is absolutely clear, Maite."

"It's not so clear to me."

"Nothing's ever very clear to you."

It's funny, but whatever you say about it, sex brings people together. It creates this weird bond. Even if you've only done it once with someone.

"I don't know how I ever got involved with you," she said.

Typical. I knew she was going to say something like that. Girls always say stuff like that.

"I don't even remember," I answered, acting real cool.

"Liar."

"Fine," I said. "I remember that you fucked Nacho over. We both did."

"Did you tell him?"

"You can fuck someone over without them ever knowing. The fucked-over part is the same. In the end, of course, it all comes out. But that's not the case here."

"Thank God, Matías. I'll kill you if you say anything."

"It's not like you still like him or anything, is it?"

"No, but I don't want him to be mad at me."

"You wouldn't want him to stop fantasizing about you."

"Maybe."

I look at Maite. Under her T-shirt I can see her bathing suit, and I try to remember her body. I never saw the whole thing. Touched it, yes, but saw very little.

"Would you sleep with me now?" I ask her.

She plays sort of hard to get, and acts all serious, really pensive.

"No, I don't think so. Maybe. I'd have to be really angry. But at the same time, I can't lie and say there isn't a little bit of chemistry between the two of us."

"Well, there isn't. Definitely not."

"More than there is between you and Antonia."

"Has she mentioned me to you?"

"She told me that you bore her. That sometimes you're sweet and everything, but that you didn't really give yourself up to her. That all you thought about was yourself, and . . . that you were way too self-involved."

I felt like something just hit me. But the pain was lighter than usual.

"So she had it all figured out," I said.

"I don't know, but, in a certain way, I agree. You are kind of self-involved. But that's part of your appeal. In your own way, obviously."

"What do you mean, 'in my own way'?"

"You're angry, Matías."

"I'm not angry."

"I know you. Don't lie to me."

"Let's make one thing clear, Maite: you don't know me. You couldn't even if you tried. And do you know why? Because I'm not interested in you knowing who I am."

"You don't allow anyone to get to know you. Period."

I left her there, talking to herself. I went down to the sand and walked along the edge of the beach all the way to El Cementerio. Now it was Flavia Montessori's turn in the game. She had chosen Yoko Ono.

"Are we going to Ritoque, Chona?" Rusty asked Nacho. Rusty thinks that reversing syllables is fun. He calls Papelucho "Cholu." Patán is "Tanpa." Me he calls Matías. Thank God. I never thought I'd be so lucky.

"Where did this asshole learn Spanish?" I ask Lerner.

"His old man works for Firestone. He's lived in Spain, Mexico. And Venezuela too, I think. He goes to the Nido de Aguilas. He's got loads of money."

"I bet."

Later, we all got into Cox's Blazer and Rusty's very own huge black Jeep, with Firestone tires. Of course.

"Let's get back before it gets too dark. I'll race you, Cox."

Pía Balmaceda got into the Blazer. In the Jeep went the little aquatic threesome, plus that slut Maite Daniels and Flavia Montessori. Before crossing the Aconcagua River, we stopped to buy pisco, drinks, and some snacks. I had sand in my bathing suit and was really pissed off. But there wasn't much I could do, so I concentrated on the pisco.

And I isolated.

Rusty won the race. Once we we reached the finish line, in

the middle of that unconquered, sandy stretch, we decided to continue the race. Everything was all orange by now and there was a motherfucker of a wind that wouldn't stop blowing. It was getting seriously cold.

"We could've gone skinny-dipping," said Rusty.

Maite smiled. Flavia didn't.

Cox decided to drive his Blazer down by the water. Rusty too. Papelucho got into the Jeep. Lerner, who'll really do just about anything for attention, got into the Blazer.

The rest of us stayed by the dunes. Nearby, there was a minivan, its owners nowhere in sight.

"I bet it's a couple, and they're fucking down on the beach," said Patán.

"It could be a couple. But one of them is in the military," said Pía.

"How do you know?" I asked.

Nacho jumped into the conversation: "It's the bumper sticker. From the navy. Look, there's a walkie-talkie inside. And a folder full of notes."

After a little while, the rest of them came back. Papelucho and Lerner were frozen solid. And soaking wet. Rusty jumped out from the window of the Jeep and fell—just right—onto the sand.

"This fucker thinks he's a cowboy," I said to Patán, but he ignored me.

"They're from the navy, Rusty," said Nacho.

"We have to do something," added Papelucho.

"No trouble, Cholu."

That was when I started to think, we're in for some trouble.

"Rusty is something else," Patán assured me. "He told me he was deported from Spain for setting his teacher's car on fire."

Luckily, it didn't cross Rusty's mind to do the same thing to the minivan whose owner, the naval officer, was out on the dunes fucking somewhere. Lucky for us the van's owner didn't show up. They just stole all his gasoline, but they didn't even fill up their own tanks with the stuff. Rusty pulled out a thick hose from his Jeep, sucked on it, swallowed a little bit of the gas, and then let the rest of the gasoline from the van drip out, for the sand to absorb.

"That was better than that time at La Reina, right, Tanpa?"

"Better."

"Let's get out of here," I said, pissed off.

They all wanted to go to my apartment, but I said no. I was scared they'd get mad or something, but Pía Balmaceda jumped in and said, "Let's go to my house. You can all shower there. There's enough food for everyone. I've got to go anyway, to close up and leave it clean."

So that's what we did. But I knew that I didn't want to be there. I said to Cox:

"I'm going to my house. I have to lock up."

"Should I come and get you?"

"I don't think so. I'll figure out how to get back."

"You're sure?"

"Yeah."

That's how I left it. I went down toward Playa Negra and walked to Higuerillas, where there was a bus that left me right in front of La Mela, half a block from our apartment.

"Hello?"

It's my father. Luckily, he doesn't sound sleepy.

"It's me," I say.

"Where are you?"

"I'm at a phone booth in La Alameda. Near the corner of Las Rejas. By the Metro station."

"You came back from Reñaca? Is everything all right?"

"Fine, I just don't have any money. I had to come back by bus. There are no buses running now, though. It's too late."

"Listen, just take a taxi and when you get here, tell the doorman to give you the money. That's why they have that little cash box. I'll repay it in the morning."

"Okay."

"Is there anything wrong?"

"No."

I hung up, walked a block, and hailed a taxi.

"I thought my father was coming to get me," I said to the driver.

"What?"

"No, nothing. Nothing new. Don't worry about it. It's nothing I can't handle."

MONDAY
SEPTEMBER 8, 1980

A few dilemmas, *serious traumas. It's decision time. What am I going to do? Take off and tell everyone to go to hell? Escape?*

What would happen, I wonder, if I did? Would anything happen? Okay, try to picture it. Think about it. Let's put things into perspective here.

What would happen? What?

Consider it: what if you went, if you just left and didn't look back, knowing that it could be a really big mistake, but knowing that you'd feel good about it? Would you still do it? You'd lose everything you've got, but so what? What does it all mean anyway? Is anyone secure? Could you truthfully say, without fooling yourself, that you feel sure of anything?

The day, once again, is a sunny one. I get off the bus two stops early. I want to be alone before going back into class, before having to confront her, before having to confront anybody, actually. So I decide to walk a little. Without knowing why, I go into a pharmacy with a Sal de Fruta Eno logo on display. I see in the window that my hair is wet. I really look terrible in my uniform. So I undo the top button and loosen the knot in my tie, to look a little less formal, less dressed up. Now I look like more of a rebel. Yeah.

Like that movie I saw on television, that night I couldn't sleep.

School. Teachers. This one in particular is boring and repressed. She looks straight at a guy in my class who rides a motorcycle and wears a leather jacket, and asks, "What do you want out of life?"

The guy, all attitude, answers:

"More than this!"

End of scene. Great scene. What do you want from life, kid? I want more, I want much, much more. Got a problem with that?

"*Father?*"

"*Yes, son?*"

"*I wanna kill you.*"

"*Mother . . . I want to fuck you . . . fuck you mama, all night long.*"

That Jim Morrison, he does it every time. He'll never go out of style.

The pharmacist turns off his radio and looks at me suspiciously, his eyes narrowing. Maybe he shouldn't play the Doors so early in the morning. The guy must think I'm a junkie, that I'm about to attack him or something. Or better, that I want speed, or downers, or a neat little cocktail of vitamin C with Percoset. Time to fix my hair. First, I muss it up, then I neaten it, and then I muss it up again, so it looks natural. There. Okay. I feel the screwdriver I had earlier taking effect. Now, there's a healthy breakfast. I idly think about what a great idea it would be to sell cocaine in pharmacies. They should do it.

"*Hello, good morning, how are you today? Would you be kind enough to give me, oh, half a gram of angel dust?*"

"*Certainly. From Medellín or Santa Cruz?*"

"*The Bolivian is cheaper, right?*"

"*Well, actually, the Peruvian is the most economical, but unfortunately, we've run out.*"

"*That's fine. Give me the Medellín. Important day today.*"

"*Wise choice. The inexpensive product always ends up costing you more in the long run, if you know what I mean.*"

"How true."

The radio is on. News. I've got three minutes before the bell rings and classes start, so I put on my new sunglasses. Excellent. *I'm* excellent. I drank the vodka with *jugo* Soprole, had half of a McKay's soda cracker (tastiest in town), some vanilla yogurt, and topped it off with half a Valium that I stole from my mother while she was in the bathroom putting on her makeup.

"Would you like something, young man?"

" *'Young* man'? Why, thank you for the compliment."

From the radio speakers I hear *El Correo de Minería.* The announcer is on the side of the "SI." People who are for the "SI" listen to Radio Minería and Radio Portales, and the more fascist types listen to Radio Nacional. Old Jorge Alessandri, hard to believe he hasn't dropped dead of old age by now, says that to vote negatively is equal to treason. Yolanda Sultana predicts a 75 percent win for the "SI"; Shara, the radio astrologer, says that the stars assure a victory for the "SI," by 80 percent, and that the President can sleep easy.

"Give me some vitamin C," I hear myself say. "And a package of condoms. Lubricated, if you have them. With room to hold semen. If you have the ones with spermicide, I'll take those. They're even better, right?"

The pharmacist pales. On the radio, they're now talking about Jaime Guzmán. They were talking about Gustavo Leigh, who's asking people to vote "NO." I hate Jaime Guzmán, I admit it. Sometimes I have nightmares about him. No kidding. I dream that I've become his twin, all white, transparent, a virgin, bald, badly dressed, and with those awful glasses. The biggest nerd in Chile.

The pharmacist brings me what I asked for, and I open my wallet to pay him. Finally, I have a little money. My father left me some bills on the night table while I was beating off in the shower. The jerk only did it because he felt guilty about not picking me up at Las Rejas last night. You know, to cleanse his conscience. Does he even have a conscience? Well, anyway, at least I got a wad of cash out of the whole thing.

"Thank you, Mr. Pharmacist," I say as I collect my change.

Then I run. I arrive right on time, just before the last bell. Some guys have all the luck, right?

Right?

I'm at the back of the classroom. From my desk I am observing the scene in English class. God, how annoying—I know more than the teacher does. She can barely turn on a stereo, probably doesn't even know what *Rolling Stone* is. That kind of thing. I shouldn't be here, I think. But here I am. Not much I can do now.

"Vicuña, would you please take off your dark glasses?" my teacher asks in English.

"Sorry, Miss, but I have an eye problem."

Or more to the point: *I have a problem.* But I don't say anything, because I don't want to take off the sunglasses, and I don't really feel like confronting the principal. I decide to keep my mouth shut for now. I should just shut up while I'm ahead, right? I have nothing to say anyway. I don't feel like talking to anybody right now, only with Flora Montenegro, but her class isn't until sixth period. I can wait until then. No problem. I just won't talk.

I'll observe.

And disappear.

You're wearing your sunglasses. You look good in them: you're a real rebel, a loner. You write something in your notebook, but it doesn't have much to do with the lecture being given by the English teacher, who can't even pronounce anything in English: she softens the "ch" sound, so that instead of saying "children" she says "shildren."

Attentive and studious, Antonia Prieto sits in the second row, seat number two, almost on top of the blackboard and the teacher's wooden desk. The English teacher talks about anything that floats into her head. Mindless prattle, but Antonia takes notes on everything she says, even when she goes off on a tirade about how terrible it is that we missed so many classes because of the trimester vacations and our trip to Rio. Then she announces that due to the political situation, Wednesday classes may be canceled. Thursday as well, even though she hopes that on Friday, despite the celebrations, everyone will come to class, because she will be going over verb conjugations. Very important, because the week after that, we'll only have three days of school because of the Independence Day break.

Antonia continues to take notes.

You continue with your observations. Farther over, in row three, sits Ignacio "Nacho" Detmers. He is a truly unpleasant character. Pathetic. He doesn't know it, of course. He thinks of himself as one of the "chosen ones," but he isn't. Antonia, on the other hand, is, but she denies it, which is even worse. Ignacio Detmers doesn't listen to the teacher either. He is secretly reading Surfer *magazine, which, as its name suggests, is about the sport, which consists of mounting a long board that navigates the waves in the ocean; a sport that those who consider themselves the best never stop—*

"Vicuña, can you repeat what I just said?"

I look up.

"No, I guess I can't."

"Please pay attention, then."

I can't bring myself to pay attention. So I get up from my desk, standing tall, and I walk up to the front of the room. I glance over at Antonia and then tell the teacher: "I feel sick. I have to leave."

"Is something the matter?"

"I feel like shit, okay?"

"Leave the room, please."

"Just what I wanted to hear. Thank you."

"Go straight to the principal's office. I've had it with you."

"Have you, really?"

"Enough. I'm in the middle of a class."

"Yeah, clearly."

"Leave my room this instant!"

I close my eyes. What luck.

I open my eyes, and in front of me is the school disciplinarian, with that burgundy apron that makes her look more like a cleaning lady than a school administrator. She stares at me, silent, checking me out, giving me the old up-and-down. I'm in a chair, in her office, flipping through a copy of *Coqueta* magazine that she probably confiscated from some lazy girl who was reading it in class. Her office is pretty small. I notice a Firestone calendar hanging on the wall. In the foreground, there's a big, clunky tire, and in the background, the bucolic Chilean countryside, blossoming into spring.

"This is the last straw, Vicuña, you know that, don't you?"

"I don't know. I'm not so sure about that." I grin.

"What aren't you sure of?"

"Well, I'm not so sure I should be here at all. Aren't I a little bit old to be punished? And marked down in your book? I mean, that's just stupid, it's stupid, the way you record this stuff in your stupid little book. It doesn't scare anyone, you know. I mean, I know my attitude isn't going to change just because you've marked me down in that thing."

"You know, this isn't a joke, Vicuña," she asserts. "I'm going to be forced to call your parents this time. You're up to your seventh offense. We're barely two weeks into the new semester, and already you're getting yourself into trouble."

"The trouble started a long time ago . . ."

"One would think that the school trip might have calmed you down and allowed you to release all of that nervous energy."

I don't answer that, because the school trip is an untouchable subject to me, sacred, in fact, and I'm not about to argue about it with this moron, who gets off on putting my name down in her demerit book.

"I'm going to have to call your parents. You've left me no alternative."

"I doubt they'll be too concerned. They're the ones who raised me this way, after all."

"We'll see about that."

"Seriously. If you call them, maybe they'll even get angry at *you*. It would be like saying they didn't raise me right or teach me how to behave or something. You yourself said I was poorly behaved, right? So, it's not just the school that will look like shit—excuse me, look poorly—but my parents will as well. And, let me tell you, ever since the two of them joined Alcoholics Anonymous, they've been especially sensitive to exactly this sort of thing. For me, all this is quite overwhelming, but, well, that's the way families are, and it's better to have a family with problems than problems without a family, right?"

I like that expression: *problems without a family*. It sounds good.

The disciplinarian gives me a superior, pitying look that says: "What a pathetic life you've got." She still marks me down in her book. My luck. Bitch.

"Stay here during the second hour of English class. I want you to think about what you've done and what you're going to do about it. Stupid you're not, but remember, some people are too smart for their own good. You're going to go nowhere if you keep this up, Vicuña. I have experience with this, you know. And take off those ridiculous sunglasses. You look like a gangster."

"Or a secret-police agent, right?"

She doesn't say anything. She just shuts the door behind her and then locks it. Great. So, if there's an earthquake or a fire, I'm fucked. I look around the room and decide to try snooping through her desk, but that's locked too. Another one of her aprons is hanging on a hook, and in one of the pockets, I find a jar of Tapal, for ovarian pain—she has ovaries?—and a cigarette. But I don't smoke, and I don't have ovaries. So I sit back down, and turn on the little electric stove in the corner of the room, just for the hell of it. And I resume my flipping through *Coqueta.*

I walk around the empty courtyard. Somehow I convinced the disciplinarian that, since she did punish me by locking me up, I should at least be able to go to the library for a little while. I don't feel like reading, though. I hate the library anyway. All the books in there stink. What I want to see are all the books censored by the Committee for Decency, the archenemy of Flora Montenegro. So instead, I walk over to the vending truck at the edge of the courtyard, but it's closed. I can't buy my Negrita cookie. I decide then to concentrate on chewing the vitamin C I bought at the pharmacy. I look at my black shoes, all shiny and new. I can hardly believe that I still have to wear that uniform— gray pants, navy-blue blazer, and a silk tie—it's so they don't confuse us with the kids from the public school.

It's a good thing I have my Ray Bans to protect me.

I go into the bathroom, and as I pee, I read the graffiti covering the walls. Almost all of it is about the teachers, and the principal, with her horrendous flannel pants. She is by far the most popular up here, along with that faggy Carlos Miller and Ximena Santander, who is—was—such a slut. At least that's what it says on the wall.

The gratuitous insult to Ximena is anonymous, like all the insults and rumors up here, but that one in particular really bothers me. I remember Ximena. She had a mane of hair like Farrah Fawcett, only jet black. I remember her well. She's not in school with us anymore, which is kind of sad, because she was—is? was?—very, very cool. She never let other people influence her, and she always did exactly what she wanted. Even though she was a few years older, she used to always talk to me, violating that unwritten law that forbids older students (especially older female students) from even thinking about associating with younger guys. I was in my first year and she, with her tight, short pinafore, was repeating her third.

Ximena was a rare bird, she was really unbelievable. I was so proud to be her friend. I almost considered myself her disciple. It wasn't like we went out together or talked for hours on the phone or anything. It was a real funny sort of a school friendship. Or maybe "cutting school" friendship would be a more accurate way of describing it. Right after classes let out, we'd meet up, and get a big group together next to that little vending truck run by Señora Gladys. She always liked us, I remember. We'd smoke—well, she did, I didn't, actually—and hang out for hours talking about life. And I always learned something from those afternoon sessions when we hung out. That's the kind of friendship it was.

When she was fourteen, her life changed. She was the "star" victim of one of the most spectacular car crashes in Chile. Her sweetheart—who was six years older than her—was driving. Seven people died: three in his car and four in the other. She was the only survivor. And practically unharmed at that. Her photo was on the front page of all the tabloids. Ever since then, she decided to live every day as if it might be her last. That's why they suspended her again and again in school. They grew to hate her.

Once we got busted together. Me for talking back to the principal. I told the old lady that she was a liar, that something she said wasn't true. The problem was, I told her so in front of the entire school. And the old bitch, she never let me forget that one. She thinks she's so aristocratic and English, so superior to everyone. Well, maybe she's English, I don't know, but aristocratic, no fucking way. Anyway, what happened was that she announced that she was a real believer of "open-door politics" and that any student who wanted to talk could go to her office and "dialogue" with her. I said—in sort of a loud voice—that she was full of it. I asked if she didn't remember the time she automatically suspended my sister Francisca for making out by the back entrance to the school. I had really wanted to get some revenge for that, because it was so totally absurd that our school—a school with a ridiculously high abortion rate—should punish someone just for kissing in public. "Well, that wasn't her boyfriend," the principal said, as if "boyfriend" and "girlfriend" represented some sort of official status that made kissing in public acceptable or not. I ended up getting busted.

Ximena Santander was in the principal's office that same day for drinking pisco and Fanta in the middle of chemistry class. So that was when and where we initially became friends. When they sent us back to class, we went to Pumper Nic for french fries. We bumped into the Garmendia twins, from the Villa María, cutting class as well. The four of us hung out together until late in the afternoon, way past teatime. We became inseparable.

"We're rebels," said one of the twins.

"And we're going nowhere fast," answered Ximena. "People like us always lose. The enemy is always around to remind us who's boss."

I looked at her with an admiration which, in that instant, I think I confused with love.

"We're two of a kind, Matías," I remember she said. "Enjoy life while you can."

I know she certainly did. She got terrible grades, but everyone knew she was a genius. She even predicted the future when she said to me, "One day I'm going to pay for being the way I am."

She was right. It all happened when she decided to have a baby. She was seventeen, an age she thought was perfectly reasonable for childbearing. The father was a German who came to the FISA convention, selling indoor sprinkler systems. Ximena met him there. She was attractive and she spoke a little English, so she had been able to get a job working the French booth (the Germans didn't want her because she wasn't blond). She met Heinz during a lunch hour. After that, she was with him for the whole two weeks of the fair. I only met him once, when I was going on the train from the Estación Central. I was with Nacho, and we had gone to buy imported chocolates and look at the cars on display. We bumped into her, and that was when she introduced us to him. I guess he was around twenty-eight.

"The truth is, I got pregnant. Knocked up, I mean, and I didn't plan it," she said to me one afternoon, leaning against Señora Gladys's truck. "But I couldn't let the opportunity slip away—Heinz was too good looking and too smart, and anyway, I've always known that I've wanted to have a tall child. So I'm looking at this as a chance given to me by God. I've been pregnant before, you know, and I had an abortion. Not this time. I'll just have the baby and then go back to school."

But Ximena forgot one thing: the enemy is everywhere. Her parents, the school, and that bitch principal, to name a few, joined up with the Ministry of Education and a few remorseless doctors, in a united front against her.

Maybe it was her fault; I don't know. It was as though she went through life acting like someone was filming a documentary about her. Scared that it would turn out boring, she exaggerated everything she did. That's why, the day after sharing the news and a Sahne-Nuss chocolate with me, she requested a meeting with the principal. Very poised, she told the principal that she was three and a half months pregnant. Then she asked for permission to continue on in school. She regretted her improper conduct, but she thought she would continue attending school until just before giving birth, and if all went well, she wouldn't miss much.

Obviously, she didn't get the permission. Instead, she caused a scandal and some pretty major humiliation. They ordered her to withdraw from the school immediately. No way were they going to allow a young girl to attend classes if she was a mother, an underage, unwed mother. What the school did agree to do for her was recommend her to a clinic, Liceo Lastarria, where she could "fix" her situation and continue her studies at night.

Well, the very next day, Ximena showed up in class. When

they pulled her out of an exam, she started screaming. And there was more. She grabbed hold of the microphone, the one the principal uses, and she launched into her whole tragic story, telling the entire school what had happened. Two days later, she jumped the fence, came into school again, and put up cardboard signs demanding justice, and accusing the school of forcing her to get an abortion. Not only was this immoral but illegal, she claimed.

Then Ximena hit the old biology teacher, who tried to take down one of the signs that I had actually hung. And that was when the principal called the psychiatrists.

I didn't see when they took her away. She ended up in the same clinic as another girl I knew. Tons of people check in there every week, for all sorts of things. From what I learned, she had a drug-induced abortion, and then they gave her a bunch of sedatives and electroshock treatment. I never heard about her again. She was there for about six months, locked up; then they sent her to Miami.

In school, they've made her out not only to be a total whore but also a raving lunatic. To me, though, she became a saint, or more like a martyr. But we weren't allowed to talk about her. She wasn't even mentioned in the yearbook, and it seemed like everyone tried to just forget she ever even existed. The enemy is everywhere, she used to say. And I didn't believe her, back then.

You have to see things to believe them, I guess.

The bell rings.

Recess.

All the assholes start coming down the stairs.

I'm sitting in a lotus position, on a perfectly shaped stone bench, facing my own little "wailing wall," absorbing the morning sun.

They all come down, lots and lots of them, perfectly disciplined and obedient, thanks to what they learned from rehearsing the emergency drills of the famous "Plan DAISY."

First, the group of "bad girls," led by Montessori, Infante, Pía Balmaceda. Then Guatón Troncoso (the Nazi, I'm still sure of it) slowly trundles downstairs. He's talking to Sobarzo, who's wearing a gray parka that shines in the sun. Maite Daniels then appears, with a notebook in her arms; she's wrapped up in a conversation with Patán and Julián Longhi. Same old same old. Luisa Velázquez, caught in her own world, walks down the stairs next to Antonia, which is sort of weird, the two of them together.

Nacho is standing over with Cox and McClure. Gonzalo's trying to act indifferent, but I see him sneaking glances over in Antonia's direction.

The whole scenario is too perfect. I can see them all, and I revel in the idea that I know a little tidbit about each one of them. Or better, I know how each one of them is connected to, or disconnected from, me. The image is slightly distorted because of the uniforms everyone is wearing. They all seem younger, less offensive, more naive, or something. There are some people that will never look good in a school uniform, I think.

Nacho breaks away from the group and walks over to Señora Gladys's truck. He buys an *alfajor* and approaches me.

I look up at the sun, right to the middle of it, until it blinds me.

"Hey. Have you got a problem or something?" Nacho asks.

Okay, I could take this as an attack or as a legitimate gesture of concern. I decide on the former.

"No. Do you?"

"Not that I know of."

"Fine, see you later. I'm meditating. No offense."

"No sweat." He backs off and returns to his little group. He must feel guilty.

"You're like a lizard in the sun."

"I like that, a lizard."

It's Luisa. One of her tights has a run, I notice.

"So are they going to suspend you?"

"No, they just told me off. Nothing big-time. It's all the same anyway, it's so stupid. I know more English than this whole courtyard put together."

"The teacher told us you have psychological problems."

"No more than she does, I can assure you of that."

"Well, maybe, but you barely saved yourself from getting suspended. You'll have to go to the Marshall School, or Liceo Eleven, like all the other outcasts, if you are suspended."

"Well, that'd be a change of scenery, at least. Right?"

We sit there, quiet for a while, as I continue to soak up the sun. I look over at Antonia, who's now sitting on a bench, with Mc-Clure at her side. Not a trace of passion. They look like a married couple.

"I was talking to Antonia."

"About me?" I perk up a little.

"Not exactly."

"About what, then?"

"About Rosita Barros's birthday. It's today. They're having a party."

"I guess she has something to celebrate, then."

"Don't be such a downer, Matías."

"I'm not. I'm not at all. You're the one who said it."

The bell rings.

"Should we go up?"

"Sure."

Everyone is talking and nobody's paying much attention when Flora Montenegro makes her entrance into the classroom. Thank God. I needed to see her. Flora Montenegro isn't exactly well-loved by her students. She's not hated either, but they don't take her seriously. They don't really understand her. She just rubs them the wrong way, and they think she's a drag because she gives out lots of bad grades and asks about things you don't usually read about in textbooks.

"I hope you've shaken the sand out of your ears," she begins. "I imagine you all had a very nice time in Rio. I can see you're all nice and tan."

She's cut her scraggly black hair into a pageboy and is wearing a pair of bottle-green pants and a plain white blouse.

"Look at her pin," Luisa whispers.

"I already noticed it."

Flora is pretty brave. On her left lapel, she's got on a little pin with Mafalda on it, holding up a little sign that says "NO." Flora, everyone knows, is a leftist, but a smart one. Maybe she's too smart for someone who has just turned thirty. She studied in Paris, lived on the island of Malta, and she's read everything. She also has this really attractive quality, sort of rough and unrefined, very sexy. And scary too.

"We're going to start this week of lies with a bit of truth. I've brought back your graded quizzes."

Flora is famous for two things: giving out bad grades and not following the guidelines laid down by the Ministry of Education. The first quarter we had her, she made us analyze *Don Quixote*, but we only read little bits and pieces of it. Then we translated it to modern times. What we ended up talking about was how the *novelas de caballería* were just like so many of the police series on television, like *CHiPS* or *Starsky and Hutch*. And about how the genius of Cervantes lay in how he instituted that entire genre. Or something like that.

But way more than *"En un lugar de la Mancha . . ."* what really turns Flora on is Latin American literature, which is the topic she teaches us in the second quarter. She's teaching it to us because the teacher that we're supposed to have next year is a backward Catholic woman who's still stuck in *Marianela* and *Niebla* and other boring crap like that. Flora, on the other hand, has made us read guys like Fuentes, Puig, and Sábato.

"It seems like you people don't even live in this country. Either that, or you simply don't know how to read. These quiz scores are pathetic, and that's putting it mildly. Antonia, will you hand them back, please?"

The quiz had been on the book *A House in the Country,* a novel, way too long and not very easy to understand, I thought. It was written by José Donoso, who is Chilean, but because—according to Flora—this country is so small, so gossipy, and so frustrating, the man is totally unable to write here. So he went to Spain. The interesting thing, though, is that all his novels are about Chile, which, to me, seems like kind of a contradiction. According to Flora, that's not strange at all because to comment on something close by, a writer needs to observe from a distance. Like in Rio, I guess. I looked at the Pan de Azúcar Mountain and I thought of San Cristóbal.

When Antonia comes near me, she's impenetrable. She looks me straight in the eye, makes a grimace somewhere between sarcastic and insulting, and hands me my quiz: a 4.9. Saved. Blue. A triumph since, in Flora's scoring system, a 4.9 is equivalent to a 6.5.

Almost everyone else got the old red mark, I noticed.

"She should have made us read *Coronation.* It's by the same guy, but supposedly it's much easier," says Luisa, who got a 4.7.

"Easier and more boring too," I say. "Flora says that *Coronation* is overrated. I actually hope we read *The Obscene Bird of Night.* It's supposed to be awesome, but it's pretty heavy stuff, and our parents could ban it."

I look over my quiz. She didn't like my answer to the question: "Despite the fact that Donoso has set his novel in an indeterminate time and place, it's obvious that he refers to a very specific historical moment. What is this moment?"

This is what Flora wrote next to my answer:

"From what can be inferred from the text, and after what we spoke of in class, it's clear that Donoso is talking about the coup d'état of 1973. Do the acts of torturing and kidnapping seem normal to you? Do you think it's acceptable for servants to violently punish children at the behest of their parents?"

The quiz, I realize, was from before the trip to Rio.

Which means it's not worth anything.

Maybe if I read the book now, I'd say something else. Who knows? Who cares?

Flora has started her lecture. She's analyzing the novel. She explains the situation with the two cousins and tells us why Donoso makes the children talk in such a strange way and why sex here isn't pornographic. She talks about authoritarianism and repression and the downfall of the establishment and the use of the fantastic and the allegorical and the parabolic interpretation of the world.

"I don't understand a damn thing she's talking about," Lerner mumbles to me.

Lerner got a 2.9. And Nacho, from what I can see, got a 4.1. Antonia got a 4.2.

I look over at Lerner.

It occurs to me that I do get it. She's talking about me. But the bell rings and that's where it ends. Class is over.

Change rooms, change classes. Now it's time for biology. After that, recess again. And after that, two hours of math with that ancient, crusty old lady who'll probably live to be a thousand.

Flora gets up, shuffles her papers, hides her copy of *Hoy,* and is about to leave. When she gets out to the hallway, I go up to her and tell her in a low voice:

"We have to talk. It's urgent. Let's have a drink. I need to speak with you."

"I can't today."

"It's really important."

"Let's have lunch tomorrow, then," she says.

"Tonight you can't?"

"No."

"Fine. Where?"

"The usual place."

"One-thirty, right?" I ask.

"Perfect."

I look at my watch: 10:50. More than twenty-four hours away.

I go down the stairs to face the biology class. With my sunglasses on, of course.

The label reads: Valium 5. By prescription only. Registered trademark.

The bottle cap reads: Coca-Cola. Embotelladora Andina S.A. Carlos Valdovinos 560. Santiago.

The newspaper says: General Pinochet announced in Talca that the new constitution "will save us from communism . . ."

Michelle Phillips, ex-member of the Mamas and the Papas, arrived yesterday from Los Angeles, California, to make a guest appearance in the new TV show *Applause,* with César Antonio Santis. The blond actress/singer returned to fame a few years ago when she appeared nude in a series of racy scenes with the Russian ballet dancer Rudolf Nureyev in *Valentino,* a film directed by the controversial English director Ken Russell . . .

Pepe Abad, the well-known news announcer of Televisión Nacional de Chile, died today.

Extremist terrorists, who were apprehended last Friday, attacked the police precinct on Calle Román Díaz . . .

On television, Ricardo Calderón is interviewing Yolanda Montecinos on *¿Cuánto Vale el Show?* Three maids from La Pintana are dressed up in long, gold-lamé sheaths, imitating the Frecuencia Mods. These three Pintana ladies have just sung "Duele, Duele," which was a hit about three years ago, when the three "mod" sisters lived in Chile. Montecinos, typically unpleasant, talks to them about the incorporation of erotica in art and awards them a pathetic hundred pesos.

On Channel 7, Enrique Maluenda has no problem with the ridiculous, and distributes cases of Té Supremo to the stagehands.

* * *

"**Are you going** to eat lunch, Matías?"

"I suppose so."

"Well, then, it's just the two of us."

Back on TV, Maluenda gives away Té Supremo to an old man from Malleco or someplace like it who's suffering from gout. When Gloria Simonetti comes out, and she starts to sing, I turn off the television.

Carmen serves two plates of celery with avocado and ham with ricotta and chives. There's also white wine and Frambuesa Andina on the table.

"Is there any milk?" I ask.

"Yes. I'll bring it over."

"Thanks."

She brings it over. Ice cold. In a tall, thick glass.

"How was school?" my mother asks.

"Fine. The same. Okay. Boring."

"That's good."

"And how was the lunch yesterday?"

"Wonderful. Very, very nice. Felipe was nothing less than a little saint. He didn't even cry once. I suppose that holy water must have done him some good."

"I suppose."

"And how was Reñaca?" she asked.

"Sunny. Lots of people, but it was nice."

"And you watered the plants?"

"Yes."

"Great, great. And how were they? In good shape?"

"I think so. They didn't look dry or anything."

"Good. You know I don't trust that caretaker out there. He's lazy, like all of them. He's not even a caretaker, he's more of a glorified security guard. María Elena Squella, on the fourth floor, the mother of Bea's little friends, told me when I saw her last time that he spends the day tanning himself on the beach. I can't believe he thinks he's getting away with something."

Carmen comes in with a tray of spinach crepes, smothered in a cheesy sauce.

"And your father?"

"I don't know."

"I thought you knew."

"He must be in his office."

"No, I called him there, but he's not in."

"Do you want some more wine?" I ask.

"No."

For dessert, we have canned peaches with some sort of gloppy meringue sauce.

"I don't want dessert," I say.

"Me neither."

"I don't want coffee either."

"Me neither."

Silence. I think about school, about *A House in the Country,* about Flora Montenegro.

"Have you read *A House in the Country?*" I ask.

"No."

"It's about the dictatorship."

"What dictatorship?"

"This dictatorship."

"It must be written by some leftist. Anyway, I hate the countryside. Do you want coffee?"

"I already said no."

"Right . . . I don't know where my head is. I'm going to take a nap. And watch the soaps. I hope *Pecado Capital* is still on."

"I met one of the actresses on that show when I was in Brazil," I lie.

"Which one does she play?"

"I don't know. She's a redhead."

"It must be Neusa Santos."

"I think that's her, yeah."

"Small world, isn't it?"

Carmen takes back the desserts, untouched.

"Where are the girls?"

"I don't know."

"You don't know much, huh?"

"Matías, I'm going out after my nap, but I'll be back around seven. All right?"

"Fine."

"I just wanted you to know. It's a charity obligation that I can't get out of. I have to help a . . . a friend in need. Some sort of crisis in a run-down neighborhood."

"Fine."

"I'll be back at seven, then."

I go to my bedroom, and after a little while she leaves.

I flip through the latest *Rolling Stone,* which just arrived. "After a long absence, the product of a self-imposed isolation, John Lennon is recording a new album in New York. It will be released at the end of the year."

My bedroom faces north, toward Arica, Iquique, and Antofagasta, toward San Cristóbal Hill. I know it's north because the sun follows its path north and continues in a semicircle, stopping only when it reaches the mountains.

The strong sunlight peeks into my room through the mini-blinds. It always does on sunny afternoons. In the summer, oddly enough, the rays don't fully penetrate, because of the sun's position. But in the winter and the spring, the afternoon light is very intense.

Like today, for example.

I open the blinds, and the sun suddenly bursts in, illuminating the freshly waxed parquet floors, and warms my bright blue comforter. *Permanent Waves* by Rush is softly playing. On the night table, underneath the Farrah Fawcett poster (the one with her tits pushed together underneath a tight red T-shirt), sits a glass containing the remains of a vodka Collins.

I'm lying in bed, faceup, with my eyes closed. I'm sticky from sweat and the remains of the Hawaiian Tropic. I'm naked except for my gray socks. I don't even have the strength to get up and clean off the warm white stains sprinkled on my chest. They've already begun to dry anyway. When I surrendered, hastily and conventionally, I was in the midst of a fantasy that will hopefully do me some good, clear my head. I feel better now. Much, much better.

I close my eyes and smell. It's intense, sticky, and hormonal. The sun feels good. Penetrating, numbing, liberating. I'm in Rio, Ipanema to be exact, in front of number eight. I'm on the north coast of Maui, El Cementerio de Reñaca, Malibu, or Zuma, on the rocky beaches of Malta.

Wrong. I'm in Santiago.

I'm lying in bed, faceup, eyes closed. I'm sticky from sweat and the remains of the Hawaiian Tropic, which is just beginning to take effect.

That smell of red, sunburned skin, the smell of Cassia, and me.

Wrong again: I'm in Santiago. Alone.

At least I'm somewhere.

Lerner comes over around six and wakes me up. My sister Bea lets him in. I get dressed as fast as possible, because none of the excuses that come to mind would sufficiently explain my sweat-stained, sun-drenched siesta. I show him my *Rolling Stone* as a distraction, turn on *The Blues Brothers* album, and then go for a shower. Twice I wash my hair, with an imported antibalding shampoo that my father brought home.

"Let's go to Rusty's house. Papelucho got some good pot. Everyone's going to be over there," he says.

I show him my Christopher Cross record.

"I was going to go to Rosita Barros's birthday party."

"Why? What's up with her?"

I feel like saying, "More than what's up with me and Papelucho and Rusty, and definitely more than what's up with me and Nacho." But instead, I say, "Nothing, really. Just something to do."

Then I add, "Anyway, Antonia's going."

"Forget about her, will you? She's not worth it, she really isn't. She's all wrong for you. For anyone, really. She doesn't talk straight. She's always pissed me off anyway—she even lies to God, man, when she prays at night."

"Maybe. But I just wanted to go to the birthday party."

"So go afterward. We'll smoke a little, and that way you'll get there more relaxed. I'll even go with you. Anyway, Nacho's also going to be there. He's probably waiting for us right now, in fact."

Pause.

"Hey, Matías, you're not mad at Nacho or something, are you?"

"No. Why would I be?"

"Well then, what is it? You don't like Rusty?"

"I think he's overrated, yeah. But no, it's not that."

"What is it, then?"

"I don't know."

"Bad vibes?"

"Yeah, I think so: bad vibes. That's all. Don't take me too seriously these days."

Bea comes into my room. I ask her to gift-wrap the record. As payment, she asks to borrow a sweater, my navy-blue one.

"Your sister's not very nice, is she?"

"None of the Vicuñas are, when you get down to it."

Bea reappears with the record, wrapped in pink paper. I give her the sweater.

"Should we go?"

"Yeah, let's."

As we're about to leave, the front door opens before we reach it. My mother.

"Hello there. How are you boys?"

"Fine."

"You see? I got back before seven. Just like I said I would."

"I'm not keeping tabs on you, you know."

"No, I know. And you don't have to, Matías. Do you want the car?"

I feel like saying to her *No! I'd rather die first!*

But instead I just say, "No thanks, we're going in Lerner's."

"Don't worry, ma'am, I'll bring him back."

This statement pisses me off. An annoying, gratuitous remark on Lerner's part.

"Bye, then."

"Bye."

"Bye."

I should say something else. But I don't.

Shortly after arriving, I realize Rusty's parents are not at home. They're in Ohio, I'm told, going over accounts in the Firestone headquarters.

"It seems like everyone's parents are on vacation," I say to Lerner.

"Except for yours."

Rusty's house is at the top of Lo Curro Hill. Through the glass door, I notice how there's almost no concrete, it's practically all windows and exposed beams and has a panoramic view of the city lights below.

Cox comes through a door, and he's dripping wet. It's freezing cold. He's got a towel wrapped around his waist.

"What's up?" I ask.

"We're in the pool. Come on," he signals me.

I go and it's totally dark except for some lights on in the kitchen across the way. Cox walks in front of me, his wet feet dripping onto the brick floors. The house is filled with these strange glass ashtrays, surrounded by tiny rubber tires.

We go down a flight of stairs and reach a huge room filled with couches, a pool table, and all these Firestone posters. There's also a neon Michelob beer sign and a gigantic *National Geographic* map of the United States. The room is carpeted. There's cushions on the floor, and a glass coffee table full of beers and Cokes, pisco bottles, and some drink I've never seen before, which looks like whiskey—Jack Daniel's. There's also a bowl with some popcorn, and the usual scrap of newspaper laid out, with pot stems and seeds sprinkled on it. Pink Floyd's *Dark Side of the Moon* is on the Technics stereo system.

"Now I think maybe I understand Rusty a little bit better," I say to Lerner.

"Don't be so sure," he says.

This living room leads onto a patio and a lighted swimming pool. The sliding glass door is open, and a cold wind rushes in. Cox takes off his towel anyway and stands there in his light blue boxers.

"Jump in. It's warm."

I watch as he disappears in the water.

Patán, Julián Longhi, and a Chinese-looking guy who I've never seen before are all in the pool.

The Chinese guy is in red boxer shorts.

"Jump in, Matías."

"I don't think so," I say.

"Get something to drink, then."

"Okay."

I pour some Jack Daniel's into a Coke and grab some popcorn. It's so salty, I spit it out.

"Where's Rusty?" I ask.

"He's in his room," says Patán before disappearing underwater. Lerner leads me down a hallway where "Money" is playing. It's coming out of a bedroom, Rusty's bedroom, obviously.

"Unbelievable," I say. "They've got speakers in all the bedrooms."

"God bless America, right?"

"I suppose," I say.

Rusty's bedroom is empty but his bathroom is full. Even the bathroom has speakers. The depressing, druggie sound of Pink Floyd mixes in with the smell of pot that penetrates everything. Another typical night.

Rusty's in his bathtub, which is filled with steaming-hot water. His hair's wet, and slicked back like a gangster, and he's smoking a joint. There's almost no light except for a single red candle that smells like cinnamon.

"This is sooo hippie," Lerner says to me.

"I'll keep my opinions to myself, thanks."

The rest of them are all hanging around this *hot* tub, I now realize. Nacho's there, wearing some pants I've never seen him in, and nothing on top. He's busy drying his hair with a scuzzy-looking towel. Papelucho, in a black T-shirt and underwear, is sitting on the edge of the tub, trying to hang up a pair of white socks with purple stripes. The three of them are singing away, like a bunch of retards. They're majorly stoned.

"*. . . Oh, how I wish you were here . . .*"

It's 7:38 P.M., I notice.

"What's going on, you lunatics?"

"Nerler, my pal, come in, come right in." We're back to the little nickname business again.

We both go in.

Nacho looks a little surprised at first and stares straight at me. Then he relaxes a little and calls out: "Matías, what are you doing here? I never would have thought . . ."

"Only because you're here," I answer sweetly.

"You want a smoke?" asks Papelucho. He hands us an enormous joint, moist from the humidity and the vapor and all the fingers that have already touched it. I take it and place it between my lips. I inhale twice, but I realize I don't really want any more. "Animals" is playing now.

"This is like a Pink Floyd marathon or something," says Lerner.

"I saw them live," says Rusty. "There was an inflated pig, a big pink thing, floating over the crowd."

"I wouldn't mind meeting Syd Barrett," Nacho says, buttoning up his blue shirt, the one from his school uniform.

"Supposedly he lives in Paraguay."

"Like Mengele," I say.

"I don't know, I never heard of him," says Lerner.

I sit down on the bidet, silent.

Rusty disappears underneath the water for a few seconds. One, two, three, four, five, six, seven, eight . . .

"What's he doing?" I ask.

"He's trying to find his equilibrium," answers Nacho, who's being more communicative than usual. It's probably from being stoned, or from having soaked his fucking head or something. Whatever. It still doesn't make him any more real.

Rusty finally emerges and gets up out of the tub, momentarily causing a minor tidal wave that splashes soapy water onto the glazed floor tiles, my shoes, and the black bath mat. He stands there for a second, getting his bearings and flexing his body in the shadows.

"I'm stoned," he says in English.

Nacho lights another joint and grabs another bottle of Jack Daniel's from behind the trash can. Out of nowhere, he pulls out a bottle of Coca-Cola.

"This is like a Cuba Libre without Cuba," he jokes.

"Aren't you the little Alejandro Paz," I say, sort of surprised at myself.

"I haven't seen that guy in a while. How is he?"

"Fighting for the 'NO.' "

"Yeah, anyway—I haven't seen him in a really long time. I don't trust him anymore anyhow. We're going to win, obviously."

He's pretty wasted.

"Hey, asshole, those are my fucking boxers! Give them back!" Rusty shouts to Papelucho.

"Fuck, man, I'm sorry. I got mixed up."

"Stupid fucking Chilean . . ."

Papelucho takes off the boxers, which have little cannabis designs on them, and trades with Rusty, who gives him back his boxers, which only have the letters of the alphabet on them.

"Sorry."

"No sweat."

I close my eyes. This is too much.

"Want some?" asks Nacho.

"No, I don't want any more pot."

Nacho turns on the light. A rosy glow washes over Rusty.

"Let's go find everybody else."

"Let's go."

In the room with the neon Michelob sign, the sliding door is closed; the shimmering pool lies just outside, empty and calm in the darkness. The steam rising from its water reminds me of the outdoor pool at the Hotel Portillo.

"It's going to snow," I say to Nacho.

"It never snows in Santiago," he answers, almost angry.

"On the mountain it does."

"Perhaps . . . I don't know . . . it doesn't matter much to me."

I decide not to say anything more. I'd like to put some kind of curse on him or something, send him the worst luck I can. *Perhaps* . . . so all of a sudden now he's a little Englishman. He's pathetic.

"Vicuña, you want more Jack Daniel's?"

"I don't know, Lerner."

"It's imported."

"Fine, whatever. Sure, pour me some." I flop down, like an existential sack of potatoes, onto a cushion labeled "Star Wars: Let the Force Be with You."

The other bathing beauties are all dressed now. The Chinese guy, I realize now, is actually an American. Half American and half Chinese. Or Japanese, I don't know.

"Charlie, help yourself to some weed."

"You bet, loco," he answers in this real rah-rah tone of voice.

A Chinese, druggie, American, bilingual, rock-star teenager. This is too much. Too much.

With his punk hairdo, which stands on its own, Charlie, the Chinese rocker, removes a Jaclyn Smith poster framed in glass from the wall and suavely places it on the coffee table. He then takes out his crocodile wallet, opens it, and pulls out a tiny piece of foil.

I think of my origami, of Cassia, and of the redhead from Leblon.

Someone plays "The Wall." This Pink Floyd shit could drag on all night, I'm beginning to realize.

The Chinese guy starts doing lines.

"We're Charlie's Angels," Cox says, trying to be the comedian.

I remain silent and sip some of the poisonous Jack Daniel's and Coke.

"Is there any wine? We *are* in Chile, aren't we?"

"I'll get you some," says Rusty, who for some reason is playing the nice guy all of a sudden.

"Rusty's parents must have loads of wine," says Lerner, as if I really care.

Charlie sniffs the first line and yells out something, but I'm not sure if it's in English or Chinese.

Everyone laughs. The Chinese guy then passes his Bic pen over to Lerner, who heartily accepts it. Right away, I notice my nose starting to tingle. But I decide not to participate in the ritual, as a matter of principle.

"Here's the wine," says Rusty, who has returned with various bottles of Tarapacá/Ex Zavala, uncorked.

I pour myself a glass and one for Patán. Rusty puts the bottles on the coffee table, then rolls up his sleeves and snorts a line.

"Is anyone cold? It's like really cold, isn't it?" he says in a nasal voice, like someone whose nose is all stuffed up.

Nobody answers him, because they're all in line to snort: first Nacho, followed by Cox, and then Julián Longhi. Rusty hits a few buttons on the wall, to turn on the central heating.

"How state-of-the-art," comments Patán.

"Don't talk to me," I answer before downing more of the freezing-cold red wine.

Rusty lowers the volume on the stereo and fiddles with the equalizer. For a second, the only thing I can hear is the sound of Papelucho snorting. Then the most famous part of "The Wall" comes on:

"We don't need no education, we don't need no thought control . . ."

"Your turn, Vicuña," says Cox.

The Chinese guy looks at me. I decline the offer.

". . . All in all it's just another brick in the wall . . ."

The Chinese guy snorts the line that was for me and sits down on the floor, closes his slanty eyes, and says in English:

"This is fuckin' great, man."

The rest of us watch him in silence. The circle is complete; the only things missing are a roaring fire in the fireplace, andirons, and trusty Boy Scout. Or maybe everyone should be in pajamas. It's the old let's-see-how-depressed-we-can-get-that'-s-what-Pink-Floyd-is-for routine.

"Mother, do you think they'll drop the bomb? Mother, do you think they'll like the song . . . ?"

This is like a religious ceremony, I think to myself. Or satanic. I've been through this scene before. I've dreamed it. I know exactly what's going to happen, I know the whole deal. This existential atmosphere drives me nuts. Gives me the creeps and actually makes me feel kind of embarrassed for them. Especially listening to Nacho singing, as if he's totally wasted, even though I know he's not. I've seen all that before. He's such a poser.

"Goodbye, cruel world, I'm leaving you today . . ."

Everything's exactly as it's supposed to look: the semidarkness, the joints, the wine, shit-faced guys flopped on the floor, the hallucinatory but melodic, suicide-inducing music.

"Goodbye, all you people . . ."

"They say Syd Barrett is still alive," says Patán in a low, almost funerary voice.

"Of course," answers Julián Longhi. "He's not dead, he's just crazy. They say he's even recorded an album, only under another name. But that it's just about impossible to find anywhere."

"I heard that he went to live in one of those Rajneesh communities, like they have in Oregon," says Rusty. "I've been to Oregon, so I know. It's full of fuckin' space cadets like that. There aren't any here."

"Barrett OD'd on acid."

"On LSD, you mean," says Charlie, who pronounces the letters like he does in English, rather than in Spanish. This interruption makes him sound like he actually knows what he's talking about, even though he doesn't.

"That's a total rumor," says Papelucho. "What happened was, the guy was schizo, and the music just made him even crazier than he already was."

"Well, I tell you what I think. I think the rumor is exactly what drove him crazy. I think Roger Waters and Syd Barrett are the same person. Or at least, Waters writes the exact same stuff that Barrett writes," adds Patán, who I've never known to be such an expert on Pink Floyd.

"I have become comfortably numb . . ."

"Total lie, Tanpa. Like the story that Rod Stewart had his stomach pumped and they found two liters of semen."

"I heard it was three, Rusty," says Lerner, who's all of a sudden some kind of statistics expert.

"Anyway, I still think it's true."

"It's bullshit."

"Like what they said about *Rasguña las Piedras* by Sui Generis," says Nacho. "And that thing about Charly García dedicating the whole thing to a 'babe' who had some kind of spaz attack and then was buried alive."

"That one's true: Charly García said it himself in a magazine article."

"I doubt it," says Nacho in English.

"They'll say anything. Buried alive, Jesus . . ." Cox trails off.

"Who's Charly García?" asks the Chinese guy, sounding kind of anxious and kind of drunk.

"He's this Argentinian singer, dude," Nacho answers in English.

"Is he any good?"

"Latin Americans like him," says Rusty, again in English.

I go over to Lerner, who's smoking a joint.

"Give me your keys, will you? I'm going to get that record out of your car. I'm leaving."

"But this is just getting started . . ."

"Yeah, so?"

"Well, how are you going to get down the hill?"

"On foot. I can walk, you know. It's no big deal. Really."

He gives me the keys and offers me a hit.

I accept, inhale, and get up quietly, carefully.

"Hey, Longhi, is it true you ate Maite out the other day?" someone asks. I can't tell who, though.

"Yeah. It was pretty bad, though. She acts like she's been around, but she's all talk. No kidding. Has anyone else here fucked her?"

"I did," says Patán.

That's not true. With Patán it was only a quickie, no sex. It happened when we were in Rio. I don't say anything.

"And what did you think?"

"The best thing she does is give blow jobs."

We all laugh, except for the Chinese guy, who doesn't understand.

I close the door behind me.

*   *   *

"Matías, what a surprise!" Rosita Barros welcomes me in.

"Yeah, no kidding . . . Uh, this is for you. I hope you don't have it already."

I hand her the wrapped-up record. The house smells like wax, that classic, familiar smell of the well-kept Chilean household.

"Christopher Cross! I love him! You're too much, Matías!" she exclaims.

She gives me another peck on the cheek.

"Mother, I'd like to introduce Matías Vicuña."

"Hello," I say to her mother, who's wearing one of those Scottish kilts, with a little pin on the side.

"Delighted to meet you, I'm glad you could come."

"Me too."

"Well, please, come in, come in." She gestures toward the other room.

"Thanks."

The decorating scheme here is definitely her mother's touch, I can tell. All the chairs have flower prints. Pastel colors, of course.

"How is your VW?" I ask Rosita, even though I'm thinking about Maite and that birthday party Virginia Infante had at the shopping center.

"Fine, fine, but it's not mine, you know. It's my sister's, the one who's studying to be a veterinarian."

"I was sure it was yours."

"No, no, next year, when I turn eighteen, they're going to give me one."

"That's nice, wow."

"Yeah, isn't it? But anyway, come in, come on in here. Everyone's here already."

Rosita really is kind of a joke, I think to myself. She'll always be Rosita, never Rosa. That's the kind of girl she is. It's like, the things she says, I can barely believe her: "*Everybody's* here."

Everybody?

Well, some of them are, that's true enough. A more-than-substantial group of friends. Antonia's here, obviously. I knew she would be, though. I just sensed it. I can feel her vibes. I go into the living room and everyone looks up at me. Some faces I recognize, others I don't.

"Hi," I say, sort of shocked, not knowing quite how to act. I start getting that awful feeling, like this was a mistake and I shouldn't have come. I look at Antonia, but she doesn't respond. The sound of voices and the radio fill the air again. I'm not the center of attention anymore.

Antonia is all dressed up, in varying shades of green. McClure is sitting next to her, although it's hard to tell if he's really with her or not. He's talking to some guy, whose hair is slicked back, all black and oily. As they talk, the guy keeps putting on and taking off these tortoiseshell glasses.

"I never thought *you'd* come. You don't usually make it to this type of thing."

It's Luisa.

"It's you. Someone I know, at least."

"Sorry to disappoint you."

"No, no, it's not that . . ."

"It's not that at all, I didn't mean it that way," she finishes for me. "I know, I know. I've heard that one before."

"I'm sorry," I say. "It's not you. It's nothing personal."

"That's okay."

"Who else is here?"

"Let's just say it's not going to dramatically alter your life or anything, Matías."

This makes me stop and think for a second: it's not going to alter your life. And if it did? If I changed my name, and my age, and I decided to become a veterinary student? What then?

"Do you want a drink?" she asks.

"Sure."

We go into the dining room, and the table is all set up, just the way a mother would do it. There's punch and pisco, and Fanta Limón and Pap and Piña Nobis and a vase with roses, and plates with hors d'oeuvres, little canapés with chicken, and chunks of cheese with pimiento, and tiny pearl onions, and a big Black Forest cake, bought at the Avenue du Bois bakery.

"I'll just have a pisco with Limón," I say.

Now I've got her from a different angle, but the deal is still the same: she's talking to a girl, one of those types from the Liceo Los Andes, probably the daughter of some old Catholic millionaire with dozens of kids.

"Where were you?" asks Luisa.

"At some American's house, this guy who has suddenly brought Santiago to its knees. I was with Lerner and the other guys."

"Yuck."

"Yeah, yuck's right."

"So why did you go, then?"

"A person doesn't always do things that make sense, Luisa."

"A person should try to, though, Matías."

"Neither perfection nor maturity is a goal of mine."

"That's pretty obvious."

"Goodbye, Luisa. I don't want to argue with you."

"Who's arguing?"

"Nobody."

I leave her standing in the dining room and walk into the other room. I sip the drink—it tastes lousy—and nod a hello to Virginia Infante, blond as always, who is immersed in a dialogue with Flavia Montessori. I sit down by the fireplace, which is crackling away. Right next to me are two guys, overly shaven and cologned, talking about some economics professor from the Católica who was recently in Chicago. On my other side, a fat girl chatters on about some computer she's planning to buy, as sort of an investment for the future.

In front of me, and just in front of the table, is Antonia, next to a little silver turtle with a tail that you can pull to ring for the maid. She's talking to McClure now. He looks over at me and smiles, although I can't really tell if he's doing it to be friendly, or to be smug, the sarcastic little *huevón*. I look at him without blinking an eye, which leads to nothing, since McClure doesn't try to start a conversation with me.

Luisa walks through the door and disappears; the living room is full of people, just like the dining room and the study, which is a little farther down the hall. To me, though, it feels as if nobody were here at all. That's the truth. Nobody worth talking to, at least. Nobody worthwhile. Except for me, of course. And Antonia, who, despite being so inaccessible, is still an obsession.

I decide to stare at her. Look her right in the eye, just like my mother taught me to do. She doesn't respond; it's as if she doesn't see me at all, but she knows she's being watched. I'm impressed by her willpower. It's not that I think she likes me, or loves me, or anything like that; I'm simply surprised that she's been able to excise me from her system. Just like that. Not that I think I was ever important to her at all. I sincerely doubt that. But I still sometimes fantasize that I was. That's a person's prerogative. The idea that if *you* feel a certain way about a certain person, that something from inside *you* managed to find its way to the other person, well, then it's only natural to imagine and hope they'd feel the same about you. For example, I bet—I'm sure, actually— that every time she eats bread with avocado, she thinks about me. Maybe yes, maybe no. I'll never know for sure, though. Even if she swore it to me, it could still be a lie. A person can never be sure. Security only comes when a person really believes in something. And I believe, I feel, I'm *sure,* in fact, that her not acknowledging me, her ignoring me, not looking at me, her total indifference toward me, is proof, positive proof, that I still mean something to her. Or, at least, that she hates me but, sometime, at some other moment, when everything was much, much simpler, she did have feelings for me.

I think that the past is much harder to hide than the present. Which is why, I think, every last person in Rosita Barros's pastel-flowered living room could put his or her hands in the fire and truthfully say: "Yes, it's true, it's clear that there was definitely something between the two of them once, and maybe there still is." Twenty years from now, I think, when she's married to Mc-Clure, or someone just like him, and she happens to hear about me, my life, and my probable failures, I'm sure that those eyes of hers will open wide with curiosity and nostalgia and maybe even a little bit of jealousy. And she'll say: "I did the right thing. He wasn't the man for me."

The saddest thing of all is that she'd be right: I'm not the right guy for her. Not anymore. Once I was, a long time ago.

Something happened, and I have to live with the consequences.

"Is everything all right, young man?" Rosita's mother all of a sudden interrupts my thoughts. "Can I get you anything?"

"No, thanks. I ate already."

"There are some tapas warming. They're splendid, I'm telling you."

"Well, I'll try some of those, then."

In an effort to abort our conversation, I take a canapé of salami and smile as wide as I can.

Right at that moment, Rosita comes in, turns off the radio, and plays the record I gave her.

"Listen," she says to Antonia. "Do you like it?"

"I love it. That song 'Sailing' kills me."

"Yeah, it's excellent, isn't it?"

"You've got to lend it to me," says Antonia. "I was going to buy it myself, I'm dying for it. Where did you get it?"

"Matías gave it to me. He's too much, isn't he?" Antonia looks at me.

"Yes," she says. "Too much. Really."

I get up; it's practically a reflex by now. I realize I've no choice but to leave. No choice at all.

TUESDAY
SEPTEMBER 9, 1980

Last night I met *Holden Caulfield. It was like a chemical reaction or something, totally mesmerizing. I really couldn't believe what happened. Now at least I didn't feel so alone—finally, I felt a little better. I had found a new friend—my new best friend, my twin.*

Finally.

It was by accident, like in the movies. It's when you think there's nothing left . . . that everything's lost . . . that you're never (not even by accident) going to get out of that black hole or lose that awful feeling of total stagnation that makes you totally, totally bored with yourself . . . that you don't care either way about anything . . . when you're just not satisfied with anything or anyone . . . that's when something finally happens to get you out of it.

Get me out of it. Kill me is more like it.

That's exactly what came about. It's as if I've known him all my life, that's what's so odd about it. It's like I recognize his voice. Although I know he doesn't really exist: he's just a character in a book.

What scares me is that Holden's a great guy, I love him to death, I admire him and all that, but he doesn't exactly end up on top of the world. He ends up a mess, a real mess, locked up in some mental institution, like Ximena Santander. And after that, who knows? It's an open ending, like Flora would say. He pays the price a person has to pay for being different.

I finally understood all of this last night. That's me, that's why I am the way I am. This realization took me by surprise, too much by surprise if you ask me, and the truth is, I'm not sure if I was ready for it. I tried to call the Great Alejandro Paz of Chile but Juancho's was closed and nobody answered at his house. Alejandro's phone number was there in the back of the book.

I try to reach Paz again from a public phone in El Faro de Apoquindo that morning around ten. I should be at school right now, but I've got too much on my mind to pay attention to useless information that doesn't interest me in the least. What I need to do is talk to a couple of key people. I've got to find out if what's happening to me is for real. There are some things you go through alone, that only have real meaning when you're able to share them with another person who's interested, who really gets it, you know? That's what I'm going through. I feel this overwhelming urge to tell Alejandro Paz about Holden and, if nothing else, at least thank him for lending me the book. It's weird how, at this early hour of the morning, I feel closer to Paz than ever before. So I call him again, but he's still not there. That's the way this world is: what you get is inversely proportional to what you want and need. That's why life is so hard.

After walking through some shops I go into the ice cream store that's just underneath El Faro, but I don't get anything. I just walk around. I take off my tie and hide it in my jacket pocket and unbutton the first two buttons of my shirt, but I've still got that unmistakable private-school image. No escape from that. The parking lot of El Faro is loaded with cars and minivans, all belonging to the legions of mothers who are taking advantage of the morning hours to go shopping. I look at a pair of sneakers and little bike accessories, just in from Italy. Next door is one of those trendy little boutiques that are all over the place, the ones that sell exotic things like Asian art and antiques. When I enter, I hear this big gong. A slutty-looking girl who's a little older than me comes out. Wearing a shiny red silk dress, she looks like she belongs in a massage parlor, rather than an antiques shop.

"Hi, I'm Jessica. Can I help you with something?"

I sort of feel the urge to say something funny or kind of crude to her, but my conscience won't let me: "I'm looking for something for my mother. She loves China. All of the Far East, actually. Except Japan, of course. I myself was born in Hong Kong."

"Really?" asks Jessica. She's all dolled up in her tight little getup.

"Well, my family's from Chile. The thing is, though, that my father has a bank and nowadays most of his business is coming out of the Far East."

Jessica's eyes widen. I've clearly made an impression on this clerk.

"And you?" I ask. "Where are you from?"

"Nowhere, nowhere, I'm just Chilean. From Renca. My family's from the south, near Osorno."

"Absolutely incredible. I was certain you had a little Mandarin blood in you."

She blushes, and I think about those mandarin shrimp they serve at that restaurant, the Blue Danube. I better change the subject, I think, because that's about the extent of my knowledge of Chinese culture.

"Well, listen, Jessica, the reason for my little visit here is that I need to buy a nice gift for my mother . . . something meaningful . . . and expensive. It shouldn't be anything imitation, you know, or anything made in Chile."

Jessica looks at me, a little surprised.

"Well, what does she need? A pretty vase, maybe? That would be a nice birthday gift."

"No, no, you see, it's not *her* birthday. It's mine, in fact. That's why I'm buying *her* something. It's an ancient Oriental tradition, the son gives his mother a present as a sign of appreciation for her having given him his life. Since I've had a pretty good life so far, I think it's only fair of me to give her something really wonderful and unforgettable. Money, Jessica, is no object, especially when it comes to family."

"Hmm, let's see," she says. "Maybe one of these nice porcelain pieces would be more fitting, then?"

I look at them and they're really cheap, they're horrible, flashy and shiny and tacky as hell. Like from a wholesaler or something.

"Oh come on. Please, can't you come up with something a little more tasteful, Jessica?"

"Excuse *me*. These have been quite popular lately."

"I read you wrong, Jessica. I thought you could tell the difference between what is really elegant and what is junk. I mean, really."

Now I've really pissed her off. Then I notice that behind a bamboo curtain decorated with these cosmetic, painted-on dragons is an old man with huge hairs sprouting out from his ears. He's staring at us.

"Well, listen, Jessica, it's nothing personal but I think I better just be one of the sheep and go for something more normal, like a Rolex or something. It's been a pleasure meeting you. Happy September eleventh. Remember to vote for the right candidate. Bye."

She doesn't answer.

As I leave the store, I hear that gong again, and then I start running, like some thief who's just ripped off a store. I've turned into a pathological liar, I think to myself, then I laugh. As I go up Avenida Apoquindo toward Providencia, I think about Jessica and my little performance, realizing that maybe it's true that Holden, or his voice, his being, really can be elevated to reality. That's the weird thing. Nothing like this has ever happened to me before with a book, or a movie, or even a record. Or even with a real person.

This little game of adopting someone else's identity does have its charm. It also scares me a little, because that whole act of lying and creating a scene is something uncontrollable and compulsive, just like playing hooky. Like in *The Exorcist:* the devil seems to have taken control of my mind . . . I don't know what's happening to me. It could also be that I'm imagining it all too. Maybe these desires and impulses are really my subconscious desire to be cut off from everything. That old saying is true, "What goes up must come down," or whatever it is that Luisa always says, but in my case it's different. Right now, Holden is more an example to follow for me, a support, a little slap on the back. He's like a shot, or a line of coke.

I see another phone booth, so I try calling Paz again. He still isn't there, and Juancho's is still not answering.

I keep walking, passing all the ivy-covered mansions, the embassies and huge buildings that all look just like my building. There aren't any other kids around at this hour, and I feel like everyone is watching me. It gets so intense that I actually start shaking when a military patrol car goes by. Then I come to my senses, realizing that the fucking military is more worried about the communists than some little juvenile delinquent like me. It's still weird to be running around when everyone else is inside. The disciplinarian will probably ask me for my excuse tomorrow. I wonder what I'll say to her. Asking my parents to cover for me is pretty much out of the question. Especially my father, who, in one of life's stupid ironies, actually drove me to school this morning. When I got out of the car, he just sped off. After he left, I saw Sobarzo and Flavia Montessori but when I saw Rosita Barros, reality caught up with me and I realized that no way, under no circumstances, could I bring myself to go in. I just couldn't do it. Without a thought to the consequences, I walked half a block, hailed a cab, and asked the driver to please take me to the skateboarding courts where Calle Tabancura meets Las Condes.

I start walking, block upon block upon block. Maybe it will help me organize my thoughts. In front of the bowling alley there's another phone but Paz still isn't answering, so I keep on going. My feet hurt a little because I've walked from Tabancura to El Faro and from there back here, but I keep walking anyway.

Maybe I should have gone to school today after all. Maybe I shouldn't go back home. Maybe I can wait for Antonia at the front entrance. Maybe I can go to Rio, in a truck. Maybe I can just exile myself altogether.

As I go by the military academy, I see the cadets practicing a march while the older soldiers, the privates, are patrolling the area. They're packing guns. I decide not to stop and watch them but wander under the huge bridge that crosses over Vespucio instead. It looks like a war zone here, they're repaving it all and there are dump trucks and tons of soil and gravel all over and debris strewn all around. The subway station still isn't finished. Posters in favor of the "SI" are plastered all over the scaffolding that surrounds the excavations for the Metro.

Away from this chaos, the residential area seems totally untouched. There, housekeepers are watering the lawns, oblivious to the drums beating in time with the soldiers' march, oblivious to the hysteria of the drilling in the street. A bit farther is Navidad Hill, possibly the gentlest hill in all of Santiago, leading up to the strangest little square in the world. It goes right up to Apoquindo, but the hill (which can't be more than two stories high) protects the neighborhood from the outside noise. The far side of the square is the heart of the whole town, surrounded by a host of busy little side streets. There's a huge old patrician mansion from the nineteenth century that's now a hospital for children with tuberculosis. The patients sometimes stick their heads out the windows and look out at all the healthy kids, who come here just to play or jump over those bouncing balls that were so popular a couple of years ago. The square itself is lush and green and filled with hundreds of tall trees, even some palm trees. It also has little hills and sand traps. An incredible spot, really, with dogs—St. Bernards, Afghans, huskies—all running around, never seeming to bark or annoy anyone.

Right now, the secluded park is empty. The springtime sun is beating hard against the light cloak of smog that has begun to invade this part of the city. I sit down on a bench, put my books down, then take off my shoes and socks. I walk up a bit then stretch out in some warm sand, sand that sticks to the insides of my toes. It's kind of nice, I think to myself; I could get used to this. It's eleven-thirty and right now I'd be in chemistry class. I'm glad I'm here, though, lying in the sand, it's almost like being at the beach. I take out my sunglasses, to face the sun with the appropriate attitude. This isn't the first time I've been here on this grassy, sandy knoll.

I used to come around to this park with the little hill when Nacho lived around here. His parents lived about a block away on El Trovador. We had a little ritual. We'd go to Nacho's house to study but we'd always end up bullshitting and walking his dog Maximiliano around the square, so that he could play with other little dogs. Nacho and I smoked—cigarettes or joints (like I said, I don't really smoke cigarettes). We'd drink beer and eat beef jerky and those little green olives that we bought at the Unimarc on the corner. This is where Nacho and I really became friends. We'd spend hours and hours lying in the sand, cutting classes or studying cheat sheets or playing with Maximiliano, who really was the best fucking dog that ever lived, as far as I'm concerned.

Thanks to Maximiliano, we got to know two girls that worked in the neighborhood. One of them was Elena; the other was Vanessa. Elena used to push a shiny chrome carriage with a little blond baby with pink cheeks. Vanessa was the hot one, she was the one who never wore anything under her apron that had little aqua-green designs on it. She walked a little dachshund that she called P.F., just like the sausage brand.

We met them right here, about two years ago. It was in November, right before we had to take all those standardized tests and aptitude exams. It was already pretty hot, hot enough for us to take our shirts off and sun ourselves in the sand. First we checked them out and then we started flirting with them a little, nudging Maximiliano to go and mess around with the little caramel-colored dachshund, which was actually kind of cute. Whenever Vanessa said, "P.F., come here!" we'd die laughing, just because we thought the name was so stupid. That's how we all became friends. It's weird to think that they were around twenty-one or twenty-two at the time. It seemed as though they had already wasted their lives away working and taking orders from everyone else. They were both pretty enough, and it wasn't embarrassing to talk to them or anything. I mean, at least they were clean, they had all their teeth, and they were actually much cooler and much nicer and funnier than most of those trashy girls we usually meet on our nights out on the Gran Avenida.

Our biggest escapade, so to speak, happened on the plaza, a bit above the hill, where there's sort of a fortress, a tower hidden between these huge gothic trees and giant boulders. We met up with them, I think it was on a Wednesday—during a historic week in which the temperature hit a record high, something like 105°, at four in the afternoon. Everyone was sure there would be an earthquake. Nacho stole a bottle of Bacardi from his father's bar, and I had a couple of joints. Our double date was for eleven-thirty, or twenty-three thirty, as he likes to say. We were a little late, but the girls were calm and happy, waiting for us on a bench that seemed to shine underneath the glow of the streetlamps. That evening, they looked different, not in their maid's uniforms but in jeans and little angora sweaters. "You look like sisters," I said to them. "You too," giggled Vanessa, who I got the feeling would be mine for the night.

The whole evening was incredible and magical and amazing because after the rum—nothing goes to your head like rum does—and the joints and the whole mood of it, we were all totally relaxed and into each other. Right above us, buses and cars whizzed by, coming dangerously close to us, going up Avenida Apoquindo. The moist, thick atmosphere gave everything a sort of hazy, dreamy quality, and the four of us ended up with our clothes off, running through the grass as if we were little cherubs on acid or something. Maybe it was the total secrecy of it all, or our collective nihilistic fear of an earthquake, but whatever, the moon was full, and the best and probably the most incredible thing was that nobody but us knew we were there. Two by two, we took to the benches and just drowned in pleasure. For me, and for Nacho as well, it was our first real, totally erotic experience. No worries, no rushing, it wasn't one against the other in a big battle, but just two couples. It turned out that the girls were the wild ones. When it was all over, I lay down on the hill and felt the sweet, dewy grass caress my back; and I remember thinking that Vanessa's breathing must be the same sound the earth makes when it turns on its axis. Between my little dreamscapes, I looked at the trees, with their fresh green leaves, and it seemed as if the stars were like little buds in the branches. Nacho, who was with Elena on the hill next to us, was like my brother then, and this encounter was our secret, our private, sacred secret.

We never saw them again, of course. Exams came, as did our end-of-the-year parties and then the summer. Nacho saw Vanessa once at Unimarc, I think, but he was with his mother, so they just glanced at each other and didn't say anything. Time passed, and Nacho left for Valparaíso. That was when I stopped coming around here altogether. I doubt Nacho will ever go back to his old house either. I also doubt I'll ever see much of him again. If I do see him, I can't imagine we'll have all that much to talk about. I mean, I don't think we'll ever go back to seducing working girls in the plaza, or lying in the sand, talking for hours about sex, about our parents, about clothes, and things like that. I guess we won't go on that postgraduation trip to Australia that we were planning, on a ship with the Merchant Marines, with our stops on Easter Island and Fiji and Nauru, an island that fascinated Nacho even more than the coastline of Maui, with its incredible pipeline and all those surfing contests.

I feel like calling him, and telling him I was here.

Maybe it's better not to call him at all. If I did, then I might start missing him, and that wouldn't be any good. I guess.

I get to the vegetarian restaurant before Flora, so I sit down and wait for her. And I order a carrot-and-orange juice to drink while I read. Supposedly it's the house specialty.

When Flora shows up, she's wearing a multicolored sweater, one of those Peruvian things that you buy in Cuzco, with a black blazer on top, which doesn't match at all. She's not in a great mood, and I can tell she's uncomfortable. Her eyes dart around, looking everywhere except where I'm standing.

"I'm sorry, Matías, but I had a run-in with the principal, that's why I'm late. I got involved defending another teacher who skipped her classes last week during the Frei speech at the Caupolicán."

"Did you go too?"

"Of course."

"Oh."

"Hey, you missed classes today too, didn't you?" she asked.

"Yeah, how did you know?"

"Well, I was looking for you, actually, to cancel our date. I asked your friend Antonia if you were in school and she said no. So, of course, I figured you were cutting, and didn't want to keep asking people and get you in trouble, so . . . anyway, what do you want for lunch? Whatever you'd like, it's my treat."

I've known Flora since last year, when she became my Spanish teacher, but I feel as if I've known her all my life. She only teaches second and third years, and this is my second year in her hands. That's the way I see it. I mean there has always seemed to be something between the two of us, much more than just a teacher-student relationship. But it's much less than a relationship between two lovers. I just mean I learn a lot from her.

More than the age difference, though, I feel like she really lives—it's like she lives so much more in one day than I ever have in all my seventeen years. Flora has traveled all over the world, with no money to speak of, but still has managed to meet who knows how many influential, famous people, and especially all the writers and intellectuals she loves so much.

"I flirted with a certain legendary lesbian existentialist in Paris," she once said to me in the Kafé Ulm, where she had invited me to this concert Capri gave, where we listened to Quilapayún, Inti-Illimani, the Jaivas, and the rest of the aristocratic communist set.

She's also been with Borges, who wrote "Emma Zunz," a story Flora once made us analyze from a feminist perspective. That was the one that Luisa actually got an A+ on for her comment that it was "dubious, from a psychological perspective." According to Flora, Borges might have been a genius, but he didn't know a thing about sex. Because of that, nothing he ever said has any meaning. He also knew nothing about politics, according to Flora. She said that to him too, right to his face, when she was in Buenos Aires. She also lit into him for having accepted a medal of honor from General Pinochet. She told us about that last year, which was a minor scandal at the time. None of us had ever heard politics being discussed so publicly. We had certainly never heard a teacher even insinuate that they didn't agree with the government on something. I always thought her opinions were gratuitous and out of place, and generally inappropriate.

"Look, I think it's pretty simple: he accepted the award because it was an honor from the country of Chile. The President is only a figurehead; he's a symbol that represents us all." That's what I said.

"Listen, Vicuña, it's one thing to be blind; it's another thing to be an asshole."

Everyone in the room fell silent, including me. After class, she said she wanted to talk to me. And she took me to a grimy pizzeria, around Calle República. For three hours, we talked about books, intellectuals, politics, human rights, and sex. In that order. She then delivered me home in her Fiat 600. She was kind of shell-shocked when she saw my building; all she managed to say then was:

"Chau, Gatsby."

Later I found out that her remark had something to do with the Robert Redford movie. I told the story to Luisa, who immediately started giving me hell about it, saying she was sure Flora was after me, that Flora wanted to seduce me. Ever since she met Flora, Luisa became obsessed with her. She admired—still admires—her integrity, and the way she's not afraid to take risks, or to do something other people disapprove of. After promising me she'd keep her mouth shut about our thing at the pizzeria, I promised Luisa that I'd do whatever I could to include her in any future chats Flora and I might have. That was when I asked Luisa what Gatsby was. She told me he was a character in a book and that she'd try to get it for me.

I read *The Great Gatsby* with dedication, the same dedication you have when you're getting ready for a party that the girl of your dreams will be at. Daisy was exactly like Antonia, and I loved the way the two mansions were right across the bay from each other. But I thought it was kind of rotten of Flora to nickname me "Gatsby."

About a week later, I saw her in the hallway and said that I had been thinking about things, and I wondered if we might meet some afternoon. I waited for her after class, next to her orange Fiat, and we wound up in that vegetarian place with the Hare Krishna motif again. I told her that even though I was only sixteen years old, even though some people thought I was just a rich kid, that that didn't make me stuck-up. Then I quoted the beginning of *The Great Gatsby:* " 'Whenever you feel like criticizing anyone,' he told me, 'just remember that all the people in this world haven't had the advantages you've had.' "

She looked straight at me, and smiled with satisfaction:

"You're right, I was only testing you. You passed."

That was almost two years ago, I think. Ever since then, we've always gotten together to hang out outside school. In her class, I'm just another student, although clearly one of her favorites, along with Luisa, who always questions everything, and Nacho, who is destined to write the next great surfing novel of the twentieth century, according to Flora. That last thing I'm not so sure about, though. Anyway, those two sometimes join in on our little extracurricular outings, but aside from them, nobody knows about us. The fear that one day we might get caught *in flagrante* drinking beers in soda glasses together may be why Flora is twice as hard on us in school, making us kill ourselves for pretty mediocre grades.

"You're sure you don't want more wine?" she's asking me now.

"I'd rather have a lemonade; I've drunk way too much already."

"Whatever you say."

Our plates are loaded with crepes, black beans, and spinach, plus a serving of brown rice, and I don't know what else. Something's distracting me from saying how I feel.

"Well," Flora says, looking at her watch, "I hope you didn't cause too much damage in Rio. Three years ago I had to chaperone a trip there, and it was a blur of spending money like crazy during the day and going to discos all night. That was when I decided to read Jorge Amado in the original Portuguese."

"I had a fantastic time, actually," I say to her. "The best time in my life."

"Are you kidding? I thought it was awful. So many tourists, as if the place weren't content with just being Brazilian. It was like Miami. I mean, if you ever really want to know Brazil, you have to go to Bahia. That's the real thing."

"Well . . . maybe so, but I had a good time anyway. The trip made me think a lot about things. Too many things, maybe."

"You'd never guess it from that tan."

"Hey, you can still think on the beach, Flora."

"About what?"

"I don't know, anything—life, Chile, anything."

"Maybe."

She's on some other wavelength right now, I can feel it. It's like we don't have that connection today. I look out the window and see the valet parking attendant counting his money. She starts talking about the corruption surrounding the referendum, the years of dictatorship that stretch out before us, and then this article she's writing for Stanford University, about Julio Cortázar.

"Are you thinking of going to Stanford?" I ask, just to have something to say.

"Are you kidding? You know better than anyone how I hate the United States. I'd die before going there. Stanford did offer me a teaching position, and I'm told it's outstanding, that their Latin American library is beyond my wildest dreams, and a few of my colleagues from the Pedagógico went into exile there, and they seem pretty happy. But my job is here."

Flora is an international brainiac. She publishes all sorts of essays and papers outside Chile, and she's even written some kind of book, an analysis of semiotics, I think, which was published in Mexico. On top of that, she's written an entire book of poetry, which she did under a pseudonym. She won't tell us what it's called, but I'm almost positive that it's a book that won a prize last year, something Luisa told me she'd read. With all that, she'd still rather stay here—where everything is dead, according to her—and teach Spanish to a bunch of spoiled rich kids, rather than teach public school kids, or students at the university, where there actually is some political action going on.

"Your parents will vote for the 'SI,' right?"

"Clearly."

"And what are you going to do about it?"

"Nothing. What can I do?"

Whenever I'm with her, things always get complicated. It's hard to explain, but they just get complicated. Like now I don't feel like I can explain to her what I've got on my mind and what has brought me here in the first place. So now, when I should say something, nothing comes. It's like I don't have a care in the world, but no, it's not that. It's as if what I'm going through recedes when it's time to say it. Or it seems ridiculous all of a sudden.

"I'm sick of losing, Flora," I say to her.

"Then make an effort to grow up."

"I don't know if that's the answer."

I think I might be right: when you overanalyze things, you reach these definitive conclusions that don't allow you to resolve anything. When you start thinking things: Why do I like this person? Why do I have the desires I have? Why do I have this inexplicable bond with Flora Montenegro? I don't even feel like I know if we're friends or confidants or what. All I know is that I've talked to her about everything. Except myself. The same goes for her.

I have this attraction to her too, which makes me kind of uncomfortable. There's definitely something there, but nothing's ever happened between us, and I don't even try to imagine if anything ever could. My guess is that it's useless and that she's not really interested. Either that, or she doesn't want to think about it either. I know there's some chemistry in the air with us. Even though most of my friends think she's pretty ugly, I don't agree with them. She's probably not my type, true, but she's got her appeal. When she talks, especially when she talks about herself, I can't help falling for her, which sometimes pisses me off, because then I start comparing all the other girls with her, which is absurd and makes no sense at all. That's the way it is: ever since I met Flora, I can't imagine going out with a girl, even if she's pretty. If she doesn't have a brain, or doesn't get excited with such outré things like German movies in black and white, where nothing at all ever happens anyway.

Lots of times when we're together, I just sit there, like a bump on a log or something. I act all interested in these things she talks about, even though they don't really interest me at all, or they interest me only mildly. I don't understand them or share my thoughts on them with her. Like that thing she says about my mother voting for the "SI" as "nothing less than a classic case of penis envy."

"So you spoke with Antonia," I say as I sip my lemonade with organic honey (not sugar).

"Yes . . . every day that girl gets more and more bourgeois. I wonder if she'll ever be able to break away from her conventional little beliefs and customs. Oh, she's messed up, I think. I don't imagine you're still interested in her, are you?"

A tough question for me to answer right now. I could launch into my "act of falsehood," as Flora calls it. So I think about it before answering, because it's all becoming clear to me now. The issue of whether or not Antonia is in my life is just another "test" by which Flora is judging me.

"Listen," she once said to me when we were talking about Antonia. "I think she's a very pretty girl, for the social mores that you aspire to. She's gorgeous enough to be in television commercials. She's not got a stupid bone in her body. That's the worst thing about her. Try and open some doors for her. Change *her* perspective. If you don't, your little romance will never go anywhere, and you'll lose out in the end, or give in to her, which would be even worse. Make her see your way of life, not the other way around. Do you hear what I'm saying?"

What does she mean, "the other way around"? What does Flora know about my "way of life" anyway? It's like, one of her stupid intellectualized theories that says if a person acts a certain way, he must think a certain way, and therefore be a certain way. Okay, so maybe she does have a point, that I'm not the same kind of person as Antonia. I'm glad about that. Really I am. Because of that, it doesn't necessarily mean I'm anything like Flora, much less an avid supporter of the far left. The two don't have to contradict each other, I don't think. I mean, maybe I don't agree with what my parents think, but in the end, you bring your dirty laundry home to wash anyway, right? I don't know. Maybe

Flora's right. She's older, she's more experienced, she's got culture and sophistication. She's about twenty times more real,
more authentic, than all my friends put together, that much I
know. But I don't know. Really, I don't.

"Last night, I reread Nabokov. I assume you've read *Lolita*?"

"Uh, no . . . I know that it was some major scandal in Chile,
yeah, I know that. That's why they call teenage girls 'lolas,' I
think. My grandfather told me that."

"You must read it, Matías. It's about the reverse exile, a fascinating subject: those who rejected communism in favor of trans-
planting themselves directly in the hotbed of capitalism. I'm
thinking of writing an essay about it, for Washington University,
in St. Louis. There's a professor there who's very interested in
the breakdown that was precipitated by that issue in the book.
And I'm thinking of relating it to the Cuban phenomenon—
Cabrera Infante, definitely, who is a grade-A *gusano*. And Jerzy
Kosinski's *Being There*—you've read it, haven't you?"

"No, but I saw the movie. With Peter Sellers. Excellent. You
know, it could make just about anyone laugh. He's so funny. Hilarious." I laugh.

"I don't agree with you one bit."

Silence. Why can't I ever satisfy her? Maybe that's why she's
become this addiction for me. Half the time, I don't understand a word she's saying. She recommends so many books to
me that if I were to even begin to read them all, I'd barely ever
leave my house again. Some of the stuff I've read, and some of
it I even like, but the truth is, I couldn't get through most of it.
To stay on her good side, though, I just agree with everything
she says, all her theories and hypotheses. It's the same thing
that I did after that Capri concert. I told her I loved it, even
though I thought it was shit. I do the same thing when I make
myself out to be this Allendista, the little leftist rebel, when the
truth is, I don't understand the first thing about any of it.
Which, of course, makes me feel like an idiot, because then it's
like I'm this hypocrite. But I'd feel even more like an asshole

if Flora were to think of me as mediocre. Mediocre. One of her favorite words. Like the students who can't tell the difference between irony and straightforward, simple sentences. They're mediocre.

"I read the most amazing book. I highly recommend it. It's called *The Catcher in the Rye.* I read it in English, but I'm sure it's in Spanish. You could have the class read it, that's how good I think it is."

"I read it years ago."

"Did you like it?"

"Not that much, to tell you the truth. It's a bit childish. It's all so obvious and so typical. Sure, Salinger isn't bad with colloquial expressions, but at this stage in the game, how much does that count? I think the book is also pretty dated by now."

"Really?"

"Well, anyway, I think the Americans have overrated it. They've turned it into some kind of twentieth-century Bible. If you're into teenage sagas, read *Huckleberry Finn.* I think you're beyond Salinger, Matías."

"Really? I mean, I don't know if it's well written or not, or what, but it was incredible. So real."

"You should reread it. I thought it was pretty disappointing, to take this character that, frankly, nobody really cares about and raise him to some philosophical, poetic, universal level. I mean, the trials and tribulations of a spoiled Jewish kid, so self-obsessed that he takes off and holes up in a hotel only because he's got his pockets lined with money. Who's really interested in that sort of thing? Maybe the book critics, who are all Jews. They're the ones who canonized the book anyway, you know."

"Flora, what are you talking about? Jews don't have anything to do with the book. Holden Caulfield is a Catholic. He's even pissed off at his church; he says so in the book."

"Well . . . maybe, sure, but Salinger is a Jew. And so is that whole supposed literary 'establishment' in New York; they run the book world there, everybody knows that. That's how Philip

Roth became famous. Or Singer, the guy that only writes about the Talmud. What a bore. Even William Styron inserted a totally gratuitous concentration camp scene in one of his books, a totally autobiographical novel at that. But he had to do it just to get *their* stamp of approval."

I look at the empty glass of lemonade. I'm not sure I want to continue this conversation. I feel crushed.

"Don't be blind to it. Almost all literature is written by the Jews. Proust was Jewish. What I really can't stand, though, is what's been happening recently. All this North American Zionism. The very best Jewish writers are precisely those who reject their condition as such. Or leftist Jews, I guess you'd call them. They represent the most delicious clash of all."

"Do you have something against Jews, Flora?"

"Is it that obvious? I can get a little carried away sometimes." She laughs a little, but she laughs.

"No, it's not too obvious," I say, getting up from the table.

"Is there something wrong?" she asks as I inch away from the table.

"Not with me. With you."

I stop for a second and look her squarely in the eye. For the first time in the two years I've known her, I've succeeded in making her squirm. I savor the moment and really get a good look at her, looking at her facial features, because I know, whatever happens, this will be the last time I'm ever going to see her. Now I'm going to have to change schools, no question. There's no other choice. Just the thought of having to look at her face again makes me sick. And sad too, because now I feel empty. There's a lump in my throat I have a tough time swallowing.

"Matías, what's going on?"

"Nothing. I was just testing you."

This must be the thirty-eighth time I've tried to call Paz today. I went to Juancho's, but some janitor answered the door and said he didn't know where Paz or anyone else was. He says that El Toro is going through some ordeal.

"Are you having lunch?" Carmen asks me.

"No, I ate already."

"You could have told me. I've got other things to do. There are people coming over tonight."

"Who?"

"Your father's uncle, the ambassador, he's being canonized or something, I don't know. A lot of people are coming over, too many people, as far as I'm concerned."

"And my mother?"

"At the hairdresser's. Where else?"

That said, Carmen leaves, shutting the door behind her. I turn on the television. Soap operas. I open the curtains to let the sun in. I'm still in my school uniform.

"Hello, is Andrés there, please?"

"He's in school. I think he has gym class today. Is that you, Matías?"

"Yes, it's me."

"You're not with him?"

"No, I've got a sprained ankle," I lie to her. "I've got a doctor's note and everything. I just thought . . . well, I guess I forgot he has gym today. I'll call him back later. Bye."

I hang up. I better start being more careful when I cut class. She could have busted me, Lerner's mother, I mean. Although I'm sure she could care less. My parents, on the other hand . . . that's different. But I can handle it. Now I have to sleep a bit, rest. Even my feet are exhausted. All of a sudden, I realize that I haven't really slept in weeks, really, but it doesn't bother me. I'm home, I'm going to start over again. This all hasn't happened. It hasn't happened at all. Okay, what I need to do is stop the chaos before it starts, before it's too late. I should sleep, I should sleep a little, that's the first thing on the agenda. Clear my mind. But I can't. I close my eyes—nothing.

I turn on the television. Cartoon hour. The Coyote runs after the Roadrunner across a red and yellow desert. The Coyote puts up a trap: a yellow-colored screen that looks like the desert floor, but in reality, he's hiding a brick wall that he's built behind it, connected to thousands of pounds of dynamite. As usual, the Roadrunner averts the trap, and in the end, the dynamite explodes in the Coyote's face. Poor guy, I think.

"I'm sick of losing, Flora."

"Then make an effort to grow up."

"I don't know if that's the answer."

Now Tom is running after Jerry. It always happens like that. Of course Jerry usually wins, being pudgier and cuter, and everyone loves him better anyway.

"Did you like it?"

"Not that much, to tell you the truth. It's a bit childish."

Bugs Bunny, to mix things up a little, dresses up in women's clothing. Fred Flintstone confronts Barney Rubble, ignoring little Gazoo, who's talking about the lost paradise. That dog, I forget his name, hugs himself with all the tenderness in the world and rises up to heaven in his own little ecstasy.

"I mean, the trials and tribulations of a spoiled Jewish kid . . . Who's really interested in that sort of thing?"

The Warner Brothers logo appears in Technicolor, and all the little monkeys in the company march onto the screen, singing: "Thhhhat's all, folks!"

I turn off the TV, throwing the remote control on the floor.

"Lerner? What's up?"

"Oh, it's you."

"Yes. Is that a problem?"

"No."

"Good, then . . . Hey, did I miss anything? Any major interrogations in class?"

"Vicuña, you're asking for trouble."

"Why? What happened?"

"Nothing, you didn't miss anything; I just don't understand what your deal is."

"Hey, come on. This isn't the first time I ever cut class."

"It's not that."

"Well then, what is it about?"

"Let's just say that I'm not getting you right now . . . I don't understand your deal."

"What do you mean, 'deal'?"

"Nothing, I guess . . . whatever, it doesn't matter, it's not my problem anyway . . . You really didn't miss anything . . . we only had a few classes, actually; everyone's thinking about the whole referendum thing."

"Don't change the subject. Come on. What are you trying to say to me?"

"Nothing, Vicuña, it's not that big a deal, it's nothing I'm losing sleep over, or anything. You can do whatever you want, it's not my problem. Look, just take my advice: you're starting to piss everyone off. I don't know what's wrong, but you're getting on everyone's nerves. Obviously something's up with you; you're really fucking everyone around, you know?"

"I'm not the only one."

"Luisa's right. You're impossible to even talk to. It's like you've totally lost it; you can't even have fun anymore. Everything's a drag or boring to you or something."

"What have you been doing talking to Luisa? And why is that bitch getting involved in things that are none of her business? You know, if there's anything that pisses me off, it's gossip. That bunch of motherfuckers, they've got nothing else to do with themselves. Me, at least I've got real problems. Serious shit. This country, I'm telling you, is really sick. It's fucked. We all are."

"It sounds like you're the sick one, Matías."

"Fine, so if I am, it's my problem. Don't get involved."

"Nobody's getting involved with you. Don't worry about that. Now I know why Nacho avoids you these days. And your little escapes, what's up with that? Why did you leave Rusty's like that? We were talking about that all last night. You even pissed off that Chinese guy. The same thing happened at Rosita's. Even Antonia was bad-mouthing you, that's what Luisa said anyway."

"And you agree with all of them. Oh . . . so now I get it . . ."

"There's not anything to get, Vicuña. You're just going through a shitty time. I'm telling you, fuck it before it ends up fucking you. It's not worth it."

"You know what, Lerner? I think you should mind your own fucking business and stay out of things you don't understand anything about. So why don't you take some friendly advice and go straight to hell."

"Fine. It's your problem."

"Exactly. It's my problem."

Someone is banging on my door. Hard. They won't stop. Each knock leaves echoes. The devil's knocking, I imagine. Even so, I don't want to wake up. I can't wake up . . . I open my eyes a little but they shut right away. It's like a playground slide I think. Once you decide to slide down it, there's no way to change your mind, so you might as well go all the way down it. There's no stopping once you've started.

"Matías, open up! Wake up!"

It's my father, whose voice pierces the viscous layer of protection afforded by my dream state. There's nothing I can do about it now. I'm awake. So I open my eyes. The sky is lit up in purple Technicolor. It looks fake. The sun set while I was sleeping. I've been sleeping for a few hours, I guess.

"Matías, wake up right this instant!"

"Just a second."

I grab the bottle of Valium—stolen from my mother's night table—and toss it in the dresser drawer that's filled with my crusty nail clippings, bus tickets, rubber bands, and a pile of old envelopes with stamps from the album *Historia del Hombre.*

I finally open the door:

"Ah . . . some of us work, and some of us take lovely long afternoon naps."

"We ran a race in gym class today. I was wiped out."

"Wash up and change out of your uniform. I want you to come with me to Jumbo to pick up some things for tonight."

"I really don't feel like it."

"It's an order."

"Give me twenty minutes, then."

"Fifteen."

"Fine."

I go into the bathroom, shower, and watch as the foam from the shampoo slides down my legs to my feet and disappears down the drain. Suddenly I'm overwhelmed by this compulsive wave of hysterical crying, like an attack of some sort racking my body, but the rushing water drowns out the noise. The hot water crashes down in short, sharp little threads onto my skin, which is indifferent now to the heat and cold. My body jerks spastically in the shower, but my sobs disappear as fast as they came when I turn off the water.

I take a deep breath.

I wipe off the mirror. My face is bright red and swollen, teetering over the rest of my pale, wet body. I feel totally weak and embarrassed.

"It sounds like you're the sick one."

That comment continues to echo in my brain. I turn on the cold water to brush my teeth, but I'm distracted by the blood that flows from my gums. Scary. I stop, not before reminding myself that what happened, happened. It's over. Starting right now, this very moment, I am absolutely, totally, essentially alone, and if I wasn't before, then it was only because I didn't realize it.

That's all. It's over.

My father is driving down Kennedy. We're in the Volvo. Something's wrong with him—he's really tense and jumpy, I can feel it. He's also not saying much. The speedometer reads 140 kilometers per hour.

"You're going kind of fast, aren't you?"

"Don't worry. Everything's under control."

I look at him out of the corner of my eye, annoyed. He's wearing my blue Polo shirt and a pair of pants that are also mine. He doesn't look as young as he usually does. For once, he almost looks like the forty-three-year-old he really is. But I'm the only person who sees that; I guess everyone else who looks at us—if they look at us at all—just see a guy, not my father.

"Are you all right?" I ask him in an effort to start a conversation.

"Everything's under control," he says as he wipes his nose with his shirtsleeve. "Relax, nothing's going to happen. Don't worry, you're the last person to be in danger of anything."

He smiles, satisfied. Laughing, even. Maybe he's only kidding around or something.

"I don't know if anyone's ever told you this, but you never smile," he then says to me.

A question not worth answering. But I answer it anyway.

"Maybe I don't have any reason to smile."

This leaves him silent for a few seconds. Then he says, "Um, what was I going to say to you?"

"I don't know."

"No, don't worry. It was nothing. No big deal."

This is pretty typical with him. Whenever he's unsure about something, or in a strange mood, or needs to talk about something uncomfortable, he replaces the awkward silence with these meaningless conversation fillers that don't do much more than exercise his jaw muscles.

"What I was going to say was . . . this attack on the police force . . . did you hear about it?"

"Vaguely."

Silence takes over the car once again.

"Hey, you gave me back the keys from Reñaca, didn't you?"

"Yeah. Yesterday morning."

"Oh, right. So did you have a good time? Did you get back very late?"

"I called you, don't you remember? From Las Rejas. Don't you remember?"

"Oh, that's right. I was thinking about something else."

"Are you sure you're all right?" I ask him.

"I said I was. Stop it already, will you?"

There's definitely something wrong. I can tell. But I can also tell that it's probably not worth it to hound him. If he doesn't want to talk about it, I'm not going to make him. Fine. There's nothing to say anyway. And I don't think he's too interested in what I'm thinking.

I turn on the radio: Grace Jones singing "La Vie en Rose." I go to change it.

"Leave it," he barks. "I like her."

"I suspected as much . . ."

He doesn't say a word, and drives even faster.

Grace Jones reminds me of Flavia Montessori. But that's ancient history now. I don't want to allow her, or anyone from that class, or that group, to enter into my thoughts right now. I've thought about all of them way too much already.

I look at the speedometer: 120 kilometers. The Jumbo is just up the street; I can almost see it. Just as the song ends, we pull into the parking lot.

"I knew this fucking place was going to be full of people," my father says as he looks for a parking spot in front of the supermarket. "These people go crazy when they shop. They say that just about anything could happen this Thursday, and that the stores might even run out of everything as a result."

We find a spot next to a lime-green BMW that makes my father frown, as if some miserable fate has come over him.

"Let's go. We don't have a lot of time. I haven't even gotten dressed yet and your mother told everyone to come over around nine."

As I grab a shopping cart, he looks the other way, so naturally I end up pushing the thing around the store. This shopping warehouse—which is what this place is—is jammed with people. There's a little musical band, all dressed up in green and white uniforms, playing this Ray Coniff type of music. I can also hear a Muzak version of some song from *Saturday Night Fever,* coming out of some overhead speakers. The saddest part of all, though, is my father. Despite his semicool cowboy boots, boots that Rusty wouldn't hesitate to kill someone for, he catches on to the tune and starts to whistle along. Oh my God. So pathetic.

"Esteban, what a surprise! What a pleasure to run into you."

As I turn around, I see my father's face take on a frozen, funereal look. It's very unflattering.

"Eynard, in this neighborhood? I thought you lived in Talca."

My father thrusts his hand forth, with an enthusiasm even faker than the models that were offering little tastes of ravioli in the front of the store. This must be the famous Eynard Enger, I think. It's not that he's that famous, actually, but there was a time when my father dropped his name a lot, always talking about his avocados, cherimoyas, and exotic nuts, as if he were some kind of god or something. That's what Eynard is famous for.

He's older than I would have guessed, but better looking too. He's got short hair, pure gray, and he's wearing a green woolen jacket that gives him this little Alpine flair. At his side, shrouded in silence, stands a short woman, with a pretty serious hair-dye job. She's probably around fifty, even though she looks like she

could be his granddaughter. It's not because she's so young looking, but she has this weird, slightly unpleasant quality that
makes her seem immature and dependent on him.

"Esteban, this is Pochi, my niece."

The woman, who has huge green eyes that dominate her entire, wrinkle-free face, looks at my father with an intensity that
can only be described as hatred.

"Hello. Nice to meet you. This is my son, Matías."

I look up in response and take a step back, leaning against our
shopping cart. She also retreats; I can tell she's pretty uncomfortable. And if I don't quite know what her anger is all about, I
can pretty well put two and two together, because without wanting to or meaning to, I am now, because of the introductions, in-
extricably linked to her.

"Matías," my father says, "why don't you run ahead? There
are still a few things we need. Pick up some things to drink—
you know how these people like to drink. You can pick everything out. We're, uh, short on whiskey, you could get some vodka
too, some gin—María Teresa only drinks gin, don't forget. Maybe
a bottle of Napoléon, I'm not sure. You go and check. And get
some snacks: some cheese, olives, you know. I'll catch up with
you in a minute."

I move away, past the recently washed and shining-as-if-they-
were-plastic vegetables. My father stays behind, talking to Eynard. Pochi, on the other hand, moves away from them. It's as if
her legs can barely support the weight of her body. Obviously,
she's Hilda Escudero's sister. Hilda Escudero, Eynard's famous
niece. That's the connection. I've never met Hilda, of course. Nobody has. Except Eynard, Pochi, and my father, of course, who
was her lover a long time ago. I know all this because he told
me himself. Not the dirty details, but I got the general story
line. He limited himself to the basic facts. He was once involved
with an older woman; an older, slightly insane woman was all
he ever told me.

"I'm only telling you this because you're a man now. These things happen with men," he said to me about two years ago. "It's not a big deal, and I don't want you to be alarmed at all: your mother and I are not getting a divorce, so don't worry about that. It was my mistake, a grave mistake, and I'm prepared to pay for it. I just wanted you to know, so if you ever hear a fight or anything, or feel like something's wrong, don't worry about it. You see, Hilda can be kind of melodramatic, and she likes to stir up scandals when she can."

Of course, she stirred this one up good.

My mother and my sisters found out, of course. It was a pretty big mess, loud and unpleasant, and totally predictable too, because it wasn't the first time my father was unfaithful. Everyone knew about that. But this was the first time that it was a public thing, because Hilda had gone around talking about it, and even worse, she fell in love with my father; so in love that she kind of went crazy.

The other thing that was different about this affair was that Hilda wasn't just anyone. Or at least, she wasn't just any common girl. She was connected to someone my father did business with, a pretty important guy involved in the import-export business my uncle Sandro ran at the time. His family (especially on his father's side) wasn't much of anything to speak of socially, but Eynard Enger had his connections and if he found out that his unmarried niece was running around with one of his colleagues, he just might put an end to all their business together and send all of them straight to hell.

I learned those details from my sister Francisca, who took on the role of supporter and advocate for my mother throughout this whole battle, which actually had to do more with pride and self-respect than true love and hurt feelings. My mother moved pretty stealthily—I think she may have even hired a private detective for a while—and found out every last thing there was to know about Hilda. For example, that she lived in an apartment complex on a squalid, run-down block near Avenida Grecia, near the Estadio Nacional, and that she worked in some kind of laboratory on the same street. This was an important piece of information, because immediately after discovering this, my mother stopped buying that company's medicine and instead bought from the competition. According to Francisca, who really got off on this whole scandal, my mother also found out that Hilda wasn't a dumb floozy at all; in fact, she worked out at a gym, she was a cyclist, and she didn't make a bad living at all, considering she had to support her mother as well as an unmarried sister who had a child of her own.

Even if Francisca hadn't told me the whole story, I still would have found out about it, since I once woke up in the middle of the night, to my mother's screams:

"How could you get involved with some menopausal middlebrow, who, to lay insult on injury, sings in a church choir? Remember this, Esteban: I will never, ever forget this happened. Really, how could you have such bad taste? This is the lowest, the lowest you've gone. How could you play games with someone like that? Hilda may not be much of anything, but at least she has a heart. And I'm telling you . . . I *sympathize* with her. She must really regret ever having set eyes on you. She really should have lost her virginity to someone with a few more scruples than the likes of you."

That legendary night marked the beginning of the end of "the Hilda Escudero saga." The final moment was when the poor woman suffered a guilt attack and decided to call my mother. The whole thing backfired on her, and whatever my mother spat out at her was enough to drive even the most remorseless person to a confessional. Hilda was no easy bait.

The ordeal ended up with Hilda fleeing to Ecuador, where she got a job working at a lab in Quito. I found that out because one day a letter for my father arrived at our house, and Carmen, who loves intrigue and gossip, passed it along to my mother, who opened it up and laughed her head off at what she read:

. . . Sometimes, I think I made the wrong choice. Ecuador is so close. I should have gone to the North Pole, as far away from you as possible. But I don't think I could ever forget about you, not even there. Every day, do you know what that's like? Every day I check the paper for flights to Santiago, and I write down the departure times. I envy all those passengers who can fly to you, even though they don't know it themselves . . .

The famous Eynard Enger broke down after that, and lost his prestigious avocado trees, cherimoya fields, and walnut groves. The notice appeared in the paper. And so ended the profitable business relationship. My father is still connected to him, though, and doesn't quite know what to do about it, I can tell.

"Would you like some?" asks a heavily tanned model.

"Sure, only a little, though. I'm not crazy about Martinis."

"But this is Italian. The real thing."

"Fine. I'll take two bottles."

The girl seems overjoyed. Like they say, it doesn't cost anything to be nice. I push the cart toward the rest of the liquor. There are two more girls standing there, one promoting Pisco Capel and one offering a selection of Mitjans liqueurs. I look at the labels: almost all imports. I pull bottles off the shelves at random: Johnnie Walker Black Label, Stolichnaya, three Tanquerays, a Napoléon Cointreau, Bacardi, four six-packs of Heineken, two tequilas with worms at the bottom.

I then make my way over to the deli counter and the cheese section where I bump into Pochi, who stumbles as she is moving toward me. I stop the cart, turn halfway around, cut through the laundry detergents and the spaghetti section, and make a little circular trip, back to where I started. Pochi continues shuffling forward, though, only this time, she's turned her back on me. She's wearing a blue overcoat. The store musicians, meanwhile, are playing military marches.

Pochi turns the corner and starts up the aisle with all the drinks, heading for the woman promoting the Italian Martini. Then something happens, because instead of talking, they start arguing. Pochi takes her handbag, and using it as a shield, pushes the startled promoter to the side and then takes advantage of the moment to suck down a giant gulp of the Martini Bianco. The woman gets really angry now and calls the other promoters over, all of whom are pretty pissed off as well. The three of them start talking, all at once, but Pochi just starts laughing. She laughs so loud that I have to look down, just out of embarrassment for her. She keeps laughing, and drinking that Martini Bianco.

"Madam, for goodness' sake, please!" the Pisco Capel lady pleads with her. "Veronica. Go call Mr. Iñiguez. Right away."

Pochi stops laughing now and looks at the promoters with the same look she gave my father earlier. This lady is definitely nuts, I think to myself. Her bright red cheeks and swollen eyes don't hide a thing.

"You bitches!" she shouts at them. "Don't think I don't know what you all really do for a living!"

Then she leaves, although not before giving one of the tables a good, hard shove, causing all the bottles of pisco to fall on the floor. A chorus of shattering glass resonates through the store, and the tiny pieces of glass scatter all over the floor.

I can barely believe what I'm watching. Pochi starts running away in her high heels, which create a slight problem for her smooth getaway. Her handbag trails behind her, like a dog refusing to go for a walk.

"The woman is drunk," the Martini lady says to me. "She practically drank everything we had. I think this was her fifth visit to our booth in the last ten minutes."

I look toward the front of the store, but Pochi is already gone. I push my shopping cart down the aisle, to the strains of salsa or Caribbean music or whatever it is the band is playing now, and then I reach the cash registers, but still no sign of Pochi. A group of customers in front of the jams and jellies confirms my suspicion. Pochi is now causing another sort of public spectacle.

There are so many people standing around whispering to one another and the music is playing so loud that I advance cautiously and put my shopping cart to the side. I push my way through the crowd to see what's happening. There she is, on top of a platform, holding a banner that says, "Happy National Holidays from the Hipermercado Jumbo." The band is now playing a limbo song, and Pochi starts dancing, gyrating her hips and moving her shoulders in perfect synchronization before my eyes and those of the flabbergasted crowd. But that's not all, she's dancing with a guy dressed up as an elephant. The guy, I realize, doesn't quite know what to do. It seems he can't see all that much from beneath his gray rubber suit and humongous elephant's trunk, which hangs almost all the way down to his belly button.

The surprised crowd of shoppers begins clapping in unison, encouraging Pochi, who then fearlessly takes off her overcoat, tosses her handbag in a corner, and starts grinding shamelessly with the elephant, who is trying to follow the rhythm of the music. This only encourages Pochi. She taps her heels against the floor to the beat of the music, then lifts her skirt up to show her underwear. Without any warning, in the middle of a fit of laughter, she suddenly grabs the elephant and wraps its trunk around her neck. The people watching stop cheering when the music stops, eliciting a deathly silence. The promoter scurries over with the store manager, and the elephant attempts to disentangle himself from Pochi, who doesn't want to let go.

My father comes up from behind me and grabs my shoulder. "We're leaving, Matías."

I'm wearing a jacket, a gray tweed thing. My mother's idea. She bought it for me, so she decided I should wear it tonight.

My father stands directly in front of me, on the other side of the living room. Recovered from the earlier disaster, I'm sure. His hair is still wet from the shower, and he's also wearing a tweed jacket, only his is brown. He's playing bartender right now, surrounded by the bottles we bought in the liquor store on Apoquindo. We left Jumbo in a matter of seconds, and neither one of us even dared to mention what we'd just seen or experienced. Now, at this party, it's like that scene never happened. All it took was a shower, a shave, and a splash of Azzaro, and now he's in perfect shape, flirting with María Teresa Ezquerra, no less, as he serves her a Tanqueray and ginger ale, plus a thinly shaven bit of lemon peel.

I'm not all that sure what I'm doing here, but it came about pretty simply: my mother came into my room and asked me if I was going out tonight. I thought about it for a second, and the truth is, I didn't know where else I could really go. So I said no, that I was staying in tonight.

"Fine, then. Put on that gray tweed jacket you never wear," she said. "If you're staying home, the least you can do is greet the guests. If there's anything I can't stand, it's those homes where the kids shut themselves up in their bedrooms when guests come. I won't put up with that kind of behavior here. Bea went to sleep over at Camila's, and Francisca is coming home late tonight, she's out studying, I don't know where. So if you stay, wonderful. But you better put an appearance in out here. And . . . put on that jacket."

It's not quite a party. A meeting is more like it. Or a dinner meeting, I don't know what the hell it is. All I know is that it's a giant waste of time for me. Everyone else seems to be enjoying themselves, though, from what I can tell.

Nobody pays any attention to me. It doesn't really matter. If it were up to me, I wouldn't say a word to any of these guests, but here I am, leaning against the wall, observing Carmen as she is serving baby plums wrapped in bacon. She's all dressed up in her formal uniform, minus her eyeglasses.

I should go back to my bedroom, I ruminate. After my father and I came home, I locked myself in there until my mother came in and started in with the tweed jacket routine. That was about an hour ago. I brought the telephone into my room—they finally fixed the wires—and started calling people and hanging up on them. I did that for about twenty minutes, I guess. First I tried calling Paz, at the number he wrote on the inside cover of the book, and nobody answered there, so I tried Juancho's, but the phone line there was busy, busy, busy, every time I dialed. Then I pulled out my pink Day-Glo wallet and my tiny address book and flipped through it from A to Z, looking for someone to call. As I was going through it, I realized that there wasn't a single person I wanted to talk to. Since I was bored and all alone, I decided to have some fun, so I called Guatón Troncoso. His mother answered the phone.

"Fucking Nazi, I know where you live."

And I hung up.

I wanted to call Miriam, but I didn't have her number; I never entered it into my little book. At that moment, I realized that I didn't have any of my friends' phone numbers, like, for example, Antonia and Nacho and Luisa and Lerner. Even Cox. None of them were in there. I guess there was no reason for them to be there, since I knew their numbers by heart. I remembered Nacho's parents' phone number, so I called him, but his father answered, so I hung up. Then I tried Luisa, and she answered the phone. And I hung up. Then Lerner. And I hung up again.

My memory, despite the Valium I had taken, remained intact. I even remembered this friend that my sister Pilar once had. She used to come over a lot, and I remember she had this little black book full of telephone numbers, but with no names. "If I can't remember the friend attached to the number, then what's the point of listing the number at all? Obviously, it would mean the person wasn't very important to me, right? Then I wouldn't really have any need to call them, would I?" she said to us one afternoon over a cup of tea. My mother, of course, decided that she was crazy. It didn't matter, though. The girl disappeared and never called Pilar again.

"Oh, Matías, there you are. Come and say hello."

My mother grabs me by the arm and pushes me into the bowels of the living room, that's glowing in the candlelight.

"Hello, how are you?"

"Hey, good to see you again . . ."

"Hey, how are you?"

"Hi, how's it going?"

"Hi, good to see you . . ."

"So nice to see you again . . ."

"Hello, how are you?"

"Hey, what's up?"

"Hi, how are you these days?"

After this series of salutations, I try to return to my original spot against the wall, but my father attacks next. I can tell he's been drinking a lot. It's on his breath.

"Matías, do me a favor. Go over to the bar, will you, and take care of the drinks. I have to go around and talk to all these people."

With no other choice, I park myself in the tiny corner behind the bar, and I begin to inspect the bottles, with much the same care and attention a pilot dedicates to inspecting his cockpit and all its dials before takeoff. Twists of lemon, lime, and orange peel. Little hunks of pineapple. Olives for dry martinis. Club soda, bottled water, tomato juice, Tabasco sauce, bitters, crème de menthe, tonic water. The works. I decide to fix myself a little Bloody Mary, *a la mexicana,* only without the pepper.

There aren't too many people here, but it's definitely the A-list, I can tell. My uncle Sandro Giulianni is here, alone, and I see my other uncle, Enrique Matte, impeccably dressed as usual. There are a few couples scattered around the room, none of whom I know, but from the look of them, I can tell they're all pretty wealthy. Negro Ezquerra is talking to someone, definitely a military officer of some sort; his haircut gives him away.

My uncle Sergio Vicuña is also here; he's the Chilean ambassador to Indonesia. The party is in his honor, and they're all treating him special because it's his saint's day. Standing next to him is his latest wife, Stella de Castro, looking much younger these days because of her recent plastic surgery. On his other side is this guy who's a dead ringer for Robert Mitchum. My uncle's regaling him with stories about the fabulous beaches of Bali. The guy is no movie actor, though; his name is Armando Ortúzar.

My mother is sitting in the middle of the room with my aunt Loreto and María Teresa Ezquerra, who's busy polishing off a glass of gin. With them is the very illustrious Meche Ellis de Ortúzar, probably the richest lady ever to set foot in our apartment. She's a millionairess, I know it for a fact. She's married to the Robert Mitchum look-alike, but everyone knows that she's the one who drives the bus. It was only because of her that he got elected to the Senate years ago. Among other things, she's also president of a foundation or two, a champion equestrienne, and the mother of two of the craziest, most fucked-up girls in Chile. Both of them were sent off to study in London years ago. Now they're back, and dedicating their lives to corrupting the youth of Santiago with their evil ways.

I prepare another Mexican Mary and eavesdrop on the conversation with Meche Ellis de Ortúzar:

"Well, I think there are different ways to go about it . . ."

"But you have to admit she's gotten exactly what she wanted," says my mother.

"Yes, but at a high price, dear, a very high price," says Meche.

"I don't know," says Loreto. "I know Aída never misses a cocktail party or a premiere, and she's always turning up in the magazines and all that business, but don't forget, she also manages to donate money to some worthy causes, which does help lots of people."

"But she's so vain and conceited . . ."

"Well, so what else is new? She's been that way all her life.

She's not totally self-involved. I mean, I don't think she's as narcissistic as you say."

"Well, we obviously don't agree, so what do you want me to say to you, Loreto?" answers Meche. "Her approach just isn't my style. In fact, I'll tell you the truth: I think it's pretty horrendous. Really, I think this entire country is letting certain values and morals slip away. This business of Regine's, for example. Don't you find it simply unacceptable?"

My mother pales visibly and remains silent.

"But it's fun," answers Loreto.

"Maybe so. But finding your photograph on the pages of *Cosas* magazine isn't exactly the height of elegance, is it? Maybe it's old-fashioned of me, but I still believe that a truly distinguished woman only appears in print three times in her life: when she's born, when she's married, and when she dies. Do you see what I mean?"

Meche Ellis might be a ballbreaker and a filthy-rich millionairess, but she's definitely not stupid. I reflect upon this as I mix myself another Mexican Mary and make a secret toast to her health. All of a sudden, my uncle Sergio Vicuña, the ambassador, barrels toward me. Abandoning my little Meche Ellis tribute, I down my drink in one gulp and prepare for his attack. He's the younger brother of an uncle of mine who died in Patagonia years ago. He drives me crazy.

"You're getting so tall, I barely recognized you, Matías."

"Well, you know what they say about weeds . . ." I counter.

"Yes, that's what they say, don't they?"

This uncle is unbearable, it's like I can't even stand to be around him for more than a few minutes without wanting to slap him. He literally makes my skin crawl. I don't know how old he is, but he's probably twice the age that he thinks he looks like. He was never very good looking, although he probably used to consider himself quite a stud. He now admits that he's old and has a round little potbelly. That's not his fault, I guess. Everyone gets old eventually.

"What can I get for you, *tío?*"

"A screwdriver."

"Coming right up."

"Make it with Stolichnaya, would you? I've been in Russia, you know."

He always aspired to be a diplomat, but according to my mother, he didn't have the brains for it. His connections and his persuasive personality usually managed to get him pretty cushy jobs at places like Lan and Codelco and the Compañía Sudamericana de Vapores. He's always lived outside of Chile. That explains his suave silk handkerchiefs, his silk shirts and straw hats.

"You know Stella has a son around your age," he says. "He lives in Boston, not far from New York. He's quite an intelligent kid. He'll be going to Harvard, which is quite a prestigious university. And you, Matías, what are you doing these days?"

"I go to high school. But mine isn't too prestigious."

My uncle never had any kids, because his first wife thought childbirth would ruin her fabulous figure, and her body had been the main reason he'd married her in the first place. She drank way too much, and her brain turned into mush. The alcohol led to a brain tumor, and the cumulative effects of her mental and emotional decadence, combined with her endless self-obsession, eventually took their tolls. She would go to parties and say really dumb things to people, and that's when everybody caught on that she was losing her mind. She'd get really forgetful. By the time she was forty-five, she had the mind of about a four-year-old. My uncle then sent her back to Santiago from wherever they were at the time, and she was put in a nursing home. She didn't die until about six years later, though, and by then, my uncle had a new wife, who was a Belgian ski fanatic. He even brought her to the funeral. That marriage didn't last too long. My grandparents died and they left him a ton of money which I guess he didn't want to share, so he decided to get rid of her and come back to Chile alone.

"You must come and pay me a visit in Jakarta sometime, Matías."

Typical. He's always saying shit like that—I don't believe a word he says. Even if I somehow made it there, I doubt the authorities would allow me anywhere near the Chilean Embassy.

"It's so far away, though . . ." I offer weakly.

"But you once said to me that you really wanted to visit. Remember? By boat, you said. We were in Reñaca, and that friend of yours, the surfer, was asking me all those questions about Bali and Nauru. He said that the two of you were planning a trip by boat, so you could stop at all the islands. You'll definitely want to stop in New Caledonia, Stella loves it there. You know, I've got contacts at the steamship company, Sudamericana de Vapores. You just say the word, and we'll get a boat, with a captain to take you around . . ."

"Thanks for offering, but I doubt I'll be able to come anytime soon."

"You could try, though, I'm sure," he says as he pours himself another healthy screwdriver.

My uncle thinks that being the Chilean ambassador to Indonesia is the epitome of sophistication. He can thank the Chilean military for that. When he arrived in Indonesia, he was working for this company, and all of a sudden his luck changed pretty drastically. An old schoolmate of his became the Minister of Foreign Relations, and so my uncle was made an ambassador practically overnight. That's how he got to go to all these exotic places: Jordan, Haiti, Kenya. He met Stella de Castro on safari in Kenya, just after wrapping up his second marriage.

I decided to mix myself another Mexican Mary before anyone can interrupt me again.

"You better eat something or else you're going to get drunk," Carmen says to me.

"What are those?" I ask her, pointing to the tray she's carrying.

"How am I supposed to know? Some American lady who spends her life making these things brought them over."

I try one of the little tan balls on the tray that are covered in tiny seeds. Meat. Raw meat. But it's not bad.

"What's the latest word on the news?" I ask Carmen.

"How would I know? I've been running back and forth between here and the kitchen. I haven't had a spare second to listen. Frei said the referendum is a fraud. He gave up the fight, and now there's rioting downtown."

Before all the guests had arrived, I had gone into the kitchen for something to drink, and Carmen had been there, mixing some salads, with the radio on.

"Frei is going to speak," she had said.

"Didn't he speak last week?" I ask.

"Yes, but that was in the Caupolicán. This is a smaller speech. It's more of a symbolic demonstration. He's joining up with some union members, Teamsters I think, at Almirante Barroso."

"So do you think the 'NO' might have a chance of winning, Carmen?" I ask.

"Listen, Matías. I'm a maid, and I'm poor, but that doesn't make me an idiot. Of course we're going to lose. That doesn't mean we shouldn't try to shake things up a little."

"You think the voting is fixed, then?"

"As my friend Iris says, this country is so corrupt that the military doesn't even need to think up an excuse for the corruption. All those fuckers will vote for the 'SI,' and so will all the rich people in Chile. In La Pintana, where I live, the majority of the people support that fucking Pinochet. You want to know why? Because he offered them some little shacks to live in. The suckers bent over and took it up the ass, and for that he got their votes. Traitors. People can be such scum. They really can. They deserve whatever they've got coming to them."

*   *   *

I pour some more tequila, add a splash of tomato juice, yet another Mexican Mary. I'm getting close to the bottom of the bottle, and I can vaguely see the worm floating around.

"Matías, be a love and pour me another gin and gin."

"Sure, no problem." I pour the drink.

María Teresa Ezquerra moves away, delighted, and walks over to Stella, whose skin is looking majorly bronzed, from Bali, I guess, or Nauru.

I finish off the tequila, bite into the worm, and take a good look around. Meche Ellis is still talking about tact and good taste, and my aunt Loreto is still trying so hard to absorb everything she's saying. I look at my uncle Sergio, who's talking with Negro Ezquerra and some military officer. I overhear:

"General Leigh announced he was voting for the 'NO,' " says Ezquerra. "Do you think he should be taken seriously?"

"The air force is completely under control, I can promise you that. Leigh made a big mistake by confronting one of my men. I'd be surprised if he's still alive right now."

"They say he was one of the tougher ones," says my uncle Sergio, just to have something to add to the conversation.

In another corner of the party, Stella is entertaining a group of women with stories about her children, who live all over the world. My mother, meanwhile, is whispering something into Uncle Sandro's ear that makes him turn red and then break into a sweat. When he realizes I'm watching him, he immediately drops my mother's hand, which he's been holding for a while.

My father then comes back into the living room and begins chatting amiably with Enrique and Robert Mitchum. Every so often, he gazes over toward my mother and Uncle Sandro, who are still deep in conversation. Both of them are pretty drunk by now.

"How is everything?" my father asks. I can tell he's come over because this is the best place to spy on my mother.

"The cops are attacking the protesters now," I say.

"I meant in here. The party. How is the party going?"

"Well, you can see that for yourself. Do you want another drink?"

I grab a glass, throw in some ice, along with a healthy splash of Johnnie Walker Black Label. Then I get a good look at him while he's not paying attention. There's a thin layer of white powder just under his nose. I move a little closer and try to wipe it off for him. Startled, he jerks back and quickly jumps away from me, looking at me like a little lost puppy. But he only lets his guard down for a fraction of a second, then snaps back right away.

"What's your goddamn problem?" he spits out at me, and then he pushes me. Hard.

That was what I was waiting for. I knew it was coming. The jerk. I can see out of the corner of my eye that my mother catches our little scene from across the room. Instead of coming over, she stands up and claps her hands, announcing gaily:

"All right, everyone, dinner is being served. It's a buffet, American-style self-service, so please help yourselves to as much as you'd like."

Carmen opens the dining room doors and turns on the light. The table is piled high with food and flower arrangements.

"Rosario, you've outdone yourself," says Aunt Loreto.

I abandon my post at the bar and head for the dining room. My father is right there, his knuckles white from gripping his drink so tightly. He's confused, all right. Uncle Sergio comes over to the table and studies the astonishing variety of meats, salads, lobster, fruit, artichokes, and every imaginable delicacy on the table.

"Who says there's no food left in Chile?" Uncle Sergio says, smiling broadly. "The nerve to say that in Chile there's nothing to eat but lamb and venison . . ."

He's so totally predictable. The rest of the guests titter at the snappy humor offered up by my uncle, the worldly ambassador. I think about it for a second, but decide there's really nothing to think about. I've got to say something, so I open my mouth:

"If you went for a drive through the slums for once in your life, maybe you wouldn't think that."

My uncle's eyes narrow, and his face turns bright red, livid. Ready to explode. Nobody says a thing, and I don't dare breathe. But I don't waver either.

"Sergio, please excuse Matías," interrupts my mother. "This child has had a little too much to drink, I fear. He's got no right . . ."

"*Who's* drunk, Mother?" I interrupt her.

"Let's end it, Matías, or we'll have a scene right here and now."

I look over at my father, who doesn't say a word. Neither does Uncle Sandro.

"Go to your room! I want you out of here this instant!" she shouts at me.

Without a glance in any direction, I leave, go through the kitchen, and head for my father's room. Calmly, I walk in, lock the door behind me, and look around for his checkbook. I find it and tear one out. It's the last check. On the night table, I spot his wallet, pick it up, and take out all of the cash inside, plus the lone little silver envelope sitting beneath it. Slightly shaking, I open the bedroom door, but nobody's there. Moving faster now, I go into my room, grab my keys, my wallet, my sunglasses, my copy of *The Catcher in the Rye,* and the Valium. Then I head for the front door.

"Where do you think you're going?" shrieks my mother in front of all the guests, who are now dead silent.

"I don't think it's any of your business."

"Esteban, say something to him. Hit him. Something."

"Matías, now calm down. Don't do something you're going to regret. Be reasonable, I know you . . ." my father stammers.

"That's a lie. No one knows me at all."

I don't even know where I am; what I do know is that I'm way out of my territory.

The bus I'm sitting on is empty, except for me and the driver, who's wearing his bus driver's black parka. Songs by Victor Jara and Silvio Rodríguez are playing on the radio—the Cooperativa, that is. Every so often, the music is interrupted by news flashes about arrested protesters and people being detained by the police.

As I look from the bus window, I see a line of shanties, lurking in the shadows, the wrecked chassis of a minivan, and endless streets of empty lots. Little groups of men are huddled together on the street corners. This must be La Pintana, I surmise, but I'm not sure. I wouldn't dare ask.

I'm at the south end of the city, near the Américo Vespucio bypass road, which we crossed a few minutes back. I thought of getting off there, along with a fat guy in a leather jacket who was the last one to get off, but the area seemed kind of sketchy. Avenida Vespucio is one of those wide, desolate avenues with creepy, dingy-yellow streetlamps. The apartment buildings lining the avenue are littered with graffiti and posters in favor of the "NO" and protesting the CNI. That's about it. As I looked out from the bus, there wasn't a single car in the street, so the idea of getting off there, alone and exposed to God only knows what, was not exactly a tempting one. So I stayed on board. Big mistake. The neighborhood got about ten times worse. No lights, no buildings, no nothing except for some scaffolding around cruddy, rubbly vacant lots, and scuzzy-looking men hanging around this shantytown.

"Okay, kid, this is it. Last stop."

"Is this a bus stop?"

"No, it's my house."

"What time does the next bus come, then? Do you know?"

"Well, we're here, and I'm done for the evening. I don't think there are any more buses from here tonight. Walk up past that bus stop up there and then keep walking straight. About twenty blocks away you can catch another one."

When I get off, the driver turns off his headlights. The more I walk, the darker the neighborhood gets. I take off my watch and take my wallet out of my pocket and stuff both of them inside my jeans. My mind is racing, and I'm freaked, terrified. I don't know what to do. They're going to kill me here. I'm surely dead, I think. This is it. Okay, what? I try to think rationally. I don't have much of a choice, so I start walking down the muddy street, making my way through piles of MIR pamphlets proclaiming the need for insurrection and revolt.

It sure is quiet here, I think to myself. The only sound is that of my feet hitting the pavement. Looking up, I see through the windows covered in plastic to the blue, glowing light and low hum of the television sets inside the houses here. Then there's the sound of the radio. Hundreds of radios, emitting protest songs, all in Spanish. Not a disco tune among them. I'm definitely lost, I think to myself as I begin to panic again. I'm really in for it. They're going to kill me, I know it. I just hope it isn't too painful.

The scene at my house was pretty heavy but I had to do it. I still think so. As I went down in the elevator, I wanted to burst into tears, but I was so confused that my mind didn't know how to react to so many impulses. When the elevator doors opened and the doorman looked up, I knew I had to get out of there, so I just ran. For blocks and blocks I ran, until finally I was sweating so much, sweating off all the tequila I drank, getting rid of it and clearing out my system. The more I ran, the freer and lighter and cleaner I felt.

I look at my watch: 1:10 A.M. Curfew time soon, and I have to figure a way out of here, to get back to civilization. I've wasted enough time already.

*   *   *

I ran and ran. I ran so much, I ended up in Providencia, until
I finally allowed myself to slow down to a walk. I wandered
around for a while, eventually getting to the corner of Suecia and
General Holley, where the pubs were all open. There were cars
and lots of noise in the street. I decided to go into one of the pubs,
you know, have a drink, use the bathroom, and then maybe get
a little hit off my father's silver envelope, but the bouncer at the
door wouldn't let me in.

"You're underage. I can't let you in."

"Here, how about some money . . ."

"You're drunk. Get out of here."

I was sweating buckets at that point, but I still made a go of it,
trying to push my way past the bouncer. That didn't work too
well, though. Quick as a flash, he grabbed my wrist and twisted
it behind my back.

"Don't be an asshole, kid. I could beat the shit out of you if I
wanted." Clearly, this Neanderthal would have no qualms about
killing me, I realized, sobering up slightly. Then I saw something
that distracted my attention. Sitting at a table, a round table
with a little candle in the center and several empty glasses
around it, was my aunt Loreto Cohn. Her hair was all messed
up, and she was wearing a flimsy, transparent blouse, not that
it made any difference since most of the buttons were undone,
anyway. Next to her was a dark-skinned guy with a steely look
on his face. He had buzzed hair, military style, and was definitely
no older than twenty-five, at the most. She was caressing his
face. He was playing the tough-guy/hard-to-get type, and she was
looking like a total slut, stroking him like that. She had way too
much makeup on, as well. A slightly more normal couple, sitting at the table next to them, watched them, visibly grossed out
by the scene they were witnessing. When the buzz head turned
away, Aunt Loreto would pull him closer to her and kiss him,
staining his neck with her hookerish red lipstick.

"Why don't you just go home, kid?" the bouncer asked me.

"Why don't you go to hell?"

I said it and then, just as fast, tore out of there. The bouncer didn't even attempt to chase me.

I ended up a few blocks away, near Juancho's, where I thought I'd try to get hold of the great Alejandro Paz of Chile, again to tell him what was going on with me right then. I didn't even know him all that well, but that was exactly the reason I felt like I could confide in him.

"Paz has been detained and is unreachable right now," Toro told me, all official. "I was talking with the cops earlier today, but there's nothing we can do right now. He's been accused of subversive actions, and supposedly, he was at some kind of illegal meeting with a group of people from the university. The cops went through his little apartment on Lastarria, and they found a bunch of 'suspicious' books and pamphlets. I think they'll let him out by tomorrow morning."

"Are you saying that Paz is a terrorist?"

"No, no, I don't think so. But he's definitely an idiot. The police have a witness who claims to have seen him around Macul, spray-painting things in support of the 'NO.' "

"But . . ."

"No buts, Matías. That's illegal. He's a university student, not a soldier. He should know better than to mess around with that. He deserves what he got."

All the people at Juancho's, and there were a lot, were dancing to Blondie, totally oblivious, as if nothing at all were amiss. I was just about to order a Mexican Mary when I noticed a new guy behind the bar, sporting a trendy blond hairdo and a smart little tie.

"Who's *that?*"

"Look, I know you think Paz is one-of-a-kind, but he's not irreplacable," said Toro.

When I turned to speak, Toro was already onto something else, so I grabbed a straw from the bar and went into the bath-

room. Empty. I closed myself up in a stall, opened my silver envelope, which wasn't an origami but a little piece of silver foil,
like those bonbon wrappers. This one, however, was filled with
three or four grams of coke. I tested the goods with my little finger. My eyes watered as the coke hit my tongue. Good stuff, I
thought to myself. Nothing but the best for my father. So with
my brain sufficiently anesthetized and an insurmountable lump
in my throat, I left the bathroom. I had no other choice but to
order from the new blond guy tending the bar: a straight vodka
and a pineapple juice on the side, which I paid for in cash. For
some reason, I couldn't enjoy the drink, couldn't enjoy the hip
little crowd in there, couldn't enjoy the music. From his DJ box,
Chalo was playing things like Boston, Yes, and a bunch of other
nostalgia tunes. Then, like a bad scene from some television
rerun, I saw Miriam making her way over to me. It was like she
just appeared out of nowhere. She had noticed me right away,
leaning against the bar. I gulped the vodka down and made my
way out of there as fast as I could. I tried to find a cab, but there
weren't any. Only buses.

I got on without thinking twice.

I didn't feel so good, so I went over to a seat by the window. I
sat there, looking outside, trying not to think about too much,
but my speeding mind kept wandering. Where did my father get
such good coke? Why was my uncle Sandro holding my mother's
hand? Flashes from the evening.

After that, I don't really remember what exactly happened. Or,
well, I remember, but I don't really understand it. It was like I
just let my mood carry me where it wanted to go, and my body
drifted along with it. Little by little, the bus moved away from
the neighborhoods I knew, going farther and farther outside the
city center. As the bus crossed Tobalaba and went past the
Grange School, I thought about getting out, but something kept
me nailed to my seat. Then the bus reached Plaza Egaña, which
was like the outer limit to me. The scene was like something out
of a Brain Damage concert, or one of those places where all those

groups from school play, like the Manuel Plaza gym. Anyway, that was where I should have gotten out, but I didn't. I'm going too far out, I thought, might as well stay on the bus until it turns around and heads back toward the center. But the center of town never came back into view, and the bus kept barreling ahead, moving farther and farther south.

As we approached these ramshackle houses, there were only a few people still left from when I had originally gotten on the bus back at the other end of Santiago. We passed by the dirty buildings around the Plaza Grecia, passed the little vending carts that sell french fries, like the ones by the beach in summertime. There, more people got on the bus, some of whom sort of scared me. None of them even noticed me, and I just sat there, looking out the window, like some hapless tourist.

"Hey, you. What time is it?"

I can't really even see the person asking me. All I know is that it's a man, and from his voice, that he's young. He's probably got a knife hidden under his pants. All right, I'm dead, it's gonna happen any second now.

"I don't know, I don't have a watch," I answer in a cold tone.

After focusing, I see that the guy is wearing an American army jacket that he probably got at some kind of used-clothing store, and a pair of clunky black army boots, of the painful but sturdy variety. He doesn't seem like a murderer, I think to myself. But then again, I can't see much of anything because of the dim streetlights around here. He looks around my age.

"You want to buy some weed?" he then asks.

"No."

"I've got good shit. From San Felipe. It's not skunk weed. Seriously, it's good stuff."

"I believe you, I just don't smoke, that's all."

"Well then, get the hell out of here, asshole."

"Yeah, all right."

The guy, thank God, moves away then. I take a deep breath.

I'm exhausted, and tired too. And cold. I have this strange combination of headache, anxiety, and this nagging, draggy feeling of depression. I keep walking; far off in the distance I can make out a bonfire. Someone must be burning paper, I guess. As I get closer and closer, I realize that it's tires. There's a lot of people milling around, shouting.

I move away and turn a corner. All of a sudden, a dog races onto the street, barking at me as if I were Jack the Ripper stalking the neighborhood or something. The sharp sound of the dog's barks cuts through the night, ricocheting off the tin roofs. The sides of all the buildings and gates in this area are covered with military signs. I don't even recognize any of the street names around here, that's how foreign it is to me. There's no people, no cars, no buses, just the sound of that dog barking away. My heart pounds like crazy.

A few more blocks of this, and then a miracle appears. Out of thin air, a rickety old Opala taxicab passes right in front of me. It's something out of a slo-mo sequence in a movie. I yell, but the driver doesn't hear me. The taxi slowly moves away. I decide this might be my only chance, so I make a run for it. I run like hell, like never before, I'm running for my life, waving my arms around like a lunatic, until finally the Opala stops.

"Am I lucky I found you," I say to him, panting.

"Yeah, but I'm not going anywhere."

"Oh, but I've got to get back downtown."

"I'm out of service. Sorry."

"Please, come on . . ."

"Well . . . I can take you as far as Departamental."

"Sir," I say, lowering my voice a notch or two. I take a few deep breaths. "I've got to get back downtown. It's an emergency, you see. There's, uh, been an accident, nothing serious, but I've got to let my parents know. My brother's under arrest. He just crashed his car into a little retarded boy who was walking in the street."

"Well, can't you just call them on the phone?"

"I tried, but it doesn't work. Please. I'll pay you whatever I have to, really."

The guy studies me. I think he can tell I'm pretty desperate, and that even though I'm obviously lying, I'm serious.

"Please, I'm begging you. I mean, you can see how important this is to me, can't you?" I plead.

The driver, who's got eyeglasses and a beard, looks at me for a second, and thinks about it.

"Here," I say, shoving some money through the opening in the window.

"All right, kid. Get in."

We take off. The Opala creeps through these foreign city streets, past the bodegas and the hardware stores. As we're driving, I take out a wad of bills and hand it to him. It's probably enough to get me all the way out to Viña, and that's including gas and tolls. But that's all irrelevant right now. I don't really care about the money, I just want to get out of where I am.

"What street are we on?" I ask the driver, just to make conversation.

"I'm about to get on Gran Avenida." The driver continues.

On the radio, it's Lonely Hearts' Hour at this time of the night, and some lady DJ with a sultry voice is reading her listener mail on the air. The letters are all about breakups, unrequited love, secret lovers, that sort of thing. The taxi driver takes advantage of the empty streets and races along, passing through red lights. I don't care, though; I barely notice. All I want to see is the Torre Entel and the Virgen de San Cristóbal. I just feel like getting back to my neighborhood.

"Where are we now?" I ask, after a few minutes of silence.

"El Llano."

I don't recognize anything at all. Maybe I've been here before, but there were more cars and noise then. I try to remember the name of a girl I once knew who lived around here, but I can't. We went to a disco that was called Kayman, or something like that. I don't know, maybe it wasn't around here at all. The taxi driver, thank God, doesn't try to strike up a conversation with me or anything. He doesn't even ask me about my brother and the retarded kid. We just listen to the radio, and I barely even hear that. I'm alive, that's what I'm thinking about, and the fresh air comes in through the open window, cooling me down and drying off my sweaty hair.

We get to the Teatro Caupolicán. The metal security gates in front of the bicycle shop still have the spray-painted "NO!" and "Viva Frei!" on them. I notice on the store's front door there's a sign that says, "Down with the dictatorship."

"Fucking commies," says the taxi driver.

"Yeah," I say, just to stay on his good side.

We're getting closer. For real. I finally close the window and feel calmer all of a sudden, but I still don't understand anything, nor do I know what I'm going to do next. So I try to clear my mind and not to think about anything for the time being.

"All right, kid. Here's where I stop. You can get around from here easy, just watch out for the curfew."

"Thank you. Really. I owe you one."

The taxi driver doesn't say a word. I slam the door and he speeds away.

I'm on the Alameda, and there's buses and taxis and people everywhere. I can see red lights glowing out the window of a bar called Indianapolis. The Bee Gees are belting out "Stayin' Alive." Back to civilization, I think. Sort of.

I cross the street and walk over to Paseo Ahumada. A sanitation truck lumbers by, swishing the streets with soapy water. Just about all the stores are closed down.

I start walking again.

On a side street, I notice a bunch of little barefoot girls, rummaging through the garbage cans behind the row of stores. Inside a café, the waiters are wiping down the tables and stacking chairs on top of them. I go into a video game arcade, which is closing. They're not selling tokens anymore, but the place is still jammed with people, all of them male, all of them smelling like cigarettes. I stare at one guy who's playing Pac-Man. He's got on these bright white, immaculate Adidas sneakers, but from his manner I can tell he's a factory worker. I look around and catch sight of an older man in a trench coat, staring at me in an obsessive sort of way.

I decide to get out of there immediately, and continue walking, toward Plaza de Armas. On Calle Agustinas, a group of really cheap-looking hookers giggle among themselves, then call out to me: "Are you alone, little boy?"

Bad scene, I think. Really not a good scene at all. My options suddenly aren't looking too good. It's way too late to go home. I've got nobody to call, and there's nothing here that's going to do me any good. On the corner of Calle Huérfanos, there's a military checkpoint with two soldiers on patrol.

I look at my watch. Forty minutes before the curfew.

I run toward Compañía to hail a taxi. Then I suddenly see a huge red neon sign on the side of a building: CITY HOTEL.

The taxi slows down.

"Sorry," I say. "Forget it."

I walk over to the building, which has a glass-covered entrance hall separating the two separate buildings that make up the hotel. Not a soul is in sight.

I walk up to the reception desk and ring the little bell.

A big fat man waddles up to the desk. He looks like he hasn't slept in a few days, but seems like a nice enough guy. He's probably around fifty.

"Yes? How can I help you?" he asks, sort of puzzled.

I'm about to open my mouth, but I don't know quite what to say. It occurs to me all of a sudden that this is sort of strange, for a kid my age to go into a hotel and ask for a room at this hour of the night. Not knowing exactly what to say, I pause, studying the decades-old chairs in the sitting room.

"Good evening. Can I help you with something?" he asks me again.

"Yes," I say in an English accent. "I'd like a room."

"For this evening?"

"Yes. A single, please."

"You don't have any luggage?"

"Excuse me?"

"Handbags. You have luggage?"

"No. I lost them. At the airport."

"I see."

There's a slight silence.

"One room. Please."

The guy then pulls out an official-looking form for me to fill out.

"Do you have any identification?"

"I don't have anything. Stolen."

"I see. What is your name, please?"

"Caulfield. Holden Caulfield."

"Country?"

"New York. Manhattan."

"Excuse me, but are you with your parents? Where are they?"

"Buenos Aires. They're in Buenos Aires."

"And all of your luggage was stolen?"

"Yes."

"And what about your plane ticket?"

"Stolen too. Braniff. Tomorrow I'll call Braniff."

"This all seems awfully strange to me . . ."

"Please, just give me a room. Okay, I'm Chilean, but I do need a place to stay tonight, maybe for a few days. I've got the money, tomorrow I'll have even more. I haven't done anything wrong, I swear I haven't broken the law or anything. It's just a problem I'm having with my father. And my mother. Please. I'm begging you. If you want, I'll pay for my room right now."

I take out my wallet, and after looking at the prices, I pay for two nights.

"I don't know . . ."

"Come on . . . what is it to you? I'll pay extra if you want."

"All right," he says, and makes a note on the form.

"Thank you, thank you very much."

"Sign here," he says.

I sign my name on the dotted line. He gives me a key to room 506.

"It's in the front building. Cross over and take the elevator up to the fifth floor."

"Thanks. Really."

"There's no reason to thank me, Mr. Caulfield. Have a good night. And get yourself a little rest."

"I wish I could."

WEDNESDAY
SEPTEMBER 10, 1980

I'm bathed in red. My whole body is, in fact. From my window, I can make out the letters *C* and *I;* molded glass tubes filled with red neon illuminate the desk, the bed, the sheets, and my hands. There's no traffic outside, so I open the curtains to fully absorb the penetrating redness. The relentless neon pierces the curfew, which will soon be over.

It's five in the morning. And I'm still awake. Well, half awake. I slept a little, thanks to the Valium and my total exhaustion. I haven't dreamed, I've barely even slept, now that I think about it. When I woke up and saw everything soaked in red light, I knew right away where I was, and I wasn't scared at all. I remembered everything. I was in the City Hotel, room 506, in the heart of downtown Santiago. It wasn't far enough away, however, from what I was trying to escape.

But it's all right. This place is okay, I think to myself as I try to snuggle with this immense, stiff, unfamiliar pillow. The room reminds me of my grandparents' house—my Vicuña grandparents, that is. Their house was on Calle Ricardo Matte Pérez, and had a walled garden full of trees. Inside there were bells all over the place, just begging to be rung. That house, with its long rectangular pool, vines, poplar trees, and lemon groves, had that historical, Old World atmosphere. It was somewhere between rustic and refined. That's what this hotel is kind of like: an antique wooden dresser with soft edges and curved drawers; an ancient Grundig television set with a radio; a massive, elegant bathroom with blue and white tiles, like a chessboard, with a useless old bidet that looks like some kind of strange porcelain sculpture and a thick, distorted little mirror above the sink.

I decide to take a hot bath, mainly because it's something I could never do at home at this hour. I get up, go into the bathroom, and turn the hot water on. I try to get something on the Grundig, but at this hour, there's nothing on the FM stations. So I try the AM, and after flipping around for a while, I find an American military station playing some early morning jazz. I open the window and stick my head out. It's totally, absolutely desolate on the streets.

When I go back into the bathroom, the tub is just about full, and steam is rising from the water. I turn off the overhead light: there's another neon light in action, coming in through the bathroom window. When it lights up, the water takes on a strange, deep greenish hue. I submerge myself, and imagine that instead of water, it's really peppermint schnapps or crème de menthe, warmed up. I close my eyes, but that doesn't really do anything: it's still dark. Better to keep them open. The green water does add some atmosphere, and the jazz playing on the radio—Thelonious Monk, according to the announcer—completes the picture. I think to myself: don't ever forget this moment. You've been wanting to do this for a while now; you should've done this a long time ago.

I **step into** one of those elevators with a metal grille and elevator operator. It's just like in those old gangster private eye movies.

"Good morning," says the elevator operator, who's dressed in a green uniform, with a hat that looks like an upside-down coffee cup.

He closes the gates and the elevator begins to make its descent.

"Excuse me," I say. "But where did you get that hat?"

"I don't know, it's from the hotel. It's part of my uniform."

"Oh . . . I've been wanting to get one like that for myself. Do you know where I could find something like it?"

"I don't really know. But the best place to buy hats is on Avenida 21 de Mayo, at Donde. It's right nearby. People around here know the place. Ask anyone on the street."

"Thanks."

"Not at all. At your service."

I get out of the elevator, cross the hallway that separates the two buildings, and realize it's colder outside than I thought. Walking into the lobby, I hand over my room key to the guy at the reception desk who is a different guy from last night. I check my watch. It's ten-thirty in the morning. I should be in Spanish class right now. With Flora Montenegro.

"Where can I get some breakfast?" I ask the guy at the desk, who's scanning the newspaper *La Tercera.*

"Right out front, in the same building where your room is."

"Thanks."

I cross through the hall again and walk into a coffee shop, which looks like something out of an old black-and-white movie. Very few people are even eating breakfast: everyone's scanning their newspapers. Everybody seems to have at least two or three different papers, all spread out, and they're all taking notes. I sit down at a little round table in the corner, which leads out to a little enclosed garden with trees. From my table I can make out the bells on the cathedral.

"Good morning, young man."

"Good morning. I'd like some breakfast, please."

"Continental breakfast? American breakfast?"

I think of those American brunches in my house.

"Continental is fine. Listen, why is everyone reading so many papers?"

"They're foreign correspondents. Journalists. They're probably reading up for tomorrow."

The waiter then moves away, leaving me all alone, and bored, which makes me kind of uncomfortable. It's like I don't have anything to do, really. Except think. And remember. Eating is another, sort of a secondary thing about living alone, I realize. I guess I'd better get used to it, but it's kind of weird.

I pull out the check I stole from my father's wallet. Now is as good a time as any to fill it out. The waiter comes back, though, with a big tray with an elaborate silver service, including a teapot, a coffeepot, and milk.

"Hey, could you lend me your pen for a second?" I ask the waiter.

"Of course."

I pour myself some coffee and a bit of milk.

"Where can I get a paper?"

"Well, which one would you like, young man?"

"All of them, except *El Mercurio.* It reminds me of my father too much."

"Yes, sir, right away."

With the pen, I fill in the check and make it out to myself. I do it for enough money to keep me busy for a few days, but not so much to cause suspicion. On a napkin, I practice my father's signature. Easy, though, because he doesn't really even have one. I've done it before, for school stuff and tests and things. I sign the check. Perfect.

The waiter reappears with an orange juice, toast, and jam, along with a pile of the tabloids I asked for.

"We didn't have *La Tercera,* young man."

I look at *La Nación* but it just makes me sick, so I throw it on the floor. I open *Las Últimas Noticias* and read about a bombing attempt—they planted one in the Jumbo supermarket on Bilbao (not at the one on Avenida Kennedy)—and I skim an article called "What Will Happen If the 'NO' Wins?" There's also a list of detained persons, but Paz's name isn't on it. I go to the section entitled "Candilejas" and look at this week's offerings: *All That Jazz, Mad Max, The Tin Drum.* I then read all about Shawn

Weatherley, a.k.a. Miss Universe, who's hiding in the Carrera and is refusing to talk to reporters.

The waiter returns:

"Sign this, please, and include your room number."

This is great—I could really get used to this sort of thing. I take another sip of my coffee; it's got the taste of freedom, I think to myself.

"Waiter, I'll take some more coffee, please."

Beyond my reflection in the window of the hat shop, I notice a little mechanical monkey, tapping on the windowpane about every three seconds or so. It's been doing it for years, I can tell, because the glass is all worn down in that one spot.

The section of town I'm in right now seems ages older than the other neighborhoods in the city center. Thousands of people are milling around in the streets, transforming the area into sort of an open-air bazaar. Street vendors line the sidewalks, and the men are yelling out to one another, over the people pushing by, who are carrying plastic bags filled with fruit and vegetables from the Mercado Central that's a few blocks away.

The little monkey—who's wearing a hat like the elevator operator had—keeps tapping on the window, but nobody inside the hat shop acknowledges him. It's as if the inside of this place has nothing to do with the world outside those glass windows. It's like a museum or something. A hat museum, full of dust, and the familiar smells of gasoline, leather, and felt. The window is the most incredible thing, though: the prices are posted there, and even they seem like they're out of another decade, written by hand on little pieces of yellowing cardboard, Scotch-taped onto the glass.

I have to buy a hat, I decide. That's what I have all this money for anyway, right? And I've got plenty. After I finished my breakfast, I went out to the street and breathed in the morning mist, which fell down onto Paseo Ahumada. The street was full of people, and I was strangely affected by the scene. Affected, really, by this whole thing of experiencing something and being somewhere that was sort of prohibited. This was precisely the time of day for taking care of all the business that I miss out on when I'm usually in school.

At a newsstand, I asked where I could find the nearest branch of the Bank of Chile. It was just a few blocks away, a grand old building that looked more like a library than a bank. I went in through the revolving door, and once again, I went through this time warp thing. I felt like I had left the 1980s behind and entered into some BBC documentary about the stock market crash on Wall Street, or some other ancient topic like that.

Unlike most banks I'd been in, this one had the teller windows in a wooden rotunda area, hidden way in the back, which made me think of those old amusement park carousels. That's what it looked like, except for no colorful paint job. It just didn't seem like a bank at all. The vaulted ceilings, with marble columns and fancy glasswork, gave it the feel of an elegant old train station. Even the people approaching the windows looked like they were about to buy train tickets, not deposit money. Underneath a tremendous clock with Roman numerals, one of the bank tellers sat underneath a window decorated in gold.

I got in line behind a gray-haired man wearing a really ancient-looking suit that was just a little too tight, and shiny. Before I reached my turn, I got off the line I was on and turned around. You can't really trust a woman, I reasoned. They're more suspicious, you know; it's that maternal instinct that gives them the power to read minds and guess what other people are up to. Even when they shouldn't. Men, on the other hand, always identify with their own kind, so to speak, even their enemies. So I looked around until I saw a male cashier, a young guy; the kind of guy that never grew facial hair, and because of that, never learned how to shave. There were lots of people on his line, but I got on anyway. What rush was I in? The guy couldn't be over twenty-three, I figured, and he looked like some privileged kid from a high-class background who'd fucked up and ended up having to get married. A shotgun wedding, I bet. As he counted out bills, I checked him out, to see if he was wearing a wedding ring, and I was right. The knot in his tie, I noticed, was a little off, which calmed me down for some reason.

"Good morning," I said to him, and passed him the check.

"Identification, please."

I handed my card over, and he didn't even flinch. He looked at the number on the back of the card, asked me to sign it, and then stamped it. Then he counted out the bills.

"Not a bad gift, huh?"

"Yeah," I said. "My father gave it to me for a school trip. I still have to buy dollars, though."

"Where are you going?"

"We're going to Rio."

"I've been to Brazil myself," he said.

"Really? What's it like?"

"Time of my life. I promise you, it's great."

"Well, good."

"There you are."

I grabbed the wad of cash, and almost left him a tip but then I thought that would be sort of weird, so I left it at that. I actually felt kind of bad lying to him. The whole thing of him remembering Rio and relaying it to me, well, it was kind of depressing. What he should have said was something about me being in my prime, the best years of my life, the peak of my teenage experience or whatever. That I was lucky enough to have a father who threw wads of cash my way. But he didn't say any of that.

Standing there in front of the hat shop, I bite into a piece of cinnamon Freshen-Up and feel that familiar squirt on my tongue.

The monkey, that really old thing, continues his banging against the store window. I go in. A salesman, with a light mustache that almost looks painted on, appears, like magic, out of the shadows.

"May I help you, young man?"

"I'm just looking for now, thanks."

"Fine, fine."

The shop is filled with ancient, slightly decrepit cardboard cartons, like the boxes on Ricardo Matte Pérez, or those jars my grandmother always used to keep her marmalade in, or those metal molds for making gelatin.

"Sir, do you have hunting caps?"

"What kind of hunting do you mean?"

"To hunt for, oh, wild ducks, maybe. The kind that cover your ears. Like the ones that Goofy wears."

"New England style, you mean?"

"Yeah, exactly."

"Well, I'll have to take a look. There aren't too many ducks around here, you know."

"I know."

When he goes around to look, I browse around a little more. There are loads of ladies' hats in this place and tons of old black-and-white photos up on the wall, of deathly pale women wearing heavy lipstick, posing in the hats like some bizarre species of Hollywood vampire. All the photos are signed by the photographer, who I guess was pretty hot stuff in his day.

"I've got this one," interrupts the salesman, who, now that I get a closer look at him, reminds me of one of those movie mafiosi from the 1940s.

He shows me a hat, more or less what I expected. It's a cap with a visor and earflaps that hang down and come together under the lining. Flannel. Blue and black, like those Scottish tartan blankets.

"You don't have this hat in a solid color?"

"I have it in red."

"Red?"

"Yes, and it's exactly the same model. Red and black, I mean. This is the only fabric we work with."

"That's fine, then. I'll take it. The red one."

When the salesman disappears, I try on another red hat, like the one John Belushi wore in *The Blues Brothers*. And then I stick on my shades. Cool, I think to myself.

"Here you go, young man."

He gives me the hat, just the little cap I was looking for.

I take off the sunglasses, hang up the Belushi hat, and put the hunting cap on, cautiously, carefully.

"How do I look?" I ask the salesman.

"It looks very nice on you. Better than the black, I think. You seem more . . . more young, I guess. Innocent."

"I'll take it, then."

The military patrol is on the corner of Huérfanos and Ahumada, with reinforcements, like a truck with a humongous fire hose, and far more cops than they could possibly use. I notice a newsstand nearby, full of foreign papers. *O Globo,* from Rio, a bunch from Argentina, and one called *El País,* from Spain, that has a huge front-page photo of Pinochet wearing black sunglasses.

I decide to take my own sunglasses off. I don't want any trouble. I also take off the gangster/John Belushi hat that I couldn't resist buying. The hat goes pretty well with my new black jacket, the one I just saw in the window of an upscale boutique in the Galerías Crillón. I went in, tried it on, and the salesgirl said I looked awesome in it, that I should always dress in dark colors, she said. So I bought it right then and there, paid in cash, and left her the tweed jacket (the one my mother had bought me) as a gift.

I'm still looking at all the newspapers: the *Miami Herald,* the *Los Angeles Times,* the *New York Post.* Among them, almost lost in the piles, I see one paper that grabs my attention: a huge one with blue lettering and a picture of a young guy on the cover. He looks more or less my age, almost bald, wearing a T-shirt with the Roadrunner on the front, and a striped tie around his neck, like the kind I wear to school. It's exactly like the one I wear to school, I realize. The guy has this smirk on his face, and instead of looking into the camera straight on, he looks off to the side. The headline refers to him: "Josh Remsen: Out There on His Own."

At the foot of the photo, a tiny caption indicates that he's the same Josh Remsen, a musician, that Paz was always telling me about. The one who said "a person only feels isolated when surrounded by people."

"Can I have that newspaper?" I ask the guy behind the counter.

"The *Village Voice* you mean?"

"Yeah."

"It just got here. You're lucky," he says, and I pay him, the equivalent of about three American dollars, which I calculate as I look at the printed American price of sixty-five cents. But I don't really care. I would have paid even more. I grab the paper, roll it up, and with my shopping bag with the hat in it and the hunting cap in my hand, I approach Paseo Ahumada, feeling a little more sure of myself now.

The street is crammed full of people, and the big cannon on the Santa Lucía Hill booms out the time: twelve noon. I calmly breathe in. The cannon is just a tradition, not a terrorist bombing or anything. The little birds who can't differentiate fly off their treetop perches, hysterical from the roaring noise, and scatter off into the smog.

I go into the Burger Inn, with its plastic tables and American movie posters up on the walls, and I order a Rover and a chocolate malt. I settle into a corner table, as far away as possible from the windows that overlook the street vendors and all the chaos on Ahumada.

I open the *Village Voice* and begin to wolf down my Rover. By page 8, I already feel like I'm wasting my life away, and that instead of dealing with this stupid shit that's happening here, I could be there, in New York, where I'd really be able to live. As I look at the movie section, it becomes even more unbelievable to me. All that in one city, I think. Then I look at the music that's playing this week in Manhattan alone, and see a notice for that CBGB place that Paz is always dreaming about. He's right, though. He and I should get ourselves there. If he ever gets out of jail, that is.

"Madam, excuse me," I say to a woman sitting near me, who's eating some french fries. "Will you watch my food while I go to the bathroom?"

I go into the bathroom, close the stall door behind me, and put my plastic straw and little silver envelope to work.

"Thanks a lot. I really appreciate it," I say to the lady upon returning.

I look for the Remsen article, stick the straw in a paper cup, swallow the slightly bitter chocolate malt, and begin reading:

Josh Remsen . . . post-punk . . . anti-disco . . . raised on the Upper East Side of Manhattan, is now a musician living in the East Village. After years of aimless wandering that took him from the marijuana plantations of Jamaica to the toughest pubs in Dublin, this fragile, tense twenty-two-year-old kid, who never finished high school but inserts James Joyce in his erratic, lusty lyrics, has found, for the moment at least, that he finally has a home—in the East Village . . . where else?

Out of pure happiness, I start to shout out loud, as loud as possible. People at the other tables stare at me, as if I'm a deranged lunatic or something. I put on my sunglasses and my red and black hunting cap, roll up my *Village Voice,* and leave as if nothing happened. But everything *has* happened. Finally.

*   *   *

I turn off the black-and-white Grundig television set. I've just finished watching *Myriam,* one of my favorite made-for-TV movies. I've seen it tons of times by now, so when I went back to my room and turned on the TV and found that it was on, it was like an instant visit with an old friend, someone who knew me and was just like me. It was kind of comforting and made me feel a little better about being by myself.

After the movie is over, I check the time. It's now four-thirty in the afternoon. I still have a little bit of the Campari and tonic that the friendly elevator man brought up to me earlier. On the folding table are a couple of plastic bags from Falabella, full of the clothes I bought: Levi's, two corduroy Wrangler's shirts, T-shirts, sweaters, a pair of Top-Siders, socks, underwear, and a pair of yellow pajamas. I also stopped by a drugstore and stocked up on a bunch of stuff like toothpaste, deodorant, shampoo, and some Azzaro cologne.

From my window I can see Calle Compañía, heaving with buses now. I can also see the marquee for the Cine Real and the Cine Plaza movie theaters, where there's a double feature, two kung fu movies. I can also see into the offices in the building straight ahead, where there's a secretary typing away, with a bored look on her face. A man is picking his nose as he talks on the telephone. I've got the radio on, but the old Grundig doesn't get Concierto's frequency, so I settle for classical music on El Conquistador.

I flop down on the bed, open up the *Village Voice* again, and reread the article on Josh Remsen.

> "Your first record, *The Sleeper Must Awaken,* is all about the theme of innocence, and the loss of innocence as well, obviously. How the only form of salvation is hanging on to innocence. Josh, it's been two years since that album debuted, are you still innocent?"

"A person can't feel the anger and frustration I feel and still remain innocent."

"Why are you angry, then?"

"That's my problem, man. Not yours."

"Well, can't you elaborate a little?"

"Let's just say that I feel betrayed. By other people, by myself even, for trusting so many people. I believed in a lot of things back then when I made that album. In those days, I believed that work, creative work, I guess, could make a difference to people. Wrong. Maybe I shouldn't be so negative about it, I mean, some asshole could read about this and commit suicide, and then I'll get blamed for it . . . but that's how I feel. True, it's only my opinion. I do get this special kind of confidence here in New York, just from the fact that you can't trust anyone here. I may not know much about anything, but I do know that it's important to see things for what they are. There's nothing worse than not being able to make a decision. Indecisive people, liars, they piss me off. They're just a bunch of masochists who'll never amount to anything, much less produce anything worthwhile. They're always the ones that latch on to you. Like leeches. That's why I can't stand groupies, and fans in general, actually."

"You've made enough decisions on your own, though, haven't you? And you've created your own work. How do you feel about your latest album?"

"This is my second album now. It's a real follow-up to my last one. It was harder to make, it's a little scarier . . . much scarier, actually. I'm happy about everyone's reaction to it, but not so happy that I forget about other things that are lacking in my life. I mean, I'm glad about how the record came out, it's the most personal thing I've ever created, and probably *will* ever create, but it's only my work. Work is one thing, you know, and life, well life is a different story. People think that it's difficult to be an artist, and it is, but as far as I'm concerned life is actually a lot harder than art. That's a totally personal opinion, though, and I don't expect too many people to agree with me on that one. Anyway, I'm the one that got into this, and I'm the only one who can get me out of it."

"Salvation is a pretty recurrent theme in your lyrics . . ."

"Hmm . . . so you've actually listened to my music. I like that. You do your homework. You're a good boy, you know that? Although you could stand to let your hair grow a little, yeah. You don't really look enough like a rock critic, more like an opera critic or something, and that could be deadly, you know? Careful there."

"We were talking about salvation . . ."

"Yes . . . yes. I think, after all is said and done, that a person can save himself. We should all hope for that, you know. I don't go around hoping to find happiness, or love, or fame. I'm just hoping for salvation, and I think I just might get it if I keep working at it. Of course, to really believe something like that, you have to be prepared for sacrifice. If I manage to save myself, well then, everything after that will just be icing on the cake. I hope."

"Save yourself from what, though?"

"Well, that's my own personal thing. Everybody has their own thing they need to save themselves from, but then, not everybody wants to save themselves. Which doesn't have anything to do with people's dark sides or crossing boundaries between reality and fantasy and drugs, and other stupid stuff like that. That's what I hate about rock and roll. Everyone thinks that it's all about drugs and sex, but that's not it at all. True, that stuff helps, it's kind of entertainment, but that's all it is. That's what I like about disco music: it's aware of its own mortality. It doesn't try to save itself. It's all lost souls, dancing however and whenever they can. Me, I'm a little more pretentious: I still think that there are other things out there for me."

"Let's talk about love . . ."

"You talk about love. Maybe you'll teach me something I don't know, something I haven't experienced. The truth is, I don't know much about it. Every day, I become more and more aware of how little I even understand about myself. And the more I learn about myself, the more I'll be able to connect with other people. I'm sick of how people love me, and I don't know how to respond to them. Being famous doesn't make it any easier. Sometimes I feel that all these people—especially girls—just want a little piece of me for themselves. Like the way everyone walks around with their opinion of things, telling me about everything. I can't ever express my own real opinion. I hung out for four months, alone on an island called Foula, far off the Scottish coast. It's a place they call 'the edge of the world.' That was where I realized that maybe I don't know much of anything. At least I know that I'm sick of fulfilling this role, of being this reflection of what everyone else wants me to be. I'd stop recording, I'd stop composing, but that would just be doing what they all want me to do. The key for me to all of this, I think, is to create and impose my own rules on myself. Impose the truth, really. Which, actually, is impossible, because the only real truth, the only one that interests me, at least, is the one that eventually hurts people, myself included. It hurts everyone. If this is achieved, pure truth, then suicide doesn't become an option anymore."

"So there's redemption."

"Yes. I'd like to think so. But redemption requires faith, which implies a certain trust."

"Speaking of faith and trust, do you think, for example, that the Coyote could really ever eat the Roadrunner, like your last album title says?"

"I guess. It would be really incredible, wouldn't it? That's what I wish, anyway. The blood's gonna flow, and heads will roll. It's about time, don't you think?"

"Do you have anything by Josh Remsen?"

"I don't recognize the name," says the saleswoman at the Feria del Disco, which is jam-packed with schoolgirls in their proper little uniforms, looking at all the tapes in the Spanish section.

"You do carry imported music, don't you?"

"All our music is imported."

"So the album *The Coyote Ate the Roadrunner* doesn't sound familiar to you?"

"No," she says with a disgusted look on her face.

"What about *The Sleeper Must Awaken?*"

"Sorry, no."

Maybe they have the album at Circus. Just the thought of having to go all the way over there depresses me, so I forget the idea. They probably don't have it anyway.

I leave Feria del Disco. Paseo Ahumada is still teeming with people. A newspaper boy yells out the latest headline from *La Segunda:* "List of Military Officers Sentenced by Radio Moscow." Unbelievably, crowds of people rush over to buy the paper.

I don't have much to do. I am getting used to just letting my body go where my mood takes it. I guess I have too much time on my hands right now, and I don't know how to use it, or what to fill it with. I've got no desire to play pinball or video games, and the idea of watching the Village People's latest movie, *Can't Stop the Music,* doesn't exactly thrill me. So I just start walking.

There's a lot of tension here in the city, I can feel it in my bones. There are just too many people in the street, and everyone is looking around, staring at one another. By the kind of look they've got on their faces, you can easily tell whether they're going to vote "SI" or "NO." There are cops on every corner and police dogs sniffing everything in sight. The sidewalks are covered with pamphlets. "Today is bad, tomorrow will be worse," "Frei sellout," "NO to fascism, SI to justice."

At the Portal Fernández Concha in front of a flour factory, there's a man selling copies of a little blue paperback book, entitled: *Constitución de 1980.* The referendum and the vote are still twenty-four hours away, but they've already printed them up. It doesn't even say "proposed" or anything like that. It's done.

I go back to Paseo Ahumada and walk among the cops and a group of old men, dressed in heavy overcoats, who are all giving each other high fives as they walk past one another. On the corner, an old man asks me if I'm interested in a shoeshine. I look down at my shoes; they're pretty dirty, with all the dirt from those streets I was wandering around yesterday.

"Sure," I say.

I step up to his stand, where two other guys are sitting.

"Excuse me, may I take a look at your newspaper?"

I open *La Segunda* and feel the old man spreading black shoe polish on my moccasins. I look down and study his fingernails and his fingers too. They're stained with a brownish tint—black and red too. His hands are a totally different color than his arms and face.

"The United Front Prays for the Country," I read in the newspaper. "Jaime Guzmán Affirms: Alessandri Advises His Constituents to Vote 'SI.' " It makes me feel like puking. So does this guy whose life is dedicated to shining the shoes of guys who could be his grandchildren. How pathetic everything seems.

"That's fine," I say.

"I haven't buffed them yet, sir."

"It's okay, I'm in a hurry . . . and please, don't call me 'sir.' "

I get up and hand him back his paper.

"Hey, who are you going to vote for?" I ask him.

"For my General."

I give him the money I owe him. And a tip, of course.

Along the same little street, in front of the movie theater, I see there's a bookstore, so I go in.

"Do you have *Catcher in the Rye,* by Salinger?"

"No, but we've got *Nine Stories.*"

"Are they any good?"

"I don't know, I've never read any of them."

"Is Holden in any of them?"

"I don't know."

I exit the store, engrossed in my recent purchase, and practically crash into a fat lady walking down the street. Then I turn down Agustinas and stop for a second in front of a travel agency, attracted by some posters of Tahiti, Venice, and the Statue of Liberty, which is green. From there, I head over to Ahumada, where the atmosphere is really unbearable. There are teams of foreign correspondents with their cameras, just waiting around to capture a riot, an assassination, or whatever on film. As I'm standing there, someone tosses about a thousand pamphlets from the top of one of the tall buildings. The sky is suddenly smothered with fluttering sheets of paper, falling like confetti. There's yelling, applause, and cursing too, but all I can hear is the sound of the soldiers' boots as they start to pound up and down the pavement.

I figure that before they can catch me, I'll go inside Café Haití. It's full of fascist men in favor of the "SI." In an effort to be as inconspicuous as possible, I buy a drink voucher, and I walk up to the bar, where men in black and gray overcoats are drinking their cappuccinos and cortados and eyeing the waitresses in their miniskirts.

"What flavor?"

"Chocolate."

The waitress retreats, and I look at her thick, firm thighs. They are like a cyclist's thighs. Next to me is a guy with gray hair, and dandruff on his shoulders. He's reading *La Segunda* through his bifocals. Just for something to do, I start leafing through my book.

"Here you are."

The waitress places a huge glass of chocolate frappé on the bar in front of me. It has a tottering tower of whipped cream. She also sets a glass of mineral water and some sugar down as well. I take the long spoon and remove some of the whipped cream, but all the people in this place are suddenly staring at me, as if it were my birthday or something. It really annoys me. Luckily, some rioters start shouting out on the streets: "Die Pinochet!" The filmy, senile eyes inside the café turn toward the scene. Only then am I able to drink some of my frappé without feeling so guilty.

"Matías! How's that dessert?"

It's my grandfather.

"Tata, what a surprise, huh?"

It's true, it is a surprise to see him here. He's the last person I thought I'd run into.

"What are you doing around here?"

"I came to see a movie," I lie. "But I also had to buy a book for school."

"I talked to your mother. She told me you left home."

I stop smiling and put on an appropriately cynical, bitter face.

"Where did you sleep last night? They've been looking for you like mad, all today and yesterday."

"I doubt that."

"What?"

"Nothing. I stayed over at a friend's house. He doesn't go to school with me. I'm okay, well, broke but okay."

"Do you need money?"

"Yes."

"When are you going to go back home?"

"I don't know if I'm ever going back."

On the other side of the windowpane, the scene is getting wilder. Cops are starting to follow people around with their clubs, and their dogs are now all barking like crazy. From Alameda, a truck with a fire hose turns onto Ahumada and begins spraying everything and everyone in sight.

"We're closing!" announces a guy wearing a Café Haití jacket. "Please, everybody leave."

"I can't believe this," Tata says to me.

"I'm getting out of here. This is too much."

"We'll go together."

I examine myself closely in the mirror. What do I see? Not much. And I really don't like what I see either. It just doesn't feel right. I don't mind what I look like, but I need some kind of a change. A radical change.

"Let's see, young man, what can I do for you?"

I'm so wired up that I can barely answer the barber. All I can do is look in the mirror, as if to remind myself that the man on my left, this person wearing a suit and a blue tie with little red dots, isn't me.

"I want something . . . different, Señor Luna."

This man, with his pasty-white skin, doesn't get it. He just doesn't understand my request.

I may have seen it in a movie, or I read it in *Rolling Stone* or something, but they say that the best way to treat a cocaine overdose is just to breathe. Breathe in, breathe out, that sort of thing. Or else get a haircut. Now that I think about it, maybe Josh Remsen said it. I don't really remember.

So here I am, looking at myself in the mirror, sitting in one of those ancient barber's chairs, like from the 1930s or something, and I'm surrounded by old men full of Brancato hair cream, in some basement barbershop.

When I bumped into Tata Iván, I already had a couple of lines of coke racing through my system. Our surprise encounter, well, it surprised me, obviously. I didn't have any way to escape from him after that, and it pissed me off; I mean, nothing pisses me off more than not being able to make my own decisions for my-self. Or having to do things other people want me to do, to avoid feeling guilty—I hate that too. But it's much easier said than done, and I couldn't break away from that stupid habit, which is why I let myself fall right into step with him.

At least, this is how I *think* it happened.

We left the Café Haití when the tear-gas explosions started, and Tata Iván started coughing uncontrollably. I really thought he was going to croak on me, right then and there, just watching his eyes tear and his face redden was horrible enough. But he didn't die, and so we started to run. I know he must have been think-ing about or remembering Hungary and the ghettos in Budapest. All I could do was grab his hand and quicken the pace a little. Only a few feet behind us, I could hear a soldier beating the shit out of some guy who was already on the ground. He was bleed-ing, like a burst pipe or something.

As we ran toward Alameda, the rioting worsened. I thought that we might be able to find shelter in the drugstore on the cor-ner, but the owner shut the metal gate right in our faces, leaving us outside in this war scene, with people yelling, sirens screech-ing, and the sounds of gunshots all around us.

"That way! That way to the club!" insisted Tata, who was sweating like crazy. His face was all swollen and red by now. We kept running, past the huge hoses that were brought out and turned onto the rioters, who were in the process of spray-painting the front entrance of the university.

"Here, here! This way!" Tata continued.

It's a good thing the club was so close by, or else my old grand-father would've probably dropped dead. We made our way up the marble staircase, and once inside, the atmosphere changed instantly. The cool surfaces of the marble columns and the fancy gilded entranceway now protected us from all of the madness outside. I went in first, pushing the giant revolving door as hard as I could. It was heavy and old.

"Young man, where do you think you're going?"

"What's wrong with you?" I managed to sputter, but that was before the doorman recognized who I was with.

"Don Iván, my God!"

"He won't let me in," I said.

"It's my grandson, you idiot."

"Excuse me, Don Iván, I . . . I didn't realize."

"Get me a chair, will you. And some water."

This was the famous Club de la Unión; I'd never been there before. I had only heard about how elegant it was, and deadly boring too. It was one of those places that only allowed men inside.

My grandfather eased himself down into a thick red velvet easy chair. The doorman signaled to a waiter, an older guy dressed in white from head to toe.

"Poblete! Bring us some washcloths. And lemons, please."

I sat down somewhere, I don't remember where, and I wiped my eyes. The silence that followed was almost unbearable. At another table next to us, underneath an enormous crystal chandelier, an old, really ancient couple sat, tucked deep into a couple of easy chairs, having their afternoon tea, looking totally calm. Bored even. They didn't have the foggiest fucking idea of what was going on outside.

"Are you all right?" my grandfather asked me.

"Yes, sir, I'm okay. Are you?"

"Better, thanks. Much better now."

I looked around. "This is like that club in *Around the World in 80 Days*. Do you remember that movie? You took us all to see it. It must've been ages ago."

"Yes, you're right, you know?" he mused. "This club is *quite British,*" he said in English, in a put-on accent.

The waiter returned, bearing his requests on a silver tray. Tata took a sip of water, noisily, and chewed hard on the little bit of lemon rind that came with it.

"Thank you, Poblete. I'd like to introduce my grandson, Matías."

"A pleasure to meet you, young man."

"Since you're over here, why don't you see if you can find one of those club ties for Matías, and some Onces. While you're at it, a San Guillermo for each of us. Matías, did you want anything . . . special?"

"Just some coffee," I said, realizing that it wasn't going to be so easy to get myself out of the current situation.

Poblete moved away, and Tata began to talk, now that he had recuperated from the scene outside a bit.

"This isn't the first time the club has saved me," he said. "When Allende was in power, I found myself in the middle of riots like that one, more than once. Well, I was a lot younger then, though. Obviously. I'm pretty sure your father went through the same thing a few times."

My father is also a member here, just like my grandfather Vicuña was, and—I assume—my uncle the ambassador still is.

Poblete reappeared almost immediately and presented me with a Givenchy tie, a blue silk thing with tiny red dots. As he handed it over, he said, "The men's room is through the far end of the hall, young man."

"Right, Matías, it's just down the hall. House rules. Everyone's got to wear a tie around here. No little rapscallions allowed into the club."

He cackled, one of those aren't-I-funny laughs, which made me want to smack him and tell him that nobody even uses that word anymore. But then I thought better of it and shut up. It would only waste time.

The bathroom was all marble. It was one of those that have all the sinks in one room separate from the urinals. I took off my sweater, pulled up my collar, and knotted the tie perfectly. I went to put the sweater back on, then I thought better of it, and left it off, so I was wearing only my new jacket. I then shut myself into a stall, which had one of those fancy, old-fashioned metal locks. I couldn't resist doing a line right there, beneath the roof of the historic club, where so many illustrious politicians had decided for so many years the fate of the country. This was as good as sneaking into the Presidential Palace, I thought to myself, as I carelessly let some white powder spill on top of the shiny white toilet seat lid. I must've lost at least a gram, I thought, as I watched it flutter away. Punishment for the sudden craving I'd succumbed to; I guess I got a little too greedy. No reason to get carried away here, though. Since I didn't have a straw with me, I rolled up a brand-new, crisp bill, and just inhaled it all in, and kept going and going until my nose (and my tongue and my gums and my throat) couldn't take it anymore.

Now I was ready to return to the great entrance hall and face my grandfather, who was still chatting away with old Poblete. He was eating some big gloppy dessert with meringue and yellow sauce, covered in nuts.

"Here, have some of this. It's a specialty here."

I had a few bites, but didn't really taste much of anything, since I was about a hundred and fifty percent anesthetized from my little bathroom binge. Still, though, the sweetness had a nice relaxing effect, and there was some fruit in there somewhere that neutralized the strong taste of the meringue. It did make me ferociously thirsty, though.

"Poblete," I called out to the waiter. "Could you bring me a Coke?"

My grandfather laughed at that, and had this look on his face that said "Isn't my grandson a little rapscallion?" Yeah, right. Whatever.

"All right, Matías," he started in. "I think it's time we talked."

"What's there to talk about? That was a really great snack. Thanks for the Onces. And the San Guillermo—excellent dessert."

"Matías, I think it's time you called home."

"Really? Why?"

"To tell your parents where you are. Hasn't that crossed your mind at all?"

"Well . . . you're going to tell them you saw me, right? I mean, if I were sick or something, or dead, they'd know about it in a second. Those kinds of things get around. I really don't have that much to report right now."

"You missed some classes at school today, didn't you?"

"Tomorrow's a holiday. Or day off, whatever. There's no school until Monday."

Poblete reappeared, bearing my Coke.

"Listen, Tata," I said, leaning back in my seat. "Why don't we just drop the whole subject? We're not going to agree on anything, and our talking about it won't get us anywhere. All I can tell you is that I need some time. That's all. You know I can't leave the country or anything without permission, right? And I don't really have enough money to get very far anyway. Time. I just need some time. Period. That's all. This morning, for example, I've just been walking around and around. I still can't concentrate on anything. I need to make some decisions here, or just get used to things. I don't know what. I just need some time to myself. To figure stuff out."

"Think about your mother . . ."

"That's exactly what I'm trying *not* to think about. Don't you get it?"

"Don't say things like that, Matías."

"Well then, don't ask me any more questions, because if we keep talking about this, I'm going to say what I really think, and that's probably exactly what you're not going to want to hear, so that won't get us anywhere, right?"

"I just don't understand you, Matías," he sighed.

"I'm not that complicated. Really."

We didn't talk anymore after that. I finished the rest of my San Guillermo cake and only managed to drink half of the Coke I'd ordered. My grandfather got up and said, "If you want, I'll take you home. I'll drop you off there."

"Thanks, but no, Tata."

"Do you need money?"

"Well, sure, thanks."

"Here, take this. If you need more, call me."

"I'll do that, Tata."

"Won't you at least tell me where you're staying, Matías?"

"No, I can't, I'm sorry. But tell them not to worry about me, okay? I know what I'm doing right now, and I know this is the right thing."

We said goodbye to the solicitous Poblete and left, out onto the Alameda, which was heaving with buses, all spewing forth their black exhaust fumes. Everything seemed a little calmer, though. I looked up at the clock on the San Francisco Church: 6:10 P.M. The sun was just beginning to set. My grandfather hailed a taxi.

"So you're not coming with me, then?"

"No."

"You sure have Hungarian blood in you."

That really struck me when he said that. I don't know why or how, but I realized exactly what he was trying to say to me then: *I can tell you're a Rothman.* He then shut the taxi door and sped off.

After he left, I didn't really have anything better to do, so I went back to the club to talk to Poblete.

"May I stay here for a little while?"

"Of course you can."

I went over to the bar, where there was a group of young executive types, busy downing dainty little drinks, like spritzers or something. Some of them were playing cards. There was a big glass window overlooking the Stock Exchange, where loads of sweating men were pushing the cops out of their way, just to get out of the building. I turned to the bartender and ordered a Campari and tonic, Josh Remsen's favorite drink. It didn't do much for me. The whole atmosphere there inside the club started to really depress me, because I started to get that feeling, you know, that everyone was watching me, and judging me, and all that, and I started to realize that I couldn't stay in there forever. After two or three more hours, I reasoned, I'd have to get out, go back to the City Hotel, and, like I said to my grandfather, make some sort of a decision. The problem was, though, of all the possibilities that lay before me, none of them appealed to me at all. In the least.

It felt like being in an airport with a free ticket to go anywhere in the world and not knowing what airplane to get on. Or worse: finding out that all the planes have been grounded. Or worse: wanting to leave but realizing you've lost your passport. I don't know, something like that, I think. This feeling turns into this self-fulfilling prophecy, like some vicious existential cycle that gets you absolutely nowhere. Except crazy from analyzing it to death. I've thought about all my possibilities: first the boring and predictable ones, then the sort of exciting and tantalizing ones, and now I realize, no matter what I think, I'm pretty much stuck.

You didn't used to be this way, Matías.

Whenever my potentially bright future is clouded over by my grim reality, and then that depressing combo is contrasted with my complicated and even more depressing past, that's when the only thing left to do is get a seriously radical haircut. That's how, really without realizing, I ended up in the barbershop. I went down to the basement of my grandfather's club and first tried to distract myself by watching all the old men playing pool. They were all trying to hit those red balls. It was from there that I noticed men going in and out of the barbershop just down the hall.

"Well, young man. Have you made up your mind?"

"Yes. Something radical. Military. As if I just came out of an insane asylum, how about that? Take it all off, but leave just enough so I'm not bald."

"So you want me to buzz it with the electric razor, then?"

"Perfect."

The barber wet my hair and started his scalping process, mercilessly. I watched him in the mirror as he did it, fascinated by the buzz of the razor, and I noticed how, little by little, the shape of my skull infused me with this strange feeling of power.

That's right about the time when my father came walking in. He edged into the shop, toward the far corner of the mirror, and came so close that he eventually disappeared from the entire picture. I decided then to close my eyes and await my new haircut in darkness. And silence.

Alone.

"You look good . . . baldy."

"Cut the crap, will you? And don't call me 'baldy.' Or 'stud.' "

"Whatever you want, peach fuzz."

"Enough, I said. All right?"

This is all getting too weird. But in a strange way, it doesn't bother me. In fact, I almost like it, in a strange, perverse way. I'm glad to be near my father.

"All right, peach fuzz, it's your turn."

"Don't call me that, all right? And don't be such an idiot. You already did three lines. We said it was two for each of us. That's it."

"But we have more, we've got enough to last us all night. So relax. You only live once. Hey, those girls are coming back, aren't they?"

We're stretched out on a huge bed, the two of us. The bed must be about the size of a giant pool table, wider even. Through the window are the neon lights of the Plaza Italia. We're inside one of the Torres de Tajamar, I'm not sure which, on the eleventh floor, I think. "Eleven, like the eleventh of September," my father said as we got into the elevator.

"Okay, go. Do another line."

So I do it. It's the kind of offer you don't exactly want to refuse.

Especially coming from your father, the man who gave you life and raised you to be a good little boy.

"Some role model I am," he sighs.

"Yeah," I agree. "Some role model. But I've seen worse. I'll be right back, okay?" I go into the bathroom to find a towel, but don't find anything, so I grab a robe and tightly wrap the belt around my waist. I leave the bathroom and head to the door.

"Where are you going?"

"To get some more to drink. And to find those girls."

I walk down the black-and-white-wallpapered hall and go into the lounge. In the center of the room, a small fountain bubbles away and one entire wall is covered with a poster of Manhattan at night, with all its skyscrapers aglow. A man about thirty years old (gray hair, no potbelly) is singing. He's got a pair of boxer shorts on and not much else, except for his shoes and socks, which give him away: a banking type, or a general manager of some sort. He's actually pretty good and is singing some old Cat Stevens song. One of his contemporaries, I guess.

"Hello?" I call out to the manager of the place, who's busy going through a bunch of credit card receipts.

"I'll take a bottle of Stolichnaya, please. And two glasses with ice."

"I just ran out of Stoli."

"Black Label, then."

"Fine," he says.

"And tell those girls to come back in about twenty minutes, to give us some time to recover, all right?"

This place is called Escort VIPs, but it's really known as Torres de Tajamar. Or simply 1104. It's all the same, really, because it's so exclusive that it doesn't really need a name. What it is speaks for itself: the Godfather's premier "evening spot," or rather Santiago's privileged class's "evening spot," if you know what I mean. It is owned by some relative of the guy who owns Juancho's, so that's the connection. That's why everything here is supposedly the best: the girls (some of them are even models

and TV announcers), the best drinks, the best rooms, the best facilities. And the lines, of course, are compliments of the house.
The guy that runs the place is my father's connection. He's got
a direct line to Bolivia; at least, that's what my father tells me.

The weird thing about all of this, though, is that I'm here,
Matías, talking with him, wearing only a gray terry-cloth
bathrobe, way past the curfew, asking him for a bottle of Scotch
during election time, when alcohol is supposedly prohibited.

But I've already made my *own* election, so to speak.

I think.

It all happened pretty fast, kind of unexpectedly. So unexpectedly that I barely had time to analyze it or question it, that's
how fast it happened. Maybe it was a mistake. I don't know.

I figured out pretty quickly that the traitor in this current little scenario had been Poblete. I can't really blame him; I mean,
he was only doing the right thing as far as he was concerned. He
called my grandfather and told him that I'd returned to the club.
My grandfather then called my father right away, of course. It
was only a matter of time before my father made his way through
the riots, by taxi, to the club, which is where he found me. Getting my hair cut.

I had no way to escape. Neither did he, though, now that I
think about it.

That's why I'm here now. That's why he's with me. He needed
to be with someone, he couldn't be alone right then. I realized
right when he walked into the barbershop. He seemed defeated,
and had no axes to grind or fights to pick with me. He just
strolled in, sat down, and watched as the little old barber finished buzzing the last of my hair away. As the scissors snipped,
and the electric razor hummed, going up and down, up and
down, my mind was racing, trying to plan an escape, some kind
of getaway, some kind of excuse I could give him, what to say,
what not to say. I just wanted to avoid any and all communication with him.

Then everything stopped. I looked in the mirror. I was done.

The barber had made me look like some army recruit heading for Vietnam.

"Good job, Panchito," my father said as he paid the barber.

Then he touched my head with the palm of his hand.

"Prickly," he said.

At first, I didn't know how to respond, but then I said, "I feel like a huge weight's been lifted from my shoulders."

"You don't know how much I envy you, kid."

He then put his hand on my back—it was a gesture somewhere between tender and forceful—and said, "Let's get out of here; it's all old people at this place. We're still young, aren't we?"

We left the club and got into a taxi, managing to escape the nighttime rioting by going down the narrow side streets. We finally reached the Parque Forestal, in front of the Museo de Bellas Artes.

"You can let us out here. We're going to walk a bit."

We got out of the cab and silently walked, underneath the huge Oriental trees that hid all the couples making out on the grass, on top of the soggy pamphlets, kissing each other in the privacy of the darkness.

"Listen," I said to him after a few minutes. "I've got to go. I've got stuff to do."

"Relax, it's early. I just want some fresh air."

"No. Seriously. I'll walk you up to the corner, and then I'm going."

"Matías, please. I want you to stay with me, and I promise I won't bother you or make you feel bad, okay? What happened, happened, all right? Let's just end it there. I only wanted to see you. I've missed you, that's all. I had no idea where you were."

I looked at him cautiously. I don't know what kind of glare I shot him, but it must've been pretty obvious what I was thinking, because he immediately said, "You don't believe me, do you? You really don't think I feel anything for you, do you?"

"Last night was a mistake, all right?"

"It wasn't a mistake, it wasn't anything at all. But I'm not talking about that. I've already analyzed everything about yesterday in my head. What I wanted to say to you . . . well, what I'm try-ing to say, Matías . . . Matías, do you mind looking at me when I speak to you? This is hard enough for me as it is, so don't make it more difficult."

I looked right at him, but inwardly, behind my eyes that stared straight at him, I held back. I was protecting myself, I guess. I started to shake.

"I'm listening."

"Don't be cruel, Matías. I know that maybe I'm not the best fa-ther there ever was . . . maybe I'm nothing at all to you . . . I know you look down on me, that you can't stand me, but maybe some-day we can get past all of that. What I won't tolerate is if *you* start acting like the father here. Don't start with that, because that's going to end up in a fight, for sure. All I'm trying to do is talk to you friend-to-friend."

I didn't quite know what to say to him after that. Or what to think, for that matter. I sort of broke down, though, just because his tone of voice really got to me, and then his eyes filled up with tears; I mean, it was all just too much for me. I felt helpless, like a little kid again or something.

So I hugged him. A real hug with no guilt and no anxiety.

"See, it's not so bad."

"I just don't understand what's going on," I said to him, dry-ing wet eyes and trying to pull myself together a little. "Well, I mean, you know, I don't like this kind of heavy stuff."

"I know. Me neither, kid."

We then walked for about five or six blocks in silence, but a natural, comfortable silence, that wasn't forced at all. It wasn't like one of those horrible, loud silences, full of pregnant thoughts that are hidden, bottled up, drowned. It wasn't like that at all. When he spoke again, he seemed like another person. Back to his old self, his usual self, only partially now, of course. It was pretty obvious that he'd never be the same after all that had hap-pened in the last few days.

"Let's go wild," he said, right there, in the middle of Plaza Italia. "I'm not going home tonight, either. Your mother asked me not to, actually, but it was kind of a mutual thing. I thought I'd stay in a hotel."

"Why? What happened?"

"Just some problems, nothing to worry about. Nothing we can't work out."

"Does it have anything to do with my taking off yesterday?"

"Well, yes, but it isn't about you, Matías. There was a lot of fighting, and your mother's not exactly in a good frame of mind right now. So we decided I'd stay somewhere else for now. Right after that discussion, your grandfather called us. I had actually thought I'd go to Reñaca, but with the referendum coming up, I have to stick around. I've got to place my vote here in Santiago."

"I'm staying at the City Hotel," I said to him all of a sudden.

"Hmm . . . they have a nice bar. Old-fashioned, the same as it was years ago."

"I took a check from your wallet. And I cashed it yesterday."

"That's all right. I would've done the same thing in your place. It's my treat now, though. I owe you. Come on, let's go."

We stopped another taxi, and it took us to where we are now, the Torres de Tajamar. First, though, we went into Kabaret 1100. One thing led to another. We got kind of drunk, laughing at the topless dancers, and the cocktail waitresses who were hanging all over us, treating us like we were brothers or something.

"Do you want to do a line?"

"What?"

"A line. A line of coke," he shouted over the music.

I looked at him, dead serious, not really understanding if it was a joke or not.

"Don't play dumb with me, Matías. I didn't care about the check you stole, but you can bet I noticed the missing coke. After today, we'll put an end to all of this. I probably should prohibit you from using coke, that's what everyone else would say. But too many things have happened between us, and I understand where you're coming from. We'll finish this stuff off together, and then tomorrow . . . tomorrow's another day. How does that sound? Tomorrow we can be sensible and organize our lives a little. Properly. But tonight let's just forget about it, okay? I can't deal with it tonight."

We ended up in the men's room, snorting away in clear view of anyone and everyone who came in to use the facilities.

"I like this. This is okay with me," I said.

"The coke?"

"No, I mean being with you. While I'm losing a little of the respect I had for you, I'm losing the fear too."

Later, around midnight, we were the last patrons in the once-crowded bar. At midnight is when the no-alcohol rule went into effect because of the election.

"Let's go upstairs."

"Where?"

"To 1104, the best massage parlor in all of Santiago. Trust me."

"The best whorehouse, you mean."

"Well, I was trying to be subtle about it, Matías."

"Don't play with me, come on."

We weren't the only ones upstairs. The man who ran the place recognized my father right away and really gave him the royal treatment. He took us down a long corridor, which led to a suite with a gigantic double bed by a window. Above it hung a huge black-and-white poster of a naked girl lying on a dune somewhere.

"Whenever you'd like, the sauna is ready for you."

"Is Rebecca available tonight?"

"Of course."

"Well, then, let's have Rebecca and one other."

Now, this was getting really sort of strange, even for me, but the coke, the vodka, and my participation in the whole scenario took my mind off the reality of it all. When the attendant closed the door behind him, my father took a mirror that was hanging on the wall and placed it gently on the bed. Then he took off his jacket, loosened his tie, and emptied out a hefty mound of coke onto the mirror. Like a pig in a pen, he started snorting away, shamelessly.

"You too," he motioned to me. "Go for it."

He handed me his little metal straw, and I snorted a few lines as he was taking off his clothes. Then it was my turn to undress, but I wasn't quite sure what to do, so I decided to strike up some conversation. I started rambling on about my wandering around Santiago, my red hunting cap, the life and times of Josh Remsen, anything that came to mind. Then, suddenly, I realized I didn't have a bit of clothing on. The truth is, it was just fine, because I felt like, what the hell, what did I have to hide from him anymore?

"Come on, kid."

We went into another room, with wood paneling and no windows, boiling hot with that raspy, dry kind of heat. There were about five other men there, in their forties, I guess, and they all looked like real moneybags. Millionaires, if you ask me. I started sweating pretty quickly and a lot. Sweating out the alcohol and the coke, that's what it felt like. After a little while, a woman came in, wearing some little see-through number, although the most impressive thing about her was the sixties-style hairdo she had going on. It practically reached the ceiling.

"Rebecca," my father said, "you were *just* the person we were waiting for."

She handed each of us a robe and then led us to the bedroom where we had gotten undressed before. There was another girl there, sniffing coke on the bed. This girl was different from Rebecca. She was much younger, and incredibly sophisticated, but relaxed about it. Like, she could have cared less that she was there.

"Hi there. I'm Solange," she said to me.

Rebecca turned out the overhead lights and turned on another, dimmer set that had this sort of suave brownish color. The new lights simply darkened things a bit and gave the room this incandescent, luminous glow. Rebecca immediately whipped off her nightgown, then took my father's robe off for him. She dried off the tiny beads of perspiration on his chest with a black towel and then set her tongue to work on his nipples.

"Relax, Matías. You know about this stuff, right?"

Solange came over to me, sat down at the edge of the bed, and took off my robe. Before patting me down with the towel, her fingertips trailed over my chest, making little designs in the rivulets of sweat that had accumulated in large amounts by now. She then pushed me onto the bed and opened her legs. I managed to get one more line in before entering her. As I was on top of her, I looked over at my father, who was only a few inches away from me on the bed. His eyes were closed and Rebecca was on top of him, massaging his neck.

"We're crazy."

"We're just hot, that's all."

The room is still dim, illuminated only by the oh-so-subtle brown light. It's a little after five in the morning, I realize through my haze. I can barely believe this scenario. There was a lot more after my little bit with Solange. I vaguely remember switching girls with my father at some point, and then the two of us took Solange at the same time, at which point Rebecca started in again on the coke as she watched us, sort of nervously.

"I don't know if I want to keep doing this," I said. "Let's wait till the curfew ends, and then I'll leave you here, is that okay?"

"I don't want to screw anymore either," he said.

"Yeah, you've screwed enough for one night, I think."

"Here, come over here."

I go over to him.

"What do you think of all this? Totally decadent, right? Do you think I'm a pathetic slob now?"

"No, no, not at all."

"You don't have to lie to me, Matías. Tell me what you really think. Seriously."

"Well, this was all kind of strange. It was pretty good. It definitely calmed me down a little, yeah. I think it was a pretty good idea, actually."

"I think your mother's leaving me," he says out of nowhere.

"Are you sure?" I ask.

"Almost positive."

"Well, if she is, clearly it's because of this kind of stuff," I say. "In a way, can you really blame her?"

"No, no, that's not it at all, God no. She doesn't have any idea about this. Even if she did, I don't think she'd even care. And that's exactly the problem, Matías. I don't mean a thing to her. In fact, I don't think I ever have."

"Listen, I don't know much, and I don't really want to get that involved, but some of the things you've done over the years, well . . . they weren't exactly admirable, if you know what I mean. That whole mess with Hilda Escudero was pretty horrible and embarrassing for all of us too, don't you think?"

"Look, Matías, I'm not trying to defend myself here, but I've got a lot of reasons for doing the things I've done. I mean, I've been behaving like this, because, well . . ."

"Because my mother doesn't want you . . . is that it?"

"Yes. But I still want her. That's the thing . . . I can't help it, I mean, it sounds really hypocritical of me right now, especially after what we've just done, but I love your mother. I love her."

"So tell her."

"I did, last night. Today too."

"Yeah, and?"

"She's in love with Sandro, and she has been for a while now. That's why he left Loreto, in fact. I didn't know a thing about it until last night. Now that I think about it, our relationship has been rocky for quite some time now. A while back, I began to notice something strange, even a few suspicious things, but there was never enough to really accuse anyone of anything, least of all Sandro. I mean, he's my friend, and my business partner."

"You're fucked." I can barely believe the words that have just come out of his mouth.

"Yeah, I know. Tell me about it. It hurts like hell."

Then he starts to cry, quietly at first, but then he lets go and really starts bawling. As I take his hand and stroke his hair, I'm looking out the window, watching the darkness slowly ebb. The only thing I hear is my father's sobs.

"Let's go home," I say. "I'm ready to go home now."

SUNDAY
SEPTEMBER 14, 1980

It rained last night, but that didn't come as much of a surprise. It didn't surprise me at all. In fact, I'm surprised it didn't rain more. That it didn't flood or something.

The sun is now shining, weakly, and the Andes are capped with snow. They are looking better than ever, actually. Even though the streets are still wet, my ride up the hill has been an easy one. Maybe that's why I've decided to go farther up, pedal as far as I can go, up, up, and away until I hit the very top. The road ends, though, and a person can't really expect to go up, up, and away when the road ends. I've gotten far enough anyway. I can't complain.

There's nobody up here today, just me, riding around and around, in circles and figure eights, playing this little game of I-can't-let-my-bike-touch-any-part-of-the-Virgin's-shadow that is covering the cracked ceramic tiles on the plaza. It's not hard. My little Benotto is easy to maneuver, and I've had plenty of practice.

It's been one week—exactly last Sunday—since we baptized my nephew Felipe. It was just like it is today, part sunny, part rainy. Sundays are always like this, they tend to have this sameness about them, even if they're nothing alike. A lot of time has passed since last Sunday, much more than just a week. It seems like years have gone by, actually. Everything seems so distant, and so foreign to me now. Foreign and detached. Irrevocable. It's almost like nothing really has happened.

Time is weird that way. Life is like, so controlled, marked by all these little intervals. It's like it's one big chess game. If you look backward, or, for example, if I look down right now, toward the city, and think about everything that's happened since last Sunday, or since the Sunday before that, when I was in Rio, on the beach, or if I think even further back, way before I took the trip, when I was only thinking about the trip, I can't help but feel like everything just suddenly—broke. Stopped working. Something.

Last night, it rained hard, but not hard enough for me. Last night it rained, but that didn't come as much of a surprise. It didn't surprise me at all. The weird thing, really, it's true, the weird thing is that we didn't get flooded. That's what surprised me.

I guess I'll have to start getting used to surprises.

I went back home. I had to, and anyway, I wanted to, despite my reservations. I still have doubts, and probably always will, but beyond the reality of it, beyond the financial, legal facts, all those things that seem so stupid and useless, but which are more deeply ingrained in me than I'd care to admit to anyone, I felt that my family needed me. Or that my father did, my father needed me, and that's a good thing, because it made me forget all the bad stuff and allowed me to even start forgiving a little. Forgiving, meaning not just my father. Me too. Or what's left of me, that is.

I guess the basic stuff is still here: my body, my frame, my brakes. The main stuff is still there, but lots of other things have changed. It's like I'm operating with a new engine, new transmission, a new set of gears now. I'm a whole different machine. I've replaced my old parts with new ones, stronger, more reliable ones. It's still not the same, I mean, how could it be? When you play rough, you end up going down rough too. You ride down rocky paths and tricky roads that you've never gone down before. How can you expect to come out of those unscarred? The frame stays the same, but the little parts rattle around, and some of them you have to change. It's never the same again, because in the end, it's the little parts, the details, that you always focus on. The details are what count.

When my father and I got back to our apartment, all I wanted to do was turn around and go straight back in the cab to room 506 at the City Hotel. Something—I don't know what—made me go upstairs, something made me stay by my father's side and go up there. My mother wasn't there, though, and my aunt Loreto, we learned, was dead. The night before, she had loaded up on sleeping pills, or really, a bunch of serious tranquilizers, and she had also turned on the gas, even though it was the pills that did her in.

The business between my mother and Uncle Sandro got around pretty quickly, and Loreto fell into the bowels of depression. She simply couldn't deal with it. She called Sandro, asked him point-blank, and he told her the truth. Then she called my mother, but my mother, with her typical intelligence, grace, and tact, hung up on her. A few hours after that, after the police found her dead, my mother left Santiago, heading for Buenos Aires. I guess she'll hook up with Sandro there. Who knows? My father and I certainly don't, and I don't think we really care anyway. My father refuses to talk to her, and they basically ignored each other at Loreto's funeral. It was short, the funeral. Not too many people came.

The burial was on Thursday, at twilight, just as the election results came through. The "SI" won, with 67.6 percent of the vote. Ironically, nobody in my family was able to muster up the desire to vote. La Alameda, of course, was packed full of people, celebrating in front of the Diego Portales building. That crowd was what held us up as we were driving toward the cemetery. There were far too many people, crowds and crowds of entire families, with their children and their grandchildren and grandparents, and everyone was running out into the street to celebrate the future, toasting the economic stability and the promise that nothing bad would ever happen to Chile.

For their sakes, I hope they're right. Really. I'd really like to think, now that the troubles have subsided a little, that we're in for some calm, maybe even peaceful times ahead.

The famous Alejandro Paz of Chile was released, and he wasn't even tortured or anything, outside of getting slapped around a little bit. He says that in Chile the worst is still to come; the worst stuff, he says, happens during moments of supposed peace, when everybody's gotten used to things.

Now that I've gotten to understand the whole political issue a little better, especially the people who voted for the "SI," I believe that maybe people voted for it as a way of keeping things the same. I know from my own experiences that the scariest thing in the world can be change.

The Great Alejandro Paz is leaving Chile. He was jailed for a little while, but that actually worked in his favor. He now has a visa to go to the United States. I hope he makes a clean break of it. I'll miss him, obviously, but if he leaves right away, somehow I think I'll miss him less. That way, his absence will just be one more element in this total void that I feel nowadays. It's not terrible, the void. I mean, it doesn't hit me as hard, or weaken me the way it might have in the past. Paz gave me a bunch of his stuff, a ton of magazines, and Josh Remsen's *The Coyote Ate the Roadrunner,* which he got just before they threw him in jail. I still haven't listened to it yet. I just haven't found the right moment. But I will. When I miss him a little less, I guess.

I'll never stop missing some things. I wouldn't want to. I wouldn't want to forget Nacho, and now I realize that even if I did want to, how could I? Same with Antonia. Just a few hours ago, before I came up the hill, I rode around to a bunch of different places, taking advantage of the silent streets, as empty as always on Sunday mornings around here. Without realizing it, I found myself at her doorstep. Something made me stop, sure, but I didn't ring the bell or anything.

"You're such a pessimist," I remember her saying to me once. I had answered her back saying that yes, I knew I was a pessimist, but there was a certain advantage to that.

"What do you mean?" she had asked.

"I always expect the worst. That way, whenever the worst doesn't happen, I end up kind of pleasantly surprised. Happy. Whenever the worst does actually come true, it happens, and I don't get depressed or disillusioned. I'm used to it by then. It's normal, it's just the way things are. It's not necessarily the way things *should* be."

It's funny, things surprise me a lot right now. In a good way. Especially things about myself. *Even* things about myself. My father, who will never be the same again, for him, things are a little better. My house, clearly, will never be the same again. My younger sisters decided to move in with Pilar for a while, so that means my father and I are alone. That doesn't scare me anymore. In fact, exactly the opposite. I mean, it's not like I know what's going to happen to us or anything, but we'll come out of it okay. We'll see, I guess. My father even said that he'd let me change schools and that I could go to Liceo 11, but I just figured I'd stay where I am. For this year at least, it won't kill me to finish the year out, finish what I started, like they say, because leaving in the middle is kind of like never having arrived. I don't really want to isolate myself from everyone for no reason, because inwardly, that's what I always seem to want to do. Running away is a hell of a lot more complicated than sticking around. I'm not ready for that yet—I don't have the strength for it. I'd rather just stay put for a while.

The sun is climbing, and the Virgin's shadow is slowly starting to creep over me.

Time to go.

I start biking downhill. The incline is steep, and with each push of the pedal, I go faster and faster. The wind feels pure, it's so cold it bites. But I keep going. I like it like this. As I go faster, I get closer to my house, and I'm feeling stronger and stronger.

It's as if the wind is purifying me, and it's as if it's pushing me to go further, to arrive, to leave behind the bad vibes and the doubt, and confront the confusion I have to face down below, in Santiago.

I guess I have made it.

For now.

About the Translator

Kristina Cordero, originally from New York City, received a B.A. in Romance Languages from Harvard College, where she wrote (in Spanish) *In the Name of the Father: The Life and Work of St. Teresa of Avila.* She has contributed to *Let's Go: Spain and Portugal, Let's Go: Europe,* and *Condé Nast Traveler.* Her first travel guide, *Frommer's Complete Hostel Vacation Guide to England, Wales & Scotland,* was published in 1996. *Bad Vibes* is her first translation; she is currently at work on her second.